5.1/12

DATE DUE

NOV 1 3 2001		
DEC 0 5 2001		
JAN 0 7 2002		
MAY 0 7 2002		
DEC 1 3 06		

LAND OF THE FAR HORIZON

Voyage of the Exiles
Angel of the Outback
The Emerald Flame

9608

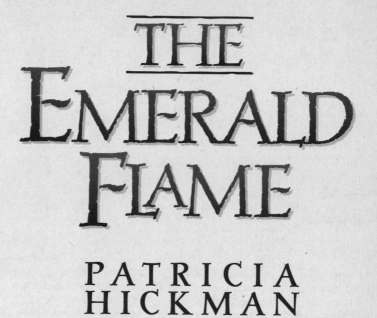

THE EMERALD FLAME

PATRICIA HICKMAN

BETHANY HOUSE PUBLISHERS
MINNEAPOLIS, MINNESOTA 55438

The Emerald Flame
Copyright © 1996
Patricia Hickman

Cover by Patricia Keay

Published by Bethany House Publishers
A Ministry of Bethany Fellowship, Inc.
11300 Hampshire Avenue South
Minneapolis, Minnesota 55438

Printed in the United States of America.

Library of Congress Cataloging-in-Publication Data

Hickman, Patricia.
    The emerald flame / Patricia Hickman.
       p. cm. — (Land of the far horizon ; 3)
    ISBN 1-55661-543-4 (pbk.)
     1. Australia—History—1788-1851—Fiction. I. Title.
II. Series: Hickman, Patricia. Land of the far horizons ; 3.
PS3558.I2296E44   1996
813'.54—dc20   96-25290
                                           CIP

To my oldest son, Joshua.

God gave you the singing voice I always longed to
have when I was your age. He also gave you a courage
and a fearlessness that I had to struggle to aquire. It seems
all that I longed to be as a youth—all my secret desires
that never culminated in me—you are. God always
saves the best for last. You are the best, son.
And you are His.

PATRICIA HICKMAN is a full-time writer and the wife of a pastor. She is the author of three books. She lives with her huband, Randy, and their three children, Joshua, Jessica, and Jared, in Florida.

CONTENTS

PART THREE
Age to Age

PART ONE

AGE OF INNOCENCE

KILDARE, IRELAND

JULY 1800

1
FAREWELL KILDARE

Twelve-year-old Kelsey McBride held a remnant of fishing net overhead, her shining hazel eyes full of fascination. Her rosy face portrayed both a strength and a delicacy uncharacteristic of a girl her age. She watched a small gray field mouse nestle into the golden hay that crowned the rolling hills of Kildare. *If I don't move, I can catch the little fellow and keep him.* A breeze, full of the warmth of Irish summer, stirred the blond curls that fell about her neck. A crimson scarf slid from the crown of her head and draped her shoulders, the fringed corners blowing precariously. But she paid no heed and let it fall, keeping her eyes on the furry prize she sought. Suddenly the wind changed direction. The mouse leaped frantically into the air, having sniffed the human scent nearby. Kelsey dropped onto the hay with her net, her hands working quickly to prevent the creature's escape. A pity swept through her when the captured mouse emitted a helpless squeal. "Poor thing," she murmured, pulling out the squirming rodent and cupping it between her long, slender fingers. "I've frightened you." Freeing her hands carefully from the net, she cradled the creature next to her pale yellow bodice and sang softly in an Irish brogue while rocking gently back and forth, as though the melody would soothe the little beast. "I'll take exceptional care of you," she vowed, her soft, oval face filled with solemnity. But the creature's eyes, tiny brown beads riddled with anxiety, aroused a tenderness that overwhelmed her. With a sigh, she opened her palms onto the straw and watched the field mouse scamper away.

" 'Tis a pity, too. Would've made a fine addition to my other secret pets." She referred to the wild animals she had rescued and now cared for in an old abandoned shed. Tending the creatures, most of which were injured or near-dead when she had stumbled upon them, occupied her afternoons, after she had completed her daily chores for the farmer and his wife. Other than her mother, Kelsey had no other family ties. She found joy and satisfaction in caring for the beasts.

Her mother, Hattie McBride, had worked as a sharecropper for the farmer for a year. Kelsey had perceived that her mother wanted nothing to do with having a husband. Not that she didn't like men, but rather she liked them only temporarily. Kelsey found she pitied her mother, for she seemed lost at times, like a wanderer in a roadless world. Her self-worth at loose ends, Hattie was ripe for the coming rebellion. Realizing the croppies had organized their numbers for a future insurrection, Hattie jumped into the boiling cauldron of Irish dissidents without hesitation. Kelsey saw a change in her mother's demeanor at once, and the distance between them widened. Hattie's covert role as a zealot with the United Irish rebels consumed her every thought now, leaving little time to spend with Kelsey.

"Kelsey McBride!" The raspy voice carried only a pale shade of femininity, and Kelsey recognized it at once.

"Coming, Mother!" Still kneeling in the straw, Kelsey awkwardly lifted her knees from the dark blue apron and brushed the straw from her lap as she stood. Running to the crest of a lush green berm, she stopped, as if spellbound by the symphony of landscape, lowing cattle, and lyrical birdsongs. The farmhouse, cradled in a fertile hollow, absorbed the sunset colors into the shingled roof. Although up close the old weathered house depicted a colorless scene, the sunset painted it bright and grandiose from a distance. Kelsey ran down the hillside toward the house, basking in the final warmth of the day.

Running up to greet her mother, she saw her grim countenance and slowed her pace. *Something's wrong.* Kelsey had observed her mother's bearing darkening over the last few weeks. She stopped at the foot of the rock stairs that graced the back porch of their country home.

Hattie McBride, a tall, stout woman, stood with her arms crossed. "I've a *meeting* again." The sun glinted against the few silvery strands woven through her unkempt auburn hair.

Kelsey swallowed hard, for she knew the meaning of *meeting.* "Couldn't it wait, Mother? Please? You promised me you'd not go again." She couldn't help but take a patronizing tone with her mother. *One of us has to be realistic*, she reasoned. "What if you're caught?"

Hattie McBride grew impatient. Her exasperated sigh suggested that the girl's words may have faintly pierced her complacent conscience. "Mind yer own, now, mind yer own!" She waved a broad, lye-parched hand at her daughter. "I'm nonetheless your mother, and you'll respect me as such." Her voice fell into a stern whisper. "I'll return in two days. Tell Mr. McGregor I've gone to attend a sick relative."

"But he'll not believe that again! Please don't ask me to lie, I'll—"

"Quiet!" Hattie's tone grew harsh. "The whole household will hear you!" She moved down to the step below.

Hattie abruptly caught Kelsey by the elbow and escorted her away from the steps. Kelsey clasped her hands, head lowered, and gazed up apologetically. "I'm sorry, Mother. But you could be killed. I . . . I don't want you hurt," she said in a tremulous tone.

Hattie nodded, allowing her rigid face to soften, for she knew well how to ply the girl. "All right, then. If you want me safe—you'll do as I say?"

"Yes." Kelsey blinked back the tears that threatened to spill over.

"Good-bye, then. I'll soon return." Hattie pressed a hurried kiss upon her daughter's cheek and then moved away, her jaw tightening.

13

Kelsey watched as her mother trudged away with a carefully bundled knapsack. The brisk kiss upon her cheek spoke more clearly than words. *Mother has more important things to tend to than an illegitimate daughter.* At the end of the farmhouse road she heard the sound of squeaky carriage wheels. Her eyes followed the silhouette of her mother hastening to meet it. "Good-bye," she whispered, her fingers uncurling in a weak farewell. A brown Welsh mare ushered the cart, but the face of the driver could not be discerned. In an instant, Hattie McBride had stolen away again to join the ranks of the local rebels, soon to be labeled spies by the British.

Over the next few days, Kelsey once again cloaked her mother's clandestine political activities with lies. But she also lived with the sickening realization that her mother would, without a doubt, soon face her adversaries. The thought frightened Kelsey. Hattie's motherly instincts had never ripened to full bloom, but Kelsey's loyalty and love had persevered throughout even the worst of her mother's decisions. Although Kelsey had grown accustomed to being left alone on occasion, her uneasiness burst into full-blown dread at the prospect of being completely without a mother. A worse title than the shameful one she now held would seal her doom for certain if she were to become an orphan. She would have to try to reason with her mother soon if they were to survive. *Please don't leave me alone, Mother. Please!*

New South Wales, Australia—Sydney Cove

Caleb Prentice, face bronzed from the Australian sun, and his young companion ran down the clay-packed roads of Sydney Cove, chasing the rusted ring from a rum barrel. He ran and tapped either side of the ring with a hand-carved gum tree limb. "Hurry, Matthew! You run like a bloomin' girl!" He shook his blond head, his dark brows and blue eyes a startling contrast against his golden bronzed skin.

"Go on, then! Show me you kin do better!" Matthew parried.

Drawing back his arm, Caleb swung around with a force

and struck the ring a resounding blow. The spinning ring bounced over a grassy berm and rolled down toward the back door of a tavern. When the ring smacked against the weathered door, the thirteen-year-old boys' evident glee burst into unbridled laughter.

Caleb had grown up in the British colony under the loving, temperate guidance of his emancipist parents. The early years in the prison colony had left their unforgiving mark on his transported family, but Caleb had shrugged off the tainted label of emancipist, choosing to ignore the colonial prejudices against "their kind." His father, arrested years ago in England for pickpocketing, had made a new life for them in Sydney Cove. Unskilled as a squatter, his father had struggled with the unyielding land until he had stumbled into sheepherding. Now the Prentices found increasing satisfaction in the simpler pleasures of life. And Caleb continued to disregard their convict past.

Caleb held up his stick in mock defense when the tavern door flew open.

"Out o' 'ere, you ruddy brats!" Weems, the pub's owner, stood in his nightshirt, his frayed red stockings and tousled hair giving him the appearance of an aged rooster.

"Sorry, sir. Didn't mean to wake you." Caleb bit his lip to stifle his mirth. The set of his chin suggested a staunch stubborn streak.

"Out 'o 'ere, I say, before I call the magistrate."

"Not likely, sir. I saw 'im meself this mornin' out in Parrametta hangin' a crawler by the neck." Caleb winked broadly at his amused companion, his delft blue eyes sparkling with confidence.

"You'll be next to go, brat! Out wakin' all the good citizens o' Sydney Cove b'fore they've had their mornin' grog."

"Let's leave, Caleb!" Matthew tugged anxiously on his arm. His dark eyes bespoke his apprehension.

"When I'm ready." Caleb persisted in taunting the pub owner. "But first I need me a bit o' rum." He wiped his mouth with the back of his woolen sleeve and sauntered boldly toward the taverner. "Drink for a thirsty traveler, sir?" The lad stretched out his palm as a beggar would do, his eyes lit with mischief. With his other hand, he held his throat as though parched.

"Trouble here, Mr. Weems?" A testy voice spoke from the outside corner of the tavern. Sitting atop a wagon was Lieutenant Macarthur with a boy seated next to him.

Caleb looked up quickly, startled by the interruption of his mischief. "No problem here, Lieutenant, sir." He saluted with an exaggerated flourish, which served him rather poorly in the matter.

"Emancipist, be on your way." The lieutenant waved his hand in a haughty manner.

"Or I'll give you a clout wi' this!" Weems held out his fist.

"How do you know he's an emancipist, Father?" The lieutenant's son, a nine-year-old duplicate of his father, eyed Caleb with an air of arrogance.

Macarthur stared the shabby boy up and down with distaste. "It's simple, John. First by his mannerisms"—he cast a displeased scowl—"and then by his common attire."

Caleb felt his throat tighten. The stigma of his father's past as a former convict continued to haunt his every move. But the shame attached to the label ignited a fire in the lad, which of late had sent him into many a tangle with the colonist children. Crossing his arms rigidly, he plunged on carelessly. "And I can tell a rat when I sees one. See the beady little eyes, Matthew?" His eyes filled with teasing laughter, he pointed first toward Macarthur and then at his son, John Junior.

"That does it!" Weems glared at Caleb.

"Let me handle 'im, Weems!" Macarthur stepped confidently from the wagon and marched toward the emancipist's son. Drawing back his hand, he swung with an angry force.

Young John Junior smacked his right fist inside his other palm. "Get him, Father!"

Caleb dodged the lieutenant's blow, crouching low and then lunging to the side when the officer came around with his other hand. "Away from me, scum!" he shouted at Macarthur, his gaiety waning and his mouth twisting into a threat.

"You'll be flogged, scoundrel!" Macarthur stretched out his sinewy hands and snatched Caleb by the collar. Shaking him vigorously, he pushed the boy backward, sending him flailing to the dusty red earth.

"What goes here?" A frail-looking man in peasant attire appeared from the alleyway that separated the tavern from the town stores. His searching blue eyes demanded an answer.

"George Prentice?" Macarthur growled and then murmured from the side of his mouth, "I might've known."

Prentice spied his son dragging himself from the ground, his clothing soiled and torn. "What's wrong, lad?" He hobbled to the boy's side and helped him to his feet.

"Lieutenant struck me, he did." Caleb straightened himself, pulling his back erect and squaring his shoulders. "An' called me an *emancipist!*" Caleb felt the bruise upon his thigh. He had landed on a hard object still pressed tightly inside his pocket. His brow knit from pain, he fingered the object. *Me knife.*

George's weathered face frowned with anger, his slightly graying brows drawing downward. "Struck me boy, Macarthur? Whatever for?"

"He'll be flogged for his offenses if I catch him being disruptive again. You'll do better to keep that boy caged with the animals where he belongs!"

George hesitated, choosing his words carefully, for Macarthur and his military monopoly wielded a power that saw no justice—only dominion. "You've no right to insult the lad!" He pushed his graying tousled hair from his face.

"I've every right as a colonist. The boy's a menace to this colony as are all you emancipists. I'll see to it he's shipped off to Norfolk if I hear any report of his shenanigans again!"

"You'll do no such thing!" Caleb shouted, pulling away from George. "I'll come at night while you sleep and cut out your black heart!"

"*Caleb!*" George lunged for the impudent boy, grasped his arms firmly, and shook him soundly. Setting his eyes once again on Macarthur, he said defensively, "The boy's angry, Macarthur. He knows not what he says. Don't hold him to his words!"

"I'll hold you to *this*, Prentice!" Macarthur held up a gloved hand, his finger pointed menacingly. "One more offense, and the boy is gone for good!"

Reaching out with steady hands, George gripped his son's shoulders. "Quiet, son," he warned in a whispered tone. "Let it go. He's not worth it."

Caleb tapped the small knife that was hidden inside his pocket, then clenched his fists at his sides. His lips pressed in forced servility, he stood silent before a man who represented the master he hated—the British military. Watching John Macarthur ride away, Caleb glanced toward the tavern owner, who stood with his arms akimbo, staring smugly.

"Your father's a crawler and you'll be one too!" He shook his finger at Caleb.

George glanced down at his boy once more. "Let it go, I say."

When the two stood alone again, Caleb pulled away from his father. "How could you stand there taking their insults like that, Papa? Why won't you fight?"

"I can fight with the best of 'em, son." He shook a fist in front of his face. "But what's the good it'll accomplish? Macarthur can send us both off to Norfolk Island with the blink of an eye. What would your mother do then?"

"If we hanged Macarthur, the entire colony would pay us a reward. Everyone hates 'im! You know it's true."

George's leathery countenance reflected an inward wisdom that weighed heavily against his thoughts. "It's not as simple as you say. If we take matters into our own hands, then we're interfering in matters that belong to the Almighty."

Caleb crossed his arms at his waist. His eyes smoldered with an unquenchable fire.

George weighed the boy's silence. "You don't understand, do you?"

"You're right! I *don't* understand! That's because I don't see God in anything here. We live in hell, and Macarthur is the devil 'isself!"

Prentice hesitated, his solemn silence saying more than words. "Don't be so quick to hand us or this country over to the devil. We've got to work the land as unto the Lord. Let our toil be unto Him." Prentice managed a faint smile, mischief playing around his lips. "And keep your tongue—for the same."

Kildare, Ireland

Within days, the news had spread throughout the boroughs

of Kildare—*Hattie McBride, arrested!* The list of arrested croppies grew, and the sharecroppers who hadn't joined in the rebellion argued amongst their ranks for both sides.

Kelsey McBride stood for the last time upon her beloved
hillside, for now her mother's arrest had labeled them both as
troublemakers. Garnered like cattle, war orphans such as she
would soon join their exiled parents as transports to a land far
beyond Kildare's horizons. Opening a small cage she had once
fashioned from wire, Kelsey set free a bird whose broken wing
she had nursed. The bird leaped onto the cool grass, keeping
near the girl who had hand-fed it every day for two months.
"Go on, now. You're free!" She blinked back a tear. "Go!" The
bird hopped around, flapping its wings, its behavior suggesting
its confusion. "Please go." She nudged the bird with trembling
hands. The small, round body lifted, fluttered back to earth,
and then, instinctively, glided into the endless sky. With a heavy
sigh, Kelsey glanced around at the empty cages. All the wild
animals and fowl now set free, she felt an emptiness inside, as
though all her worth had flown away with the birds. The government wagons would soon come for her, and she would be
taken to join her mother to await transport. A large shamrock
tickled her calf. Kneeling down, she plucked the Irish symbol
from the moist earth. Carefully bending the stem in half, she
tucked it into her pocket. Perhaps taking along this tiny memento would hide a part of Kildare inside of her where no intruder could reach.

Kelsey peered down the other side of the hill and beheld the
neighboring farmhouses. The other families' homes, so unaf-
fected by the rebellion, mocked her with their serenity. If she
ran to one of them with her plight, would they open their doors
to her, or would they send her away? Some of the families
might offer Kelsey the security she had never known. She recalled that once she had assisted a friend's family, the Fitzgeralds, with the storage of their winter food. The memory of that
day had left a pleasant and lasting impression. She had observed the close-knit family working in harmony for the good
of all, showing affection for one another, and having the nur-
ture of both a father and a mother. Secretly, she had envied her
friend's affinity with her parents. And more than once the realization had struck her mind like a hammer that her world

sadly lacked what many other children took for granted. *Would the Fitzgeralds take me in?* The thought encouraged her, but then a pang of guilt echoed through the chambers of her conscience. *What would you do without me, Mother?*

The sound of wagons and horses abruptly awakened her from her bittersweet daydream. She saw the flash of red coats and knew at once that the British military had come for her. She glanced longingly again toward the Fitzgeralds' farmhouse. But the thought of her mother alone without her on a transport ship came vividly to her mind, and she hurtled back to earth as harsh reality struck. *No*, she reasoned. *I cannot leave my mother.* Then, clasping her hand around the shamrock in her pocket, she trudged down the green hills of Kildare for the last time.

The days since the mass arrests stretched into weeks. The Irish rebels, loaded into the squalid hulls of cramped ships, found themselves snatched from their beloved homeland and bound for a distant horizon that welcomed not their massive numbers.

A single lantern flame glimmered on the deck of the *Friendship*, a dim reminder of the night that blanketed the harbor with bleakness. A shipmate walked the forecastle, listening in the silence. Finding the black night air without complaint and being glad of it, he pushed back on a wooden stool and prepared an evening smoke. He heard not the oaths spoken beneath the ship's fasteners.

"God, bring down your wrath on these persecutors!" a voice prayed, condemning the captors. Down in the belly of the ship, the holds groaned with the weight of the Irish transportees— all political or social exiles from the splintered rebellion. If placed in the hands of the local government, the arrested Irish rebels posed a threat to the civilian magistrates. Thus, goaded by consequence, Mother England deported the entire disorganized rebellion. Along with thousands of others, they exiled a most dangerous fanner of the flames of defiance, a Protestant United Irishman by the name of William Orr.

The anarchist, who was being closely watched by the British military, squatted in contemptible silence next to common thieves whose allegiance was pledged only to themselves. He kindled no ire in their company. As he looked around, Orr contemplated the matter. *Throw me in with the rubbish. A useless ploy!* And so, the Irish exile waited in sure anticipation of the next day when he could stealthily spread his rancorous doctrine to the other banished outcasts who waited for the ship to weigh anchor. Then, one by one, with deliberation he would plant his seeds of propaganda. *There is nothing surer than that Irishmen of every denomination must stand or fall together!*

In a different hold, a surly Irish woman chided another for her want of sleep and demanded complete silence. "Keep your girl quiet, I say, and leave me to rest in peace!"

"She's but a child and frightened by the whole of our situation. An' you'll find no peace on this hellship, so keep your complaints to yourself!" Hattie McBride threatened, while adjusting her scratchy prison garment.

"Don't, Mother, please," Kelsey pleaded in a soft, whispered tone, her face streaked with tears no eye could see for the darkness. Now old beyond her twelve years, she well knew her mother's quick temper and wanted no conflicts on her account. "I just couldn't help but to cry," she continued in a broken whisper. Her jaw rigid, she held in her tears with all the force she could muster. "I want to go home to Kildare. I want to see Ireland again." Pained emotions sent a piteous quiver through her tone. *I should've stayed behind*, she chided herself.

"Hush yourself!" the old woman barked again.

"It'll do us no good, Kelsey, to wish for things that can't be." Hattie's voice, strained from frustration, punctuated the air with a finality. "We belong to the United Irish, and we die with them, as well."

Kelsey drew up her knees next to her chin. She had heard the terrible news that filtered down through the British rank and file to the prisoners. The winds of change had rocked even the tranquillity of Kildare, drawing both peasant and middle-class Irishmen into a rebellion against England that flared from county to county, leaving all of Ireland in a state of martial law. Kildare, she'd heard, now lay smoldering in ashes.

Kelsey recalled the dreadful events of the last few days. When the disorganized croppies summoned Hattie to aid in the harboring of the revolting soldiers, she brazenly hid them in the barn of her employer. Hattie's loyalty to the croppies single-handedly helped two hundred United Irish slip through the hands of the surprised British. Unaware of the rebels' strength and fervor, the British scrambled to muster their troops, eventually organizing and stiffening them to quell the momentum of the Irish. The captured dissidents, along with Hattie, had then been arrested. Kelsey and Hattie were eventually reunited, although their impassive reunion offered less than a pleasant memory for Kelsey. She recalled finding her mother standing among the other prisoners, her face contorted with hatred for her British captors. She had hoped that Hattie would at least demonstrate a hint of relief that she had found her, or reflect a grain of approval that she had loyally chosen to follow her in spite of the appalling circumstances. But upon running up to meet her, Kelsey had stopped within inches of her mother, seeing that Hattie's thoughts and interests were occupied elsewhere. Kelsey had taken her place uncertainly beside her mother, her cheeks flushed with disappointment, and a stab of fear pricking her heart.

Hattie now cocked her head against the wall and crossed her arms across her chest, humming a bit and then breaking into a song of treason:

"It was early, early in the spring.
The birds did whistle and sweetly sing,
Changing their notes from tree to tree,
And the song they sang was Old Ireland Free."

Much to her indulgence, the others in the cell joined in the song, their voices rapt with the strong tipple of rebellion.

"It was early, early in the night,
The yeoman cavalry gave me a fright.
The yeoman cavalry was my downfall,
And I was taken by Lord Cornwall."

The song served only to dampen Kelsey's spirits all the more. Pulling a wayward strand of blond hair back to tuck into her frazzled braid, she silently vowed in her childlike way to find a means to return to her homeland. She had searched the watery horizons that stretched eternally from dawn until dusk each day and had wearied at the overwhelming sense of hopelessness weighing against her thoughts. "Does anyone know where this Sydney Cove is? Is it far from Kildare?"

The old woman sighed, a new pity for the girl arising in her anxiety-fraught mind. "As far as the east is from the west. It's an eternity child—it's forever from Kildare."

2

BRIEF ENCOUNTER

"Land ho!" shouted the sailor stationed above the topsails. The noisy clamor atop the deck went undetected by the convicts below. The prisoners knew only that the ocean had shifted, lifting the ship up and then dragging it down into the hollow of the waves.

Morning came earlier aboard ship than on land. Kelsey McBride awoke, stretched herself, and rearranged her fragile weight against the rolls of smelly cloth where she slept. Musty aromas of rum, mixed with mold and dust, sent a grimace across her pale countenance. She sat on the edge of the disheveled rags in a daze, the muffled sounds overhead shattering her dreams and dragging her back into reality. Kelsey McBride was still on the *Friendship*, still a prisoner bound for Sydney Cove, along with all the other convicts who crowded the ship's holds. Pulling the rags around her, she felt the dawn's chill that moved in across the Indian Ocean.

A golden stream of warmth broke through the dark cubicle. "Move out, wenches!" a surly voice barked from above. "Land ho!"

Kelsey surveyed with loathing the countenance of the brute who glared down upon them. "I will, sir," she answered quietly, fearful that the slightest hint of contempt in her tone would send the fiend into another of his raging fits. "Wake up, Mother. They've sighted land." Impatient with her unkempt braid, she began to undo the flaxen strands.

"Where are we?" a convict woman questioned sleepily.

Stretching herself to her petite height, Kelsey allowed her thoughts to drift back to gentler days when her mother carried her on her hip like a limp doll along the roadway that led to the farm. She remembered Mother complained little to her but had kindled the wrath of the farmer from time to time. Hattie, known well among the croppies as a scrapper, held her own in spite of her gender.

"Where's me grub?" the old convict woman yelled up to the mariner.

Kelsey glanced toward her mother, but then glanced away pursing her dry lips. She had no reason to expect a nod of encouragement. Since the day Hattie joined the civil band of rebels, Kelsey had perceived her mother taking less and less notice of her. Hattie McBride now drew her strength from a cause that Kelsey scarcely understood.

"We're hungry, blokes!" Hattie called up as well.

"You'll get your grub, wenches, an' a new job to boot af'er sundown. Now move out!"

Hattie's eyes narrowed. Under her breath, she muttered, "I'll get that lout before the day's end."

Running nervous fingers through her tousled locks, Kelsey urged her mother with a longing face. "Don't be angry, Mother. You'll just give 'im another reason to cut your rations."

"All convicts out o' the holds!" The order was repeated in an even more threatening tone.

Climbing up the ladder, Kelsey squinted against the bright sunlight, her eyes tearing instantly. But the crisp salt air had a cleansing effect upon her thinking. She spotted the peak of land rising ahead of them, and a surge of hope filled her heart. "Maybe Sydney Cove's like Kildare. We could make a new beginnin', Mother. No more farmers to toil for."

"No, just the military," the mariner laughed. "An' these is

your new jewelry." He thrust the rusted shackles toward the girl.

Kelsey drew back in alarm. Icy fear twisted around her heart.

"Leave 'er be!" Hattie barked. "She's no convict, she's just a child."

"Come 'ere, pretty miss," the mariner persisted, eyeing the child with interest. "Ol' Jones could use a girl like you fur 'is own, he could."

Hattie's tone grew taut with threat. "Don't you touch 'er!"

The exiles who had already fallen into line turned and muttered among themselves, for Hattie's reputation aboard ship was no different than on land.

"Off wif ye wench! Or you'll suffer a rakin' at the cat!"

"Now I wouldn't be no good to you, then, would I, *Mister Jones*?" Hattie stood between herself and Kelsey, her face softening and her tone mellowed. She poised her hands upon her hips and allowed a coy smile to dimple her cheeks. Kelsey noticed with confusion how the tension between the two began to melt.

The mariner crossed his arms, his eyes regarding the convict woman with a marked fascination. "Eh? Wot's that?"

"It's been a while, ain't it, mister?" Hattie winked. "Been needin' a little company to keep you warm at night?"

Kelsey gripped the back of her mother's garment and twisted it. "No, Mother!" she whispered, her face tense. She leaned into the curve of her mother's back, attempting to change the will of a woman who knew no resolve except to take matters into her own hands.

"Line up fer grub!" a corporal shouted.

"Let's go and get our rations," Kelsey persisted.

The mariner reached out and gruffly grasped Hattie's sun-parched wrist. "Come wif me, then," he growled.

"No!" Kelsey clung to her mother's prison garb, feeling herself being dragged along helplessly.

"The girl's comin' wif us?" Jones rubbed his bristly jowl, a smile creasing his baked cheeks.

"Go, Kelsey!" Hattie turned and yanked her daughter's hands from her prison gown. She shoved her toward the rations line. "Join the others—now!" she demanded, a strange anger marking her tone.

"Come here, Kelsey," one of the Irish convict women called out. "Do as your mother says." Kelsey felt a sickening tremor shake her frame. She mouthed one last silent plea as Hattie disappeared around the forecastle with the mariner. "Please, Mother, no. . . ."

A blanket of fog veiled the harbor of Sydney Cove. A brisk chill sent the harbor frequenters hurriedly about their day. A few stood upon the landing, their eyes trained on the new prison transport ship, awaiting its arrival.

The moorings of the *Friendship* groaned against the soaked wood of the dock while the convicts filed out onto the moss-coated landing. Kelsey stood at the end of the string of weary survivors and peered around the adult prisoners who ambled out with a heavy, somnolent air of indifference. She pushed her hair away from her face and allowed it to tumble carelessly down her back. On the dock, a group of settlers milled about, talking quietly among themselves while sizing up the health of each convict. Her brow pinched with worry, Kelsey turned and gazed up at her mother who had not made eye contact with her all morning. "What are those men doing out there, Mother?" she asked softly.

Hattie sighed, glanced toward the settlers on the dock, and shrugged. "Takin' some of us home, it seems." Placing her hand upon the girl's shoulder, she bent and whispered into her ear. "If you're chosen by a settler, then go with him and don't give no thought to me. I don't want you in one of those Godforsaken prison cells if I can help it at all."

"I want to go with you—"

"Hush yourself!" Hattie stared straight ahead, her eyes steeled against emotion. "Doesn't Hattie always have the last say?"

Kelsey swallowed hard, fighting back the tears that only the night before had flowed freely down her cheeks in the dark hold of the *Friendship*.

"Where in the bloomin' world is Jones?" The captain

stormed toward the stern of the ship, his pipe leaving a trail of smoke behind him.

The Irish convicts stared straight ahead, their staid expressions suggesting they'd never before heard of Jones. Kelsey noticed William Orr had caught her mother's eye, his dark snappy eyes staring out from a sun-toughened face. She felt her mother's grip tighten upon her frail shoulders as if to keep her looking straight ahead. She did not move, but her eyes narrowed and her heart pounded against her chest, a faint twinge of fear rising inside of her. *Where is Jones?* She swallowed hard and glanced up at Hattie once more. Troubled by the morbid look that seemed to strangely soften her mother's face, Kelsey battled the curiosity to know the truth. Hattie's solemn expression implied that a peace rested with her. Kelsey allowed her gaze to wander out to the sea's horizon, where for a fraction of a moment, she spotted a lifeless body riding upon the crest of a wave before it disappeared from sight. Kelsey unfolded her mother's hands. Seeing a tinge of red along her frayed cuticle line, she turned away. "Don't tell me anything. I don't want to know." Horror knotted inside her. She withdrew into her own private world, her thoughts running to the place where little girls played with dolls and nursed broken wings and hid green shamrocks in their pockets.

"Look! It's her!" Caleb shouted, waving his cap wildly. "It's Rachel!" He had waited beside his parents, George and Amelia Prentice, tarrying for what seemed like hours at Sydney Cove's harbor.

Amelia squinted, rubbing her eyes. "Caleb, don't make such a scene! That woman can't be Rachel."

Caleb stepped toward the four-masted passenger ship that anchored beneath the clouded bay sky.

"Rachel Langley!" he called, waving his tricorn cap. "We're over here!" He gazed upon the family friend he hadn't laid eyes on in over five years. Rachel stepped gracefully down the ship's plank. Her bright auburn hair, coifed elegantly atop her head, gleamed with shadows of rich red. Her face, well modeled and feminine, now appeared so composed. Caleb remembered her as a Cockney emancipist who had fought to aid the sickly young boys in the prison colony's contagion wards. When she departed for England years ago as a witness for the murder of a friend, Caleb recalled that his parents worried they would never see her again. But Rachel, vigilant to stay in contact with them through her letters, finally wrote that she would return soon with important news.

Rachel lifted her gloved hand to acknowledge them all with a wave. She carried herself confidently, aware of the admiring glances but not at all proud. Finely dressed in a laced gown of celadon green satin, Rachel stepped from the ramp onto the dock, her slender frame poised. The dress, of impeccable design, trailed behind her as did several young boys loaded down with her trunks and boxes.

Swiftly turning, Rachel handed a package to one of the youths who assisted her. She carried herself with a strength that did not lessen her femininity. Facing her waiting friends, she strode briskly toward them, all but running in anticipation.

"It *is* her, Amelia!" George grinned boyishly, his face beaming. "It's Rachel!"

Caleb eagerly preceded his parents as they approached their long-awaited guest. His mouth fell open as she drew near. "Look at you, will ye!" he exclaimed.

"It can't be . . . Caleb Prentice?" Rachel drew up her hands beneath her chin, musing at the sight of the lad. Her eager smile bespoke her joy, and her green eyes glistened.

Amelia curled her fingers around her husband's wrist. "Would you look at this fine young lady!" She shook her head in disbelief, although her joy proved evident. "My, you're a sight, ain't you, all frilled up like a gentlewoman."

" 'Cause she is one." George's paternal affection for the girl radiated in his periwinkle blue eyes.

"Dear me, how I've missed you all!" She kissed Caleb gently upon the forehead and turned to embrace Amelia warmly, wrapping her arms around Amelia's slim, middle-aged frame. Caleb's cheeks tinged with pink, he shoved his hands in his pockets when Rachel held him out at arm's length to study his handsome young face. "You're so grown up." A swath of silvery blond hair fell casually on his forehead.

"Rachel, we need to hurry you along. We've a big feast waitin' on us at Rose Hill." Amelia turned to wink at her, her large green eyes full of humor. "An' a certain minister's wearin' a hole in the rug just waitin' for your return." She tucked a loose strand of hair, auburn flecked with silver, into her white laced cap.

"Heath?" Rachel's eyes glistened. "So he isn't—"

"Married?" Amelia made a dismissing gesture. "All other beauties pale at the mention o' your name, that's wot!"

"Such flattery." Rachel laughed. Her eyes moist, her face was full of strength, shining with a steadfast peace. "I've yearned to be with you all. Remember those mornings we would rise, Amelia, to make biscuits just the way George liked them?" she asked, reminiscing on the past.

"He was a willful one about 'is biscuits and still is." Amelia eyed George wryly, her pale pink mouth pressed into a girlish pout.

"Now she makes 'em for me, as well." Caleb crossed his arms in a cocky fashion, always the one to draw the conversation back to himself.

"Oh, we'll talk Rachel's ear off." Amelia bent to retrieve a piece of baggage for the young woman. "We've so much to catch up on. Let's make fast for the carriage, and you can tell us everything along the way."

"I'll tell you *almost* everything," Rachel hesitated, her eyes lit mischievously toward Caleb. "I've a surprise for you all *and* for Reverend Heath Whitley."

"Tell me first!" Caleb blurted. "Wot is it?"

"Patience, my dear, though it never was your virtue!"

Upon hearing Rachel's retort, Caleb hefted the heavier trunk over his stout shoulder. "I can wait, then, if you won't say." He awkwardly attempted to conceal his inquisitiveness.

"All right," Rachel smiled, her full rosy lips pressed demurely. "You'll just have to wait."

Caleb blew out a frustrated sigh as Rachel passed by him, walking briskly aside his gaily chattering parents. He wanted to blurt out a plea for Rachel to satisfy his curiosity, but his need for dignity roused, he positioned the trunk squarely across a shoulder and trudged behind them. *I can wait. I can,* he assured himself.

"Hear now, watch where you're goin' wif that. . . ."

Caleb turned to find old man Weems, the tavern owner, crossing his path.

"Pardon me!" he muttered between clenched teeth.

"Oh, it's you!" Weems snarled. "Out makin' trouble again, I see."

"No such thing!" Caleb gripped the trunk, which teetered precariously. "Just passin' through."

"You'll wait fer yer elders to pass first, I vow. Now back away, waif, and allow us through!"

Caleb planted his feet, his anger seething. Then he caught the eye of his father, who shook his head in warning. Pressing his lips together, he gave a surly nod to the tavern owner. "Go on, then, and pass."

"Hurry it up!" Weems called to several servants he'd just selected from the incoming Irish transport ship, *Friendship*. "Don't take all day," he commanded, his manner condescending.

Caleb felt the weight of the trunk creasing his shoulder. Vexed, he lowered the burden to the ground and waited for Weems and his small entourage to go by. Weems passed with his chin up and waving his black cane, while behind him trudged several Irish convicts, weak from the journey. A small girl trailed behind the others.

Caleb looked ahead to see his family waiting for him and bent to reposition the trunk. But the sight of the young girl caused him to stop. She was a slight youth who looked to be about his age. He guessed that it was the length of the journey that had left her in such a ragged state. But beneath the soot and soil of the trip, a loveliness shone through the girl's countenance. Seeing her with Weems, he was swept with sudden pity and felt an urgency to speak. "Hello," he called out brazenly.

Surprised that the boy addressed her, the girl clung to her bundle and stared back in bewilderment.

Caleb couldn't help noticing her hair, which hung down her back like strands of flaxen glass. "Lovely day, ain't it, now?" He forced a smile.

The Irish girl gazed upward in perplexity and studied the thick, gray clouds that hung low over the harbor. Her brow furrowed. "Lovely?" The light of humor glinted from her transparent gaze.

Caleb glanced up at the darkening sky and smiled sheepishly. "Or, maybe it was yesterday. . . ." He hesitated, realizing how foolish he must sound. He then paused to regard her captivating face once more. The animation of her character was enchanting. "That's it! Lovely day it was . . . yesterday."

A smile creased the corners of the girl's oval face and a small dimple appeared. At this response, Caleb smiled as well, tipped his hat, and finished lifting and settling the trunk once again upon his shoulder.

Kelsey McBride watched with interest as the cocky young man plodded past.

"Don't dawdle, Kelsey McBride!" Weems barked again.

Caleb turned and winked, his eyes lit with mischief.

Kelsey took a slow, servile step toward the sound of Weems' voice, but her eyes remained on the audacious youth who marched away with his trunk, turning as he went to see if she watched. By this one simple act, she carelessly stepped out of line with the others and into the path of a wheeled cart.

"Hey, look out!" a cockney merchant yelled. Kelsey jerked around, the air about her filled with the clucking and screeching sound of flapping hens rudely jolted inside their wooden cages.

"Wot's this?" Weems stood with his lip protruding, a callused hand tapping the black cane against the dirt.

"Hurry along, son!" Amelia called out worriedly to Caleb, seeing his attention drawn toward the conflict.

With a half-obedient nod, Caleb frowned, his thoughts focused on the scene before him.

Kelsey backed away from the angry merchant. Turning to step in line with the others, she caught the eye of her red-faced employer. "Sorry, sir." Bowing her face, she made haste to correct her mistake, but Weems charged toward her like an enraged bull.

Caleb turned abruptly and shoved the trunk onto the back of Papa's wagon. Hearing the commotion heighten behind him, he whirled around and beheld the girl standing helplessly, surrounded by several angry-looking men.

"Jump in the wagon, Caleb!" George called out in a warning. "We've folks waitin' for us at Rose Hill."

The youth glanced up, biting the inside of his cheek. His mother and Rachel Langley had already seated themselves next to George. Turning her genial face, Rachel smiled at him, her brows arched. "Coming?"

With a quick nod, Caleb leaped into the wagon in one swift movement. At once, he returned his somber gaze back toward the Irish girl who now stood alone before the hostile Weems.

George flicked the reins and the wagon lurched forward. Caleb watched in horror as Weems drew back his cane in anger at the girl whom he had now forced to kneel at his feet.

"Stop, Papa!" Caleb shouted.

The old horse whinnied, jostling its head when George instinctively yanked on the reins. "Caleb!"

Caleb leaped from the wagon bed, his intent evident. Racing toward the scene, he charged ahead without thought of plan or scheme. "You!" He pointed at the tavern owner. "Weems!"

The churlish man gazed up at the youth running fast toward him. "It's the imbecile boy again," he muttered. "Halt or I'll call the authorities!" he warned, holding up a stubby finger.

Caleb positioned himself between Weems and the girl. "Don't strike the girl!" he demanded. "It was me own fault she stepped in the cart's path. I caused her to turn aside."

"Might've known," Weems muttered. He crossed his arms, his chin lifted in a patronizing manner. He could see the pleading in the Prentice boy's eyes. "So"—he contrived a new strategy—"you'll take the beating for the girl?"

His fists clenched at his sides, Caleb looked purposefully away from the girl.

She slowly shook her head at him, whispering, "Don't—"

Weems drew back his cane again, making steady his aim for the girl's back.

"Don't strike 'er, Weems!" Caleb shouted. "I'll do it," he said, staring down at the ground. "I'll take the beatin'." He gazed pitiably upon the girl who continued to plead with her eyes, although her lips could form no words.

"On your knees, boy!" Weems growled. He lifted the cane in readiness.

Caleb bent first one knee and then the other. Casting his

eyes downward, he couldn't bear the stares of the tawdry females and churlish men who gathered to gawk at the spectacle.

"Stop it! Stop it, I say!" George Prentice ran into the crowd, with Amelia and Rachel following close behind. His weathered face reflected a paternal concern, marked by a bridled anger. "What're you doin' to me boy, Weems?"

Caleb heard his father's voice and stood at once. "No, Papa!" he cried.

"Caleb!" Amelia called out fearfully.

Caleb warned, "Go back to the wagon! Please!"

"Wot's he done, Weems?" George confronted the tavern owner.

Weems calculated his reply, then answered, "Ask 'im yourself."

Caleb faced his parents, and then saw Rachel standing behind them, her face taut.

"I caused this girl to walk out in front of the butcher's wagon. I'm takin' the beatin' for it."

"Your patience, sir!" Swiftly George Prentice shoved his way through the throng. Eyeing the butcher who still held firm to his wagon, he called out in a reasonable tone, "Any harm done, sir?"

"No." The man shook his head, his lips pursed with resolve. "No harm, sir."

George glanced down at the hens that nestled quietly in the straw of their cages. "No recompense needed, then?"

Red-faced, the butcher shook his head. "No."

George turned around and spoke gently to the accuser. "No recompense, sir. No punishment needed."

Weems clutched his cane tightly, repressing his rage at having been halted in meting out the punishment he so readily inflicted upon those under his control. He trained a glare upon Caleb. Then with bottled anger, he commanded, "Get up, McBride!"

Caleb bent to offer his hand to the girl who still knelt in the dust. "Miss McBride, are you all right?" He slid an object into her hand.

She nodded. A strange light sparked in her eyes, an acknowledgment of the exchange between them. "Thank you."

Caleb watched as she clutched his prized possession in her

hand—the small knife he had always carried in his pocket.

She gazed up at George, who came up behind his son and placed his hand upon his shoulders. "To you, too, sir—"

"Into the wagon!" Weems bellowed. "Now, McBride!"

Pressing his lips together, Caleb dared not be dragged into another confrontation with Weems. "Much obliged, miss."

"Let's take our leave, Caleb." George patted the boy's back, an urgency in his voice.

Caleb walked swiftly behind his parents. With the conflict quickly resolved, the disappointed onlookers dispersed, fanning out into the harbor square.

Climbing awkwardly into the wagon behind the grumbling Irish convicts, Kelsey McBride glanced toward Weems, who was busying himself next to his driver on the front seat. Turning her face quickly toward the family, whose name she didn't know, she waved meekly. They never saw her meager gesture or heard her whispered call, "Good-bye."

Caleb allowed his family to rush him toward the wagon. Unable to resist the temptation to glance back, he turned his face.

"Don't look, Caleb." Amelia tensed her hold around his shoulders. "We can't help her now. She can't be helped."

3
ATTACK ON ROSE HILL

The sun began to set soon after the early festive suppertime at Rose Hill. The bleating of sheep on the hillside grew silent, and a rooster tucked its head inside a red-tipped wing. But the unfinished farmhouse glowed with the warmth of a lantern and filled the pastureland of Rose Hill with sounds of merriment.

Inside the Prentice home, the evening's entertainment commenced with a neighbor sliding his bow across a sour violin, although no complaints darkened the light hearts present. Another musician vigorously fingered a hornpipe. A sense of frivolity had overtaken everyone's senses, and the ladies prevailed upon George to dance the popular hornpipe.

Launching into the spirited dance with a nod and a wink to his wife, George kicked as sprightly as a young man, and the sight of his spindly legs sent the older women into spasms of laughter.

"Oh, Papa!" His daughter Katy cupped her dainty hands to her rose-tinted mouth, a comely blush coloring her cheeks. "Such an embarrassment!" she exclaimed laughingly, although few things in life truly embarrassed her. She was a fair-faced young woman in her mid-twenties with oddly patrician features. She sat beside her jaunty emancipist husband, Dwight Farrell. On his knee he bounced their two pudgy toddlers, Jared and Donovan.

Dwight and Katy had met with some difficulties early in their marriage. But the determined young husband had sought the wise counsel of his mother-in-law on more than one occasion and found her intuitive understanding of Katy's character to be sound. His young wife's headstrong ideas overwhelmed him at times, although he would never admit to defeat.

"Don't stop, George! You're a master at the dance, mate!" Dwight clapped his hands to the lively music, urging the man on.

Caleb sat cross-legged in the corner of the room, filling his insides with extra portions of herbed potatoes and hot buttered bread. He nodded slightly to the music, although his true interest lay in the food heaped on his plate. He chuckled when two young ladies twirled in front of Amelia and then surprised her by grasping her wrists. "You next, Mrs. Prentice. Dance with your 'usband!"

"Dear me, no!" Amelia pulled a lace kerchief from her bodice and fanned her cheeks. "I'll faint."

"Come on, now!" George kicked his way toward his aging wife. "It'll do your heart good, Amelia!"

"Yes, Mum!" Katy jumped to her feet, hands clapping next to Dwight. "Please!" Others also entreated Amelia to join her husband in the dance, and the room soon rang with the sound of giddy laughter and song.

"Oh, you'd think it me last chance, all o' you!" Amelia finally acquiesced.

Caleb looked up when Rachel Langley strode from the small unfinished dining hall, cupping a glass of punch in her hands. Her dress of cranberry brocade glistened in the candlelight, and her red hair cascaded in brassy ringlets around her neck.

Rachel laughed at the sight of the two young women pushing Amelia out onto the floor. "What fun!" she exclaimed.

"What now?" The Anglican minister followed close behind Rachel, his dark eyes flashing, beholding the evening's spectacle with sure delight. He spooned a large helping of Amelia's hot apple tart, dripping with cream, into his mouth.

"Please deliver me, Reverend Whitley!" Amelia called to Rachel's handsome escort. "It ain't Christian, I tell ye!"

His mouth quite full of hot dessert, Heath Whitley made helpless gestures with his hands and shrugged his shoulders, playing mute as the guests laughed gleefully.

"You've no aid for poor Amelia?" Rachel pursed her full lips into a pout. "Is *this* how you assist helpless ladies?"

With embellished theatrics, Heath set aside his tasty dish and made haste to form a reply. Tossing a gleaming black curl from his tanned forehead, he bowed humbly before the lovely red-haired woman. "I am but your undying slave, *madamoiselle*. Speak the word and I will wrench the woman free from her evil captors!"

Caleb rolled his eyes, slightly embarrassed at the behavior of the adults, yet sensing a bit of the frivolity in his own soul.

Rachel flashed a broad smile and glanced toward Amelia, who now twirled from the extended arms of her husband. "No. Let them be. I've never seen the two of them so happy."

Sliding his broad hand down her arm, Heath Whitley clasped Rachel's gloved fingers in his own. "Nor will you ever see me as happy."

Turning from the gaiety, Rachel gazed into the minister's eyes and clasped his other hand with her own. She stilled the trembling in her hands, set off by the warmth of his touch. "Nor I, Heath. It's a miracle you waited so long for me."

Heath didn't speak, as though doing so would break the spell this beautiful woman had cast over him.

"Tut, tut! What 'ave we 'ere?" George shouted above the singing and laughter. He clapped together his browned, callused hands. "I believe Miss Langley 'as an announcement to make!"

Caleb quickly set aside his empty dish and stood to squeeze his way past the visitors to better his chances of hearing of Rachel's surprise.

Amelia grasped a small china bell that sat atop an oak stand. Tinkling it overhead, she brought the room to order. "I can't wait another moment, Rachel. You must tell us your news."

Rachel stood tall while Heath Whitley released her hand and placed his arm behind her. "All right, if you insist. I wanted you all to . . . see my new dress!" She twirled, chuckling merrily to herself.

While the guests murmured their disappointment, Amelia chided the young woman. "Rachel Langley never did give no importance to fancy frocks an' such." She rested her arms across her bodice. "What is it *really*, Rachel? Tell us your secret."

Caleb nodded his agreement.

"Oh, I'll tell them if you won't." Heath pulled indignantly on the corners of his black woolen vest.

Rachel curtsied fashionably, her eyes lit with mischief. "It's nothing, really," she chided affectionately. "But while I stayed in England, I met a most gifted surgeon, Dr. Ranier. He allowed me to study under his careful tutelage."

"Don't say!" Amelia's smile broadened in approval.

More than anything else, Caleb found himself impressed with Rachel's quiet confidence. "Don't tell me. I can guess."

The beginning of a smile tipped the corners of Rachel's mouth. "Tell us then, Mr. Prentice."

"You're a bloomin' doctor!"

"Doctor?" Amelia again fanned her face, allowing George to draw her next to him.

The guests whispered among themselves, their shock evident.

Rachel attempted to interject. "No . . . wait . . ."

"Hear, hear!" Heath lifted his cup of cider. "A toast to Dr. Langley!"

A hush fell across the room, and a man's mutterings punctuated the stillness. *"A woman doctor?"*

"Please . . . wait!" Raising her hands, Rachel once again attempted to protest.

"A toast indeed!" George lifted his cup and eyed his wife, who lifted her glass in kind.

The guests slowly responded one by one, and a cheerful Cockney girl broke into applause. "Three cheers for Dr. Rachel!"

"Hooray!" others cheered.

"You're a-a bloomin' doctor!" Caleb shook his fist in victory.

"If I may speak, please?" Rachel asked, raising her voice confidently. "I, of course, am not a doctor."

Silence fell across the room.

"I am a midwife. But nonetheless, I learned a great deal under Dr. Ranier's instruction. Perhaps the most important thing he passed on to me was a deep compassion for those who suffer." She added with firm conviction, "Doctor or no doctor."

Heath's supportive gaze remained fixed on Rachel's earnest countenance. Without a word, his arm found its way around her shoulders.

"Of course, I also learned new medical procedures, a number of techniques for treating wounds, and some effective curatives for illnesses." She paused while those around her murmured quietly. "I realize I've been gone a long time." She glanced at Heath and couldn't help but smile when her companion regarded her with amusement. "Too long, really. But while I was away, I had much time to think of all the young convicts who are locked up with those sickly prisoners. I personally know their despair. They need"—she glanced up demurely at Heath and smiled prettily—"they need *us*."

"You're a godsend, Rachel." George nodded his affirmation. "Without you, the common folks'd be doomed, that's fer certain."

"Thank you, George. You all have given me so great a hope and a faith I'll always cherish."

"I don't care wot you all say. I still say she's Doctor Rachel!" Caleb crossed his arms at his waist.

Before Rachel could raise another note of protest, George lifted his glass once more.

"So be it, son. To all of us emancipists, she shall always be Doctor Rachel!"

Rachel's cheeks burned red and she glanced down at the floor. Taking a step back, she reached to grasp Heath Whitley's hand once more and said, "But that was only one of the reasons I returned." She faced the minister. "I believe our good Reverend has an announcement of his own."

"Oh!" Amelia's eyes lit with glad surprise.

Caleb frowned. Greatly vexed, he'd noticed the minister had occupied all of Rachel's time during the entire evening's affair. With hardly a chance to speak to her, he was jealous of her time. He longed to hear of her years while studying in England almost as desperately as he longed to go there himself.

With no hesitation, Heath gazed warmly at Rachel and then politely at the guests of Rose Hill. "I am pleased to announce that I have asked Miss Langley to be my wife."

Amelia shouted, "Glory be! It's a miracle from heaven!"

Waving his hands in a futile attempt to silence the gleeful women, George turned his attention again upon Heath Whitley. "Good enough, good enough! But how did the *lady* respond?" He tipped his head, his gaze skeptical.

Heath gazed back at Rachel, his eyes wide and his handsome face full of anticipation. Rachel answered on behalf of the minister. "I said yes, of course. I consented to Reverend Whitley's proposal of marriage."

Thunderous cheers filled the quaint farmhouse as guests gathered around the joyous couple to congratulate them.

"But wait!" Caleb pushed his way through. Tugging on the minister's sleeve, he called brazenly, "You never kissed Rachel. I never saw it."

The guests applauded the youth and chuckled at his mischief, while his parents shook their heads at his impertinence.

"It is true, Reverend Whitley." Rachel feigned diplomacy.

"Not proper t'all!" gasped one of the women guests.

Heath beheld the anticipation in the eyes of the onlookers. Turning, he cupped his hands aside his fiancée's rosy cheeks, all the while more women were emulating horror at the prospect of viewing an improper display of affection. Then, bending toward her face, Heath placed a delicate kiss upon her forehead, much to the delight and relief of all the ladies present. "There. My bride-to-be has been officially kissed." He laughed upon seeing the disappointment in Caleb's young eyes. "Patience, lad. I've waited longer than you'll ever know," he whispered.

The evening's affair soon ended. The guests offered their gratitude and fond farewells, departing two by two for their wagons. Reverend Whitley, ever popular among the emancipists, had rounded up several of the neighbors in his own wagon and made haste to escort them all back home. "If you would accompany me, Miss Langley, I will, on my sworn honor, deliver you promptly back to the Prentices' doorway before the hour of midnight."

"Don't believe the scoundrel, Rachel," George chided affectionately.

Rachel held up a long, slender finger. "I'll keep you to your honor, dear Reverend."

Caleb, feeling bored with the entire affair, turned at once and made haste to the rear porch where he'd hidden a pair of his comfortable trousers. Peeling off the dress-up attire his mother had fashioned for him from remnants, he quickly slipped into clothing more suitable for a midnight fishing excursion. "I'm going up to bed. Too sleepy!" he called to his parents. Grabbing his hand-carved pole, he ran from the house down the path that led to the pond, unaware of the eyes that watched him from the dark woods beyond the farmhouse.

Kelsey finished sweeping the shards of broken glass from behind the bar. The racket inside the tavern annoyed her, and weariness overtook her mind. She would normally have been counting stars beneath her windowsill by this time. But as other merchants trimmed their wicks, the taverner added coals to the fire and kept his guests' cups filled to the brim with grog. Frowzy barmaids ran to and fro from the heavy wooden tables to the bar, sloshing overfilled pannikins of rum.

"Can I go to my bed, now, sir?" Kelsey stood before Weems, her countenance a portraiture of innocence.

"I told you to rest this afternoon," he snapped. "These is our customers, and they don't take no likin' to me closin' the doors too early. Night is their day."

"I can't stay awake, t'all. I'm weary from the trip, sir. Please. Only this once allow me to rest." Kelsey felt intimidation issuing from the man's face, but not even fear could overrule her fatigue this night. She felt his angry hands grasp the worn red smock she had been given by one of the older servers. Drawing her hands to her face, she felt one stiff clout delivered across her left ear. Whether from the man's blow or her own fatigue she never knew, but Kelsey crumpled limply to the floor. She relaxed in the arms of two sympathetic barmaids who carried her from the room, a faint hint of amusement dimpling her cheeks.

Caleb had no sooner wetted his line than drowsiness overtook him. Resting against a tall evergreen, he closed his eyes, assuring himself he would not fall asleep. But his lids grew heavy, and even the distant sound of bleating sheep did not arouse him. Nor did the muffled sound of men's voices.

"Over 'ere, mate!" A convict long since escaped from the prison compound emerged from the bush with four others. Their eyes, glistening with hunger from one too many months in the bush, peered out from their partly masked faces like skulking beasts. "These folks is busy with their party. Let's rope this fat one over 'ere an' be done wif it."

"No. Takes days to trek back here from the wilderness. I say let's take two or three, an' one o' those chickens to boot!" another convict argued, his lumbering presence drawing stares of intimidation from the others.

"I still say *one* o' these'll do." The first one pointed to a large white sheep.

"I hear tell one o' the mates out back is a cannibal. We should take an extra from the flock, just in case we needs to appease the lout."

"I don't believe those tales."

"I saw a dead man's bones meself," another added, "all circled about a campfire. If we don't take extra vittles, he might eat us instead."

The others chuckled as their leader grew frustrated. "No time to call a parliamentary vote. Let's rope the big one before he sees us."

"What about the waif?"

The fifth convict came tramping back through the thicket. "The lad's gone sound asleep. He's no bother to us."

The convicts made swift work of roping the large sheep, which all the while bleated loudly in protest. One man acted hastily and ran off into the underbrush, pulling the animal behind.

Three of the escaped prisoners hastened down the path in

pursuit of two more sheep. A fourth convict, holding a squawk-
ing chicken under each of his arms, panicked and allowed one
of his feathered prizes to escape. The first man called out from
the blackness, "I told you to forget the hens. They're too
bloomin' loud." He peered toward the farmhouse and spied the
figure of a man gazing through the window. "Run! Someone's
comin'!"

A flock of galahs, small gray and white cockatoos, uttered
their grating cries from the brambled grottos of an ancient eucalyptus.

Heaving a drowsy sigh, Caleb stretched himself, his mind
floating out across the pond. A slight wind stirred the surface
of the water, causing the moon's reflection to shimmer like
spun silver. A movement caught his eye, and he saw his pole
quiver between the two stones where he had secured it. Swiftly
he crawled toward the rod, grasping the thick end of the pole
as gently as if it were a delicate china cup. Fixing his body behind the hand-hewn fishing pole, he tightened his grip in anticipation of the next strike. The pole shuddered between his
two hands, then abruptly the tip curved down toward the
pond's mossy surface. "Got it!" Caleb whispered, his teeth
clenched. He yanked the rod with all the strength his stout,
youthful frame could muster. The fish, larger than any he'd ever
imagined, dove downward and would've taken the pole, but the
boy dug his heels into the mire and held fast.

Caleb heard his mother's voice call out from a distant point.
It had an odd ring and he imagined she was calling to his father
from the kitchen entrance. But he would not release his trophy.
When he heard his own name called out, he decided his fate
would be improved if he were to return with a fish for the table.
The string stretched out tautly in front of him, and he reasoned
that wrong maneuvering could cause the line to break. So he
stood to his feet determined to weary his catch. He waited and
the guileful fish curved in and out until the line snagged on
something beneath the surface. The water stilled. Fearing his
prize lost, Caleb waded carefully into the chilly water, keeping
watch for crocodiles that from time to time found their way
into the pond. He followed the line and found it wound around
a dead gum tree. He dipped his fingers beneath the surface and
followed the line, finding part of it slackened and pulled away.

from the trunk. "I've lost it," Caleb concluded and reached into his pocket to retrieve his knife, but found it gone as well. *The girl.* He remembered giving away his prized possession in his moment of weakness. A sigh pursued Caleb's frustration. Not wanting to leave behind his pole or his own line, he began the task of freeing the string from the water-logged trunk. His fingers worked quickly. At last he untied the final knot that released the line from the rotted wood. Lifting his pole, he wound the line around it until he felt his fingers suddenly squeezed where the string encircled them. "Wot's this?"

The line jerked with such a force it sent the pole slipping from his grasp. "The beggar's still on the line!" Caleb lunged for the pole, the splash of cold water jarring his senses. He retrieved it and the battle raged once more between boy and fish. The discharge of a musket from the wooded glen beyond the pond caught his attention briefly, but he continued to wrangle tirelessly, the promise of a catch fortifying his vigor. The fish soon tired and Caleb dragged the beast to shore, delighted to find its size equaled its fight.

Sizing it up with his eyes, he then lobbed the line with fish intact over his shoulder and made straight for the farmhouse. His father's pride in his catch would most assuredly outweigh his mum's displeasure at his rebellious excursion.

A musket fired again but sounded closer this time. Caleb stopped abruptly, realizing a hunter could be trespassing. He deliberated upon running back to the farmhouse and retrieving his firearm or confronting the hunter directly. Taking a step in the direction of the farmhouse, a faint groan sent a chill through him. *Papa?* He listened intently. Only the sound of a lone bird trilled through the stillness of night. Then, when the human groan again issued from the deep forest, Caleb ran toward it without further delay.

Pushing his way through uncut bramble, he scratched his face and winced at the pain. The fish and pole tangled at once in the density of the woods, and Caleb dropped it without thought. Men's voices shouted back and forth to one another and then grew faint as though they ran faster than he. Caleb listened, intent upon finding his father. Forcing his way into a clearing, he stopped abruptly when he saw the moonlight pointing to a still figure crumpled on a bed of forest leaves.

"Papa?" he shouted, his heart pounding in his ears.

The body did not stir. Caleb began to move toward it, but then heard the sound of approaching footsteps. He dove into the nearby thick underbrush and waited soundlessly.

He could not see, but he heard the cry of his mother coming from beyond the clearing. *No, Mum. Go back!* He clenched his fists as though by sheer will he could send his mother back into the safety of the farmhouse. "George! Caleb!" Amelia cried.

It's me own fault. She's lookin' for me. At that moment Caleb hated himself for his headstrong ways.

Close by he could hear footsteps pace slowly and then turn in Amelia's direction.

His own safety now secondary, he made his choice and battled a useless urge to cry. Hearing a pop of twigs as the footsteps cracked through the brittle underbrush, he thrust himself from the foliage and waved his arms wildly. "Run, Mum! Run!"

The convict jerked around, his anger evident. "Silence, you"—he wielded a knife—"or you'll get this!" He twisted the knife in the air and the blade glinted menacingly in the moonlight.

Amelia called out again, her voice coming closer. "Caleb, where are you?"

"Caleb, eh?" the bushranger grunted morosely. "Tell 'er, son." He cupped his fingers outwardly. "Bring the wench to Papa," he sneered in a whispered tone.

"No." Caleb shook his head, keeping his voice muted. "Kill me. But leave 'er be."

The convict stepped toward Caleb, his arm extended with the blade gripped firmly. "Your Papa killed me mate. Guess I'll 'ave to kill you."

Perplexed, Caleb glanced toward the body. A mixture of elation and fear swept through him upon realizing the body on the ground was not his father's. The convict drew closer and Caleb froze. He knew that one sound would send his mother tearing into the clearing. Swallowing hard, he closed his eyes and prepared for the inevitable.

"Stop, you fool!"

Caleb opened his eyes. Behind the bushranger stood his papa, musket aimed and ready to fire.

"Papa!" He felt the first tear trickle down his cheek. "You're alive!"

"George!" The limbs of a shrub stirred. Amelia emerged with bewilderment marking her gaze.

"Don't move!" George threatened the convict. Turning to face his wife, George spoke breathlessly, for he'd been running. "Bushrangers. They stole our sheep, they did. This man"—he pointed to the body—"tried to take me rifle. It misfired and shot 'im. Shot 'im dead."

"I knew you couldn't—" Caleb shook his head, his anger kindled at the vagabond convicts.

"I could, son," George corrected the boy, "for two reasons." He gazed first at his wife and then back at Caleb. Regarding the convict, he said regretfully, "Your cronies got clean away, I vow. Stole a sheep an' two o' Amelia's prize hens."

Amelia cupped her hands to her face. "Who cares a shillin' about the hens, George Prentice? At least you're alive!" She turned toward Caleb. "And you, young man—"

Instantly, the felled convict groaned.

"He's alive!" Caleb exclaimed. "I'll run and fetch Rachel. She'll know what to do."

George bent to examine the man's chest. Feeling the warmth of fresh blood, he lifted his hand and worried at the musket wound gaping near the man's heart. "You'd best hurry, son. He ain't with us for long." Before he could stand, the other convict whirled around and bolted into the darkness.

Caleb flinched. "Look out!"

"He's getting away!" Amelia shrieked.

George trained his eyes on the blackness, the weapon steady in his grasp. He sighed, then dropped the musket to his side. "Too late. I'll tell the military tomorrow, and they can organize a search party." He mopped his brow. "I'm too weary to take another step."

"Why did you come out after them?" Caleb asked, perplexed.

Blowing out an exasperated breath, George eyed his boy. "I found my scoundrel son missing. When I heard the commotion, I feared the worst."

Amelia took her place next to George and stooped over the convict. "You'll be the death o' me, Caleb Prentice, that's wot."

A sickening feeling swept through Caleb. "You both could've been killed. It would've been my fault . . . all my fault."

"Don't, son," George answered resignedly. "Just go an' fetch Rachel and Reverend Whitley. If we save this one, per'aps he'll lead us to the rest."

Amelia stood and grasped George's hand. "Afraid not." She glanced down at the lifeless body. "This one's already gone."

Caleb eyed his parents soberly, then turned to tread back toward the farmhouse with a lingering memory of one prize fish that hung dead somewhere from an unknown tree limb.

4
THE FLAME
KINDLED

Reverend Samuel Marsden sat across the desk from John Macarthur. He fingered a small purple velvet pouch drawn up with a gold braid. "It is my feeling, Paymaster, that the whole of the settlement's problem is the convicts' inability to conform." The coins inside the pouch clicked together like brass buttons.

"To say the least." Lieutenant Macarthur studied some figures from his personal supply list with a looking glass.

"It's my opinion, therefore, that the whole of their problem is their heathen roots."

"I see." Macarthur laid aside his looking glass. "And you are proposing what?"

Stuffing the pouch inside his cloak, Marsden held up a recently penned document. "I'm proposing mandatory church attendance by all convicts."

"Your pulpit, I presume?"

"Well, yes, of course."

Macarthur frowned. "You believe that convict church attendance would solve the colony's ills?"

"Most assured of such an objective."

A sardonic smile curved Macarthur's face. "For that new church building of yours, it would certainly improve your numbers—"

"I'm not concerned with my numbers, sir!" Marsden pulled a handkerchief from his pocket, dabbing his upper lip in quick succession. "The poor beggars couldn't even tithe. They've no money. But I've been appointed here to bring change, and change I'll accomplish if allowed to do so by the military."

"So it's your reputation that's important to you?"

Growing weary of the lieutenant's innuendo, Marsden paused. Then gazing up at the man, he retorted, "Don't be overly concerned with my motives, Lieutenant, until you've evaluated your own."

"I don't hide my ambitions behind a Bible, sir," Macarthur spoke candidly. "My task is clear, my goals predetermined."

Marsden calculated his gaze, allowing his eyes to peruse the ornately decorated office. "Heaven help you."

Ignoring the minister's pointed stare, Macarthur clasped his hands calmly below his brass insignia. "When speaking to *me*, there'll be no cause to conceal your aspirations with religious dialogue."

Gazing down at his hands, Marsden replied, "And no cause for insult." Well acquainted with Macarthur's savage temperament, he pulled on his gloves and drew himself up with a staunch finality. "If you wish no help from the Anglican church, then I wash my hands of the matter—"

"Not so hasty, Reverend. I'm a man to lay everything on the table, that's all I'm saying. You can say what you want behind your pulpit, but don't try to ply John Macarthur with your religious pomp."

"Even John Macarthur is a man in need of religion, I'm sure. However pompous you make it is entirely up to you." Marsden settled himself back into the chair. He knew Macarthur's tactics for maintaining control had left him with an unshakable reputation as that of a dictator. But Marsden himself was well acquainted with control and was equally successful in having his way. "So you might find some importance in cooperating with the church, yes?"

Macarthur nodded. "Possibly. Are you suggesting the military escort the crawlers to and from your services?"

"It would do them a world of good."

"What about the Irish Catholics?"

"They're the worst sort of heathen. They should comply with the ruling as well."

"I hope to see immediate improvement in the behavior of the prisoners."

"You shall." Marsden grinned broadly. Placing his gloved fingers upon the documents, he shoved them slowly toward the paymaster. "Sydney Cove will be a paradise. I guarantee it."

Kelsey McBride rode behind Charlotte, a young Cockney woman, straddling the stocky horse owned by Weems. Charlotte had secured permission to visit a relative in the countryside in addition to tending to the domestic affairs of the taverner. Kelsey, with great relief, had been granted permission to accompany the servant and assist her in any way needed.

"Where are we?" Kelsey asked, studying the blue afternoon sky.

"Parrametta. We'll be at Aunt Frieda's house before long."

"How did you come to have a relative so far from England?"

The girl stiffened, steadied the reins when the steed increased its gait, and answered quietly, "You kin keep a secret?"

"I swear it."

"Frieda Mercer befriended me aboard the transport ship I was shackled on. She's a good woman—good as gold, good as any gold. She married up with a military man and got 'er pardon right away. She's done a lot fer me, her bein' freed an' all. I wanted to do somethin' fer 'er, seein' how it's 'er birthday."

"What did you make for her, Charlotte?"

"Made 'er a rhubarb pie an' a new apron."

"Aye, she'll love it! You're a good friend, at that."

Suddenly preoccupied, Charlotte's tone grew somber. "Horse is actin' strange. Must smell water."

Kelsey peered around Charlotte and studied the horse. "How can you tell?"

"I been takin' care o' Weems' livestock six years now. This

one an' me can read each other's mind."

"Do tell!" Kelsey laughed. Her cheeks flushed pink, and she realized the mirth did her well. Charlotte reined the horse to a stop and dismounted. Reaching up, she assisted Kelsey down, and then removed the satchel of food she had prepared for the trip.

After walking across a field and beyond a stand of trees with Charlotte leading the horse, Kelsey laughed at seeing a stream stretched before them. "If I didn't know a wee bit better, Charlotte Hampton, I'd say you're a witch." Her crisp Irish brogue snapped off the phrase with an air of mischief.

"Watch your tongue, girl." Charlotte made a cross over her heart and touched a knee to the ground.

"You're Catholic?" Kelsey asked with interest.

"No, but I seen a nun do this, an' I figure it wards off evil."

Kelsey laughed again and raced the woman to the water's edge. Bending at the stream's bank, she scooped up the water with both hands. Tiny wet rivulets trickled down her dusty wrists, leaving irregular white paths. She caught sight of a small fish moving slowly through the narrow crystal waterway. Leaning forward on her reddened knees, she followed its movement with fascination. "There's a fish in this stream, Charlotte. Let's catch it."

"An' how you goin' to catch it?"

"I don't know. But wouldn't it be grand to take a fresh fish to your aunt Frieda?"

"No. Carry a smelly fish in this heat? Let's go, Kelsey." At the finality in Charlotte's tone, Kelsey sat back on her legs. "Let's go, let's go," she mimicked Charlotte under her breath. She was fast growing weary of having no time to call her own. Even when her mother was a sharecropper, Kelsey had cherished unfettered moments and lazy afternoons when she could run freely in the fields and hollows of Kildare's woodland. She found herself envious of the fish for its freedom. Kelsey watched dispiritedly as Charlotte led the horse back through a thicket of trees to readjust the traveling pack under the cool shade. Deciding to steal one more glance at the fish, she peered again into the glittering surface. But instead of the fish, two eyes, blue as a robin's egg, stared back at her. "Who're you?" she gasped. Instantly, Kelsey toppled backward, startled by the human face reflected in the stream. With her heart pounding rapidly, she sat up and modestly straightened her skirts. Frowning in annoyance at the boy with laughing eyes who stood across the narrow water's curve, she exclaimed, "How ill-bred!" She stood up, awkwardly freeing her worn boots from the loosened hem of her faded blue skirt. "Frightening a young woman so!" Hesitating, she studied the youth's jovial face. "Why . . . it's you!"

"Bah!" The surly Irish convict woman hurled the tarnished dish across the prison compound's stone path. "Not fit for rats!" The dish slammed against a wall and ricocheted onto the flinty pathway like a tossed coin, its cold, mealy contents scattering across the barren ground.

"Don't throw it away, wench! At least pass it me way if you won't eat it yourself!" a convicted thief complained as he sat cross-legged, gobbling his mash beneath the building's sagging eaves.

"You're nothing but a dog if you eat the poison the British blackguards dish out to us. I'll starve first!" Hattie McBride crossed her arms at her waist, stubbornly ignoring the hunger pangs that clawed at her stomach.

Across from them, William Orr quietly lifted his spoon to his parched lips, his shackles jangling like bells. His face astute, he waited for Hattie to glance his way, then lifted his chin in affirmation of his desire to speak to her. His gray eyes glanced first at the unsuspicious prisoner who licked at his dish like a ravenous beast and then back to Hattie, his gaze conspiratorial.

Freed temporarily from her chains, Hattie pushed herself from the hard ground and slowly made her way toward Orr. She bent to retrieve her dish, as though the task demonstrated her sole intent. Then, seating herself comfortably within the Irish dissident's earshot, she muttered, "You got something to say?"

"The United Irish are in need of you," Orr whispered.

"And what good is Hattie McBride now, I ask you?"

"*They* are becoming more comfortable with you, shall we

say." Holding up his shackled wrists, Orr's once-confident face betrayed his frustration. "But not with me. I'm guarded by Macarthur's hawks." He pointed with his eyes toward a soldier stationed within feet of him.

"Yes, but"—Hattie lowered her voice, her emotions yielding to a sickening helplessness—"since I lost my own daughter, I'm useless even to myself, William."

"Kelsey's in safer hands than if she'd been thrown in this devilish abyss. Be thankful, Hattie, be thankful."

"Thankful! I curse the God or devil who doomed me to this place! I'd be thankful if the guard would finish me off with that musket he totes around as though he's the king."

Orr, using his shackled legs for mobility, pushed closer to the woman. "Don't say such things. We need you. We need arms."

"How, William?" Hattie's face grew ashen. "One step toward that arsenal building and they'd pick us off like flies."

"They wouldn't suspect *you*."

"Then what? Say I snatch a few muskets. What next?"

"We rebel. We're prisoners of war. Can't you see that?"

Hattie studied the fervor in Orr's face. "You mean it, don't you?"

His lips pressed tightly, Orr drew near the vulnerable woman's face. "Unconditionally."

Hattie felt spellbound by his penetrating and powerful eyes. Her gaze riveted to his as he glanced back toward the guards. She couldn't help admiring his bold profile, which spoke of power and strength.

"Attention!" A corporal entered the compound where the prisoners sat eating. "All convicts assemble at once!" he barked.

Hattie heaved a sigh, her glare resistive, while the others around her rose instantly. "Tame ponies," she growled through clenched teeth. "British pets!"

William Orr shifted forward, his eyes casting covertly about. "Don't bring attention to yourself, Hattie," he coaxed in a low hiss. "Cooperate."

Bewilderment seized Hattie upon hearing Orr's request. But without further hesitation, she stood at once, astonished at his power over her. Orr stood next to her, leaning against her as though afflicted. Hattie gripped his arm and assisted him in standing upright. Their eyes locked and Hattie felt empathy prick at her heart. *He needs me!* she thought, astounded at the sudden realization.

The corporal shouted, "By order of the paymaster, Lieutenant John Macarthur, all prisoners of His Majesty's Navy are hereby ordered to attend the religious services held by the distinguished Reverend Samuel Marsden."

"Anglican services?" Orr's consternation evident, he gazed around at the other surprised Irish Catholics with narrowed eyes, controlling their reactions with his glance.

"Full cooperation has been granted Reverend Marsden by the military. All prisoners are commanded to accommodate with equal cooperation by way o' their attendance."

"Excuse me, Corporal, sir," a hapless convict called out.

The officer nodded to him indifferently.

"Wi' all due respek to the reverend, not all us prisoners is Protestant."

"Orders are orders. You're all expected to comply." The scroll snapped up into his hand. "The wagons will arrive Sunday morning at sunrise to escort you all"—the corporal grinned ruefully—"to church." He whirled around and departed without ceremony.

Hattie felt her cheeks flush, her anger kindled. "Trying to turn us all into Protestants, are they?"

"Surprised?" Orr's voice rumbled quietly.

Turning to face him, Hattie nodded her affirmation. "I'll do whatever you ask, William. Just tell me what to do."

Seeing the girl's distressed face, Caleb grew somber. "I apologize, miss, if I caused you alarm."

Kelsey wrapped her arms about herself. Her cheeks reddened, she gazed back down at the bubbling water. "No." She shook her head. "No alarm at all," she lied.

"It is you, isn't it?" Pulling up his trouser leg, Caleb dipped one bare foot into the shallow stream. "You're the girl from the market with Weems?" He pulled up the other trouser leg. "McBride?"

Nodding nervously, Kelsey allowed a faint smile to play around the corners of her face. "Yes. I suppose I'm indebted to ya. You were a brave one to face that horrible man."

"Why do you work for 'im?"

Kelsey shrugged, not at all wishing to divulge the nature of her dreaded situation.

Discerning the girl's cautious demeanor, Caleb approached her slowly. "You're Irish?"

Breaking into a broad grin, Kelsey spoke with an exaggerated brogue. "Now, how did you know that, laddie?"

"Lucky guess, I vow. Just lucky." Stopping midstream, he lifted his hand in friendly invitation. "Join me?"

Kelsey turned and saw Charlotte already making her way toward the dirt road. "I can't. I have to go with Charlotte. We're running errands for Weems."

"You can't join me for a swim?"

"Oh no. This is my only dress. It'd be soaked and I've nothing else to wear t'all."

His eyes wide, mocking innocence, Caleb reached to unbutton his shirt. "We don't swim in our clothes, foolish girl."

Kelsey gasped. "You're a brash young man! Away from me!" She backed away in alarm.

Realizing he had carried his folly too far, Caleb lifted his hands in surrender. "I . . . I didn't mean it, miss! I would never do such a thing, either." Now it was his turn to lie. He stepped from the stream onto Kelsey's side of the bank. "Please forgive this brash fellow?" He knelt on one knee.

Kelsey hesitated, keeping her distance. "You're sure?"

Making a gesture across his chest, Caleb nodded assuringly. "Cross me heart, hope to die."

Filled with relief, Kelsey smiled. Her heart gladdened upon finding him so affable. She asked, "What be your name?"

Reciprocating her trust, Caleb answered jovially, "Caleb Prentice. And what're you called?"

Kelsey hesitated. Her mother had firmly cautioned her to trust no one.

"Surely you have a name?"

She nodded, answering reluctantly. "Kelsey McBride."

"Right fine name."

Remembering the day in the market, Kelsey reached inside

a pocket and pulled out the knife. "Look. I still have it."

With slight regret, Caleb nodded. "Oh, good." He attempted to sound cheerful.

Her eyes wide, Kelsey held out the knife. "You can have it back, of course—"

"No, no. It was a gift." Caleb regretted his prior decision but refused to correct the matter. "You keep it. Really." He felt his ears redden.

"Kelsey?" Charlotte called from the road. "Where in blazes are you?"

Kelsey dropped the knife back into her pocket. "I must leave, Caleb." She started toward the road.

Sighing in frustration, Caleb attempted to follow her. "But we've just met. Can't she come for you on the way back to Sydney Cove?"

"No. We're staying the night at her aunt's house."

"Who's her aunt?" Caleb seized the opportune moment. "Per'aps I know the lady."

"Woman by the name of Frieda Mercer."

"I *do* know the Mercers. Live right down the road from Rose Hill."

"Kelsey!" Charlotte's tone grew agitated.

"Coming!" Kelsey shouted her reply, then glanced back toward the boy. "Rose Hill?"

"Yes, Rose Hill. That's where you're standin'—on Rose Hill. Me parents' land."

"What?"

"We're sheep farmers. Rose Hill is our land."

Gazing around the lush landscape, Kelsey commented sincerely, "Rose Hill is a lovely name for a lovely place. You're fortunate, y'are."

Seeing the strange sadness in the girl's eyes, Caleb felt the same melancholy rise up that he had felt for her in the marketplace. "I'll come to visit tomorrow at the Mercers."

"*Kelsey!*"

"Good-bye, Caleb," Kelsey called over her shoulder as she ran into the thicket of trees and disappeared.

Cupping his hands to his mouth, Caleb took a deep breath and shouted, "Expect me tomorrow. I'll be there!" With the girl completely out of sight, he bent to wring the water from his trouser cuffs. Denying her seeming rejection of him, he turned confidently to cross the stream.

"I'll be looking for you!" Kelsey's voice resonated from the road. Whirling around, Caleb spied the young Irish girl riding on the saddle blanket behind the woman she'd called Charlotte. They trotted down the road with Kelsey waving timidly toward him. He chastened himself for the foolish exuberance he felt from her acknowledgment. *She's only a girl.* He could imagine what Matthew would have to say about the matter. He finished crossing the stream and ran down the bank to check his fishing lines. But then, Matthew didn't have to know everything.

5

EMERALD FIRES

Caleb waited impatiently, settling himself upon the steps of the darkened stairwell that led to his room. He had hoped to speak to Reverend Whitley, but finding the minister preoccupied with Rachel all evening, anxious thoughts filled his mind as Whitley prepared to take his leave of Rose Hill.

The matter of marriage being settled, Heath Whitley visited Rachel at Rose Hill without inhibition. Stepping out beneath the unroofed verandah, he guided Rachel through the front door behind him. "Good night, again."

"Good night, Heath." Rachel started to release her grasp but smiled when his strong hands enclosed hers. "I—"

"Let's not say good-bye. It saddens me."

"Why is that?"

"Because I can't bear to leave you again." Heath stepped toward her. Gently, he cradled her arms in his hands. "As a matter of fact, let's run away tonight. To the magistrate."

"Awaken David Collins?"

"He wouldn't mind. You'd be my wife . . . tonight."

A smile broke across Rachel's face. "I'm as anxious as you, Heath Whitley. But what of all the plans Amelia's made for a church wedding for us. We wouldn't want to disappoint her, would we?"

Heath waited, the longing in his face an almost pained expression. "Perceptions! Why must we allow what others think to dictate—"

"Reverend Whitley?" Caleb's young voice broke the silence. Heath and Rachel turned at once to see him standing in the doorway. Rachel sighed, although her eyes lit with affection for him. "We thought you'd retired for the evening."

"I needs to ask the reverend somethin'."

Heath nodded patiently but maintained his grasp around Rachel's arms. "Go on."

"I'm needin' to go by the Mercer place. Would you be goin' that way?"

"Yes, but it's much too late to awaken those good folks tonight. I could bring you back tomorrow on my rounds." He turned to face Rachel. "It would give me a good excuse to return to Rose Hill."

Caleb contemplated the matter. "I've no chores tomorrow wot with it bein' Saturday an' all."

"Ask your papa if you could accompany me tonight then. You can sleep on my floor."

Caleb calculated the time it took for his father to fall asleep. He heard no snoring emanating from upstairs. "I'll run ask him and fetch a clean shirt for tomorrow." He made haste to scramble up the stairs. He found his father walking around in his nightshirt and bearing a bright candle that illuminated his sleepy face. Caleb made a great show of the fact he wished to accompany the minister to his home and join him on his rounds tomorrow. George complied reluctantly and turned to curl sleepily around his wife in their soft feather bed.

Snatching his best shirt from atop the mattress on his floor, Caleb clambered down the stairs again. Sliding across the floor in a buoyant manner, he stopped upon seeing the silhouette of the minister embracing his bride-to-be under the glow of the moon. *He's kissin' 'er!* Lingering in capricious anticipation, he crept up to the doorway and crossed his arms at his waist. "If I was you, Rachel, I'd smack 'im across 'is face," he called.

"Teach 'im a lesson, it would!" He chuckled mischievously.

Gently lifting his face, Heath acknowledged Caleb with a wink. Then, without hesitation, he bent and placed a final soft kiss upon Rachel's lips. Stroking her face with his hands, he turned and nodded diplomatically. "Ready to leave, lad?"

"Yes, sir." Caleb strode past them, making fast for the carriage while the couple lingered over their parting.

After a while, Heath made his way toward him and stepped up into the carriage, seating himself next to Caleb. "I'm exhausted."

Sighing, Caleb retorted, "It's no wonder, the way you carry on so with Rachel. An' you a respectable minister!"

"Do you blame me?" Heath allowed his gaze to follow the graceful young woman stepping into the farmhouse. "I'm obsessed. I admit it."

Caleb rolled his eyes. "I'll never allow a woman to drag me out this late at night, that's wot."

The reins firm in his grasp, Heath flicked his wrists. Studying the dark road ahead, he commented casually, "So, young man, what does bring you out so late on this night?"

Caleb remembered his promise to Kelsey, but then his own words flew at him. He blushed, but grateful for the dark, he took a deep breath and chose his words. "I promised to do some chores for the Mercers."

"Mr. Mercer came calling?"

"No." Caleb fidgeted. "Yes, that is—"

"Ah, lad, your sins will find you out. Time to confess now. Why call on the Mercers?"

"I ran into . . . an old friend. Sh-she's staying with the Mercers, and I promised to come and visit. No problem with visiting a friend, is there?"

"Surely not." Heath enhanced his words with mock sympathy. "And never, repeat, never allow a woman to drag you out late at night. But an old friend, that's different, eh, lad?"

Caleb nodded, the lie in his throat choking his words.

Kelsey arranged a bundle of twigs beneath the large iron kettle. Charlotte had retired for the evening, but Kelsey enjoyed the company of Mrs. Mercer and found excuse to stay awake. "There, now, Mrs. Mercer. We can start our cooking early in the morning. The kindling's all ready for you."

"That's a dear. Thank you, Kelsey." The older woman lifted herself from a straight-backed chair. "But do call me Aunt Frieda. Everyone else does."

"I'll do it," Kelsey answered sprightly. "How I wish you had been the one on the dock to take me home." She frowned, the dread of returning to Weems' dank tavern already overshadowing her trip.

"Now, don't fret. Perhaps Mr. Weems would consider a proposition." Frieda Mercer ambled toward the room where she and her husband slept.

Kelsey hesitated, hoping her ears did not deceive her. "Proposition?"

"I'm gettin' slower these days. Could use an energetic girl like yourself to help me around the kitchen."

"Oh, could you now?" Kelsey's face brightened. "I'd work harder than anyone you've ever seen, ma'am! I'd—"

"Don't overexcite yourself," the old woman chastened. "Weems is a hard man. He'll be a difficult ol' codger to quibble with. Might not consider the trade at all."

"Trade?"

"He's been eyein' a milk cow o' Edgar's for some time now. An' I'm needin' kitchen help—"

"Swap me for a cow?" Kelsey stood contemplating the thought and then cupped her hands to her mouth as she laughed. "Wouldn't my mother think it folly?"

"Folly or no, it's the only idea I kin think of."

Whirling around Kelsey clasped her hands atop Frieda's weathered fingers. "It's a wonderful idea, Aunt Frieda. And begorra, you're a saint, that's what!"

"I'm no saint, child, but it gives me a fright to think of you slavin' under that tyrant. Now off to bed with you."

"Good night, Aunt Frieda." Kelsey kissed the woman aside her cheek and stepped with a springy bounce toward the back porch. She made haste to unroll the bundles of blankets left for her on the frayed rug. Undressing quickly, she donned an oversized pink gown that Charlotte had loaned to her for the trip and then knelt upon the folded blankets. Finding the windowsill an agreeable place for reflection, she rested her arms upon the unpainted wood and gazed upward. The stars, brilliant and cheerful, lit the dark landscape like candles on a Christmas tree. As she bowed her head, petitions lined up in her mind like untended soldiers wounded in battle. She hadn't said her prayers since the horrible afternoon she had bid farewell to her mother. Inside her stirred a mixture of resentment and affection for the woman as well as for God. *Hattie McBride, what have you gotten us into now?*

Realizing her mind drifted, she drew her thoughts back to her prayers. "Please get me away from Weems, dear God," she whispered. Fearful her words fell upon deaf ears, she continued with fervor, and each request built courage in her heart. "Take care of my mother. She's in trouble." Kelsey opened her eyes and found them clouded by tears. "Horrible trouble." She blinked and then remembered the beating she would have taken had it not been for the Prentice boy. "Please look after Caleb Prentice." She dropped all ceremony, the intensity of her requests more paramount than tradition as the stars became her focal point. "Thank you for sending me a friend. Thank you for sending me Caleb Prentice." Kelsey, overtaken by fatigue, curled up on the blankets and drifted off, her countenance reflecting a renewed sense of tranquillity. *Tomorrow he'll come.* "Father, Son, and Holy Spirit." She gestured crossways with her fingers. "Amen."

"I can't drive another mile." Heath shook his head and flicked the reins, urging the horse to quicken its gait. "Give me strength, Lord." A halfhearted prayer quietly escaped his lips.

"I can drive, Reverend Whitley," Caleb offered sleepily.

Heath had felt the youth's head lean against him more than once. "No, you rest. If I see a parishioner's lantern in a window, I'll pull aside and request lodging. They're always more than happy to oblige."

The horse and buggy jaunted along the dark passage of road for another hour. The comfortable silence between the two gave the minister time to reflect upon his wedding day. A smile curved his lips, and he resisted the temptation to turn his carriage around and head straight for Rose Hill again. A glimmer caught his eye. Heath squinted. The pale glow ahead grew, so he turned his horse to the right to make way for the carriage heading their way. "Look yonder. Another carriage approaches," he said to Caleb. He looked to the side and found Caleb sound asleep next to him. The clip-clop sound of horses' hooves neared their buggy.

"What hail!" a raspy voice called out.

"Hello, who's there?" Heath hailed the oncoming carriage.

"Reverend Samuel Marsden. Who be ye, sir?"

Heath paused upon hearing the minister's driver make known his rider. The fellow Anglican minister, albeit the new head of the first Anglican church in New South Wales, brought a sigh to his lips. "Reverend Heath Whitley, sir. Greetings."

Marsden's driver pulled his team to a halt. "It's the good Reverend Heath Whitley, sir," he called down to his master.

"Invite him in." Marsden's voice sounded unanimated and as weary as Heath's.

Heath dismounted the buggy and strode to the carriage door, where the driver allowed him access. "Greetings, sir," he said, climbing into the minister's conveyance.

"What brings you out so late, Whitley?" Marsden pulled tediously at the fingers of his gloves while the minister sat across from him.

"My bride-to-be, Rachel Langley. I've been visiting her at a farm where she'll stay until our marriage."

"Splendid." Marsden gazed ahead unseeing for a few moments. His mind was obviously preoccupied with some troubling matter. "I've two places to be at once and am at odds with my situation," he said at last.

Heath sat forward, hoping his face reflected concern. "How so?"

Pulling a wax-sealed note from his cloak, Marsden waved it impatiently. "I'm needed at the prison compound at once. Some of the convicts need a good lesson from their parson."

Heath's jaw grew rigid. "They summoned you?"

"Yes. Seems a little rebellion is stirring, but I'll quell their passion straightaway. Nothing a good flogging won't cure."

Unable to hold his words, Heath replied, "I don't know that I agree that flogging is the answer."

"What, then?" Marsden slid his glove through his fingers, wringing the tips. "You've a better solution, Whitley?"

"Our Lord has called us to feed His sheep, sir, not flog them."

"Don't be so pious, Whitley! These aren't the Lord's sheep. They're nothing but beasts. And beasts must be taught a lesson. They don't think as rational, civilized human beings, you know."

Unwilling to agree, Heath conveniently remembered the young man left asleep in his buggy. "I really must be going."

"One moment. Don't be so hasty. I believe it's providence that we crossed paths." Pulling a poorly scrawled note from his pocket, Marsden held it out to Heath. "I received this note upon my door this afternoon."

Heath obligingly unfolded the crumpled letter. It read:

Dear Reverend Marsden, I am a poor widow lost an hungry. If I do not find food for myself and my wee babe soon, I shall end our lives by midnite on this nite in the portals of your church. Plese help this lost soul find its way before its tew late.

Heath pulled his watch from his pocket. "Dear sir, it's but half past eleven at this moment."

"You see my dilemma." Marsden nodded.

"But why travel out to flog prisoners when a widow needs food?"

"The church has loyalties to the British Navy that we must fulfill. But you can assist me with the remedy."

"Which is?"

"Take that turn in the road—the one you just passed by."

Heath leaned out the door. "The bend ahead of you now?"

"Yes. It's a shorter path to the church. There's food locked in a larder in the back room of the church. Here's the key." He lifted a large key from his pocket and handed it to Heath.

"You wish for *me* to meet the widow?"

"As our Lord commanded." His smile sardonic, Marsden trained his gaze on the younger minister.

Heath felt his eyelids drooping, as was his spirit. "As you wish, sir." His fatigue weakening his inhibitions, he spoke forthrightly, "And may we stay for the night in the church? I'm wearied to the bone and have a young lad with me who also needs rest."

Marsden sighed impatiently. Tugging a glove over his pudgy hand, he acquiesced. "All right then. Take your rest upon the large bed in the eastern room. Some generous ladies in our church provided the room for weary travelers such as yourself."

Mixed relief swept through Heath. "Thank you. Now about the widow. Is all of the larder's food for her and the child?"

Marsden shook his head vigorously. "No, heavens no. I take some of it for myself. Just give her enough to last a day or two and send her on her way. Such a woman can become a nuisance."

Heath felt a twinge of remorse at having agreed to accommodate the minister. *I'll see she leaves with extra*, he decided.

Caleb sat up in the wagon, rubbed his eyes, and blinked at the darkness. The dark road appeared unfamiliar to his groggy mind. *Where are we?* He glanced at the empty seat next to him. Then looking ahead, he spied a driver atop a well-lit carriage, his hat cocked over his eyes. "Sir?" Caleb called out.

Startled at the interruption, the driver sat forward and eyed the boy. "Who are ye?"

"Caleb Prentice. Have you seen a Reverend Heath Whitley—"

"In the carriage with Reverend Marsden." He jabbed a finger toward the carriage door beneath him and pushed his hat over his eyes again.

Caleb squinted toward the carriage door, surprised that Reverend Whitley would acknowledge such a pretender to the pulpit. But soon the door creaked open and Whitley stepped out, his trudging gait attesting to his exhaustion. "Reverend Whitley?" Caleb's voice squeaked with fatigue.

"I'm here, son. We'll be making a brief detour, but we'll gain an earlier place to rest in the bargain." Pulling himself into the seat, Heath nodded politely at the driver and gestured for him to pass first. "I'll explain along the way."

Caleb watched Marsden's carriage pass, curiosity etching his face. He sat silently while Heath maneuvered the horse and buggy around a flat stretch of ground next to the road and then aimed the rig in the opposite direction. Settling himself against the cushioned seat, he allowed his mind to drift. The Irish girl filled his thoughts, and he worried for her well-being in the

hands of the vicious taverner. Soon his attention drew back to
the minister, who had begun to explain Marsden's dilemma. He
noted the frustration in Heath's tone but kept his opinion to
himself, too tired to debate Marsden's motives. *Whitley's a
kinder one than me*, he thought, remembering the selfish way
that Marsden had manipulated his way into obtaining a new
church building, while Reverend Whitley stubbornly refused to
accept the corrupt military's handouts.

The time passed more quickly than Caleb anticipated. Soon
the square broke into view, and the church's steeple could be
seen outlined in the dove-white moonlight. "Straight ahead,
Reverend." Caleb sat up, anticipating the comfort of a feather
bed. Once they arrived, he made haste to act as livery for the
minister, unharnessing the steed and leading the animal to the
trough for water, while Whitley combed the church grounds
searching for the woman and her infant.

Caleb found a spreading tree behind the church where he
tied fast the horse. Then he and Whitley positioned the buggy
west of the church building. "Where do you suppose she is?"
Caleb crossed his arms, wanting nothing more than to be the
first beneath a clean blanket. He followed the minister's gaze
to the wooded tract bordering the church grounds. Proceeding
close behind Whitley, Caleb trudged toward the black woods
until the sound of a twig's snap brought him to a halt.

"You heard that?" Whitley whispered.

Caleb nodded.

"Who's there? Come out now. Don't be frightened." Whitley's calm tone soothed Caleb's tense nerves. A movement
caught both their eyes. A tree limb quivered unnaturally, followed by the rustling of shrubbery leaves. The lad swallowed
hard but clenched his fists in anticipation. Suddenly the realization that he'd left behind his rifle struck his mind. *How foolish!* he chastened himself. But the sight of a lone, hooded female emerging from the woods quelled his anxiety, and he
commented quietly, "Look, Reverend. There's the lady."

"Hello, madam," Heath called out warmly and, out of respect, bowed slightly.

Caleb strained to make out the woman's features but could
not for the dark. She moved slowly, as if afflicted, and held a
small motionless bundle in her arms. "You the Protestant min-

ister?" Her raspy voice carried a tone of desperation.

"I am." Heath offered no explanation for Marsden's absence, desiring to dispense swiftly with formalities and fulfill the widow's needs so that he and Caleb could retire. "You are the widow who penned this note?" He held up the wrinkled paper.

The woman nodded slowly but gave no reply.

"Is that your baby, ma'am?" Caleb inquired.

Again the woman nodded. Caleb took another step toward her, concerned that the infant made no stirrings.

"You really shouldn't use the threat of harming your child to elicit food from the church, madam," Heath chastened gently. "It isn't necessary. The church will give you food and plenty. I'll see to it personally."

The woman leaned forward as though weak, and her arms trembled in front of her. Caleb grew alarmed when the bundle tumbled from her grasp. "Your baby!" He ran forward as did Heath Whitley.

Reaching the bundle first, Caleb lunged for the infant while keeping a cautious eye on the widow. He felt a chill touch his nerves. *There's nothing here!* The blanket's empty folds revealed the woman's deceit. Then horror struck his mind when the woman raised her arms and shrieked, *"Now, laddies! Now!"*

Heath backed away. "What's this?"

"It's a trap, Reverend! Run!" Caleb saw dark figures, bearing torches, bounding toward them from the bowels of the dark wood. He whirled around and ran fast for the buggy. Thinking the minister behind him, he increased his speed and turned the corner, shouting, "Run! Run!" the entire way.

Rounding the church's cornerstone, Caleb's mouth fell agape when he saw the buggy unhitched from the horse. So weary from the midnight trip, he scarcely remembered unhitching it. He jerked around and to his dismay saw no sign of Heath Whitley. Creeping with his back to the wall, he peered again around the corner. He saw a ring of angry men surrounding the minister, their taunts rising around him.

"Dear God, help me!" Caleb felt his throat tighten. He fled from their sight and scrambled into the buggy, searching for something he could use for a weapon. Under the seat he located a wooden box. He had noticed it on many occasions but

had never looked inside. He flipped open the cover and found
a pistol with several rounds of ammunition. *Good man!* He
reached for the weapon and, finding it loaded, scrambled from
the wagon. The sound of shouting increased, and he could see
the rear of the church grounds lit by blazing torches. He crept
down the dark side of the building, gripping the weapon with
both hands. He heard Reverend Whitley call out once, but the
cry pierced his heart with terror. *They're beating him! God!
Please* . . . Caleb's mind filled with panic, and he could not think
how to pray. "So many of them"—he held up the weapon—"and
only one musket," he whispered with dread. The sound of
splintering wood caused him to stop again. Through a window
he could see the men entering the back of the church, the fire
sticks held high in their grasp. The sight of Heath Whitley's
bleeding and bruised face sickened Caleb in his soul. *Don't let
him die, Lord!* Suddenly his mind filled with angry vengeance.

The men hurled Whitley to the floor and kicked at him until
he lay motionless. Caleb ran to the rear and aimed the musket
overhead, hoping the sound of weapon fire would scatter them
in a panic. Just before he squeezed the trigger, he heard a man
with a thick Irish brogue cry out, "Throw down your torches
and run!" *They're setting fire to the church!* Caleb pressed his
back against the stone structure, hoping the dark would conceal his presence. The men filed out quickly, but one turned un-
expectedly to inspect the yard. Caleb heard approaching steps
and made ready the musket. Holding it up, he steadied his aim,
determining to hit his mark if necessary.

"See anything?" the woman's voice, now strong and surly,
called out with confidence.

"No, Hattie, looks as if the boy escaped."

"Give another walk around the church, just in case."

Caleb could hear the pop and sizzle of burning wood and
smell the sickening odor of the flames.

Just as the Irish convict appeared to be marching toward
him, the man stopped, drawn by the sound of Whitley's neigh-
ing horse. "Here's me something to ride." The convict turned
at once. Caleb could hear arguing between the woman called
Hattie and the man regarding the danger of being found with
the minister's horse. Finally the woman won the argument, and
the retreat of the mob sent a rush of relief through Caleb. He

crept around the building and found the Irish gang had disappeared into the woods.

"Reverend Whitley," he called out feebly. But the doorway was filled with flames, and he could find no safe passage through the rear. Making haste for the front, he rounded the west side of the building. But he froze abruptly at the sight of the hooded female who stood before him, arms folded.

"Thought you might be around," she chuckled. "Heard you shuffling about." She stepped toward him.

Caleb lifted the weapon. "I'll shoot!" he threatened, studying the woman's weathered face and the small eyes that shone out from beneath the hood.

She displayed no fear but smiled smugly. "Can't have any witnesses about, now, can we?"

Caleb felt a sudden thunderous blow to his head, and then his world grew black.

6

SECRET OF THE HEART

The pain in Caleb's head hammered incessantly, and he could not think rationally. He slowly raised himself up from the floor of the church, but his nostrils stung with searing pain. He could not see except for the blurry image of fire dancing around him like tendril-shaped demons. Widening his eyes, he struggled to discern the events of the last few moments. Seeing the limp form of Heath Whitley jolted Caleb to his senses, and holding the back of his head to ease the pain, he stumbled to the minister's side. "Reverend—" he rasped out, then coughed and could not form any more words. Feeling for Whitley's wrist, he found a weak pulse. He grasped both arms and attempted to drag him toward the front door, which creaked partly open, the doorknob hanging loose from the wood. But he could only inch Whitley's body forward in minuscule increments. He felt his limbs weaken, his senses spinning from the suffocation of the smoke. *We'll both be dead within minutes*, he concluded dismally.

Collapsing next to Whitley's body, he heard a muffled groan.

He blinked his eyes and saw the minister's body stir. "Sir—" he attempted to call out.

"Caleb—"

"You're hurt. We've got to get out of here." Caleb felt his last breath being sucked from him, the remaining bit of air licked away by the flames. Abruptly, he felt his arm gripped by a trembling hand, and he opened his eyes partly.

"Get up, Caleb. You can do it!" Courage and strength welled within the youth's chest. He rolled his body toward the door. A bit of air circulated through the crack in the door like a dim, hopeful ray of light. "This way, Reverend!" He saw Whitley lift himself from the floor, but it proved to be Caleb's last image of him. A black cloud of smoke descended on Whitley, and Caleb lost sight of the man. "Follow the sound of my voice!" he cried. "Follow me! I'm here! I'm here!"

Feeling for the door, Caleb thrust himself through the opening and coughed violently, the fresh air filling his lungs. He kicked at the door and peered inside as the flames engulfed the edifice. Smoke billowed from just beyond the chancel where he last had spied the minister. He stretched his hand through the doorway and then lost all awareness. The hours of the night ticked on like seconds. Caleb's eyes opened and closed, and the night became fragmented images. He felt his body lifted by strong arms. He saw stars veiled with sooty clouds and then black tree limbs etching toward the sky like menacing warriors. No longer inside a burning church, he lay on the cool ground, but dreamed of the feather bed he had not yet laid his head upon. Soon a soft bed swallowed him up like a whirlpool, and chaotic dreams became his reality. He longed for sanity. The black world of unconsciousness became his solitude, and the struggle to awaken, his nightmare.

The soothing words of a girl's gentle voice began to penetrate the haze, and his head felt a cleansing spray of water. He opened his eyes, but the vision before him blurred, and he closed them again. His voice mumbled words, but he could not discern them. How he longed to be free from the torture of his semiconscious state. For a moment, he even longed for death.

"Caleb."

His own name called out to him from the depths of an ethereal well. His mouth, cottony and desert-dry, fell open, but he couldn't reach back from the depths with words. He commanded his senses to respond, fighting the urge to fall asleep forever. The touch of his own hand against his bruised right side told him he had not died. He muttered and his voice sounded loud to himself.

"He's coming around."

Caleb, encouraged by the words, opened his eyes. He blinked, certain that the image before him was a bright angel. The girl smiled and bent to stroke his brow. "Can you hear me, Caleb?"

Seeing a small tear trickle down the girl's rosy cheek, Caleb forced himself to nod. "Kelsey?" he whispered.

The girl glanced around the room and then bent so no one would see. Caleb felt her lips purse and brush against his own, and then he fell peacefully asleep.

"To your feet, crawlers!" The guards rushed the prison compound, their boots pounding the ground and their clubs beating against the individual doors of the cubicles. They shouted oaths and struck the doors with violent blows. "At once! To your feet, beggars!"

Inured by the cruelty of the guards, the convicts lethargically arose from their scrubby mats on the floor. But a few of the Irish cellmates remained on their beds and did not stir, fearing their own faces would betray them.

"They know!" one frail woman whispered through bared teeth. "They've come fer us!"

"Shut up!" Another leaped from her mat, clamping her hand over the woman's mouth. "They'll hear you, fool!"

Waiting until the guards had passed, the first woman stood and gripped the barred window, peering out with haunted eyes. Seeing the guards busy mustering the convicts several cubicles away from them, she turned and with her voice quivering, asked, "What do we do?"

"Act as though you were just born. You know nothing."

The woman wrapped her arms about herself. "But, Hattie, I'm afraid. Me own John's always been a poor liar. They'll see it in his eyes. They'll kill him. They'll kill me John."

Hattie bore down on the woman. "And well they should if he can't keep his tongue in his head. Now, if you want to protect the man, shut up!" She could hear the sound of boots approaching their cubicle again. "Here they come!" she whispered. "When they summon you out, yawn as though you've just awakened. Pretend you fancy not why they've awakened us so. *Understand?*"

The door shook before them. Angry guards jerked the chains and lock from the fastener and burst their cell door open. The soft, dusky remainder of moonlight swept into the dark cubicle, and Hattie McBride stepped out, beguiling as a serpent. "Whatever's the difficulty?" she bustled. "Waking good folks before daylight like this!"

The balmy dawn sky arose over the rocky ledge that shadowed the Mercers' farmhouse. A thick black-gray ripple of smoke lifted on the horizon, an unbidden reminder of the previous evening's fire.

"The boy's stirring, Charlotte." Frieda Mercer blew across the top of her china cup, then inhaled the strong aroma of black tea. "Look, there." She pointed toward the lad who slept on a mattress she had pulled out the evening before.

"When will his papa and his mum be here?" Charlotte lifted herself from the chair, laying her mending aside.

"My husband's gone for them. I expect the Prentices anytime now." Frieda straightened herself, reaching to grasp a fresh cloth she had just dampened for the boy's bruised head. "Tell me now, how does Kelsey know the lad?"

Charlotte crept toward Caleb Prentice. She spied her young charge, Kelsey, sleeping soundly upon her bed on the rear porch. "How does Kelsey McBride know anyone? She vows she met the boy some time ago, when first she arrived in Sydney Cove." Pulling her skirts gently around a small table, she commented, "She stayed up half the night just watchin' the lad breathe."

"If he asks, don't tell him about the minister, Charlotte," Frieda cautioned. "Not until he's better, at least."

Caleb's lids fluttered, bringing Charlotte to kneel quickly at his side. "Good mornin', young fellow."

His throat stinging, Caleb coughed and tried to speak, but he could form no intelligible reply. He struggled to recognize the young woman who stood before him. But her oval face and brown calflike eyes brought no recollection to his mind.

"Tut, tut." Charlotte pulled a bottle of laudanum and a silver spoon from her pocket. "Take a bit o' this, love. It'll put spark back in you, an' you'll be yer ol' self once more."

Caleb parted his lips slightly and allowed the woman to tilt the spoon into his mouth. The foul taste drew a sour grimace to his face. "No more," he muttered.

"Swallow it all, or ol' Charlotte'll give you another dose, I vow."

Caleb allowed the woman to dribble the remaining contents of the spoon into his parched mouth. He shuddered and glanced around the room. His mind still jumbled, he held only vague remembrances of awakening and falling asleep. Then, suddenly he remembered the fire as clearly as the morning sunlight that now shone through the window. "Reverend Whitley!" He tried to sit up, but searing pain shot through his chest.

"Don't fret yourself, young man!" Charlotte chided. "Doctor says you should lie still, an' I'm the one to see that you does!"

"Doctor?"

"Doctor White from the military. He's gone to see about the minister." Charlotte slanted a glance at Frieda, her eyes rolling sheepishly at her own slip of tongue.

"So . . . Heath Whitley . . . he's alive?"

"I 'spect he is." Charlotte pulled the blanket up around Caleb's chin. "Now, we'll find out about all that business later. First we 'as to get you well."

"Caleb?"

The voice startled Caleb. It sounded like an angel from one of his dreams. He looked up at Charlotte to see if she had heard his name called. He followed her gaze and saw her mouth widen in a friendly smile. "Good mornin', lass," he watched her call gaily. He turned his face slightly and saw the girl whom she called out to.

"It *is* you. So, it wasn't a dream?"

"Glad to see you're awake." Kelsey clasped her hands in front of her. "Mr. Mercer helped out with the fire. He brought you here and then rode back to help the others."

Swallowing with great difficulty, Caleb pushed himself up-right against the feather pillow. "Me parents, they—"

"Mr. Mercer's gone for them. They should be here soon, lad," Charlotte affirmed.

"An' Reverend Whitley?"

Charlotte glanced back at Frieda, her brow pinched with concern. "That's . . . that is, Mr. Mercer's gone to see about the minister as well. Now you lie back and rest." She glanced toward the window so that her eyes would not betray the facts.

"You're hungry?" Kelsey leaned over the lad, her face reflecting her sincere concern.

Caleb nodded wearily. "Not a lot, though."

"I'll whip up some bread and beans." Charlotte reached to retie her apron.

Kelsey smiled down at him, reaching instinctively to feel his forehead. She then withdrew her hand awkwardly and asked, "Do you remember what happened?"

"I believe so. Heath Whitley saved me life—carried me from the burnin' church."

Kelsey bit her lip. "Let me make him something to eat, Charlotte. You've worked all morning. Go and rest now."

Charlotte patted her shoulder. "Thank you, love. I'd like to prop up me ol' tired feet." She joined Frieda at the table for a cup of tea.

Kelsey acknowledged Caleb with a half nod. "I'll return shortly."

Gazing into her large hazel eyes, Caleb nodded and watched as Kelsey smiled bashfully, turned, and walked into the kitchen. She had a graceful gait, he noted, and she appeared to bustle energetically wherever she went. The girl was not overly delicate, and the gentleness that pervaded her personality appeared to be seasoned with a hint of stubbornness. Not long after she left, she returned with a large platter in her arms.

"Fresh biscuits—not warmed over—and gravy. Some fruit . . ."

He watched Kelsey's large eyes again, which gazed heedfully at each item on the platter as she described it. The delicate, dark brows outlined her eyes and complemented her fair complexion perfectly, as though brushed on by a master artist.

As she stooped beside him to place the food on a nearby table, he felt a strange urge to reach out and touch the golden locks that cascaded around her face. Not prone to self-control, he lifted his hand to do so, then seeing her glance up at him, he hesitated and drew his hand to his face, rubbing his nose instead.

"Can you sit up on your own?"—Kelsey stood upright and crossed her arms at her waist—"or do you need my help?"

Caleb frowned. Of course he could sit up. But then a voice inside him stirred a different response. "Well, would you mind? I—"

"Not at all." Kelsey stooped once more, placing her hands behind his shoulders where the pillow rested against him.

Caleb felt the touch of her hands against his shirt. He placed his weight against her and turned his face slightly so that her hair brushed his cheek. He closed his eyes and inhaled slightly. "Flowers?" he whispered.

"Beg your pardon?" Kelsey stood up once more, her arms akimbo.

"Nothing really." Caleb smiled at the slight blush that rose across her cheeks, as though they had been kissed by the sun. "Your hair . . . it smells like flowers."

Kelsey stroked a strand of her own hair, inspecting it curiously. "Oh, that. Aunt Frieda loaned me some scented water. I washed my hair with it, that's all."

"Your aunt is charitable." He gazed into her eyes again until doing so became uncomfortable. Sitting forward to grasp the plate of fruit, Caleb busied himself with breakfast. "Why don't you join me?"

"I'll eat later on. I'm never hungry right away." Kelsey pulled the apron over her head and folded it. "I'm going for some water now. I'll return shortly to clear away the dishes."

"Please don't go."

Kelsey pursed her lips and gazed down at Caleb curiously. "I don't wish to bore you."

"You don't. That is, I shouldn't be left alone what with my condition and all."

One graceful brow arched cynically. "Oh?"

"It's true." Caleb coughed, but only slightly, not wishing to overplay his hand. "But don't stay if you'd rather not. I'm certain I'll be all right." He pushed his plate aside and sank down against the pillow, closing his eyes. The room grew silent momentarily. He parted his eyelids slightly, peering out between his thick brown lashes. The room appearing empty, he opened his eyes and sat up, disgruntled at his obvious abandonment. But a sudden movement caught his eye. Turning his face, he saw that Kelsey had drawn up a chair close to the mattress and settled herself with a book. Hiding his surprise, he asked, "What's that you're reading?"

"It belongs to Mr. Mercer. It's his Bible."

"Me father owns one. Katy—me sister—taught me to read from it."

"I learned to read in Ireland. A minister's wife opened a small school in her husband's church. I love to read anything I can get my hands on. Sometimes, when no one's looking, I read the prayer books in church."

"Me parents take us all to the Anglican church."

Kelsey hesitated, lifting her face piously. "I'm Catholic."

"That's all right by me. I only go because I'm made to."

"I've not been in a while. I used to go with a neighbor . . . in Kildare . . . in Ireland. . . ." Kelsey's voice trailed off, along with her thoughts.

Caleb noticed the faint trace of pain in her eyes. "Why are you here, Kelsey? Can you tell me?" Shaking her head slightly, Kelsey's brow knit. "It doesn't matter. I'm here, whether by providence or accident." She closed the Bible, tucking it beneath her arm. "I really should go and fetch the water."

Caleb watched the girl rise and place the chair back against the wall. His mind raced. He tried to think of another excuse to keep her at his side. "May I ask you something?"

With a nod, Kelsey stepped toward him, her face poised.

"I had a dream that you—"

"Dreams mean nothing." Kelsey held the Bible close to her, pressing her lips together.

"Was it a dream? Did you kiss me?"

The room grew silent. The youths, both motionless, locked eyes for a moment until Kelsey finally stirred. "Why would I do such a thing?"

"I believe that if someone kisses another . . . well, it's because he wants to do it. Makes sense to me, anyway."

With a hard swallow, Kelsey cast her eyes shyly to the floor. "It was only a dream."

Caleb's face drew up dubiously. Crossing his arms at his waist, he conceded with a nod. "Surely. Just a dream."

The distant sound of a horse's neigh broke the intensity of the moment, and they both looked toward the window. "It's Mr. Mercer." Kelsey stood up on her toes. "Your parents are with him, Caleb."

Caleb sat up and peered out through the glass. "You're right," he acknowledged. But a slight pang of regret gnawed at his stomach. He would have to leave with them, of course. He glanced back at the girl.

The chairs in the kitchen bumped against the wooden floor. "Prentices are here!" Charlotte called out.

"I'll bring them in for you," Kelsey volunteered.

Caleb thought he detected a sudden relief wash across her countenance. He hurriedly finished off the biscuit and the last bit of fruit. Briskly, he brushed away the crumbs that fell upon the blanket as his parents entered the room with Kelsey close behind. "Hello!" he called out cheerily.

"Looks as though they've treated you like a king, son." George laughed jovially.

"Mercy me!" Amelia's eyes grew misty.

"I'm all right, Mum." Caleb immediately saw his mother's anxious expression. "Not to worry."

"Worry is all I do with you, Caleb George Prentice!" Amelia handed a large basket to Kelsey. "This is for your mother, dear. For all you've done for Caleb."

Kelsey grasped the basket sheepishly. "Thank you, Mrs. Prentice. But . . . the Mercers . . . they're not my parents." She glanced around the couple and saw that the Mercers stood outside with Charlotte discussing the events of the day.

"Oh, I'm sorry," Amelia apologized.

"Quite all right." Kelsey turned to take the basket back into the kitchen.

"Such a comely young girl," Amelia said, nodding at her son. She swept the blond wisps of hair from his eyes. "Pity she 'as no family."

"I agree." Caleb bit his bottom lip. "She appears to take all life in stride, though." He attempted to encourage Mum with his words, but his own worries about Kelsey only increased.

Kelsey busied herself with storing the jars of homemade jam inside the Mercers' larder, all the while keeping her ear tuned to the happy reunion. The sound of their cheery laughter brought a smile to her face and an aching warmth to her heart. *Caleb's blessed with a wonderful family*, she decided. But then their voices grew somber, so she crept toward the doorway to listen.

"Can you remember anything at all about the woman, son?" Amelia pled with Caleb.

"They was Irish, all of 'em, Mum. The lady wearin' the cloak had large hands, I remember. An' she wasn't totin' no infant in that blanket. It was all a lie to trick us into comin'."

"The authorities think that the Irish rebels intended the harm for Reverend Marsden, not for Heath Whitley, that's wot," George interjected.

Amelia persisted. "You said they called out to the woman. Can you remember her name?"

Kelsey clasped her hands beneath her chin. A sudden panic seized her mind. "Don't let it be so," she whispered, holding her breath.

"I can't remember." Caleb shook his head. He sighed and pressed his head against the pillow. "It's all so foggy."

"How about letting me fix you all something to eat. Can't let this delicious food go to waste, can we?" Kelsey called out sprightly.

"Dear me, no, child. You've done too much already." Amelia shook her head.

"No bother at all." Frieda Mercer bustled into the room. "We insist. Charlotte and I can whip you up something hot and good in a moment's time."

"Might as well let them, Amelia," George conceded.

Straightening the blanket around Caleb, Amelia sighed. "If it isn't a bother," she answered, her brow furrowed. "And if you'll let me help out."

"Come join us." Frieda smiled gaily.

"I'll be right there, ma'am." Kelsey curtsied to Frieda. "But first I'll clear away Caleb's dishes." Kelsey waited until the women scurried from the room and George had joined Mercer on the front porch. "I'm . . . glad that you're starting to remember," she said weakly.

"Remember?" Caleb's brows arched curiously.

"About the rebels who started the fire."

"Oh, that. I can almost say the woman's name now."

Kelsey's face grew faintly anxious. "You can?"

"Something like Maddie, or—"

"It's all right. You need to rest yourself—"

"Hattie! That's it!" Caleb sat up. "I remember!"

Kelsey glanced quickly toward the kitchen and then the front porch. "Caleb, don't!"

"Fetch Papa! I must tell him!" Caleb threw back the bedding.

"You mustn't get up!"

"I'm fine. Help me to the porch," Caleb persisted.

"No!" Tears rimmed Kelsey's eyes. "You can't, Caleb! Please!"

"What's wrong with you? Don't you see?" Caleb tried to decipher the worry in the girl's face. "I know the name of the arsonist."

"I know," Kelsey answered, her words tinged with bitter tones. Between faint sobs, she whispered, "I know her, too."

Caleb sat back on the folds of the blanket. "Impossible! How could you?"

Kelsey studied the perplexity of his gaze, but even shame could not hold back the truth. "Hattie . . . Hattie McBride. She's my mother."

"No!"

"It's true. I can't deny it." She drew close to Caleb's face. Brushing away the tears from her cheeks, she implored, "Please don't tell anyone. You can never tell, Caleb. Promise me?"

The truth of Kelsey's words evident, Caleb pulled her close to him. Shaking his head, he spilled out his regretful reply. "I can't, Kelsey. It's wrong. I can't."

7
REBEL TRAITOR

"Reverend Whitley is what?" Caleb sat at the breakfast table. Several mornings had passed since the fire, and his persistent questioning had worn down his father's defenses.

"He's not doin' well at all, son." George curled the pages of his Bible, allowing the thin paper to shuffle at his fingertips. "He's been unconscious since they dragged him from the church."

"But if he didn't rescue me, then who did?"

"A farmer saw the flames from his homestead. He assembled a group of neighbors to put out the flames. It's a miracle they found you at all," George reasoned.

"Can I see 'im? Will they let me see 'im?"

"Soon, son. He's staying at Doctor White's place. If there's any change, they'll send for us."

"What about Rachel?"

"She's at his side, of course. I'm sure she'll not return to Rose Hill unless matters change."

"He's not goin' to die, is he?" Caleb gripped the edge of the weathered table.

"Don't worry about the good Reverend Whitley." Amelia's assuring voice lightened the tension in the air. "He'd be a hard man to put down, that one."

Caleb remembered the night he first saw the couple embracing on the Prentices' front porch. Heath had begged Rachel to marry him at once. Caleb, believing himself clever, had interrupted the impetuous proposal. "If they had married that night, this would've never happened," he concluded sadly.

"What's that?" George asked.

"Nothin', sir." Caleb completed his meal in silence.

Marsden mopped his brow. Pacing back and forth in front of the paymaster's desk, he fumed, "Not enough control! What if it'd been me in that burning church building?"

"We don't yet know that they targeted you, Marsden." Macarthur made a futile attempt to quell the vicar's temper. "We've possibly cornered one of the perpetrators. They're questioning him now. A few rakes at the cat'll loosen his tongue soon."

"Give me an hour with him and I'll see justice is done!"

"We prefer to handle the matter in our own way, Reverend. The church has its place in society, and we have ours."

"You've called me in on every other matter. Why should this one be any different?"

Pursing his lips, Macarthur's eyes glinted with a sardonic light. "Shall we say, the convicts may have a small *vendetta* against you?"

"Poppycock!"

"Don't misunderstand my meaning, Reverend. We do see the benefit of an alliance with the church. But our Irish Catholic inmates have grown somewhat restless of late."

"They're barbarians!"

"They believe themselves religious. Just as you yourself believe—"

"Surely you wouldn't compare my faith to that of those beasts?"

"Surely I wouldn't." Macarthur sighed, his face bland. "But I would suggest you stay clear of the prison compound for no less than a fortnight."

"Samuel Marsden does not cower!"

"You know the risks. Have it your own way, but security in this wilderness is limited."

"Limited? Sir, I say it's preposterous, even ridiculous. But limited? Let us not oversimplify the matter."

"You believe you can manage the convicts better than the military?"

"Most certainly I do."

"Very well. You're granted your wish, sir. I will see that you personally oversee all convict discipline for a time. But if matters do not improve—"

"They will, sir. The church will prevail"—Marsden brought his fist down upon the paymaster's desk, his dark eyes narrowing contemptuously—"or my name isn't Samuel Marsden!"

"Give me some time to think! I need time, Aunt Frieda." Kelsey wrapped her arms about herself, her hands trembling.

"What is it?" Mercer emerged from the field into the quaint parlor. "Who just departed? I saw a rider at our doorway."

"It was a message delivered from the prison at Sydney Cove. Kelsey's mother—Hattie McBride—has been arrested."

"It isn't true!" Kelsey crumpled the message with her hands. "It's a mistake!"

"Kelsey," Charlotte spoke gently, "you've told me some things yourself about her. You know it's possible she's gotten herself into trouble."

"It . . . it's that English boy! Caleb Prentice did this to us."

"Caleb?" Frieda stepped toward the girl. She clasped her fingers around Kelsey's slender arms. "How could that child have anything to do with this arrest?"

"He told me he would tell. He thought my mother started the fire. But he's wrong!"

Frieda eyed her husband, their faces revealing their shock. "Caleb Prentice knows?"

Ignoring their reactions, Kelsey muttered mostly to herself, "How could she set the fire? She's locked up in a prison cell!"

"Unfortunately, those prisoners escape all the time." Charlotte heaved a heavy sigh. "No lock can keep them in if they decides they wants out."

"But Mother wouldn't do this to us . . . to me."

"Let's sit, child." Frieda's brow lifted, her voice continuing in a reasonable tone.

Kelsey slumped down on a chair in the parlor but stationed her eyes on the floor.

"You need to face the truth about your mother, child. She's not like you or me. She's a woman searching for something— who knows what?"

"She's just a little confused, that's all." Kelsey's hands clenched atop her lap. "If they would just let me see her—"

Mercer inhaled a long draft from his pipe. Resting his stout arm upon the chair arm, he nodded. "And well you should. I'll go in tomorrow and arrange a visit for you."

"You'd do that?" Tears coursed down Kelsey's face. "Thank you, sir. You won't regret it. I believe she'll listen to me."

"If she doesn't," Charlotte warned, "know this. You've got a home here."

"That's true," Frieda agreed. "Remember our little proposition?"

Kelsey looked first at one sincere face and then the other. But she couldn't pretend to belong to someone else's family. *They're all so well meaning.* She was determined to right the wrongs in her life and bring restoration to her disjointed family. "Mother needs me. I can help her, I'm sure."

Mercer stooped in front of the fireplace, tapping the contents of his pipe into the cold ashes. "Then somehow, we'll try to help." Holding out little hope for the girl's expectations, he narrowed his eyes at his wife and shook his head.

Caleb scattered grain across the packed earth beside his parents' house. He listened to the busy sounds as two neighbors assisted Papa with the completion of the interior of the house. The monotonous hammering of the carpenters' iron tools against the wood created a pleasing rhythmic sound across the yard that blended well with the clucking of the hens and the bleating of the sheep. Purposefully, he allowed the grain to trickle across his bare feet. Six hungry chicks, yellow as farm butter, hopped around his feet, pecking at the food. "Don't act like pigs!" he teased the young birds. Lifting his toe, he watched as one of the fuzzy tufted chicks slid across his foot, making high complaint with its undeveloped squawks.

"Caleb!" Papa called out.

Caleb glanced up to find his father standing on the front porch. His trim frame struck a handsome pose as he wiped the sweat from his brow. "Yes, sir?"

"We could use your help about now. William's ready for a rest."

Nodding agreeably, Caleb sighed inwardly. The new house had taken over a year to build due to limited finances. His family, anxious to move out of the wattle-and-daub shack that was their first home, had all agreed to exercise patience as the walls slowly went up around them. With the kitchen now completed, they slowly worked their way to the upstairs. It seemed the carpentry work would never end.

"May I use William's tools?" Caleb asked. "They're so much better than ours."

"Yes. They're lying at the foot of the stairs."

Caleb nodded and ambled past, his eyes to the loam.

George uncrossed his arms and reached out to pat Caleb's shoulder as he stepped up onto the porch. "Everything all right, son?"

"Uh-huh." Caleb nodded, but his eyes betrayed him.

"Something's wrong, isn't it?"

Shrugging indifferently, Caleb turned to face his father. "I'm worried about Kelsey McBride."

"Why? She seems to be in good hands at the Mercers' place."

"But she's—" Caleb hesitated. He hadn't brought himself to tell Papa about Hattie McBride yet. Once he did, he knew his father would insist upon taking the news to the military authorities. "She . . . well, shouldn't we go and see about her, since she did so much for me and all?"

One brow arched, George allowed a faint smile to cross his face. "You're concerned about her, I can see."

Caleb nodded.

"She's a pretty lass, that one."

Casting his eyes back down to the newly laid wood of the front porch, Caleb drew his arms about himself. "That isn't why I—"

"No need to explain." A low chuckle emanated from George, and his eyes sparkled. "At times I forget how fast you're growing up. Shall we pay this Miss McBride a visit?"

Caleb lifted his eyes, a new hopefulness rising in his face. "Could we?"

"We can. Let's complete the wall in the upstairs hallway and then clean up for a visit to the Mercers."

"I'll send a loaf of bread!" Amelia's head appeared around the corner. She winked at George.

"Eavesdropping, Mum?" Caleb's brows lifted in suspicion.

"Eavesdrop? That's a fine thank-you for all I do for you." Amelia lowered her voice, casting her eyes inside the house and then back to the front landing. "Besides, there's not too many girls as pretty as that one, an' wot with you being marryin' age in a few years."

"She's me friend, Mum, that's all." Caleb rolled his eyes.

"Know this"—Amelia shook her finger at her son—"when times is hard, the best one to be married to is your best friend."

George patted his wife's backside. "You tell 'im, love."

"George Prentice!" Glaring at George, Amelia blushed. "Forevermore!" Whirling around she disappeared from view.

"Let's hurry!" Caleb rushed his father through the door. "Per'aps they'll invite us to supper."

The sun not quite set, the moon made its mark in the sky, a faint white disk that soon disappeared behind a cloud. The evening settled slowly over the government building, and the last hour of the working day, usually the quietest, erupted noisily. Through the back doorway, three privates ushered in six surly members of an Irish chain gang.

"Let us go, scum!" A churlish man of enormous build threatened the military guards. "We'll mark down your names. You'll regret this, I say!"

"Shut up," one of the guards barked, "or I'll flog ye meself!"

"Bring them in!" a commanding voice called from inside the

portals of a large office. "Line them up in front of me!"

"Who is that?" a convict queried the others.

"Marsden. It's Samuel Marsden wot's called us all out like this."

"He's alive?"

"Quiet, idiot!" A female stood with stooped posture. Her face hidden from view, she pushed her way in behind the others, feet and hands shackled by rusted irons.

Marsden stood, his scowl marked by a self-satisfied smirk. As the convicts settled in front of him, he paced slowly, his authority evident. "I'm certain you all thought you'd gotten away with your filthy scheme."

The five convict males muttered to one another, but the female said nothing.

"Quiet!" The sound of a whip snapped behind the criminals, and the room grew harshly silent.

Continuing with his speech, Marsden cleared his throat ceremoniously. "But we have a willing witness. You see, the loyalty you tout among your miserable pack of thieves is quite flawed. Corporal?" Marsden turned pompously and faced the office's back doorway.

The door opened slowly and a man trudged in, his face swollen and his shirt in shreds from the brutal flogging he had received.

"Corporal!" Marsden barked.

The officer guarding the prisoner, along with two other guards, shoved the Irish witness out in front of Marsden.

Marsden stood back from the convict, as though standing close would dirty his hands. "You've something to say, Mac-Gregor?"

MacGregor tried to pull himself erect, but the beating had left him weakened, and his legs would barely support his bruised body. At seeing the eyes of his comrades, a look of shame crept across his face, and with trembling lips he struggled to speak.

"Come, now!" Marsden continued the interrogation in a patronizing manner. "You've already confessed. We have the names of all the arsonists who set fire to the Anglican church. Can you point to the persons involved?"

Not knowing whether to fear the military or his rebel comrades the more, the convict began to tremble, his eyes moist.

"Just point!" Marsden bellowed.

Lifting a bloody hand, McGregor swept a finger through the air and muttered weakly, "It's all of them. They're all here that set fire to the church."

"God help your soul!" One of the accused cursed and shook his chains.

The woman lifted her face, and McGregor beheld the fierce countenance of Hattie McBride. "They made me confess—"

"Traitor!" Hattie hissed. "Devil!"

"Take them all to separate cells, privates." Marsden maintained a cool demeanor. "They'll all be shipped off to Norfolk in three days."

"You'll die for this, MacGregor!" Hattie shouted, attempting to lunge at her former comrade. "I'll cut your throat, you blackguard!"

The sting of a whip ripped across Hattie's back. She pulled herself erect and marched unflinchingly behind the others. *It'll take more than a whip to break the will of Hattie McBride!* she vowed.

The convicts filed silently into the wagon as the moon seized its nightly reign over the dark harbor.

8

A Fig Tree Shaken

"It looks like a tree, kind of like an old oak tree." Wick Mercer stood over Kelsey's shoulder observing her rough landscape sketch. "You're pretty good—quite an artist, little miss."

"Thank you, Mr. Mercer." Kelsey kept her eyes on the sheaths of paper he had picked up for her from the general supply store. "It was kind of you to buy these for me."

Mercer clasped his fingers at his chest. "Nothin' o' the sort. I'm just tired o' seein' you scribblin' all over me newspaper." The fondness for the girl reflected in his gaze, his tone feigned discontent.

A funny pang hit Kelsey. She felt a broad smile creep across her face. Mercer had such a way about him, always thinking of others in his bashful way. "I sometimes wonder what it might be like to be an artist, or a writer," she confessed. "But not many females do that sort of thing, do they?"

"Horsefeathers!" Mercer muttered under his breath. "Who're you to try an' be like other ladies? Most of 'em strut about in finery with not a sensible thought in their heads."

"What're you sayin' to the girl, Wick?" Frieda spoke absentmindedly, busily stirring a large simmering pot on the cookstove.

Mercer blew out a white stream of pipe smoke. "Teachin' the girl the ways o' the world."

"Hah!" Frieda waved her hand mischievously. "A man teachin' a woman how to be a woman?" She bent astutely toward Kelsey and winked. "You pay him no nevermind. He's one to be talkin' about the ways of the world!"

Kelsey pressed her lips together, her eyes alight. She loved the playful bantering between Wick and Frieda Mercer. *So like the family I've dreamed of having.* But the attention shown to her by Wick especially drew a fondness from her. She could speak to the man for hours on end, listening to his stories of the war. Keeping a chary watch, she leaned toward Wick when Frieda turned back to her cookstove. She lifted her chin and, with face animated, parried in a faint whisper, "I agree with *you.*"

Wick nodded jovially, cutting a knowing gaze toward his wife. Then, with a sigh of great satisfaction, he leaned back into his chair.

Kelsey dipped the quill again into the ink and made a graceful stroke across the paper to define the picture's horizon.

"Hills . . . oak trees . . . where is this place?" Mercer's tone, quiet and assuring, broke the silence of the kitchen.

"Kildare," Kelsey answered with a long sigh.

Mercer nodded. "Oh, your home."

"Not much left of it by now, I'm certain." Kelsey fidgeted. Her drawing appeared so cold and flat compared to the rich memories that stretched across her mind. She made some strokes across the base of the hills, but the changes didn't satisfy her. "It's terrible!" She tossed the quill down and crumpled the paper with her fingers.

"Kelsey!" Frieda jerked around.

With a huff, Kelsey dropped it onto the floor.

"Don't destroy it." Wick Mercer bent to retrieve the drawing. "Little miss"—he took great care to open the paper and smooth out the wrinkles—"you're too hard on yourself." Adjusting his spectacles on the end of his nose, he examined the sketch. "Right nice work 'ere. What if you're throwin' away a masterpiece or somethin' like?"

Kelsey rolled her eyes. "Not likely. She crossed her arms, then her face grew more somber as the distant sound of horses' hooves caught her attention. She craned her neck. Standing slowly, she said, "Wagon's pulling in." Her voice reflected curiosity.

Wick studied the girl's delicate frame. She reminded him of a small fig tree he had nursed as a boy. Though bantered by the storms and wind, the tree had endured. He knew Kelsey would endure, too.

Charlotte stepped in through the rear doorway, her arms brimful of fresh laundry. "It's Weems' liveryman, Kelsey."

Kelsey turned to look at Wick and Frieda. "No . . . please . . ." Her voice trailed off.

Governor Hunter sat before the assembly of military officials and politicians. Bewigged in the fashion of high-ranking British nobility, he stroked his age-ripened face, his shoulders sagging as though heavy from the weight of responsibility. "This meeting of inquiry . . ." He hesitated, perusing the notes his assistant had garnered from the army officers' complaints. The officials seated around the room awaited the aging governor's comments, all eyes fixed piteously upon his. Governor Hunter began again, "This court of inquiry, gentlemen, has been assembled to determine whether or not the Irish prisoners sentenced to Sydney Cove or Norfolk Island are a serious threat to our colony. There are those"—he cast a leery eye toward Marsden, who sat behind the large wooden table directly in front of him—"who believe that the Irish convicts may be planning a clandestine rebellion. If such speculation is correct, then we as leaders must take certain precautions to quell any acts of insubordination. However, to scatter seeds of alarm among the colonists could prove quite damaging. Perception, as most of you are aware, is everything."

The tedious inquiry proceeded with first one army official taking the floor, followed by several others. Seated next to his Rum Corps cronies, Macarthur muttered, "He'll not make a decision in our favor, Foveaux. He's navy—we're army."

Major Joseph Foveaux sat erect, arms up, with his hands clenched tightly in front of his face. He nodded his agreement. "They had to dust the cobwebs from his coat before they carried him in here." He scowled with contempt. "Hunter's weak, not at all a competent leader."

Macarthur glanced first at the officer to his left and then back to Foveaux. "We need a change."

"Gentlemen," Hunter rambled in a monotone, "after hearing the various observations—although appreciated—I feel further investigation is needed before a decision can be established."

Marsden heaved a heavy sigh. Rolling his eyes, he stood and then made known his wish to include his own comments. Acknowledging Hunter's permission with a nod, he interjected, "As minister of Sydney Cove's first established Anglican church"—he cleared his throat and continued—"I'm in hopes that my opinions are held with some respect."

The governor nodded. "Indeed. Let the record show that Reverend Samuel Marsden is highly respected among the citizenry and the government of New South Wales."

The feathered tip of the court scribe's quill scratched across the court documents in response to Hunter's words.

"I believe that a rebellion among the Irish convicts is imminent, and that to delay with further investigation could find us all in the midst of an unexpected clash—one our dear colonists may *perceive* as being mishandled, shall we say, by our leadership. That is, unless we take prudent, albeit immediate, action."

Hunter's eyes remained fixed on Marsden. The minister's implications stirred a petulance within him. "What action do you propose, Reverend? Your flogging is renowned in the colony as the direst form of punishment next to hanging."

A dark chuckle rippled throughout the room. Marsden, drawing himself up, took a deep breath and proceeded. "I propose that every Irish rebel and emancipist be shipped off to Norfolk Island at once!"

"All of them, Marsden?" Macarthur sat forward with interest, a gleam of humor lighting his gaze. "Rather drastic, I would say."

"Not too drastic for these beasts." Foveaux allowed his fist to drop to the wooden table to confirm the minister's pronouncement. To his colleagues, he whispered, "Letter of the law has been too lax in this colony."

The army officers and politicians argued among themselves, while Governor Hunter dropped his face slightly, his eyes peering up wearily.

"Order! Order!" A court official brought the assemblage into submission.

Anticipating the silence, Marsden leaned over the table, his hands pressed against the large Bible in front of him. "No power on earth can tame the evil of these rebels. I, for one, should know. I've done everything possible to help them. We're casting our pearls—"

"I say stronger punishment!" Foveaux interrupted, his brow arched and his eyes reflecting a keen pleasure in power.

"More time." Hunter's tone, though quiet, carried the weight of his authority. "We must study the matter." Taking careful control of the meeting, Hunter remonstrated the error of those who had reacted too quickly. A silent frustration fell across the room, the officials each finding their own argument with Hunter's impeded findings futile.

Collecting his papers and Bible into his arms, Marsden relinquished the floor. Dismissing himself politely, he retired his restrained presence from the inquiry. Marching down the corridor, he shuffled his papers and hesitated, his ears straining to listen. The meeting being convened now abated into mannerly conversations and, he imagined, old war stories. He shrugged off his frustration and resolved to increase his presence and the voice of his whip inside the prison compound.

Taking a few more steps, he placed some distance between himself and the meeting room. Beyond the cheaply tempered glass of a tall window, he saw a wagonload of convicts rumbling through the borough. At the sight of them, intense feelings of ill will rose up in him.

"They should all be taken to the sea and drowned like rats, eh, Reverend?"

Marsden cut his eyes to the one who had walked up behind him. "A rather grim solution, Foveaux."

"But it's as you say. They're a blight on this colony. How will history record it? That Australian blood be traced hereafter to outlaws?"

"Not all of us are convicts."

"But we're tainted by them." His jaw set, he added darkly, "I despise them all. And what if we *do* ship them all off to Norfolk. Such a desolate little island, eh? The French could join with the Irish rebels and stage their own take-over, yes? Where would that leave us, pray tell?"

Marsden studied the callous mien of the officer. Foveaux had a vicious bent about him that caused the minister to stiffen. "I should be going now, Major. Good day." He tipped his brimmed hat to the man.

Foveaux nodded in kind. Staring through the glass, he noticed the convict wagon had disappeared from sight. His whip secured at his side, he whirled around and made fast for the meeting room. Seizing the opportune moment, he spread himself among the gentry, making certain the name Joseph Foveaux grew as common to them as that of their favored child.

The Prentice wagon jostled along the cattle trail that was quickly becoming the main roadway in Parrametta. Caleb held the reins, allowing his father to rest, his hat cocked over one eye. "We're almost there, Papa. The Mercers' place is just ahead."

"Five more minutes o' rest. 'At's all I ask."

Caleb saluted. "Granted, sir!" He inspected the basket snugged next to his worn boots. His mother not only had prepared some bread but also had sent along a remnant of cloth for Kelsey. He imagined her need for clothes to be immense. Perhaps Mrs. Mercer would assist with the sewing. Turning down the path that led to the farmhouse, he detected the pleasing aroma of smoking hardwood. "Mr. Mercer's smokehouse must be nearby."

"Pity, too, with so many starvin' outlaws an' emancipists runnin' about." George sat up. "They'll loot the smokehouse before it's finished the job."

Caleb nodded. "Most would kill for a side o' bacon." He recalled the night the bushrangers attacked Rose Hill. "You think they'd ever try an' kill us?"

His brow furrowed cynically, George crossed his arms. "Who?"

"Bushrangers an' the lot."

"Not wif ol' George Prentice on the job. Why I'd—"

"Wot?" Caleb winked at his father. "Preach 'em to death?"

"I kin handle a musket if I 'as to. Don't you worry about me."

Caleb chuckled. "Look up ahead." He pointed with his eyes. "Mercers, they got 'em some visitors."

Both cast an inquisitive gaze toward the wagon stopped beside the house.

"Someone's leavin'—a man," Caleb commented.

"An' the girl. Look yonder." George lifted his hand and pointed a bony finger. "She's goin' with 'im."

"We'd better hurry, then." Caleb snapped the whip and brought it down upon the mare's flank. He watched ahead as Wick Mercer lifted the girl into the wagon. Drawing near, his heart sank. "Look, Papa! It's the taverner's liveryman. He's come for Kelsey."

"Don't jump to no conclusions, now. Let's see about the situation for ourselves."

A rose hue settled across the landscape as the Prentice wagon arrived with the last warmth of daylight. Caleb stood and waved, not wanting the liveryman to pull away. Pressing two fingers against his lips, he whistled and then shouted, "Kelsey McBride! Wait!" He smiled broadly, believing the girl would be happy to see him.

Kelsey turned at once. Her eyes met with Caleb's, and she turned her face from his. "Let's go—quickly!" She draped a shawl about herself, taking her place next to Charlotte.

"No, wait!" Charlotte begged the driver. "We've some visitors, *Kelsey*. It's the Prentice boy." She stared at the girl in disbelief.

Caleb leaped from the wagon. He quickly lifted Mum's basket and carried it with him toward Kelsey. "You're leaving?"

"Afraid so," Charlotte replied sadly. "Weems has sent for us. One o' his girls is sick, an' he needs help right away."

Frieda stepped from inside the house, followed by Wick. "Kelsey, don't forget—oh, look! Caleb, George! I'm so glad you arrived in time to say good-bye."

George tipped his hat to the couple. "Yes, but we had no idea the little girl'd be leavin' us so soon."

Leaving the adults to chat, Caleb carried the basket to the wagon and lifted it up for Kelsey's inspection. "Me mum baked you fresh bread. An' see here! A bit o' fabric to make yourself a dress. Pretty blue, ain't it?"

Kelsey didn't look at Caleb but spoke only to Charlotte. Through clenched teeth she muttered, "I don't want it!"

Charlotte gripped the folds of Kelsey's dress, her eyes wide with shock. "Kelsey McBride!"

"But—" Caleb felt his mouth go dry. The anger of her tone confused him.

"Charlotte, let's just go!" Tears brimming in her eyes, Kelsey hid her face in the woman's bodice.

Charlotte's face filled with remorse. "I'm sorry, Caleb. Please don't blame the girl—"

Caleb drew the basket back to himself. "It's all right. No need to explain. I'll give it to Mrs. Mercer." He hardened his face and held his words. Not wishing to deal with the pain just hurled at him, he turned on his heels and walked away from the wagon. "Mrs. Mercer?"

"Yes?"

"This is for you. Me mum sent it." He finished the task at once and purposefully kept his tone cheery.

George glanced at his son, certain the basket had been intended for Kelsey. But seeing the strange demeanor of the lad, he kept his silence.

"Papa, I'll just wait in the wagon."

"But you should stay for supper," Frieda tried to insist.

"Thank you, ma'am." With deliberate control, Caleb looked away. "I'm not hungry."

Wick glanced toward the wagon at Kelsey and then at the boy who walked away from them. In a low voice he explained to George, "The girl's not herself right now, George. It's her mother. She's an Irish convict and she's been arrested."

"I'm sorry," George whispered his reply. "We didn't know."

"I believe the lad knows." Frieda placed her hand upon George's arm. "Maybe you'd best talk to him."

George expedited his polite farewells, and tipping his hat to

Charlotte, he joined his son in their wagon.

Kelsey sat rigid on her seat while the liveryman drove them away from the Mercer homestead. Feeling the chill of evening prick her arms, she drew the shawl more tightly about herself. But the chill in her heart could not be blanketed with any sort of comfort. Guilt soon crept into her thoughts, and she hated herself for her unthinking actions.

"What did the lad do to you? He's innocent, Kelsey." Charlotte attempted to reason with her.

"You don't know that. He blamed my mother for setting the fire—"

"An' if she did, what then? Should she go free only because she's your mother?"

"I thought you, of all people, would understand." Kelsey longed to be alone. "Then, let's not discuss it, shall we?"

With a heavy sigh, Charlotte grew silent.

Kelsey grew equally silent. Charlotte's words had pierced her conscience. *What if Caleb is innocent?* "But he's the only one who knew," she whispered to herself. She adjusted her shawl, turning her face slightly, while the Prentice wagon plodded away in the opposite direction. For a brief instant, Caleb glanced her way, and then turned his face back to the road. Kelsey observed their silhouette dimming with the violet horizon.

Now her foolish mistake hounded her. *Why would he drive all the way here if—* Sudden understanding illuminated her thoughts. *Someday, Caleb Prentice,* she vowed, *I'll ask your forgiveness.* She gazed again behind their wagon, but all that she longed to see was masked by the night.

9

COME BEFORE WINTER

"I don't give a hang what the Mercers say!" Weems swilled down the last drop of rum from his pannikin and then plunked it down upon the bar.

Kelsey stood before Weems, holding out the letter that Wick had written on her behalf. "But the Mercers are willing to trade—"

Weems yanked the letter from her hands. "Trade? I need labor, now!" He crumpled the letter and tossed it behind the bar. "Now get busy cleanin' up this mess!"

Kelsey surveyed the large hall, now quite empty except for a drunkard who was slumped across a back table sound asleep. "Aye, sir." She didn't bother to complain about the weariness of the trip or the fact that she had hoped by now to be packing up her bare belongings to return to Wick's farm. But this Tuesday had passed as all the other days at the tavern, leaving her future no different than the days prior. "Right away, Mr. Weems," she answered politely, although her eyes held a spark of contempt. The taverner, too inebriated for reasoning, might be capable of making a decision the following day if she would cooperate for now.

But she did not cower as she had in the past. Spending time at the Mercers had given her a new confidence in herself. She planted her eyes on Weems, seeing him in a new light. *Why, he's detestable—not frightening at all.*

She watched as Weems leered at Charlotte, who was stooped over the floor in the corner of the tavern next to the scullery maid. Quickly dispensing with formalities, Charlotte had made fast use of her time. Cleaning the stone floor in the darkened tavern sometimes took several hours with four women working. Now with only three of them, it could take until dawn if they delayed. And what with the neglect the room had suffered since Charlotte's leave, their work had doubled. Kelsey watched Weems make his way to the rear of the room. *Most likely he'll badger Charlotte now.*

Kelsey attended her chores at once and began by gathering up the dirty mugs and pannikins that littered the long rows of tables. The grimy lantern globes nailed along the dank walls gave off a faint glow, but the room maintained its cryptic appearance. *Not at all like the cheery evenings we spent sitting around the kettle, listening to Wick's outlandish tales*, she thought. Gathering the vessels onto a large serving tray, Kelsey found that keeping her thoughts upon her time spent in Parrametta encouraged her and made the task seem lighter. Secretly, she even enjoyed allowing her mind to wander back to the time she spent caring for Caleb Prentice. Realizing a smile had spread across her face, she glanced up to see if anyone had noticed. Finding no one had spied her moment of recollecting, she basked in the memories and realized that her task of clearing the tables had ended. *I'll go and help Charlotte next*, she decided.

She spotted Charlotte crouched low, her face down. Weems stood over her, Kelsey observed, and stretched out his hand to grip her arm. Her shoulders rigid, Charlotte was glaring up at the man with firm determination.

"Need some help, Charlotte?" Kelsey drew near but kept her caution because of Weems and his sharp tongue.

"Go away, girl!"

Kelsey stood her ground. She could see that Charlotte's face held a gravity and her eyes sent a clear warning. "I don't want to go away." Kelsey crossed her arms at her waist.

"What?" Weems whirled around, his arm lifted to strike.

"You're bothering her. I can tell."

Weems swung his hand, and Kelsey felt a harsh sting across her face. But she planted her feet and did not stumble.

With fearful eyes, Charlotte reached out to her, angering the taverner all the more. Weems drew back his foot and kicked the woman fiercely in her stomach. He slid his hand around the pouch secured at his waist.

His dagger! Kelsey felt her heart pounding in her ears.

"Stop! Please, Mr. Weems!" Charlotte whimpered, her arms cradling her abdomen.

The scullery maid cried out and ran from the room. Seeing that Weems followed the maid with his eyes, Kelsey reached into her pocket and drew out Caleb's small knife. Fear rang through her, but she dared not hesitate. Weems would kill them both and justify the action as self-defense. Lunging at him with all her strength, she slashed his forearm and then leaped toward Charlotte, who lay slumped on the floor. She could hear the man's cry, but unheeding, she wrapped her arms around her friend.

"I'll kill you!" Weems shrieked. Hysteria overtook him upon seeing a thin stream of red run down his arm.

"No, please, Mr. Weems!" Charlotte pulled her bruised body upright from the floor. "She was only tryin' to help me!"

"Come 'ere, waif!" Grabbing Kelsey's long hair, Weems yanked her close to his face, his eyes wide with frenzied revenge. "I'll finish you off at once!" He knocked the knife from her hand, and it skittered across the floor and stopped where Charlotte knelt.

Kelsey felt his fist at the back of her neck holding fast to her hair, but she refused to cry out. Weems held his blade to her face and then placed it at her throat. She could hear Charlotte's scream, and she struggled to break free. But his grip held her too close for retaliation.

Suddenly, she heard a voice shout, "Weems!"

She glanced sideways and saw two military guards running toward them. Following close, the scullery maid bolted to her employer's defense.

"It's the Irish girl. She's caused all this!" Entering slowly behind, an army officer peered curiously through the doorway.

"I found 'em drivin' past, Mr. Weems!" The scullery, anxious to find her employer's approval, made certain her involvement proved just.

"Thank you, Theresa." Gratification gleamed from Weems' eyes. "Yes, Privates, I'm just 'avin' a bit o' trouble with this one." He yanked Kelsey around to face the guards. "McBride's 'er name." He held out his bleeding arm. "She attacked me with a knife."

Kelsey spied the expertly attired officer, who stood calmly assessing the scene.

"Arrest her," Weems demanded angrily.

"Don't let 'em take 'er, Mr. Weems!" Charlotte stood and all but fell on the man. "She's just a child—"

"Shut up or you'll go with 'er!" Weems muttered.

"McBride did you say?" The officer approached Weems.

"That's what I said, sir. Kelsey McBride's 'er name, an' she's been nothin' but trouble since I took 'er in offa that transport ship!"

"Want us to arrest her, Major Foveaux?" One of the guards gripped Kelsey's arm, digging into her flesh.

Addressing Weems, Foveaux rubbed his gloved fingers together. "We're transporting an Irish convict woman to Norfolk. *Her* name's also McBride."

Kelsey felt a chill run down her spine when Foveaux studied her face.

"That's 'er convict mother!" Weems nodded. "They're all nothin' but trouble, the Irish!"

"I must agree."

Kelsey hated the way the officer regarded her with contempt. The thought of going with him sickened her, but she knew that staying behind now with Weems would bring her certain demise. She turned to part ways with her friend. "Good-bye, Charlotte. If you could get a message to Wick Mercer—"

"Get 'er out o' here!" Weems growled, but not before Charlotte could acknowledge Kelsey's request with a nod.

"I'll do it!" she vowed.

The guards jostled Kelsey from the tavern under Foveaux's watchful eye.

"Looks as though we'll be reuniting a family," Foveaux joked casually with the guards. "Norfolk Island should be a lovely place this time of year."

The square around the government building bustled with a strange new sense of activity on Wednesday's dawn. One naval officer quipped glibly to another, "The old man's finally retired."

"It's a miracle. I hear he's already boarded a ship for London."

"And none too soon. His age—'tis a pity. We'll all reach that hill someday, I vow."

The other officer nodded, drew in on his roll of tobacco, and gathered his papers to report to Philip Gidley King, the newly appointed Governor of New South Wales.

King had bided the years under Hunter, filling his office as commander of Norfolk Island. Although the island provided fertile soil for crops, the flax mill had repeatedly failed under the poor working conditions with convict labor. King accepted the commission sent from England with great relief.

"Welcome back, sir!" A cocky naval corporal entered the room. He had been aboard the First Fleet's flagship, *Sirius*, where King was a lieutenant. "Good to have you aboard!"

"Thank you, Corporal Frederick." King assumed an immediate authoritative air with the corporal, although he had always been fond of him. "There's much to be done, but in time, we'll have it all well in hand." He saluted formally.

"Yes, sir!" Frederick returned the formality.

"Are you aware of the status of the Irish transports being shipped off to Norfolk?"

"As aware as any, sir."

"Has Foveaux's ship been readied?"

"I can answer that, sir." Foveaux stepped forthrightly into the governor's office.

"Greetings, Foveaux." King lifted his face to greet the major.

"Your belongings have been delivered to the transport ship, I trust?"

"All secured, Governor." Foveaux approached the large desk.

"Norfolk Island's convicts are some of the worst. I'm certain that as new commander of the island you've been made aware of the problems."

Without emotion, Foveaux acknowledged, "That I have."

"I've administered my command of the island with a certain amount of . . . shall we say . . . clemency. The convicts are flogged from time to time, but I've found that offering a measure of tolerance brings its own rewards."

Foveaux pressed his lips together. "Certainly, sir," he fabricated his answer. "I can assure you that Norfolk Island will be commandeered with equal ability."

King heaved out a breath, clasping his weathered hands in front of his black coat. "I trust so, Major."

"We've rounded up the Irish rebel convicts for transport. Had to quell an uprising headed for Parrametta."

"You're certain of a planned uprising?" King's brow lifted dubiously.

"Positive. I realize Governor Hunter had his doubts, with all due respect, sir"—Foveaux kept his tone moderate, his gaze one of surety—"but I must assure you that with the uprising being imminent, we had no alternative except to ship them off to Norfolk."

"You'll have your hands full with that lot."

"No more than I can handle, sir." Foveaux met his gaze with full confidence. "If there's nothing else, sir, I will humbly take my leave."

King nodded. "Dismissed. And—"

"Sir?"

"Remember . . . clemency, Foveaux."

"Naturally." Foveaux snapped his salute and turned to walk briskly from the building. He found himself flanked at once by a military escort. "All transports secured in the holds?" He resumed his autocratic manner.

"All secured, Commander."

"Have you separated the Irish leaders?"

"Done, sir."

"Good man. Have the captain inform his men that the Irish convicts should be treated to immediate punishment of one thousand lashes at the cat if one hint of insurrection is discovered."

The guard hesitated. "One thousand, sir?"

Foveaux turned instantly, his eyes narrowed. "Do not question me, Private. Understood?"

"One thousand lashes. Yes, sir!" The private responded at once but shook his head in disbelief when Foveaux turned his back.

Foveaux stepped up into the black carriage that awaited him. Glancing for the last time upon the government building, he allowed a cunning smile to crease his cheeks. Now matters would finally be settled according to his own aspirations—in formidable military style. "Remember, Private, no clemency."

Caleb felt the household change of mood from his bed. Awakening to the dawn, he could hear his parents' voices rising to a heightened pitch. His mother, usually having called up to him by now, could be heard speaking loudly with a visitor in the front room.

Snatching up his trousers from the floor next to his bed, Caleb jumped inside them and threw on a brown woolen shirt. Slipping a pair of stockings over his feet, he ran from the room, his feet barely making contact with the stairs. He could hear his mother offering a polite farewell, which was followed by the wooden slam of the door shutting. Sliding across the floor to meet her, his face was filled with curiosity. "Who was that?"

"Rachel sent a messenger. It's about Heath Whitley." Amelia turned to regard George somberly.

Caleb drew his arms about himself. He feared the day Rachel might send regretful news. "Please tell me, Mum. I want to know."

George stood next to Amelia, and she wrapped her arms about his waist, her eyes moist. She swallowed, dabbed her face with a cloth, and lifted her eyes to meet Caleb's. "Heath Whitley is conscious again!"

"What?"

George reiterated. "He's goin' to be all right!"

"You mean, he's not—" Caleb shook his head.

"What did you think?" Amelia's eyes sparkled. "That Reverend Whitley would let a little fire stop 'im?"

Relief washed through Caleb and he chuckled. "I guess not. He wouldn't at that!"

"Rachel wants us to ride out to the surgeon's place. We can see 'im now."

"Well I'll be jiggered!" Caleb shoved his hands inside his pockets and leaned back, his face beaming. "Ol' Whitley's all right!"

A gay laugh spilled from Amelia's lips. "And more good news"—she reached to place her hands aside Caleb's shoulders—"they're goin' to be wed tomorrow!"

"Finally tyin' the knot!" George quipped.

"Rachel said they'd waited as long as they could wait." Gazing through the glass of their front window, Amelia smiled and slid the letter inside her apron pocket. Then her face grew pale. "Oh no!" she exclaimed. "Dear me, no!"

"What, Mum?"

"A wedding tomorrow? I've not finished her dress yet. And what of all the food? They *can't* get married tomorrow!"

"But they want to!" George spread his arms. "Let them, Amelia."

Amelia schemed quickly. "This is what we'll do. You and Caleb ride out to the surgeon's place to see them. Tell Rachel that I'll need her back before nightfall for a final fitting."

"But, Amelia—"

"Don't argue, George Prentice!" Retying her apron, Amelia opened the front door. "Now scoot!"

Knowing Amelia's bustling demeanor was not one to be reckoned with, George lifted his hat to his head and glanced resignedly at Caleb. "Run fetch your shoes if you're comin', son."

Caleb soon returned and joined his father out in front of their home. "This is a good time for us to talk." George gestured for him to join him atop the wagon.

"Talk about what?"

"Rachel's always loved you, son. You know that, don't you?"

"O' course I do. She's like a sister."

110

"She and Reverend Whitley have asked to assist with your education."

"But I go to the school in the borough, just like I promised Katy."

"Not that kind o' education. A *real* education." George glanced out over the land, dotted here and there with his struggling herd. "One that I can't give you, Caleb."

"You give me all I need, Papa."

"No. Listen to me, now."

Caleb nodded, but confusion darkened his gaze.

"They want to send you to France."

"But you need me here."

"I can hire an extra hand, and Dwight's all but running the affairs of the farm now. I want more for you than I ever had."

"You want me to go?"

George nodded. Caleb thought he detected a moistness around Papa's eyes. He sat back against the seat, his thoughts churning. Seeing a cloud of dust rising from the road leading into their farm, he glanced back at his father. "Someone's comin', Papa." The carriage drew closer, and Caleb saw straightaway that Wick Mercer drove it.

"Hello, neighbor!" George called out.

Mercer nodded, but a grave countenance replaced his usual friendly manner.

Caleb soon found himself hearing a story that sickened his heart. *Kelsey McBride is being sent to Norfolk!* He whipped around to face George. "They can't, Papa! Kelsey's only a girl. She'll die there!"

"Calm yourself." George gripped the boy's arm. Addressing Mercer, he asked, "Has the girl been transported yet?"

"By noon today, I believe," Wick answered.

Caleb grew anxious. "Are *you* goin' to the harbor?"

Mercer nodded. "On me way now, I am."

"Papa, I must go with him!"

"But what about Reverend Whitley an' Rachel?"

"*You'll* see to them! Please let me go!"

The pleading face being more than George could bear, he nodded and heaved a heavy sigh. "Go on, then. You'll be back before sunset?"

"I'll have 'im back, George," Mercer agreed.

The ride into Sydney Cove brought forth a rising frustration in Caleb. He crossed and uncrossed his arms numerous times, and his feet shifted restlessly. "What if we're too late? What if Kelsey's gone?" he worried.

"Not to worry, lad. Worry never gets us anywhere, eh?" Mercer assured.

"Weems should be hanged, that's wot!" Fury began to build inside of him, threatening to explode.

"Kelsey's a strong girl. Don't think she'll buckle under all this." Mercer attempted to calm the boy.

"But why can't she live with you an' Mrs. Mercer? That's what she wanted, you know."

"We've tried. We offered the man our best cow, but he wanted the young laborer."

"Where's Charlotte?"

"I can't tell you that."

"She's run away?"

Mercer glanced covertly at Caleb. Shrugging, he drew in on his pipe and winked. "I didn't tell you that, did I?"

"Kelsey should've run away, as well."

"I can't say as I disagree, knowin' all we know now. But circumstances fall beyond our reach sometimes."

Caleb disliked the hopeless tone of Wick Mercer's voice. At least when Papa addressed a problem, he quoted the Bible or offered a ray of hope. Mercer, albeit a good man, did not have the faith Caleb's parents had. He kept to his thoughts until the sounds of activity in the borough caught his ear.

Pulling out his old watch, Mercer checked the time. "Eleven-thirty. I believe we made it, lad."

Caleb sat forward, anxious for the masts of the harbor to appear. Passing the government building, he noted another wagon that was filled up with convicts. "Per'aps they're bein' sent to Norfolk, too."

"Not likely. Look at their prison garb. British jails use those garments. They're dressed like new transportees, not like New South Wales convicts t'all."

Within the next few minutes, the harbor's fishy smell sent anxiousness through Caleb. Before Mercer could rein the wagon to a halt, he leaped onto the pebble-spangled ground and ran for an officer who stood on the dock. "Sir!" he shouted boldly.

The man gazed insipidly, his regard for an emancipist child no different than that for a dog.

Undaunted, Caleb stopped in front of the officer. "Has the transport left for Norfolk Island?"

"Which one?"

Rubbing his palms nervously, Caleb struggled with an answer. "The one wot's got those Irish rebels aboard!"

His impatience evident, the officer crossed his arms. "Again I say, which one?"

Consternation filled Caleb's senses. How would he find one small girl among the ranks of the callous and indifferent? He left the officer behind and determined to find a ship's captain. Perhaps a ship's roster would be available. He queried two mariners, who shrugged him away—one with an insult and the other with a curse. *God, please help me!* he pled from his heart.

"Caleb!"

He jerked around. There was no one in sight.

"Caleb!" The call came again.

"Where?" he shouted. "Where are you?"

"Up here!"

He lifted his face and saw Mercer leaning against the rail of a ship. "Mr. Mercer! I can't find 'er!"

Without another word, Wick Mercer made a broad gesture with his arm, indicating Caleb should come aboard.

Caleb ran around the dock in search of the ship's gangplank that Wick had boarded. Finding it without a guard, he dashed up it. Relieved to see Wick's confident smile, he ran to his side. "You found 'er?"

Wick nodded toward the forecastle of the ship. A guard appeared from behind the mainmast. Ambling slowly, he guided Kelsey around the rigging.

Caleb felt his heart pounding in his chest. Kelsey's cheek, sporting a small blue bruise, caught his eye first, and the rage inside him released. "Wot 'ave they done to you?" he exploded.

Not knowing why the guard had summoned her from the hold, an apprehensive surprise spread across Kelsey's face when she beheld Wick and Caleb. She stopped, not knowing whether to run away or to weep. Drawing a trembling hand to her face, she spoke softly, "Caleb?"

Shoving his way through a circle of ships hands, he made his way toward her. "Wot's happened?"

"Weems . . . I . . ." her voice broke. "It's my own fault."

Turning to assist his mates at the capstan, the guard ordered gruffly, "Stay put, girl!"

Kelsey nodded fearfully.

"No, let's run!" Caleb whispered. "We can hide you out at Rose Hill!"

Drawing her finger to her lips, Kelsey cautioned, "There's no place to escape. Believe me, I've examined every exit from the ship. They're all heavily guarded."

"But I came on the ship without so much as a nod."

"You're not wearing this." Kelsey pointed to the gray and yellow tunic. She ambled toward the gangplank. "Watch me."

Caleb followed closely behind. As Kelsey neared the gangplank, a mariner stepped up at once, his musket at his side. "Back the other way!" he growled.

Kelsey turned around, her eyes wide and hopeless. "I'm the same as dead."

"Who could we speak with?"

"You can't stop it. You can't stop them."

"Then I'll come for you. I'll find a way!"

A gentle resignation softened Kelsey's worried brow. "Thank you, anyway, for coming. I still can't believe you're here."

Caleb warmed at the faint smile that played around her lips. "Of course I'm here."

"I thought by now you hated me for—"

"Forget all that. For now, we need a plan." He gazed into the distance. "I'll tell Papa. He'll think of a way."

"Tell your parents good-bye for me."

"I'll not give up. You'll see. I'll come for you. I'll come before winter."

At once the yellow flag was hoisted, indicating the captain's intent to set sail. The mates scrambled around the ship, carrying out the orders the officers barked at them.

"All convicts in the hold!" The guard reappeared.

"I should go and say good-bye to Wick. He's been so good to me," Kelsey said wistfully.

Glancing toward Wick Mercer, who waited patiently off to the side, Caleb nodded his agreement. Helplessness swept through him. He wanted to grab the girl and run with her. "Kelsey?" He hesitated. "I must know."

She stopped. "Yes?"

"That morning after the fire . . . was it you? Did you . . . did you kiss me?"

A subdued chuckle preceding her answer, Kelsey planted herself gracefully in front of him. "First, you answer me this."

"Go on."

She lifted her fragile hands to the sides of his face. "Did it feel like this?" Drawing him toward her, she closed her eyes and pressed her lips against his.

Caleb felt his cheeks redden. He couldn't move or react to Kelsey. He simply stood still while she kissed him in front of the entire world.

Opening her eyes, she smiled. "Was it like that?"

He nodded, as though every thought had been emptied from his head.

Laughing gently, Kelsey whispered, "Good-bye, Caleb Prentice. And thank you for befriending the daughter of an Irish convict."

Caleb's mind raced. He couldn't find voice for the words he longed to say. All he could do, all his confused mind could muster was to nod a feeble farewell.

Placing a kiss upon Wick Mercer's cheek, Kelsey McBride disappeared into the crowd of mariners, who shambled her away to the crowded holds below.

Caleb found himself shuffled off the ship, along with Mercer. He hated himself. He hadn't looked into her face long enough or said any of the things he longed to say, but instead, he had sent her away with a dumbfounded nod of his head. "She . . . did you see, Mr. Mercer?" he touched his lips, still warm from the kiss.

"I won't tell," Mercer winked.

Caleb watched with dismay as the deckhands cast off the moorings, releasing the ship from the dock. It bobbed farther and farther out to sea. "How far to Norfolk Island?"

"A thousand miles."

"I could make it in a good-sized boat."

"Never. No one goes to Norfolk but British military and convict laborers. They fear outsiders might attack the island and take it over. It's our main source o' food for the stores now, and as such, it is kept heavily guarded." Caleb followed Wick Mercer through the throng of harbor frequenters. They purchased some fish and some extra meat for the wedding and then made their way back to the wagon.

Turning to face Caleb, Mercer reached into his pocket and drew out an object. Placing it in the boy's hand, he made ready for departure and snapped his whip across the horse's flank.

Caleb unclasped his hand. "Me knife?"

Mercer shrugged. "Thought you'd need it again sometime."

"Where did you find it?"

"Charlotte asked me to give it to you."

Caleb cradled the returned gift in his hand and turned to watch Kelsey's ship ride the waves toward the darkening horizon. *I'll come for you, I promise*, he vowed. *I'll come before winter.*

PART TWO

COMING OF AGE

JUNE 1804

10

ROSE HILL'S NEW DAWN

"Kick the ball! Now run!" Caleb, enjoying his seventeenth birthday, called after one of the youths stationed out in a field not far from Rose Hill. "Forevermore, Matthew! You still run like a blooming girl!" His own movements were swift, full of grace and virility.

"My turn!" yelled Caleb's cousin, Grant Hogan.

Caleb punted the ball to Grant and watched as he whisked past Matthew with the speed of a musket ball. "Now that's running, if I've ever seen it!" His face bronzed and handsome, it kindled an easy light of humor. His hearty laugh echoed down through the vale.

Grant drew back his foot and assailed the ball with a final blow.

Caleb leaped in the ball's path and secured possession before falling into a roll along the grassy berm. "I've got it!" he cried out victoriously. His brilliant blue eyes reflected his easy conquest as well as the sky overhead. He lay for a moment cradling the ball and staring up at a small cloud bank in the shape

119

of a sailing vessel gliding across the cerulean sky.

Not a day had dawned over the past four years in France that Caleb hadn't thought of the Irish girl, Kelsey McBride. If she had ever received his letter from France, she hadn't acknowledged it. Their brief moments spent in innocent friendship lingered in his thoughts and stirred his young senses. But his anxiety regarding the impossible distance between them had soon waned, and he had allowed the guilt and pain of her memory to fade along with the flowers planted atop his father's grave.

Leaning back on his elbows, he felt the tickle of the grass on his muscular neck while he listened for Grant and Matthew's approach.

"Stand up, fool!" Grant demanded, issuing a mock order, "and take your punishment! It's a duel I'm calling for!" he announced in crisp boarding-school English.

Caleb straightened and, with an indifferent sigh, stood to his feet. The blond locks of his childhood had darkened to a soft auburn and hung loosely above his shoulders. He had grown to a height of over six feet, towering above most of the youths his age. "Don't frighten me so," he answered in feigned fear, but his eyes held a half-real challenge.

Grant glanced up at his cocksure cousin. Although himself a muscular lad of seventeen, he could not outwrestle Caleb Prentice but would suffer much punishment before confessing such a thing. He drew up his fist and delivered a friendly punch to Caleb's stout arm.

Matthew wiped his brow. His round, boyish face dripped with sweat. "I'm bored. What now?"

"Let's go to my house," Caleb offered. "Tonight's Katy's party. If I'm late for another of her social get-togethers, she'll have me hanged!"

"But she's giving the party in honor of you, true?" Grant arched one brow. "Your birthday—"

"So she says. But my sister needs little excuse to drag me into another of her social settings. She's trying to marry me off, you know."

"Since when do you allow your sister to order you around?" Matthew pressed his lips together disdainfully.

"Since Katy took over running the household affairs, she's

more fierce than Mum ever threatened to be," he said flatly, then rubbed his stomach. "But a man has to eat."

Grant chuckled. "I suppose if you're promised to Trula Hill, you'd best be skilled in catering to women."

A deliberate hesitation gave Caleb a moment to consider his answer. "Catering? Don't be so hasty." He posed his face in an assuming manner. "I've made no agreements as yet. And if Miss Hill wishes to make her future at Rose Hill, well, then, she'd best take her place as a woman."

Matthew rolled his eyes. "Her *place*? She'll most likely make her place ruling the roost if you're not careful. She already believes it's by divine providence that your parents' farm bears her name."

"Silly rumors, my good man! Trula's not entrapped me yet. I'm not that easy to snag."

"She's a comely young woman, Caleb. Surely you'll not let this one pass you by?" Grant crossed his arms, his brow arched. "Sydney Cove's not running over with beauties, you know."

"Sydney Cove's not the entire world."

Matthew asked cynically, "When are you goin' to see the entire world?"

"Soon," Caleb answered steadily, but a flicker of uncertainty glinted from his eyes. "I've seen a good share already. I've paid my dues in France. *J'ai trop observé.* In time, I'll take my rightful place at Rose Hill. But first"—he thrust a finger in the air confidently—"it's off to England for me, that's what!"

"Well, say hello to England for me," Grant said dryly. "I'm bored with England."

Matthew shot out a challenge. "Hang England! If you're not interested in Trula Hill, then let me have her!" He jabbed a thumb toward himself.

Caleb studied Matthew's face. He still retained the soft kittenlike facial hair above his lip and had close-set eyes, yet in a boyish way he held a handsome appearance. "Trula Hill doesn't want a boy, Matthew, she wants a man!" His left brow lifted in a definitive manner.

"We'll just see *who* Trula Hill wants!" Matthew retorted.

"Well, while you're both sitting on your intellect, perhaps I'll steal her from under your noses." Grant smiled smugly.

Sighing, Caleb retorted, "Another minute in this pasture debating you two fools, and I'll be dead for certain, if not by Katy's hand, then from starvation." He gripped his throat.

Grant nodded. "I must start for home as well. I'll meet you both at the party, though. Give Aunt Amelia a kiss from her favorite nephew."

"I'll ride with you, Grant." Matthew plucked the ball from under Caleb's arm. "My ball!" he reminded them in a self-satisfied way. He turned to go and untie his steed from a tree limb. Caleb waved absentmindedly and then scooped his tan-colored hat from the ground. Placing it atop his head, he allowed the neck loop to fall loosely underneath his chin in Australian style. He had ridden the new young stallion Dwight and Katy had surprised him with when he had returned from France. He strode quickly toward the brush where he'd tied it. Pressing his boot inside the stirrup, he leaped onto the saddle. He squeezed his knees against the stallion's gleaming black withers, and off they galloped, his hat bouncing loosely against his broad shoulders.

The brisk ride did his heart good. His mind preoccupied by the many changes that had come into his life since his father's death, he found a temporary peace whenever he rode, especially when he and Dwight made the frequent treks into the outback to inspect their flocks. After returning from France, he had found Rose Hill flourishing. Their stock had increased fourfold since Dwight and Katy had assumed the management responsibilities, and the increase in income had been welcomed by them all. But Caleb couldn't help but feel a nagging, senseless guilt. Papa's ways had never brought them great wealth, but he had resided over Rose Hill with integrity and honesty. Caleb missed the quiet talks he and Papa often had regarding the importance of godly living. Never completely embracing Papa's faith, he had absorbed the tranquillity that pervaded their family life and took for granted that the same peace would always remain.

Caleb turned the steed toward the high hilltop that overlooked the now completed farmhouse. The young horse plowed into the incline with great force, and Caleb pressed his body into the saddle horn for balance. He reached the crest within minutes. Soon, the farm became a lush green valley spreading out magnificently before his eyes. He dismounted and left the steed to nibble on a mound of spinefax. The hill's edge made a wide plateau, surrounded by large boulders—a shelf perfect for a grave. His abrupt return and brief stay two years ago had not allowed him to expend the grief he held inside, and the promise he had made to Papa to fulfill his education in France had become a painful burden. After George's interment, he reluctantly kissed the tear-streaked faces of his mother and sister and sailed away again. "Papa would want it this way," Katy had assured him. Caleb had chosen his father's resting place himself, knowing George Prentice would've been pleased with the view of Rose Hill. He knelt quietly at the graveside, plucking a few weeds from around the flowers Amelia and Katy had planted and nurtured for the last two years. With a shiver of vivid recollection, he recalled how Dwight had related the account of his father's death. It was bushrangers who had ended the life of George Prentice. Such deviant minds would never understand the family bond they had destroyed.

"Farm's doin' well, Papa," Caleb began, then stopped abruptly. Papa wouldn't want a progress report. "The sky is blue today, Papa," he began again. "Robin's-egg blue with a cloud or two." He seated himself beside the grave. "I never heard back from Norfolk Island. I know you prayed a lot for the McBride girl. But I can't . . ." He paused and sighed. "I can't make things right again, Papa. Don't know how. Besides, I'm almost grown now, and a young woman has entered my life," he said in a discontented voice. "I believe you'd like her. Name's Trula Hill—like Rose Hill." He tried to recall the girl's lovely features, but his mind was so weighed down by a permanent sorrow that he proceeded with other thoughts. "Katy was with child and would've loved a daughter, but she lost the baby. Don't worry about Katy, though. She's doing well, Papa, very well. She's so strong, like Mum."

A cluster of white lilies began to flutter as a gentle breeze blew across the high plateau. Caleb ran a sun-bronzed hand down one of the stems and plucked it from the base. "For you, Papa, for your love of life," he mused with fondness, then sighed. Standing slowly to his feet, he brushed the sharp pebbles from his trousers and turned in a circle to regard the warm mound of earth. "I'll come again, soon. Good-bye, Papa." He mounted the stallion and descended the hill. The day had been a good one, spent freely with his convivial comrades. But with all levity now behind him, he felt an old anxiety rising up again. Unexplained, the disquietude usually began as a stirring inside him that swelled into his chest and left him feeling troubled and alone. *Why did you have to go, Papa?* He tilted his face to the sun and allowed the horse to bear him toward the farmhouse, knowing the beast could find its way better than he.

The shearing of the sheep had become an annual celebration at Rose Hill. The number of farmhands had increased fourfold, and Dwight and Katy Farrell felt the workers deserved to end their labors with a feast. So Katy allowed and included in the celebration of her brother's birthday a generous feast for the shearers and sheepherders.

With their aprons flying, the extra kitchen help scurried about the newly installed stove and cooking area. Amelia contributed to the feast with her own brand of pastries, while Katy delegated tasks to the small staff of maids and cooks. Lifting a large spoon to her lips, Katy sampled the hot fruit that simmered in a pot. "Mmm. Delicious," she murmured, closing her eyes and inhaling the sweet aroma. "Perfect, Mum." She tapped the spoon on the pot's edge and laid it aside.

The stairs thundered with the sound of pounding bare feet. "You boys," Katy shouted. "Stop running up and down those stairs, at once!"

It grew quiet upstairs. Katy huffed about while Amelia winked in a grandmotherly fashion. "Jared and Donovan are growing so fast. What'll I do when they outgrow me?"

"Cut a bigger switch!" the plump cook interjected, wiping her face with a towel, her features drawn up in a scowl.

Amelia pressed a piece of flattened dough into a large dish. "They're good boys, Katy. You and Dwight are doin' a fine job rearin' them. An' a good job with the sheep farm, too. Such a blessin' the way you've taken over."

Katy waved her hand dismissively. "Oh, everything's just improving now, that's all. New South Wales is growing. Lots more folks coming over from England. Even your own sister and her husband moved here. You know if the Hogans put their stamp of approval on this place, it must be improving."

"Yes, but that 'usband o' yours has his way with both man and beast. He's the best sheep farmer in New South Wales, if you asks me. The very best!" Amelia beamed.

"Thank you, Mum." Seeing a figure moving across the distant landscape, Katy whirled on her feet. "Caleb's coming in early for once. That's a miracle."

"Suppose it's that young woman? Do you think she's made a change in him?" Amelia took a knife and fluted the edges of the pastry. "I know France has changed him."

Katy shook her head. "It's so difficult to say. Trula Hill is a lovely person. But she's . . . well . . . a bit possessive of him, or am I misjudging her?"

"Not entirely. I've seen it as well. But Caleb's made no complaints, an' he's a grown man now. He'll have to decide for himself about the girl."

"I know this is all so difficult for him. He always had Papa to discuss his decisions with. Dwight's made himself available for him, of course, but Caleb doesn't divulge a great deal of his thoughts to my husband." With a fork, Katy plucked a piece of hot potato from the cook's bowl. She nodded approvingly to the woman, who smiled warmly and then returned to her recipe. "But Caleb's not been the same since Papa died. He seems happy enough, but I can still see the pain in his eyes."

"He an' his papa were close." Amelia shook her apron and a cloud of flour filled the air around her. "But Caleb's never been one to discuss his thoughts or his faith."

"That's where Dwight and I have failed him, isn't it? Our faith?"

"Don't condemn yourself. I've struggled with God, too. But it's brought me closer to Him. Your papa an' me, we had our hard times, we did. But then we had the best o' times, too, right 'ere at Rose Hill. My George finished the race first, is all. He's doin' now what he always did best."

Katy gazed reflectively at her mother. "And what is that?"

"Praisin' the good Lord with all 'is might!"

A sweet laugh spilled from Katy's lips. "Of course."

"Smells heavenly, ladies!" Caleb burst through the door, his eyes full of humor but tender. "I've put all duties aside to assist with the laborious task of sampling the cooking." Before Katy could raise a note of protest, his hand lifted defensively. "No need to talk me out of it. I realize no others will avail themselves in such a manner, so here I am!" Stooping to kiss Amelia's forehead, he placed the lily in her hand. When he stood erect, his nose was white with flour.

Katy and Amelia burst into laughter, while the Cockney maids simply shook their heads.

"All right, you scoundrel!" Katy succumbed to his charm. "One taste of Cook's hot curried potatoes. Just one, mind you!"

Laying a large hand against his forehead, Caleb sighed. " 'Tis a laborious task I now must face, but someone must bear the load!"

"Oh, posh!" The cook wiped her hands upon her apron. Throwing up her palms in mock surrender, she turned on her heels and waltzed toward the stove.

Caleb scooped up a kitchen utensil and dug into the steaming bowl of potatoes. "Unbelievably good!" he mumbled with his mouth full.

"Oh, go wash up and put on a clean shirt!" Amelia commanded, her eyes sparkling with affection. "Katy's worked so hard for your birthday. The least you can do is change your shirt."

"Am I too early?" a well-modulated voice asked.

At once, every eye observed the beautiful young woman who strolled gracefully into the room.

"Hello, Rachel!" Caleb spoke first.

"Of course you're not too early," Amelia retorted. "You're family, Rachel."

Rachel pressed a hurried kiss upon Caleb's cheek. "Happy birthday! I see you've come to sample the cook's fare." She regarded Caleb with amusement.

"You know me better than I know myself, my friend." Caleb always enjoyed her gentle sparring as much as she did.

Rachel held a stunning plum-colored dress across her arms. "Amelia, I thought I'd change into my gown a bit later. That way I can help you with the banquet for now."

"It's magnificent!" Amelia stood to admire the brocaded fabric. She ran her fingers across the lace-covered bodice, glancing obliquely toward Caleb. "From France?"

Rachel smiled sheepishly. "No. From me. I sewed it myself."

"Don't tell anyone. Let them think it's from Paris, and they'll all be jealous!" Katy laughed.

"Where are your children?" Amelia glanced around Rachel into the parlor.

"Luke and Ariel? Their father has them. Heath will bring them later tonight."

"Such sweet babies!" Amelia beamed. Reaching to assist Rachel with the dress, she offered, "Let's lay it across Katy's bed upstairs, then you and Katy can dress together later. I'll show you her new gown." She winked conspiratorially. "We made it as well."

"Mum!" Katy feigned horror.

"It's our secret." Rachel held a finger over her lips. "I'll return in a moment." She smiled at Katy and turned to follow Amelia from the room.

Katy, momentarily preoccupied with the current tasks, returned to see that each maid's and cook's helper had every chore well in hand. Finding the banquet festivities flowing smoothly, she turned her attention to her brother, noting at once his strangely quiet mood. Caleb stood leaning against the large washbasin, his eyes seemingly fixed upon a point beyond the window glass. Katy walked up behind him and gently looped her arm through his own muscular arm. "Excited about the party tonight?" she asked softly.

Caleb voiced no immediate reply, his eyes transfixed by unspoken thoughts. Then he broke his gaze and shook himself from his troubled world. "I'm sorry, Katy. What was that?"

"The party—you're excited about it, aren't you?"

Opening his mouth to speak, he fumbled for a proper answer. "Of course. I'm truly looking forward to it," he said evenly.

Katy knew her brother quite well. His eyes betrayed his heart. "Caleb, why don't you tell me what you're thinking about?"

"What do you mean?"

Heaving a sigh, Katy released his arm and turned to face him. "Are you or are you not in love with Trula Hill?"

In a low composed voice, he said, "Trula will make a wonderful wife. She's mad about me, or haven't you noticed?"

"But what about you, Caleb? Do *you* love *her*?"

"In time—"

"No! Not in time! Marriage is forever, Caleb." Katy's worries spilled over into her words. "Dwight and I have had our share of disagreements, and without the bond of love, we would never have the strength to go forward at times. But I *love* Dwight. Now, answer me truthfully. Do you love Trula?"

Caleb shook his head. "I . . . I don't know." He could no longer bear Katy's penetrating eyes. When he spoke again his voice was warm but authoritative. "I have to dress now, Katy, for the party." He patted her shoulder but directed his gaze toward the kitchen exit. "Wouldn't want to disappoint Trula, now, would I?"

Katy crossed her arms over her apron. Her stubborn brother had once again averted her attempt to corner him. But she knew that Trula's arrival might soon expose his motives. *We'll see if Miss Trula Hill can flush you out, Caleb Prentice!* Exasperated, she turned her thoughts upon the banquet and allowed her frustrations with her brother to temporarily subside.

11
UNEXPECTED
VISITOR

A crimson sky crowned the horizon above the Blue Mountains with a temporary elegance. The sunset, offering a farewell performance for the end of day, melded with the twilight and flashed a brilliant display of gold above the summery green meadows of Australia.

The sound of bleating on the pastured hill beside the farmhouse grew sporadic. The sheep had gathered for evening protection, their freshly shorn pink hides blended as one. Caleb stood watching the gentle breeze bend the few tall grasses around him that had not yet been grazed upon by the flock. He had donned a fashionable dark suit, but upon trekking out of doors, he immediately removed the jacket and tossed it across one shoulder. Only half listening to the sounds of laughter now floating across the cooled air, he gazed away from the farmhouse. The party had commenced, but he found no kindred spirit of frivolity lightening his senses.

"Escaping again?"

Turning to acknowledge the intruder, Caleb stopped and smiled faintly. "Hello, Trula."

"Happy birthday!" The young woman lifted her skirts slightly to step gracefully around the mounds of grass. "Katy told me I'd find you wandering among the sheep. You must prefer the beasts to humans, eh?" Her elegant style announced a regal certainty.

Caleb regarded the young woman respectfully but inwardly wished that she had left him to his private thoughts. "I prefer sheep in place of only certain humans. None compare to your beauty, *mademoiselle*." He hoped the words sounded sincere and not as forced as they truly had been.

"Thank you, Caleb." Trula's long dark lashes waved demurely, and she lifted her face boldly toward him. "But do you truly think me beautiful in the inward sense? Or only as an *objet d'art* to be admired from afar?"

The young woman exercised little patience when matters turned to courting, Caleb had realized none too soon. Nevertheless, he found her presence strangely exciting. He acknowledged to himself that he would make no attempt to deter her flirtations. But rather, he encouraged her with his own overtures of affection. "Take a walk with me," he invited. Strangely flattered by her interest, he drew near to her and cupped one strong hand at her waist. "That is, if you dare." He lifted a brow teasingly as if to offer a challenge.

Trula raised a lace fan to her face and covered her rose-tinted lips, feigning a blush. "You think I'm afraid?"

"I think you're irresistible." Caleb gazed intently at Trula, wickedly enjoying the way this confident young woman melted in his presence.

With a sardonic smile, she retorted, "That is exactly why I shouldn't go with you." She started to pull away, but her eyes became locked on his. She hesitated. "Oh, Caleb. You're much too handsome for your own good!" Her eyes took in his powerful presence.

His lips pursed, Caleb maintained his grip around her waist and then drew her closer by placing his other hand firmly around her right side. Now his curiosity as well as his vanity was aroused. No longer caring about what was considered proper, he smiled, knowing his control over the girl's feelings had greatly improved. Her face now within inches of his, he stopped just short of kissing her waiting lips. Then, without a word, he released his hands from her diminutive waist. A strange light sparked in his gaze as once again his thoughts grew uneasy.

Trula stared up at him through tortured eyes. "What is it, Caleb? What keeps you from loving me?"

The word startled him. "Love?"

She shook her head, her eyes rueful. "You don't know what love is, do you?"

With the fire drained from his countenance, Caleb drew his face from hers and turned his attentions again upon the flock.

"Or what's best for you." She placed her hands on her hips, the lavender satin of her dress glistening against the sunset.

"What *is* best for me, Trula?" he asked, veiling his troubled eyes from her probing look.

"Can't you see that *I* am what's best for you?"

"I've heard rumors of that." He made a weak attempt to lighten the moment.

"You're taunting me!" She lifted her face defiantly and turned to run back to the farmhouse.

Seeing at once that Trula's temper had flared, Caleb's mind raced for a gentlemanly solution. Katy would never forgive him if any of their guests departed on such bad terms. Nor would his conscience allow such an incident, no matter how sporting it seemed to his indifferent mind. "Don't leave." He softened his tone. "Please forgive me. I could never taunt you."

Trula stopped but merely looked toward him, her dignity shaken.

Caleb paused, hoping to see the light of forgiveness in her eyes. But her expression remained solemn. "I know that when love happens to me, Trula . . ."

Her brows lifted hopefully. More hopefully than Caleb could resist.

" . . . that you will be the recipient. Will you please . . . could you give me more time?" He hated himself for the words he had just spoken. Wanting to appease her, he had gone too far, sounding more promising than he had intended. "I'm not as easy to understand, I realize, as Matthew or some of the others. My life has been rather complicated—"

Trula now had all the encouragement she had hoped for. "Of course I'll forgive you, Caleb." She beamed her approval and strode gracefully toward him. She lifted two fingers to his lips. "Say no more. I see in your eyes the truth of what your heart is trying to say." Her smile shook his sensibilities. "And of course *you're* more complicated than Matthew. He's a mere boy." Her confidence spiraled upward. "I promise you all the time you need, Caleb Prentice. We shall allow our love to grow together." Her strength gathered as the words flowed freely. "And you've promised me a walk."

"You'll join me for a walk?"

"Absolutely! We've much to discuss about our eventual future."

Caleb felt her slender fingers interlock in his own. He forced another smile and began his descent down the sloping knoll with Trula Hill at his side. Her perfume filled his senses, but his thoughts remained troubled. Entering the pathway that serpentined through a wooded glen, he scarcely listened to her chatter. From time to time he would nod approvingly and then wonder almost fearfully to what he had agreed. "Watch your step. There's a tree ahead near the stream," he cautioned.

Trula stopped in front of the fallen tree trunk. She was about to attempt to walk the length of the tree and go around it, but Caleb gripped her arm. "Allow me." He lifted her effortlessly, placing her feet atop the tree's algae-covered side. He lifted one long, muscular leg over the tree and stopped to regain his balance before sweeping her, weightless, into his arms. Trula locked herself into his embrace. "Look, Caleb, I'm not running away. Not this time. Not ever." Her large shining eyes met boldly with his.

The intensity in her lowered voice paralyzed him momentarily. Now straddling the trunk, Caleb stepped away from the tree and clasped her body close to his. "So I see." He felt her long lashes brush gently against his cheek. With such a beautiful young woman in his arms, he would not allow another moment to pass without incident. He allowed her to slide gracefully to the leaf-covered forest bed but did not release her from his muscular grasp. His hands glided up her arms and then slowly to her face. "Miss Hill, may I kiss you?" he asked, allowing an artless innocence to color his desire.

Powerless to resist, Trula nodded slowly and closed her eyes, lifting her face in expectancy.

Caleb pulled her to him and pressed his lips against hers masterfully. He felt Trula's arms slip around his neck as she yielded to his embrace.

Drawn into the stream's current, a lifeboat nosed into a froth of brackish water and then meandered around the curving rivulets. The sun no longer lighting the way, the boat glided effortlessly into the darkened woods toward Parrametta. A thin hand appeared over the stern, trembling fingers curving to grip the boat. Slowly a head raised and then lowered again, the hair matted green with seaweed. Then both hands appeared, white-knuckled, as the passenger struggled to sit upright. Startling a flock of water fowl, the boat's bow rested upon a sand bar. A faint groan emitted from the passenger. Struggling to lift a weathered oar from inside the boat, the figure leaned out from the bow and labored to free the lifeboat from the shoal. The heavy-bottomed boat did not move on but stuck fast in the sand. "God help me!" The feeble cry struck the deaf ear of hollow silence and floated away. After a time, rushing water caused the sand beneath the boat to shift. Aiming the bow deeper into the wooded bowels of forest, the passenger slipped exhausted back into the lifeboat and grew silent, while the moon settled darkly gold inside the branches of the pale eucalyptus.

"I should escort you back, Trula." Caleb mustered an ounce of chivalry. He felt her heart pound against his chest.

Trula straightened her shoulders. Her hair, which moments before had been neatly coifed atop her head, now hung in tendrils around the nape of her neck. "You must think me terrible."

"Not at all. We've done nothing wrong. It was just a kiss of friendship, so what's to criticize?"

She lifted her lips to his again. "The wild thoughts whirling in my head."

Caleb swallowed hard but composed his voice. "If I don't

take you back now, I soon won't be able to turn back." The smile in his eyes contained a passionate flame.

"Let's don't, then!" Pleased with their initial intimacy, Trula grasped for any remaining opportunity to be near him.

Caleb smiled, the warmth of her touch mesmerizing his senses. But he knew the young woman would wish for nothing better than to entrap him. He held her out at arm's length, having no intention of falling under her spell. Staring wordlessly across at her, he allowed his hands to drop at his sides.

Trula stepped closer, her dark blue eyes glowing with a sheen of purpose and determination. "You're so wise." She flattered him. "So strong for both of us. Now please help me with my hair, sir," she said coquettishly, then turned her back to him and placed her hands atop his.

"I don't believe I'm skilled at this sort of thing." Caleb chuckled awkwardly at the request.

"Just lift up my hair and help me tuck it inside these pins," she instructed, but her voice still held the coy flirtatiousness that sent warning signals to Caleb's mind.

He realized another ploy had arisen, but he simply did as he was asked. Soon the loose strands had been smoothed as well as he knew how. "All done, *mademoiselle*. No one will be the wiser."

Trula stepped away, her face brightening. "You've such gentlemanly ways about you. Ways that certainly reflect the life of your dearly departed father."

Caleb thanked her politely, but the same painful void he had felt while standing over Papa's grave stirred again within him. He felt a strange sensation settle in his thoughts like a black cloud. Feelings of guilt and reproach for Papa's violent death lingered like the echo of cannon fire off a hillside. He despised the fact that Trula had brought up the grievous subject. "Let's head back, shall we?" he asked tersely.

"I've said something wrong?"

His gaze wooden, he responded, "Not at all. The evening's been delightful."

Trula retrieved the fan that she had tossed atop a shrub. "I'm sorry."

Caleb reached platonically for her hand. "No apology necessary." He buttoned his coat and ran his hand down the nape of his neck to smooth his queue. A flicker of moonlight glinted off the stream and caught his eye. He started back on the pathway but then stopped abruptly.

"Something wrong?"

He glanced at Trula, frowning in puzzlement. "Did you see anything near that stream bed?"

"Don't tell me!" Panic etched her face. "A crocodile?"

"I'm sure it was nothing," he said, trying to assure her. But then his curiosity got the better of him, and he whirled around. "Stay here!" he ordered. Ignoring her protests, Caleb stepped around the wet brush and slippery rocks that lined the stream. The water slowed at this point and would eventually empty out into a large billabong just a mile from where he stood. With only the moon to light his way, he crept closer. He watched the tall grassy fronds dip and then rise again, as though bowing to a regal presence. Caleb separated the swampy foliage that impeded his view. Then he beheld what he thought he had seen moments earlier. A large lifeboat slid across the water's surface, stealing slowly away, quiet as a water snake. He would have allowed the vessel to pass, but a stirring across the rim of the bow gave rise to his curiosity. He found himself quickly removing his coat and rolling up his trouser legs.

"Caleb, please don't!"

He ignored Trula's pleadings and tossed aside his boots and stockings. Using a long stick to determine the water's depth, he ventured out into the dark, murky stream bed. The water current ebbed around him as did the slithering plant life around his bare legs. Lunging toward the lifeboat's stern, he gripped the wooden rim with both hands, but the rotting wood gave way beneath his grip. He secured a better hold and used the force of his weight to aim the bow back toward the bank.

Trula stood ashore shaking her head. "You're so stubborn! And for what? A useless, leaky old boat."

"Grab the bow!"

"But my dress!"

"Do as I ask!"

Trula lifted her skirts uncomfortably and tried to bundle the satin and taffeta into one arm while reaching out to grasp the bow with the other. "I can't reach it. I'll fall in."

Caleb shoved with all his strength until he heard the bar-

nacles scraping against stone and sand. Then finding his footing upon some large rocks near the shore, he lifted himself over
the bow. Landing with sure footing inside the boat, he stared
in bewilderment. Even Trula's constant barrage of questions
didn't bring him to speak. Instead, he bent down and placed
his arms under the frail bundle of human life who had first
caught his eye.

"At least make way," he instructed, "if you can't help!" His
annoyance with Trula's helplessness at its peak, he balanced
himself against the side of the boat. Stepping carefully athwart
the bow, he balanced the still form close to his body.

"What is it?" Trula held her hands to her lips.

"A woman."

"Is she alive?"

"I believe so." Caleb looked down at the pathetic castaway
with deep pity. The faint moan she uttered stirred an unexpected compassion within him. "But we'd best get her some
medical help right away. Let's take her to the house so Rachel
can see her."

"But you can't take this . . . this *female* into the party."

"She's a person, Trula. In need of our help."

"But she's probably an escaped convict or something worse.
Just . . . oh, turn her over to the authorities." She tried to smile
prettily. "Then we can join the party again."

His anger kindled, Caleb took charge of the matter. "Run
ahead of me, now! Run and fetch Rachel Whitley at once,
woman!"

Trula gasped at his sudden outburst. "We should've gone
back earlier," she shot back, her tone full of possessive desperation. "Now the night is ruined!" She burst into tears and ran
wailing toward the pasture.

Caleb slipped his bare feet into his boots. Then reaching
cautiously so as not to disturb the woman, he retrieved his coat
and draped it gently around her trembling frame. "Hold on,
miss," he whispered, "help is coming." He glanced with apprehension toward the pathway where Trula had just disappeared.
I hope.

12

THE REFUGEE

"She's probably a convict escaped from the prison!" Trula's words were loaded with ridicule as she stood before Katy and Dwight Farrell in a room away from the guests. The raucous sounds of laughter filtered in from the parlor.

Katy's pale blue silk dress rustled as she somberly seated herself upon an oak settee. With calm composure, she gazed up at her husband. "We'll have to summon Rachel from the party. She'll know what to do."

"I'll fetch her." Dwight nodded politely at Trula, his tone ladened with concern. "Thank you, Trula." He departed quietly, closing the door behind himself.

Trula's face hardened. "What shall I do about Caleb, Katy? He's so . . . well, difficult to understand."

Her face softening, Katy's eyes sparkled knowingly. "That I must agree with. But Caleb's not been the same since Papa was killed. We've all tried to be patient with him. I suppose you'll just have to exercise the same forbearance." She lowered her voice. "But you can't fault him for helping this young woman now, can you?"

Trula fought to hide the bitter edge of cynicism in her voice. "I suppose not." She smoothed her skirt and strode over to the mirror that adorned a small bureau. "Could you please help me, Katy. I do look a fright." Her eyes wide with sincerity, she hoped to evoke sympathy from Caleb's sister.

Katy smiled broadly. "Of course." Standing gracefully, she retrieved a small hair comb from inside the bureau drawer. Poising herself behind Trula, she began rearranging and smoothing the mussed strands of hair. Then she stopped as a thought struck her mind. "What on earth were you doing out by the stream bed, anyway?"

Trula paused to form words that would present herself in the best light. "Why, your brother wanted to discuss some matters that trouble him. You know, deep dark secrets," she lied.

Winding a curl around her finger, Katy speculated upon her words. "*My* brother?"

Trula lifted her brows and nodded. "Yes."

"Well, he never mentioned anything to me about secrets."

"Well, of course not. You're his sister. You know how little brothers can be." Trula pressed her lips together and lifted a small pot of pink cosmetic from the stand. "I believe he's beginning to trust me." She smoothed the color onto her lips and then touched the remainder to her cheeks.

Katy nodded, although her eyes drifted away. "Surely. I understand." Her face brightening, she returned her gaze toward Trula's mirrored image. "I'm *glad* you're getting to know each other," Katy added, her voice tinged with resignation.

Her lips pursed in a pout, Trula's eyes sparked with mischief. "So am I."

Katy turned her face toward the door. "I believe Caleb's arrived. I hear his voice." She finished with one final curl and then stooped to brush away pieces of dried grass from the hem of Trula's skirt. "There now! You look lovely, as always." She beamed. "Let's join my *difficult* brother, shall we?"

Caleb stood in the entry, the soaked bundle of woman snugged close to his body. "Rachel! Are you here?" he called wearily.

The guests gasped and murmured among themselves. Some backed away while others drew near to observe the spectacle. Dwight politely made his way through the curious onlookers with Rachel Whitley close to his side. "Let me pass please!" he exclaimed.

Ignoring the gawkers, Caleb turned to convey the woman upstairs to a more private room. "This way!" he called to Rachel. He trudged up the stairs, his boots squeaking from the wetness of his feet. Standing in front of his own bedroom entry, he lifted his knee to nudge open the door.

"I'm right behind you!" Rachel bounded up the stairway. "Heath's gone for my medicinals. I left them in the carriage."

Katy followed Dwight up the stairwell. "I'll find her some fresh clothes."

Rachel ran ahead of Caleb to draw back the bed sheets. "After I examine her, we can change these." She turned up the wick on the bedroom lantern, and the yellow light illuminated their faces. Gently, Caleb laid the woman atop the bed. Seeing her for the first time in the light, he studied her face and her frail frame. She had the appearance of a young woman whose plight had aged her beyond her years. "She's a mere girl," he commented quietly.

The young woman lifted a trembling hand to her lips and then let it drop limply, her eyes never opening. She stirred no more while Rachel began taking her pulse and Katy began washing her mud-streaked limbs. "We'll need to undress her," Rachel said firmly.

Her brow arched to add decorum to her manner, Katy lifted her hands toward Caleb and motioned him toward the door. "Out!" she ordered affectionately.

"I believe they're ordering us away, Caleb." Dwight patted Caleb's back.

"But I can't leave her—" Caleb towered over the bed protectively.

Mouthing silently, Katy assured him, "Not to worry."

"Trust us." Rachel smiled and then turned to receive the bag holding her medicinals that her husband now handed to her. "She's in good hands."

Hesitant, Caleb turned to follow his brother-in-law from the room.

Reverend Whitley followed them both and suggested, "You've some guests who are in need of an explanation. Let's assure them our visitor is safe and sound." He put an arm around Caleb's shoulders in a heartening grip.

"I'm certain Amelia would appreciate knowing as well. Thank you, Heath," Dwight concurred.

As Caleb rounded the doorway, he all but ran straight into Trula Hill. "Pardon me—" he began to apologize.

"I need to talk to you." Trula's voice, hushed and mysterious, beckoned him to follow her.

Dwight nodded. "Go on with her. I'll handle the guests and your mother."

Caleb followed Trula reluctantly into another bedroom but carefully left the door open behind them.

Once inside, she turned to face him and hesitated. "Are you all right?" she asked rather sheepishly.

"I'm perfectly fine, Trula." In spite of his reserve, a hint of annoyance had entered his tone.

"Please don't be upset with me." She lowered her face to allow her large wide eyes to gaze up apologetically. "I'm sorry I panicked so. I was too caught up in having you all to myself tonight. Will you forgive me?"

"I will." Caleb agreed to accept her apology but could not allow the moment to pass without chastening her behavior. "But a word of warning about me, Trula. I despise selfishness, and I won't be controlled—especially by a woman."

Taken aback by his words, Trula pulled out her fan for lack of a better response. "I . . . I don't know what to say." She lifted her chin defensively, her eyes wide with disbelief. "Surely you're not accusing me of being a selfish person?" She fanned her face rapidly. "I'm as generous as the next person."

Not desiring to become entangled in an argument with her, Caleb ignored the comment. "My father always said that I could best determine a person's character by observing them when things went awry. He pulled those little tidbits from his favorite book."

"Which book?"

"The Bible."

A quiet exasperated sigh escaped Trula's lips as her blue eyes shot up at the ceiling. But she regained her composure quickly and then stretched a smile across her face. "Are you also religious?"

Caleb stood quietly, reflecting upon her words as though he

checked a vast library of forgotten memory. "I should be, I suppose. I do live by my father's words. They've become inescapable to me. And Papa patterned his life's choices from the simple life of a carpenter. In that sense, I suppose I am religious, as you say."

"Caleb?" Katy's voice came from the hallway.

He whirled around at once. "Yes?"

"Rachel says you may come in now. We've bathed your mysterious guest and changed her attire."

"Thank you." Caleb walked briskly toward Katy and then stopped. "Pardon my manners, Miss Hill. Would you wish to accompany me?"

Trula snapped her fan closed and slid it through her gloved fingers. She strode quickly to his side. "Of course. Let us pay a visit to our little mystery guest." Her voice lilted unevenly.

Once inside the room, Caleb quickly left Trula's side and joined Rachel at the woman's bedside. "Will she live?"

Rachel nodded confidently. "I'm sure of it. She's a strong woman. But she's been through some sort of ordeal. Most of her problems are related to fatigue and lack of good nourishing food."

"How old is she?"

"My guess is that she is about your age."

Caleb studied the young woman's face again. She looked completely different now that she had been bathed. Her hair was still matted about her neck, but her cheeks had gained a soft pink glow.

"I've given her a dose of laudanum. She'll sleep for a while."

"May I stay with her?"

Trula's hands gripped at her sides. Standing behind Caleb, she shook her head at Rachel.

Rachel raised her brows in askance. "We can all take turns if that would help."

"No. I'd rather see to her myself, at least until she's awake. I must insist." Caleb lifted a chair and carried it to the bedside.

"There's no arguing with him once he's made up his mind." Katy dramatized her brother's chivalry by her tone. "He's inherited Mum's stubborn nature."

"As though you haven't." Caleb crossed his arms at his waist.

"But I thought you might see me home." Trula picked at an imaginary speck on her glove.

"Reverend Whitley and I can see you home, Trula," Rachel offered. Glancing at Caleb, she lifted her brows in question. "That is, if you don't mind, Caleb."

Caleb, pleased at Rachel's offer, smiled. "That would be a great relief. That is, knowing that Miss Hill is in such responsible hands."

Her lip protruding in a pout, Trula snapped around and marched from the room, her skirts bustling around her. "Good night, Caleb Prentice!"

Keeping his eyes to the floor, Caleb pressed his lips together in a half smile and bowed in farewell.

Katy bit her bottom lip and waited for Rachel to depart behind Trula. "Caleb, you really must try to be more sensitive to Trula's feelings."

Caleb tucked the sheets around the young woman. His brow pinched together in disapproval, he said plainly, "I'm as polite as I know how to be."

"Polite, yes. But can't you see the girl's falling in love with you?"

"How would you know that?"

"She hangs on your every word. She adores you."

"She doesn't love me. She only sees me as she sees all her material belongings—as a possession."

"Have you given her a chance?"

"I kissed her," he answered nonchalantly, "if that's what you mean."

"Then you're leading her on!"

"I could've gone much further, Katy." He answered in a tense, clipped voice that forbade any further questions. "Trula Hill will find more than she's bargained for someday if she pushes the wrong man. But I don't propose to be her next dupe!"

"Calm down, brother." Katy massaged his shoulders. "I apologize for interfering. Why don't I go and fix us a plate of food before it's all cleared away? After all, it is your birthday."

With a gentle nod, he agreed. "That would be appreciated. I'm famished."

Katy kissed his cheek and patted his head as she always had

done when he was a youngster. "I'll return shortly."

With a sigh, Caleb leaned back into the cushioned chair. He found his eyes returning to the young woman's face. The small upturned nose, soft brown brows, and long lashes looked somewhat familiar. *Do I know you?*

The young woman stirred from time to time but did not awaken.

Katy entered shortly with a tray of food for the both of them. "The poor girl must be exhausted." Her face drawn with worry, she bent over the bed and felt the young woman's forehead numerous times.

"Why do you think she chose *our* stream?" Caleb mused.

Blowing across a cup of tea, Katy's brows lifted in a questioning manner. "*Chose?* I'm sure it was purely a fortunate accident, don't you?"

"I don't know." His voice gravid, he picked at the food Katy had handed to him. "Do you think we might know her?"

"She doesn't look familiar to me."

"Look at her again. Doesn't she look like someone we once knew?"

Setting the teacup aside, Katy leaned over Caleb's shoulder. She studied the girl's face more intently. "Perhaps. I'm not certain though." Looking down at her brother again, she smiled faintly. "You're serious, aren't you? You really think this woman is someone from the past? Who?"

"Kelsey McBride."

Katy paused, reflecting upon his words. "You mean the little Irish girl who was shipped off to Norfolk years ago?"

"Maybe she's come back searching for us."

"If Kelsey McBride survived Norfolk, she'd hardly come running back to New South Wales. More likely she would return to Kildare in Ireland, from what I remember about the girl."

A heavy sigh escaping his lips, Caleb settled back in his chair. He reached up to grip his sister's hand. "Why would I wish for such a thing?"

"Is that what you wish for? Kelsey McBride's return?"

"I don't know. I've always prayed that God would protect Kelsey. Just the thought of her returning . . . well, it gladdens me." He reached for his own cup of tea. "I don't know why."

"You thought you loved her in those days, didn't you?"

"I was a boy. What did I know of love?"

"Perhaps more than you know now."

"Don't taunt me. You'd quickly marry me off to Trula Hill and be finished with me, if I'd only cooperate."

Katy drew another chair up beside her brother and seated herself. "Don't be so sure. I have my reservations about the girl."

"You?"

"I can't say for certain, but she has her ways—some good, some not so good. But she's won Mum's heart."

"Mum fears I'll be a decrepit old bachelor if she doesn't intervene." He noticed the young woman's eyelids quiver and lowered his voice. "If she'd only awaken, perhaps our mystery would be solved."

Katy took a deep breath and turned to face her brother. "She'll have more than one mystery to solve."

"Why is that?"

"When Rachel examined her, she raised some medical questions of her own. Under the circumstances, I feel I should tell you."

"Tell me what? What's wrong? Is she ill?"

"No, Caleb."

"What, then?"

"Your mysterious lady is with child."

Caleb choked down the last of his tea and pushed the tray of food aside. He held his breath as the girl's eyes fluttered open, and she gazed up at him. Swallowing hard, he struggled to form the name. "Kelsey? Kelsey McBride?"

13

BROKEN
PROMISE

The first thread of morning sun spun a silvery light across the cotton sheets of the bed. Caleb lifted his face from the side of the bed and found Kelsey McBride's presence to be quite real and not a dream as he had first imagined. After awakening the prior evening, Kelsey had struggled to speak, her words mere mumblings that neither he nor Katy could decipher. She had acknowledged his suspicions that she indeed was Kelsey McBride. But how she had arrived at Rose Hill or survived in a lifeboat at sea remained a mystery to them both.

Lifting his hand, Caleb lightly stroked her face, pushing a strand of matted hair from her eyes. The aroma of breakfast wafted up the staircase, but he wouldn't leave her side until she awakened. Subsequent to her mysterious ordeal, he dared not allow her to awaken in a strange room with no one present.

"Good morning! How's our little patient?"

Turning to acknowledge the familiar voice, Caleb answered somberly, "Good morning, Rachel. Kelsey's still sleeping."

"So I've been told. It's amazing that you recognized her after all this time. But there was always a special bond between the two of you."

Choosing not to answer, Caleb returned his gaze to Kelsey, letting out a long audible breath.

"We need to encourage her to eat some broth, but not much more until she regains her strength. I need to know how long it's been since her last meal."

He nodded. "And she'll need some clothing."

"Katy and I have already thought of that. I brought some things from home, and Katy's selected some dresses from her own wardrobe. Between the two of us, we have provided for Miss McBride's apparel, at least for a few months."

Caleb smiled warmly. "Thank you. You're a godsend."

"And you as well. Does she yet know that you were her rescuer?"

Shaking his head, Caleb pushed away from the bed and ran his fingers through his tousled hair. "I'm certain it makes no difference. She probably hates me by now." His dark brows slanted in a frown.

"Why would you say such a thing?"

"I abandoned her. It's my fault she's gone through all those tormented years."

"You were just a child, Caleb. How could you have intervened? She was a thousand miles from Parrametta, and you were in France."

"I never tried. I gave up. The same as when I abandoned Rose Hill to go to France—".

"Surely you don't blame yourself?"

"Papa needed me—"

"Caleb!"

"I wasn't here."

"I knew it!" Rachel tossed the reddish gold hair from her shoulders. "You've blamed yourself all along for George's murder, haven't you?"

"I shouldn't have agreed to go and study in France, as grateful as I am to you and Reverend Whitley."

"And if you had stayed?"

"He'd still be alive!"

"Or you'd both be dead! Caleb—"

"Rachel, you can whitewash the truth all you want, but I

know what happened. I should've been with him." His voice dropped in volume. "What if—"

"What if, Caleb? What if? We've all had to deal with our own inadequacies. What about me? I tended your father before he died. But I couldn't bring him back no matter how hard I prayed. You can't live under the burden of guilt. George wouldn't want you to, would he?"

Inhaling deeply, Caleb settled himself against the chair once more. "Papa could never change the past no matter how hard he tried. Nor can I."

Rachel blew out a breath, positioning herself over the bedside. Her eyes softening, she allowed a smile to play around the corners of her mouth. "You're exasperating." Taking Kelsey's pulse once more, she lifted a cloth from the pillow. "This cloth has dried. Could you wet it for me, please? It'll help to cool her brow."

"Surely." Caleb turned to retrieve the water pitcher from the table where Mum had placed it the night before. He saturated the cloth over a dish and then wrung the excess water from it. Striding to Rachel's side, he bent and placed the compress across Kelsey's forehead himself. Taking a deep, unsteady breath he stepped away. "Katy told me about her . . . her situation."

"She's pregnant, if that's what you mean."

"Perhaps she's married."

"Let us hope." Rachel set aside her bag. "Kelsey." She gripped the girl's shoulder firmly. "Time to wake up, young lady. Breakfast is ready."

Caleb felt his body grow tense, his hands clenched tautly at his sides.

"Kelsey McBride. Wake up, my dear," Rachel persisted.

Taking several quick, shallow breaths, Kelsey stirred, her eyes opening and closing wearily.

Caleb opened his mouth to speak, but no words emerged, and his mind became seized with anxious helplessness.

Her fingers gripping the sheets, Kelsey moaned and struggled to awaken. "No . . . no . . ." she said, then muttered more indiscernible words.

Poised to react, Rachel stayed close to her side, her hands

gently stroking her arms. "It's all right, Kelsey. You're among friends. You're safe."

Drawing closer, Caleb worried that Kelsey grew close to hysteria. "Perhaps we shouldn't awaken her . . . we—"

"No!" Kelsey cried. "Leave me . . . leave me be!" Her eyes flew open. She froze, her hands trembling at her breast.

"You're all right. We're your friends." Rachel's voice soothed the girl.

"Wh-where am I? Tell me, I say!"

"Remember?" Caleb spoke in a hushed tone. "Last night you spoke to us. Kelsey?"

"No! I don't remember! Are you with the military? Tell me!"

"Absolutely not," Rachel quickly reassured the girl. "There's not a military person in sight."

"How do you know my name?"

First regarding Caleb with her eyes, Rachel then looked sympathetically at her. "You told us your name last night. We—"

"It's all right, Rachel." Stepping forward, Caleb reached to grasp Kelsey's hand. "Your boat found its way down our stream. This is Rose Hill. And I'm Caleb Prentice."

Kelsey withdrew her hand from his and pulled the sheets more tightly around her face. "You're lying. Caleb Prentice is a mere boy."

"And Kelsey McBride was but a mere girl." He smiled and surmised appreciatively. "But now she's a woman."

"Prove to me . . . prove that you're Caleb Prentice."

Glancing at Rachel, who appeared to be somewhat amused with the situation, he crossed his arms. "I'll try," he said matter-of-factly. He knit his forehead in concentration and looked around at the small bureau near the bed. "Ah, here we have it!" He pulled out the top drawer and withdrew a small box. Fidgeting with small gadgets and mementos of his boyhood, he closed the lid and turned to gaze seriously at Kelsey. "It isn't a happy memory, Kelsey. But I have the proof you've requested."

"Show me, then! Let me see it, I say."

Slightly hesitant, he opened the box again, reached into it, and pulled out a small knife.

"Where did you find that?" A faint thread of hysteria returned to her voice.

"It's mine."

"No. It belonged to me!"

"To both of us, actually."

Her eyes grew moist and a cloud settled over her countenance. "Caleb?" Her voice cracked as though a war of emotions raged inside her mind. "Is it . . ."

He affirmed gently with a slight nod.

Suddenly her mood veered sharply from sadness to anger. "Why didn't you come for me?"

The silence that ensued tossed a multitude of accusations at Caleb. He dropped his hands at his sides as defeat swallowed him wholly. "Because . . . because I was a fool, Kelsey. An ignorant fool."

A wisp of steam curled out of Katy's large kettle. She stirred the hot soup once more, then ladled it out into a small bowl. Her cook and maid had gone for the day on personal errands, and Katy found quiet enjoyment in bustling about in her own kitchen again. Jared and Donovan could be seen riding along the ridge, their two stout bodies following closely behind their father's. Katy chuckled at the sight. "You both look just like your papa," she whispered to herself. Gazing through the window, she watched for a moment while Dwight supervised the mates that tended their ever expanding flocks. Dwight—forever in the fields—had turned her father's struggling plantation into a thriving sheep ranch. But she had worried in their earlier years about him being away from their sons so much. When the boys had come of age, Dwight assured her that they would accompany him. So now they rose early with their father, scurried about to complete their farm chores, and mounted their ponies just like proud little men. But Katy, glad of their admiration for their father, still struggled with her own worries. Even the assurances Dwight had promised for their sons satisfied little in the way of her own relationship with him.

A rap sounded at the front door, and she set the bowl atop a table.

"Hello?" A voice called from the front room.

"Coming." Katy turned and didn't bother to untie the apron from her dress.

"It's only me, Trula Hill."

Concealing the mischievous smile that crept across her face, Katy strode quickly through the large rooms and into the front room to greet Trula. "Good morning," she called out before she reached Trula, who stood impatiently in the entry. "You're up and about quite early."

"I couldn't sleep." Trula stretched a worried frown across her face. "That poor woman we rescued last night—I knew she might be a burden to you all. I must insist upon offering my services to you."

Katy's brows lifted, but not at all in surprise. "How kind of you. Caleb will be *moved* by your gesture of good will."

"The poor dear. Did Caleb sleep at all last night?"

"Actually, he sat at her bedside the whole evening." Katy slid her arm through Trula's in hopes of steering her toward the kitchen. "Come. Let's have some tea together."

"Dear me, no! I should be upstairs at Caleb's side."

"Actually, you could assist me greatly before I take a tray up to him and Miss McBride."

"McBride?"

"Oh, that's right. You didn't actually meet our guest, did you? She . . . well, we knew her once. She and Caleb played together as children."

"She knows Caleb? Is that why she came here?" A probing query rose in her eyes.

"The details are unclear at this time. Rachel Whitley feels we should give the girl more time to gain her strength. I'm certain that she'll tell us all about her ordeal over the next week or so. In the meantime"—Katy gave her a pointed stare—"let us all exercise patience."

"Of course." Trula lifted her chin with a small degree of justification. "I agree. And I shall make myself readily available for such a cause."

"Good! I'm glad to hear of it." Katy led her through the front room by way of the parlor and finally into the kitchen. "Since you have made yourself so readily available, as you say, would you mind washing out the linens? That would be the greatest service to us this morning."

"The linens?"

"Yes." Katy turned her face away to hide the humor she found in the situation. With great ceremony, she turned the latch that opened the rear kitchen entrance. "Our maid simply insisted upon the afternoon off—what dreadful timing! Here we are in desperate need of help, but isn't it provident that you would show up for such a time as this?"

"Where are the linens?" Trula's voice wavered uncertainly.

"See the small shed?" She pointed with her eyes while Trula nodded. "All the linens lie bundled in several large baskets. And the lye soap is in a bucket next to the baskets."

"*Several* large baskets?"

"Um-hum." Katy's voice was melodious. "We've a busy household." Before Trula could raise one note of protest, Katy made a great show of her gratitude. "Thank you ever so much for your sacrificial services. God sees all that you do in His name."

Trula pressed her lips together and marched stiffly from the house toward the laundry shed.

Ignoring the pitiable frown on Trula's face, Katy quickly arranged a bowl of broth alongside a cup of tea on a tray and prepared to take it upstairs.

"You still look pale to me." Rachel cupped Kelsey's chin with her fingertips. "Are you queasy?"

Kelsey nodded, her eyes wide with worry. "Yes. I can't hold down anything, it seems."

Rachel seated herself next to the girl. "Are you aware . . . did you know that you're expecting a child?" Her eyes clung to Kelsey's, watching her reaction.

Kelsey looked away, her face growing grim. Inhaling a sob, she sought to fight back the tears, but to no avail. "I knew that something wasn't right, but I kept telling myself otherwise."

Rachel clasped her hand over Kelsey's. "Is there someone I should contact for you? A husband perhaps?"

"No." Her eyes filled woefully with more tears, and she avoided Caleb's probing gaze. "No husband."

"What about your mother?" Caleb's voice was smooth, but insistent.

The hesitation in Kelsey's eyes bespoke her pain. "My mother . . . she died months ago after a flogging." She ran her fingers nervously over the coverlet. Her mood veered sharply to anger. "Those beasts!"

"I'm sorry." Caleb offered his condolences, although he knew that Hattie McBride had probably deserved such a lot. "Who . . ."—he stumbled over his words—"who is the father, if I may ask?"

"An Irish transportee, Jack Keegan. He promised . . ." Kelsey's words were suddenly bathed in uncontrollable sobs. "He promised that he would take me to Kildare . . ."

"It's all right, dear." Rachel patted the girl's hand reassuringly. "No need to say any more. There are so many unscrupulous beasts these days. There's no need to feel guilty."

"Guilty?" A cloud settled over her face. "He forced himself on me. I—"

"No more!" Caleb turned away. He struggled to keep a civil tone in spite of his anger. "Where is Keegan? I'll have the beggar hanged for this!"

"No! I must find him myself. He promised to take me to Kildare, and he'll do as he promised. If he discovers that I carry his child, then he'll bring me no harm. I know him."

"I don't understand." Caleb rested his hands atop the coverlet next to her.

"You couldn't possibly understand. Your world is surrounded by family. Mine is controlled by politics. Jack Keegan and I, we know only one love—Ireland."

"He'll use you again if you go to him. Why not stay here at Rose Hill among friends?"

"You belong to Rose Hill, Caleb Prentice. *I* belong to Kildare—*and* to Jack Keegan. I'm his property. My mother offered me to him before she died."

"Kelsey, can't you see that what you're saying is madness? This man can't own you like a slave."

"It's an arrangement my mother made with him."

"And what is his side of this *arrangement*?"

She paused and continued in sinking tones. "That I can't tell you." Fidgeting uneasily, she no longer looked at Caleb. "But he's here somewhere in Sydney Cove. I'm sure of it. And he'll fulfill what I ask. You'll see."

Caleb rose in one fluid motion and turned to look forlornly at Rachel. A sorrowful realization penetrated his mind. *I no longer know this Kelsey McBride.* An odd twinge of disappointment flickered inside of him. She obviously wanted no help from him. "I'm weary," he said, offering a frail excuse to Rachel. "If you'll see to our guest, I'm going to sleep a few hours in the room next door." He strode mechanically toward the doorway before gazing back one last time at Kelsey. "I'll see that you have all you need, Miss McBride. But I'll certainly not be a bother to you. I'll stay out of your way until you so request. Good day." Walking quickly from the room, he closed the door to muffle the tormented cries that suddenly burst forth from the confused young woman.

14

STRANGER IN
THE LAND

Stooped over a washtub, Kelsey slowly dipped her hair into the soft rainwater. Once she had removed the seaweed and debris from her hair using Katy's soap and a bottle of lavender water, she squeezed the moisture from her hair and combed through her blond tresses. A relief-filled sigh escaped her lips as she sat basking in the sun. A real bath had not been available to her in the years on Norfolk Island. She stroked her hands, feeling the roughness from the calluses on her palms. Slowly tilting the bottle, she dribbled the perfumed water onto her hands. She stroked them gently and then held one hand beneath her nose. *Still reeks of Norfolk. I'll never be rid of the smell*, she complained bitterly to herself.

"I've a freshly ironed dress ready for you in the guest room. I'll show you to your new quarters when you're ready, miss."

Kelsey glanced up at the maid who smiled down at her. She could've easily been one of the convicts assigned to Norfolk Island, for all she knew. It seemed odd to her that the woman would be serving her now. "I can do my own ironing, miss. No need to bother with me."

"I work for the missus, Miss McBride. She wouldn't 'ave it any other way than this, that's wot. Might as well go along with Mrs. Farrell. She's a headstrong lady, but, don't go sayin' I said that. I'm grateful to the Farrells for givin' me work. They's decent folks."

"Of course, I'll not say a word." Kelsey's crisp Irish brogue preceded a warm smile. She added reflectively, "You said I have a new room. I suppose Mr. Prentice would appreciate sleeping in his own bed again, aye?"

"I don't rightly know, miss. They just had me do up the guest room for you this mornin'. I don't ask no questions about why."

Kelsey tossed her damp hair over one shoulder. "I'd be better off if I would learn to do the same, I suppose." Lifting herself up with one hand, she found her balance and stood politely before the maid. "I'm coming right behind you, then."

"Thank you, miss."

Kelsey followed the maid through the kitchen and upstairs to the guest room. The home appeared to have changed a great deal since she had last seen it. Caleb had mentioned to her that since George Prentice had died, Dwight and Katy had persevered to complete the house that George had started. Tasteful drapes cascaded down the windows now instead of remnants of worn fabric. The walls had all been painted and were adorned with ornately framed paintings. The house bustled with the activity of servants and occasional laborers who tramped through on errands for their bosses, Dwight and Caleb. Kelsey spied Amelia Prentice, who sat rocking in a sunny front room chatting with her two handsome grandsons.

"Hello," she called out politely.

Amelia turned her face around. Her eyes crinkled at the corners when she smiled, causing Kelsey to reciprocate her sunny response. "Sorry. Didn't mean to interrupt."

Amelia smoothed the worn pages of her Bible. "No, not at all. You're no bother. So glad to see you up and about now. We were all so worried."

Kelsey felt odd that someone would worry over her. Recalling life with her mother and their days on Norfolk, she realized no one had ever expressed such concern about her. "Thank you for your care. I'm much better now." She eyed the writ in Amelia's hand. "Do the boys like your reading to them?"

"They loves for Grandmama to read to them." Amelia regarded Jared and Donovan warmly with her eyes. "If you plant the Scripture in children's hearts, you'll reap a godly harvest one day, I believe."

Pondering her words, Kelsey bit her bottom lip.

"You're welcome to join us."

"Oh no. I couldn't—"

"Another time, then?"

Kelsey struggled with her answer. Then she found herself nodding agreeably to the friendly woman. Amelia had such a generous way about herself, opening her world to a complete stranger. "I must finish dressing." Kelsey held out a damp strand of her hair. "It felt so good to bathe."

"Help yourself to all those things Katy left in the room and make yourself at home. We like it that way, you know."

"Again, thank you."

"Oh, and, Kelsey?"

"Yes?"

"I'm praying for you, lass."

All she could think to do was nod. Dismissing herself, she continued toward the stairwell. Glancing around the room, she continued to assess the changes. Not one corner of the house had been left to circumstance. Katy Farrell had gone to great pains to see that each room was finished out with tasteful detailing. But Kelsey sensed a void in the home, which she attributed to the death of George Prentice. She, too, had been somewhat saddened by the news. But death had surrounded her world so frequently at Norfolk that numbness had taken rule over her emotions. Her thoughts withdrew to Norfolk uncontrollably at times. The blood-red scenes of torture returned to her mind, growing and magnifying the fear that she might be forced to return to that abominable place. She shuddered at the memories of the horrors of prison life. She had learned to live in constant fear. And now, although free, she still felt imprisoned by her past. Memories of the punishment meted out by the blood-thirsty guards would give her nightmares for the rest of her days, she was certain.

Putting away her painful recollections, Kelsey turned to address the maid walking dutifully at her side. "Where are the others?"

"Out drying the wool."

"So early?"

"It gets awfully hot around here by midday."

Kelsey nodded and followed the maid into the guest room.

The room smelled of candle wax and leather, of fresh air and wild flowers. Caleb Prentice had slept in the room for several nights while she had recuperated. He had been solemnly silent, not asking any questions or making any demands of her. His distant mien had saddened her to some degree. Her childhood memories had painted him quite differently. Kelsey glanced around the neatly arranged room—the soft ivory coverlet on the cherry wood bed, ecru curtains billowing gently in front of the open window. " 'Tis a lovely room. I'll be thanking you for your hospitality."

"More than welcome, miss. An' 'ere's the freshly ironed frock." She lifted it from the wardrobe and laid it carefully near the foot of the bed. "It's a pretty one. Belonged to Mrs. Rachel Whitley. Now there's a lady o' taste if ever I've seen one."

Kelsey eyed the dress the maid had spread across the bench near the bed's footboard. "I . . . I don't know what to say."

"No need to say anythin' at all. Mrs. Whitley does for folks all the time. It's a wonder she has a stitch o' clothes to 'er name, I vow."

Sliding her fingers beneath the finely stitched fabric, Kelsey examined it with great care. "I've never seen such a beautiful dress. Rather a deep shade of violet, I'd say."

"Like a delicious plum." The plump maid's cheeks stood out like cherries.

"And look at the stitching around the neckline." She turned to hand the dress back to the maid. "I could never accept it. 'Tis too nice for the likes of me. Doesn't she have something a wee bit plainer?"

"Mrs. Whitley would be offended if you didn't accept it, miss. Please put it on, an' then I kin be about me chores again."

Kelsey sighed. "Then I'll only accept it as a loan until I've secured some work to pay her back."

"I beg you to just accept the dress, so I kin tell Mrs. Farrell how pleased you are with it."

Bringing her hand to her lips, Kelsey's countenance grew apologetic. "I'm sorry. Of course I'm pleased with the dress. 'Tis stunning to be sure. Please tell your mistress that I'm beholden to her."

"As you say, miss." The portly maid curtsied and departed the room. "I'll return shortly to see if you'll be needin' anything else."

Observing a quaint vanity near the window, Kelsey stepped toward it. But then a wardrobe caught her eye. Opening the cedar door, she glanced inside and saw a few shirts and a pair of boots. *Caleb left those behind*, she determined. She ran her fingers down the cotton sleeve of a nut brown shirt. She lifted it to rub the worn fabric gently between her fingers. Having seen only military uniforms and coarse prison garbs for four years, she enjoyed the normalcy of observing men in work shirts and ladies in printed dresses. She pondered keeping the shirt, although she couldn't determine why. The fabric held a musky, earthy aroma she found pleasing to her senses.

Instantly a flash of loneliness stabbed at her heart. She had related the bouts of depression that would suddenly hit her to her mother's death. Her mother, a fighter to the last bitter breath, had died so suddenly after the cruel flogging. She recalled how her proud countenance had gradually diminished under the power of the whip. Kelsey wanted to forget the memory of how Hattie had died. She hadn't been given a chance to say farewell, much to her misery, and feelings of guilt returned to her often while she slept. She would bolt upright in bed, taunted by her mother's lonely death. Arriving at her mother's bedside too late to talk with her, Kelsey found that only William Orr had spoken to Hattie before she died. Entering the musty tent where the guard had led her, she could find no words to speak over her mother's lifeless body, so she had departed the convict tent in despair. By the time she emerged from her cell the following morning with eyes swollen from hours of weeping, her mother had already been buried in a common grave with many others. *Mum wasn't even given a proper burial*. Kelsey shuddered inwardly at the thought. She had seen too much cruelty and suffering, had witnessed too many painful deaths. Finally, she knew she had to close her mind to the atrocities occurring daily around her, and the thought of returning to Rose Hill became a driving force thereafter. It was something to plan for, something to live for. But now that she had returned, reality was beginning to disillusion her. Things were not at all as she had hoped them to be. Although she dwelt in Caleb's home, she felt disconnected from him.

The clip-clipping sound of the maid's shoes could be heard nearing the doorway. Quickly, she placed the shirt back inside the wardrobe and closed the door.

The maid entered with a fresh pitcher of water and some towels. "To wash up later, if need be."

"Thank you." Kelsey stood in front of the vanity mirror for a long time holding Rachel Whitley's dress in front of her. "I do look a fright." Finding the vanity top well supplied with combs and lotions, she set about to use all at her disposal. But when her awkwardness became evident, the maid stepped in and began applying ointments to her skin.

"Like this," she said, chuckling.

Kelsey basked in the attention. While the maid applied perfumed creams to her face, she rubbed more lotion upon her own hands until her skin gleamed from the treatment. "Where did Katy find all these dainties?" She pressed her fingers against the bulb of an *eau de cologne* bottle. The cool fragrance that misted her neck refreshed her senses. Then she watched the maid delve into the small pots of cosmetics, lightly adding color to her wan complexion.

"Now we'll do something with your hair." Lifting Kelsey's softened tresses of golden curls, the maid pinned her hair up in a becoming fashion, allowing soft, shiny curls to cascade about her neck.

Kelsey pulled the dress across her lap and allowed her fingers to rest inside the folds of the stylish brocade. She could hardly believe that she had finally reached the haven that had haunted her sleep for so many years as she labored in the island prison. *At last, at long last.* She felt the muscles in her body begin to relax for the first time in a long while.

The Prentices had become her one last hope, for the final letter she sent to the Mercers had been returned to her. A note scrawled across the envelope—"Family returned to England"—informed her of the regretful news that she had no one to return to in New South Wales except for the Prentices. She guarded the thought until it formed fully in her mind. *I must return to Rose Hill.* It would become the sanctuary for which she longed. But no satisfaction welled in her heart as she had anticipated it would. She had envisioned a more joyful reunion between herself and the Prentice family, but Caleb seemed to have changed so much. He was now a gentleman, but yet he seemed so *distant*. They were worlds apart. The realization struck her heart that Rose Hill had been a child's dream and would never be hers to enjoy. Observing the changes that occurred in her absence, the evidence rang clear—she had never belonged here. *What a fool I am!* She clung to the reality that loomed before her. Nothing would prevent her from reaching the only place she now could call home—*Kildare*.

"Mr. Prentice? We could use another hand this way." A shepherd stood in front of Caleb, wiping his sweat-drenched brow.

"I'll offer a hand, mate." Snugging his gloves onto his tanned fingers, Caleb tipped back his hat and glanced at the midmorning sun. "It's heating up like an oven. We'll need to rush things up a bit." He pressed his heels into the horse's flanks, and riding over to a group of laborers who were struggling to unload some wool from a wagon, he dismounted, landing squarely on the dusty ground.

"Need any help?" Dwight hollered from behind a fence post.

"Don't bother." Caleb waved his broad palm. "We'll have it out quick as a whip." He barked out orders, and within minutes the tired crew had reassembled and intensified their efforts to complete the task. The final load of wool now unloaded, Caleb met with the shearers to organize the spreading of the wool onto the tarpaulins. "It's a sunny day," he instructed one of the new hands. "After it's all spread out on the tarpaulins, it'll dry, and then we'll gather it up again."

"Water? Anybody thirsty?" Katy walked toward the men, her hands gripping two sloshing pails of water. Some of the hands dropped their tasks and ran to line up with their tin billies in hand. Katy held up one of the water pails while the men scooped up the water with their billies.

"Freshly baked tarts anyone?" Trula, finding her place quickly at Katy's side, lifted a large wooden tray before the laborers. Glancing sideways, she caught Caleb's eye. "You'd better hurry or they'll all be gone." She flashed him a disarming smile.

"Good show!" Caleb clapped his hands together to beat the dust from his gloves. "I'm famished!"

Pleased at his approval, Trula handed the tray to a worker. "Pass these out, please," she ordered coolly. Then she gathered several pastries from the platter and took them to Caleb. She stood waiting at the fence post while he leaped over the barrier in one swift movement. She drew her skirts away when he landed in the dust. "I thought you'd be hungry by now," she said demurely, watching as Caleb removed his gloves.

"Close to starvation." He gathered the pastries into one hand and began stuffing them into his mouth, one by one. He rolled his eyes with ecstasy. "Delicious! Katy, did you bake these?"

"Not I, dear brother." Katy pointed toward Trula with her eyes.

"You, *mademoiselle*?" An artless yet surprised smile spread across his tanned face.

Trula curtsied in a coquettish fashion while answering with her limited knowledge of the French language. "*Oui, monsieur*. For your pleasure."

"Thank you. I shall be ever indebted." His voice was velvet edged and strong.

"Don't eat too many of those tarts. Katy's arranged a sumptuous meal for us all. Besides, I wouldn't want to spoil you, or you might take me for granted."

"Not I." His tone was incredulous, although his eyes flickered in a toying manner. He drew his fingers to his mouth to taste the crumbs left behind. "I want another."

"All gone!" Katy took the empty tray from the farmhand.

"Ride with me back to your house, will you?" Trula looped her arm through his, her face thrust toward him anxiously.

"What about my horse?"

"Put one of your men to work."

He lifted an eyebrow and smiled boyishly. "Of course."

The scenic ride to the farm aboard the buckboard lifted Caleb's spirits. While Dwight tossed witticisms, the four of them rocked the wagon with their revelry.

Dwight whispered into his wife's ear, and she pursed her

lips, looking away with a blush.

Caleb smiled wryly and then chuckled.

"Look at you now," Trula remarked quietly to Caleb. "When you laugh you look years younger."

"I am years younger." He beat his chest.

Trula hesitantly moved closer to him in the rear of the wagon. "I love it when you're happy."

"And why wouldn't I be? I'm going to be rich!"

Trula's eyes lit at the thought.

"By this time next year, I'll be in London."

"Not likely!" Dwight's humorous tone was tinged with sarcasm. "You'll be mannin' the helm, and *I'll* be in London!"

Caleb tipped his hat over his eyes. A knowing smile crept across his face. "Not likely," he whispered. He gazed out from under the sweaty hat and winked at Trula.

Watching reservedly for his reaction, she inquired, "May I ask you something?"

He shoved back his hat brim with one finger and then crossed his arms, self-satisfied. Pinching his brow in mock somberness, he drew his lips together. "Certainly."

"The young convict woman. Has she . . . are you troubled by her?"

Caleb gazed speculatively ahead and shook his head. "Not at all. We seldom cross paths. Katy sees to her mostly now."

"I know all that. I'm not being clear. What I mean, Caleb, is she someone from your past? Have you feelings for her?"

"I feel sorry for her. I feel she's troubled."

"That's all?" Trula's eyes locked on his, probing his thoughts.

"What would cause you to ask such a thing?"

Trula lifted her face toward his. "Because I feel I should know." Her lips spread into a simpering smile.

He reached up with one finger and gently tapped her nose. "Not to worry, *mademoiselle*. No convict woman will find her hooks in this man!" He chuckled in a teasing manner, but affectionately and not maliciously as he had done in the past.

"I'm glad to hear it."

"All out!" Dwight called, his hand cupped aside his mouth. "Last call for transports to Rose Hill!"

Katy grimaced. "*Transports?* Oh, Dwight, please don't use

that hideous word." She chuckled, but her intent was clear. Since her parents had been transported to New South Wales from England, she took every opportunity to distance herself from the stigma.

"Sorry, my dear." He tipped his hat apologetically.

Caleb assisted Trula from the wagon and then, in a gentlemanly fashion, escorted her through the home's rear entrance. The aroma of roasted pig permeated the kitchen.

The cook ran past holding an apron full of potato peels. "Make way!" she shouted before flying past them and disappearing outside.

Trula gasped. "You really should encourage Cook to conduct herself in a more genteel manner."

"A Cockney thief?" Caleb subdued his laughter. "It would take a stronger man than me to accomplish such a change"— he grasped the door handle and winked—"or woman. If you don't mind, I'll escort you to the parlor. I should go upstairs and prepare before dinner."

Trula nodded and smiled up sweetly at his handsome face. "Whatever you say."

After completing his formalities with Trula, Caleb walked swiftly toward the staircase. Rounding the corner, he gripped the wooden banister and then stopped. "Oh, hello," he greeted Kelsey, his tone friendly but the surprise evident. "Good day, Miss McBride."

Kelsey halted halfway down the staircase. "Hello, Mr. Prentice." She bit her lip, uncomfortable with formalities. "Am I in your way?" She stepped aside, her stunning skirt billowing about her slender frame.

"Not at all." Caleb studied the lovely sight before him. Her face radiated a youthful beauty, her eyes magnetic and compelling. He could not allow her to realize his assessment of her, but he couldn't tear his gaze from her profile.

"Is there something wrong?" She had noticed his hesitation.

"No." He chuckled warmly. "I'm just . . . well, you look so . . ." He stumbled over his own words. "You look quite fashionable." He soon found a platonic description, although it was a far cry from his true estimate. *You look beautiful, Kelsey McBride!* was what he thought. He glanced away to hide his pleasure.

"Thank you. Rachel Whitley gave me the dress. I could never repay her, though."

"She would never allow it."

"She must be a wonderful person."

"Close to angelic, I'd say." He lifted his boot onto the next step. "If you'll excuse me, I must dress for dinner." He climbed a few more steps until he stood next to her. Now within inches of her, the memory of her twelve-year-old innocent face tugged at his emotions. "You are joining us, of course?" His tone was gentle.

Nodding politely, Kelsey smiled. "Thank you, yes."

"Hello, Miss McBride." A coolly impersonal voice broke into the conversation.

Caleb glanced down and found Trula glaring up at them.

Kelsey nodded to acknowledge her but didn't smile. "Good day."

"I thought I'd see what was keeping you." Trula spoke to Caleb, but her eyes stayed fastened on Kelsey. "Now I see you've been detained," she said tartly.

"Not at all." Caleb frowned. "And I asked that you please wait for me in the parlor, Trula." He shot a warning glance with his eyes.

"I was bored."

"Don't let me keep you, either of you." Kelsey felt her cheeks blush pink. She wanted to return to the guest room. "I'm sorry."

"No apology necessary." Trula stretched a smile across her face. "As a matter of fact, I'd be delighted if you'd be seated next to me at dinner. I've so wanted to get to know you better."

Kelsey lifted her eyes to meet Trula's, her long lashes casting shadows on her cheeks. Then her face softened. "Why, thank you. I'd love to join you. It seems I see you often here at Rose Hill."

Trula composed a self-satisfied look. "My father owns the neighboring sheep ranch. Since our courtship was announced"—she cast her eyes demurely at Caleb—"I take every opportunity to assist Caleb's family. He sees me home each evening."

Kelsey nodded that she understood but pursed her lips uncomfortably. "I shall look forward to our chat at dinner tonight."

"Good. It's all settled then." Trula maintained a friendly but patronizing tone, her crisp formal English controlling the conversation.

"Oh, and I meant to tell you—" Kelsey turned to face Caleb. "Yes?"

"You left some of your personal belongings in the guest room. Would you want me to fetch them for you?"

Trula stiffened and started to speak, but Caleb took command. "Excellent, thank you." He ignored Trula's cold stare. "Just bring them to my room before I dress."

Kelsey nodded in compliance. "Certainly." She beamed. "I'll join you shortly then, Miss Hill." She followed Caleb up the staircase and disappeared from the accusing glower of Trula Hill.

15

NO PRINCE FOR A PAUPER

Although Katy Farrell had set the tone for gaiety around the evening's meal, an unsettling anxiety had settled over the faces around the small dinner party. Cook graciously carried a large basket around the table, offering generous portions of hot bread to each guest, paying special attention to both Trula Hill and Kelsey McBride. Kelsey smiled warmly, accepting each serving with sincere gratitude.

Trula, however, ate little as she sat between Caleb and Kelsey. She picked at some hot vegetables, all the while eyeing the young woman seated next to her. "I've been so anxious to get to know you." She started her conversation in a matter-of-fact manner. "You've obviously known the Prentices for a long time, which means that you and I should become friends."

After buttering her yeast roll, Kelsey acknowledged Trula with a polite nod. "As you wish."

"It must have been difficult living with all those convicts. Norfolk Island is reserved for only the worst of offenders."

Sitting forward anxiously, Katy prepared to speak, but Kelsey responded with swift dignity.

"My mother was a political offender. England deals severely with such cases. Unfortunately, our lot was such that we were thrown in with common thieves."

"Most humbling, I suppose," Trula said, purposefully avoiding Caleb's censuring stare.

"We're a humble people to begin with." Kelsey had readied herself for such questioning. "But we pride ourselves in our homeland, Ireland."

Trula inhaled deeply and impatiently. "How did you keep from falling into despair? I understand patriotism is a noble cause, but didn't you wish to escape?"

"The boats were the only means of departing Norfolk. To manipulate passage would've cost me more than I was willing to sacrifice." She glanced a chary eye around at the others. "If you understand my meaning?"

Katy nodded. "We understood before you ever spoke a word. Details aren't important."

Ignoring her hostess's pleading eyes, Trula barreled forth. "So how did you escape?"

"I had fulfilled my sentence. I'm not an escaped convict, as you suppose. I was a mere child and gave them no cause for concern. Before my transport landed, I used Jack Keegan's name with a few Irish emancipists aboard ship. They secured for me the johnboat—the one in which you found me."

"But why the boat?" Trula persisted. "Why didn't you simply secure a wagon ride out from the harbor to Rose Hill or to wherever you felt your destination would take you?"

"I had no money. The Sydney Cove harbor is no place for a woman unless her aim is to earn her way in an unscrupulous manner."

"We're relieved that you found us, Miss McBride." Dwight gently tapped at the tabletop and bit his lip while glancing uneasily at his other guest, whose impertinence troubled him.

"Most assuredly!" Caleb lifted his water glass and spread a smile across his face.

An exasperated sigh escaped Trula's lips. "I apologize, Miss McBride, if my questioning is too pointed," she interjected plainly, "but I feel that your answers are not complete."

"Trula!" Caleb shot a warning glance.

"Please—" Kelsey lifted a slender hand of protest. "I don't mind her questions. You've all been so polite to me, asking nothing. Perhaps my answers will serve to put you all at ease. She turned back to face Trula. "I realize that you only have the best interests of this family at heart, but know that I, as well, carry the same interests. I plan to stay here only a short amount of time, just until I secure passage back to my home in Ireland." She pressed her lips together, her eyes full of apology, her language transparent. "I came here because I sought the security of our friendship until I could locate Jack. I fully understand that we're all like strangers now." Careful to make eye contact with each Prentice, she confessed, "'Twas my girlish idealism that brought me here. But my mistake will be rectified soon."

"You made no mistake in coming here." Caleb lifted his napkin from his lap and tossed it to the table.

"Aye, I made a grave misjudgment, my friend." Kelsey settled back against her chair, her face lifting with deliberation. "But it's our mistakes that bring us back to wisdom and reality."

Composing herself, Trula ran her fingers up her neckline to smooth a loose strand of hair. "So your mission now is to locate the father of your unborn child?" Her eyes, sharp and assessing, darted questioningly.

"If you wish to call it a mission—so be it. My passage to Ireland should be paid by the man to whom I am betrothed. It is his duty."

"And if he doesn't, would you expect the Prentices to pay?"

"That is quite enough!" Caleb ordered.

Her humiliation renewed, Kelsey looked away. Katy Farrell hid her face in her hands.

"You're accusing me of what?" Trula turned a vivid scarlet while she paced across the rear verandah. "Of attempting to expose the tru—"

"You purposely baited her!" Caleb interrupted her vehemently. Whirling around, he placed his hands on his hips. "Admit it!"

"I didn't!"

"You embarrassed my family and me, Trula! First you

played up to her to win her trust, then you targeted her like . . . like a viper!"

"How cruel!" Tears spilled from her hardened eyes. "Can't you see that I've been right all along? This convict woman has come between us now. I warned you!"

"How could someone come between us, as you say? There's nothing to sever."

"You don't mean what you're saying! You're simply angry with me. Please don't say that you hate me!"

"Hate you?" He crossed his arms and held his back rigid. "Why, I've no feelings at all."

Her mouth fell open, stunned by his bluntness. "Then I'd rather you hate me." She turned from him and leaned against the porch railing. In one instant, she crumpled against the rail as though all strength had drained from her. Uncontrollable sobs spilled from her lips as her wrists dangled limply over the balustrade.

At the sight of Trula so emotionally helpless, Caleb closed his eyes, utterly miserable. Remorse cut at his heart. He contemplated running to comfort her, but the events of the last few moments only served to fan the fires of anger she had sparked inside him. "Will you not admit your error?"

Stifling a sob, she lifted her face and struggled to form a reply. With a tremulous nod, she answered, "I must protect you. I'll do whatever it takes."

"I don't need protection."

"Then tell me, dear sir, exactly what you do need!"

Caleb glanced out across the pastureland cultivated by his family. He could see Kelsey standing beneath a flowering myrtle, her head bowed. "Honesty," he finally answered. "Seems a rare quality these days."

Leaning against the balustrade, Trula stood in as dignified a manner as she could muster. She lifted a delicate hand to her face and gracefully wiped the tears from her cheeks. With Caleb seemingly unmoved by her sobs, she straightened herself as best she could and stepped toward him. "I want you to forgive me."

His gaze momentarily locked on a distant figure, Caleb had to shake himself from a troubled meditation. "Pardon me?" He was quick to maintain his defenses.

"I'm apologizing, Caleb." Trula lifted her fingers to each side of his face to turn his eyes upon her. Her eyes glittered prettily. Her demeanor as meek as a dove's, she asked once more, "Will you forgive me? Please?"

Caleb, caught off guard by her humility, took a short breath. "Of course I'll forgive you." He lifted his hands to clasp hers and drew them down between them both. "You're truly sorry?" His eyes penetrated hers for signs of duplicity.

She nodded, slowly lifting her face toward his. "So sorry," she whispered alluringly. "I'll do whatever you ask." Her lips drew near his.

Caleb turned his face momentarily to glance again toward Kelsey. Facing Trula once more, his brow furrowed. "Then you'll apologize to Miss McBride?"

Swallowing a lump in her throat, Trula's face tightened. But seeing his attention drawn away again, she smiled serenely and yielded. "I promise." Her arms slid around his strong neck.

His skin tingling at her touch, Caleb smiled faintly. A spark lit his gaze, betraying his ardor. He touched his lips to hers, soft as a whisper, and then succumbed to her allurement. He did not see the Irish girl disappear across the pastureland and into the darkness of the woods.

A strange, sickening feeling swept through Kelsey. The Prentice's guest, Trula Hill, had humiliated her badly enough during dinner. But the shock of seeing Caleb embrace her directly afterward had delivered a blow from which she was quite sure she could never recover. She had heard him defend her in front of his family—*as though he cared about me*. No longer able to bear seeing them embraced upon the verandah, she tore herself from the scene and raced into the woods. *I never should have come!* She chastened herself again for running back to Rose Hill. Perhaps she had been dishonest about her own motives for coming, but her mind refused to believe what her heart told her. *I've no feelings for him! I cannot possibly love Caleb Prentice!* She assured herself that he was merely a distant dream for a frightened little girl, an imaginary shelter from the maelstroms of her violent world. She now realized that princes did not appear on the horizon for foolish paupers such as she. She had to find the father of her child at once. The answers would all be clear once she found Jack and returned home to Kildare.

"Will you go to him, Dwight? Caleb will listen to you." Katy paced the parlor floor, her skirts rustling against the tapestried floor.

"He's more stubborn than you. Why do you think he'll listen to me?"

"I was slow to realize that Trula Hill is a vicious woman. Surely you can see I am right."

"Caleb has to recognize that on his own, Katy. If we try to pull him away from her now, he's sure to run to her. Give him time."

"Time? They're out on the verandah now, and I'm certain she's beguiled her way out of this last little affair. I've never known Caleb to be manipulated by anyone. Now he seems almost blind to her ploys. This woman is frightening."

"Don't be hasty—"

"You think I am hasty? Are you blind as well?"

"Katy!"

Her fists clenched, she stamped the floor with her heel. "I don't want this woman in the Prentice family!"

"Kelsey McBride, then?"

Lifting her hands to her face, Katy searched her mind for answers. "She's not the same little girl anymore, Dwight. She's—"

"A convict? What about me? Your parents?"

"That's all in the past!" Her eyes grew misty.

"Isn't Kelsey entitled to the same mercy?"

Inhaling deeply, Katy withdrew from him and turned to face the tall open window. "You sound like Papa."

"Your papa was right about people, always right."

With a tremulous nod, Katy choked back an emotional sob. She allowed her eyes to search the rocky cliff where George Prentice had been laid to rest. She longed to speak to him one last time as she had wished for so many sleepless nights in the past. "What now, Papa? What now?" she whispered.

16

An Unholy Alliance

On the day the farmhands loaded the dried wool onto wagons, Kelsey jumped aboard and stole a ride on the back of one of them. She left quietly. It wasn't because the Prentices kept close watch of her, for they didn't, nor was it because she was questioned by them, for she wasn't. But rather, she wanted to avoid the possibility that one of them might wish to accompany her into Sydney Cove. For on this day, she desired to privately make her inquiry into the whereabouts of her fiancé, Jack Keegan.

Drawing her feet into the rear of the wagon, she watched as the foreman swung the gate closed and locked it behind her. She gazed up at the sky and sighed. The ride would be hot and dusty. She checked the canteen inside her bag of belongings as well as the food Cook had given to her. Bending to secure her personals, she stopped with her mouth agape and gasped, "Oh!" She felt a pang in her abdomen. Glancing to see that no one had noticed, she pressed her fingers against the small life that grew inside her. Rachel, Caleb, Katy, and Dwight had du-

173

tifully concealed her secret from the rest of the household. If she didn't reunite with Jack Keegan soon, the whole colony would know of her shame.

"Hold up!" The driver called to the others who had mounted their rides. "Owner's approachin'."

Her brow pinched with anxiety, Kelsey peered around the large mountain of wool. *Caleb!* She quickly drew back and kept her face from sight. She could hear Caleb conversing with the foreman and the driver about the negotiations for the sale of the wool. Lifting her hand to wipe her brow, she blew out a breath, the heat causing her to feel faint. Then hearing a rise in Caleb's tone, she flinched.

"What? She's on *this* wagon?" A rein snapped and horses' hooves sent a cloud of dust encircling the wagon. Kelsey bit her lip and soon found herself gazing up into Caleb's inquisitive face.

"Hello, Mr. Prentice." Her tone was subdued.

"What on earth?"

"I . . . I didn't want to be a bother."

"Bother? You've scarcely been afoot." Caleb lifted one suspicious brow. "I'll secure a private carriage for you with a driver."

"Please, no."

"I insist." Caleb smiled, but his eyes narrowed. "Bailey!" he called. His black stallion nickered beneath him and tossed its head.

"Sir?" The foreman answered promptly.

"See that Miss McBride has an appropriate carriage and driver." He glanced at her face once again as though he harbored a question. Then, thinking better of it, he added, "Tell him to take her anywhere she desires."

Her cheeks flushed, Kelsey started to stand, but dizziness gave way. She felt a queer sensation, heard voices, then became vaguely aware of her body crumpling against the wool.

"She's fainted! Blast it, Bailey! Never let anything like this happen again!" Caleb leapt from his mount. "Frank, get me water! At once!"

While the panic-stricken driver ran for water, Caleb opened the rear gate. He studied Kelsey's pale face, white as moonstones. Seeing her motionless form, he was seized with worry.

Quickly sliding his brawny arms beneath her, he lifted her effortlessly, snugged her limp body close to his, and made haste for the nearest barn. Kelsey moaned faintly. Once inside the cool shade, he lifted a saddle blanket from a rail and cradled her head against it on a pile of clean straw. "Kelsey," he called her name softly, then took the water and a fresh cloth from the distraught driver. "Kelsey McBride." He continued speaking to her calmly as he washed her face with the cool water.

A bead of water trickled from her brow, and her eyes slowly opened. "My head," she muttered and coughed at the dust rising from the hay. "I fainted?"

Caleb nodded. "I'm taking you back to the house."

"No, please. I must find Jack Keegan."

"Not today."

Kelsey tried to push herself up with trembling arms. "I can't stay here forever, Caleb."

"Why not?"

She allowed her head to rest against the brown woolen blanket. Her eyes studied his intently. "Because I don't belong here." Her voice was fragile and shaking.

Lines of concentration deepened along his brows and under his eyes. "You're regarded as a family member here. Why can't you believe that?"

"You sound as though you believe what you say. But we aren't the same as we once were. We're under the same roof . . . yet so far apart."

Caleb glanced out of the barn's front exit. He avoided her penetrating eyes. "I'm not sure what you're saying."

"What you just said only proves me right. You avoid me. I know you're disappointed in me."

"How so?"

"Look at me. Unmarried and expecting the child of a stranger."

"You're a victim."

"You paint me as a noble woman. But are you certain you believe that?"

"I take your words at face value. I've no reason to do otherwise."

Inhaling a deep breath, Kelsey pulled herself upright. "You

promised me a carriage and a driver. Aye?" Now it was she who chose to be evasive.

"Surely you aren't serious?"

"I'm feeling better now. I swear it."

"I want someone to go with you. Let me ask Katy."

"Please. I must insist on privacy. Keegan is a mistrustful man. He'll not see me unless I go alone."

"What if he tries to harm you?"

"He won't. Not when I tell him that I carry his child."

"But the man should be behind bars for what he's done to you," Caleb said with the sense of conviction that was part of his character.

"I'll not have the father of my child jailed." Now Kelsey looked away, fearing he would read her thoughts. She could show no signs of relenting no matter how deeply it pained her to argue.

Caleb spoke again, but his tone revealed he had withdrawn from her once more. "Your carriage will be ready shortly. Do you wish for a maid to accompany you?"

"No, please. Only the driver."

"Very well. G'day, then, Miss McBride."

Kelsey felt an overwhelming sense of loneliness envelope her as she watched him mount his steed and ride away.

"I have my reasons for asking, Private. Will you call your superior, or shall I go in search of him myself?" Trula pulled the braided drawstring on her purse.

The private turned his head to spit his tobacco juice. "No one goes inside unless Corporal Chilton is expectin' them." He turned his face toward the office door and then gazed back indifferently toward Trula.

"I have a paper right here. See?" She held out a document for the private to read. "Signed by Lieutenant Macarthur himself."

The private sighed, annoyed. Official documents had floated around Sydney Cove for years—all worth whatever the bearer had agreed to pay for the paper. Ready to be rid of the young woman, he turned and rapped on the corporal's door. "Corporal Chilton?"

"Yes, Private? What is it?"

"Lady 'ere to see you. Says 'er name's Trula Hill."

After a moment's hesitancy, the corporal called out, "Allow her in, please."

Trula bustled past the private without so much as a polite acknowledgment.

The peppery-haired corporal stood politely when she entered. Gazing at her as she approached, he quite openly studied her. "You've business with the military, miss?"

"Possibly." Trula strode gracefully toward a table ladened with old weapons and ammunition. With a black-gloved hand she reached down and stroked her finger across the barrel of a rusted musket. "Antique?"

"Not quite. You've an interest in old weapons?"

"No. Just antiques." She smiled benignly. Without further hesitancy, she announced, "I have some information that may interest the military."

"Regarding?"

"A young convict woman recently *arrived*, shall we say, upon the land of a friend. She says that she's been released from Norfolk Island. But her strange arrival has given rise to my suspicions."

"How so?" The corporal's brows raised with interest. He opened his palm and gestured toward a tufted chair.

Trula seated herself. Eyeing the corporal, she moistened her lips and continued. "I think it odd that she would arrive alone on a flatboat, half-starved, and floating down a river that runs through private property."

Blowing out a breath, the corporal shook his head. "I've heard much stranger tales."

"But in a boat marked with military insignias? Wouldn't such a thing cause you to investigate? I believe the boat was stolen."

"Possibly. Where is this convict woman now? You haven't given me her name. An examination of our rosters will reveal whether she's escaped or been formally released."

"Momentarily, please. First, I want to be certain that the landowners aren't held responsible for harboring a criminal. If she's lied to them, one can hardly blame them for believing her story. True?"

"Good enough. Your friends will not be blamed."

Trula extended her slender hand across the officer's desk. "Your handshake is my assurance against such matters." The corporal nodded and shook her hand, his eyes narrowing with a hint of impatience.

"Thank you." Trula lifted her chin, her eyes hopefully alit. "The young woman's name is Kelsey McBride."

The corporal shrugged. "Never heard of her." Suddenly becoming bored with the whole affair, he flipped through a few pages of his roster as she continued to speak.

"She says she's searching for her husband-to-be, an Irishman by the name of Jack Keegan."

"Keegan?" A flame kindled in the officer's eyes. "Jack Keegan, did you say?"

Glad the name had sparked his interest, Trula shifted forward in her chair. "Yes. You know Keegan?"

"He's a notorious leader of the United Irish Rebels. Second in line only to William Orr."

"I've heard of Orr, that he's planning an uprising." Quite pleased with herself, she feigned her rejection of the idea as absurd. "All silly rumors, I'm sure."

"I wouldn't be so hasty to disregard the rumors, miss. I don't trust an Irishman no further than I kin throw him."

An atrocious thought entered her mind, but yet, a thought that pleased her. "Surely you wouldn't suspect Miss McBride of taking part in this *rebellion*?"

"If she has ties to Keegan, you can wager she has a part."

"Dear me, I never dreamed that I'd be bringing this much trouble to Miss McBride. Perhaps I never should've divulged her name at all." Her eyes wide, she skillfully hid her delight from the corporal. "I should leave now."

"Not so hasty, Miss Hill. You could be of great help to the government of New South Wales."

"How so?"

"Don't tell anyone of our conversation. Perhaps this McBride woman is exactly what we've been needing. She could lead us straight into the heart of the rebellion. Just tell me now where she's staying."

Biting her lip, Trula swallowed hard and then answered, "Rose Hill. It's a sheep farm owned by the Prentice family in Parrametta."

"And she found her way out there by johnboat, you say?"

"All on her own, she says."

"We'll see. The Prentices are probably being duped into believing such a thing."

"I'm afraid I've suspected the same." Trula stood, straightening her lace gloves. "I hope I've not caused harm here today." She basked in the knowledge of her power.

"On the contrary. You've given us the tool we've desperately been seeking. That is, *if* we can count on your loyalty."

"I swear it." A lethal calmness spread across her face. "Mum's the word, Corporal."

The ride into Sydney Harbor had developed into a more pleasant affair than Kelsey had first anticipated. Under the cover of a fine two-wheeled carriage, she rested most of the way, basking in the solitude she found on so beautiful a day. The abdominal cramps had subsided, and the dinner that Caleb had insisted be brought to her had energized her spirits.

"Where to now, miss?" The driver, Frank, spied the gulls circling overhead, which indicated the close vicinity of the harbor.

Good question. She sat forward, her eyes scanning the landscape. "To the printmakers. You know of one?"

"Right down around the borough and near the harbor. There is but one I knows of, miss."

"Good man. Take me there, please." Her posture growing tense, Kelsey fidgeted nervously with her bag. Her brow pulled into an affronted frown. Since her mother's death, dark moods had crept upon her without warning. She often felt an acute sense of loss. No matter how much Hattie McBride had disappointed her as a mother, she couldn't help feeling lonely for her company. She glanced out at the isolated landscape. The hurt and longing lay naked in her eyes. Finally, desperate to quell the overwhelming pain, she forced her thoughts elsewhere.

Within a quarter hour the driver had parked the wagon to the side of the small building where the Sydney Harbor print-maker and his apprentices labored. Kelsey accepted assistance from the driver to alight and then strode toward the open door-way. Upon hearing the clanking sound of the hammers pound-ing against the iron, she stopped, fearing her determination had faltered.

Noticing her hesitation, Frank asked quietly, "Somethin' wrong, miss?"

"No." Kelsey shook her head slightly. "Would you mind, please, waiting for me in the carriage?"

"Mr. Prentice ordered me to stay at your side." He politely lifted his hat.

"Look, the carriage is so close. You wouldn't be disobedient to wait nearby, would you?"

Bowing slightly, the driver reluctantly complied. "As you wish."

"Thank you." Kelsey turned to walk into the printmaker's shop.

A hefty older man, balding atop his head, glanced up at her as she entered. Laying aside his tools, he wiped his blackened hands upon his apron. His surprise at seeing a woman enter the shop evident, he pressed his lips together and then barked, "Lost, are we, miss?"

Not one to be intimidated, Kelsey lifted her face in expec-tancy. "Not lost. I'm seeking a certain person. Perhaps you've an apprentice by the name of Jack Keegan?"

Rubbing his bristly jowl, the printmaker shook his head. "No. You've come to the wrong place."

Believing she detected a hint of censure in his tone, she per-sisted. "He's an Irishman, quite good at his craft. Are you cer-tain—"

"As I said"—the printmaker narrowed his eyes—"I never heard o' the man. You're certain o' the name?"

"Aye." Her eyes examining the entrance to the room next door, Kelsey glanced toward the floor and slowly stepped to-ward the room.

Taking one long sidestep, the printmaker blocked her way. "I'm needin' to return to me duties"—he stared pointedly at her—"if you've no other business with me today."

His distrustful gaze chilled Kelsey's nerves. Fear and anger knotted inside her. The incessant pounding of the tools and the apprentices being blocked from her sight sent an uncontrollable emotion through her. "Jack!" she shouted. "Jack Keegan!"

Angered, the craftsman bared his teeth. "Out o' 'ere, before I throws you out!" He took a threatening step toward her.

"Miss McBride?" Kelsey heard the concerned driver call out to her.

"I'm all right, Frank," she answered promptly in an attempt to offer assurance as she backed away from the irate printmaker. "Please, sir." She attempted to reason, but the man now drew near, his angry gaze swinging over her. She swallowed the despair in her throat.

"Mulligan! Mr. Mulligan!" a voice called out, stifled and unnatural.

Drawing her hands to her lips, Kelsey watched as the printmaker swung around.

"You've lost your mind!" he growled at the one who had emerged.

Stepping around Mulligan, Kelsey strained to see the man. "Jack? Jack Keegan?" she called out both in fear and hope.

The apprentice, his face smudged in ink, stood assessing the woman critically. Drawing his arms about his waist, he nodded resignedly toward the printmaker. "Let her come, Mulligan. I know the woman."

"*This* woman?" Mulligan eyed her expensive dress.

"Yes." Jack Keegan tossed aside a filthy rag. "Mr. Mulligan, meet my wife-to-be, Kelsey McBride."

17

THE RIGHTNESS OF THEIR WRONGS

A soft mist of rain sprayed the pastureland at Rose Hill. The fine droplets fell from an almost cloudless sky, ushered to earth by golden beams of sunlight.

Inattentive to the change in weather, Caleb paced the floor of the study, absorbed in one thought. Kelsey had been away for hours. He had busied himself for some time, but now a worry began to surface that harm might have come to her. *It would be my fault. Why did I allow her to go?*

"Here, now, you'll wear a hole in me rug, son." Amelia leaned against the doorframe, her green eyes gazing around the partly opened door.

With no desire to express his worry, Caleb stopped at once and crossed his arms reservedly at his waist. "I'm pondering the sell of our wool."

Her sharp eyes assessed his face. "Posh! Lie to your own mum, then."

Realizing that Mum had read his thoughts, Caleb sighed. "Miss McBride has gone into Sydney Cove Harbor. I ordered the driver to see that she was returned before sunset."

"He still 'as a bit o' time, then. Stop your worryin'."

Clearing his throat indignantly, Caleb turned his face to the side. "Worried? Who said—"

"You're as nervous as a cat, y'are."

"I merely feel responsible. That's all I mean to say." He brushed at the lapel of his light gray coat. "If that Keegan character has dealings with the United Irish, which I oddly suspect, then Kelsey McBride could be in danger. They're a risky lot."

"True, but the girl's been on 'er own for some time now. If she's mixed up with the rebels, then it's by 'er own choice."

"Not entirely true! Kelsey's life has been one long series of choices made for her far beyond her control." There was a spark of some indefinable emotion in his eyes. "Hattie McBride's control."

Amelia's forehead knit in thought. "You have feelin's for Kelsey, don't you?"

"She's always been the same as a sister to me. You know that as well as I."

"Do I?" Amelia made her way to his side. Clasping her hands calmly in front of her, she smiled but made no further comment.

Caleb answered her silence. "If I needed a wife—and I'm not admitting I do—I would certainly choose a more stable life's mate. A woman whose feet are planted solidly on the ground."

"Like Trula Hill?"

Lifting his firm chin, Caleb blinked. "Possibly. That matter is yet to be debated in my mind." His arms crossing his broad chest, he turned to face her. "But it's certainly not up for discussion."

Staring wistfully out the window, Amelia affirmed, "Trula's a beautiful girl. A bit headstrong at times, but a practical choice."

Caleb nodded, but her comment stabbed at his conscience somewhat. "Is that what you were to Papa? A *practical* choice?"

Amelia chuckled. "It didn't matter either way. We had fallen in love. No disciplines of courtship could've kept your papa away from me doorstep." She smiled with candor.

Contemplating her words, Caleb's luminous blue eyes widened in realization. "Driven."

Amelia pressed her lips together, her eyes misting at the rims. She nodded in agreement but again made no reply. Then her eyes clouded with wordless pain.

Caleb noticed the sudden change in demeanor. His face softened. "I apologize, Mum. I shouldn't bring up the past."

"No," she said, her tone insistent. "I want you to discuss Papa with me whenever you wish. It's good for me, I'm certain."

Caleb slipped his arm about her shoulders. He allowed his fingers to become intertwined in the black silken fringe along the borders of her shawl. "Papa bought this shawl for you, eh?"

"He did," Amelia mused. "Haggled a good half hour for it down at the harbor."

The remembrance evoked an odd sort of discontent in Caleb. Just like the rug they now stood upon and other various objects Katy had placed about the home, Papa had a hand in many of their belongings that had brought comfort and beauty to their world. Papa had selected the site for building the house, their first real home at Rose Hill. Throughout the years, threads of remembrance had been woven together that brought recollections, both painful and joyful, of the godly man who had plowed through the rocky furrows to forge out a future for the next generation.

Caleb formulated a most difficult decision. "You're right, Mum. I shouldn't worry needlessly. Miss McBride is not under our wing for long. Our only duty is to offer her the food and shelter needed until she can return to Ireland." Caleb swallowed hard, the final realization piercing his senses.

"More than that, we should pray for Kelsey." Amelia spoke in a gentle tone. "She'll need God's wisdom over the next few weeks. She 'as a little one to consider."

Caleb shrugged dismissively. The best thing to offer for his own peace of mind would be to put the young woman out of his thoughts altogether. He had more important matters to settle. Within the next few months, he would make his first trip to London. *It's settled then.* The thrill of seeing England for the first time would be the catalyst for his future plans. Rachel had returned from this distant land a midwife, he reasoned. But he sought more than just a title. He would make trade connections that would place Rose Hill at the apex of the sheep industry. Then, the Lieutenant Macarthurs of New South Wales could no longer deride the people referred to as "crawlers." Instead, *Macarthur will be forced to crawl to me!*

"How did you find me?" Keegan had led Kelsey through the rear of the building to a dank alleyway.

"You aren't difficult to locate, Jack. You're as transparent as glass."

"Does anyone know that you've come here?"

"No one knows I'm here, except for the driver."

"Humph, a driver, you say?" Keegan's sooty eyes sparked with anticipation. "Are you tellin' me you've come into some money, lass?"

"No, I wouldn't be standin' here if I had the means to leave for Kildare, now would I?"

"You've some wealthy friends, then, eh?" He studied her intently.

"What's it to you, Jack? You'll be rid of me soon enough when you've settled our arrangement."

"Not so hasty." His eyes narrowed. Glancing uneasily up and down the alley, he lowered his voice. "The United Irish has need of you, lass. Your brothers—"

"My brothers, did you say?" Kelsey's temper flared upon hearing his words. "My brothers who would abandon me and leave me for dead with a child on the way, on Norfolk Island, no less? Not brothers, Jack—*devils!*"

"What is it you're sayin'?" His eyes widened with interest. "You sayin' you're with child?" A strained laugh followed his words, but his eyes remained fixed upon her.

She looked away, hating his scrutinizing stare. "It's yours, Jack, your child." Turning back to look into his glacial gray eyes, she struggled to hide her contempt for him. "Now what will you do with me? How will you satisfy your vow to Hattie McBride to send me back to Ireland?"

"My vow was to the living. Hattie McBride is dead." He shrugged indifferently.

Kelsey backed away, her anger forcing tears to the surface. "You always were a liar"—her eyes flickered pensively—"and a man of no honor."

"Shut up!"

"I'm leaving." Kelsey started to turn away but felt his hand grip bitingly into her forearm. "Let me go!"

"I thought you wanted to return to Ireland with me. Walk away now and you'll never see Kildare again."

"I'll find another way."

"Two days in this colony and you'll be selling yourself like the other worthless females. You'll die in the alleyways of Sydney Cove along with the rest of the rubbish."

"I'm not like you."

"You've always put on your airs, Kelsey McBride, stepping around us all like you was better than the rest. But if you was better, then you wouldn't be crawlin' to me now, would you?" He grasped her other arm and yanked her toward him. "You belong to me—to *Keegan!*" he barked. "And you'll do as I say, or I'll not be responsible for what happens."

"You're threatening me?"

"You turn your back on the United Irish, and I can't promise you protection." A muscle flicked angrily at his jaw. "But do as you're told . . ." he paused, his eyes assessing her reaction, "and I'll take you back to whatever is left of Kildare."

Uncomfortable with the fact that he'd spoken the truth, Kelsey battled to maintain her fragile shell of composure. "When?" She felt tears trickle across her cheek. She hated the control he held over her. But helplessness now enclosed her as she realized that she was without defense. For a traitor, the United Irish executed a revenge far more damaging than their rebellion. She momentarily entertained the thought of running to the Prentices for help. Then she remembered Trula Hill's accusing words, "Would you expect the Prentices to pay?" She could never ask Caleb to help her now. Jack Keegan was her only way out of New South Wales alive. "When will you send me back to Kildare? What must I do?" Resignation filled her eyes.

Seeing compliance softening her gaze, Keegan whispered, "That's a good girl." He rubbed her arm with a coarse hand.

Kelsey couldn't help but look away again. She remembered how much she had loathed the first time he touched her. She had desperately wanted to run away, but he had overpowered her. *I hate you! How I hate you, Jack Keegan!* But she knew that to divulge her thoughts would only mean the end of her hopes of ever seeing her homeland again. Allowing her eyes to follow his hands up his sinewy arms to his shoulders and then to his unshaven face, she forced a wooden smile. "What must I do? Just say it."

"Where are you staying?"

"Rose Hill. A farm in Parrametta."

"Whose land?"

"The Prentice family. I've known Caleb Prentice since we were children."

"We could hide supplies on this land somewhere?"

She shook her head. "I can't use the Prentices, Jack. They're good people."

"Like us? Good people who have been used as British slaves to colonize this land for them?" He spat at the ground and cursed. "If they're English, then they're the enemy."

Kelsey nodded, but her heart did not agree with her head. "Go on," she said resignedly.

"If I hide an arsenal near here, it'd be the first place they'd look. They would never suspect you or this family in Parrametta."

"Arsenal?" A shadow of alarm touched her face.

Keegan hesitated, seeing the worry of her gaze. "Surely you realize that a rebellion requires weapons."

"I won't help you if it places the Prentices in danger."

"We'll not involve the Prentices." His impatience grew evident. "We'll plan our invasion elsewhere."

"You swear it, Jack?"

"On my own mother's grave." He composed his face with an indefinable sense of rightness and crossed his fingers in front of himself. "Then as soon as we've freed ourselves from British rule, we'll be married. I'll buy the finest plot of land that Kildare has to offer."

An emotion more bitter than sweet swelled in Kelsey's heart. She wanted the news to gladden her, but a nagging sense of hopelessness drained her of any satisfaction. She felt herself shrinking from the cold gray of his watchful face. Gathering her wits, she spoke with detached inevitability. "How can you hide an arsenal on this land? Rose Hill is teeming with laborers."

"Surely there's a remote area, an unused shed of some sort. You'll find out?"

Kelsey nodded, but regret welled up inside her. She felt more like a traitor now than ever. "But the Prentices—"

"You're Irish, not British." His reasoning clear, Keegan lifted his face as a patriot and chuckled coarsely without a smile. "We stand or fall together."

"I hear what you say." She sighed inwardly, for her loyalties were tangled inside her feelings for this family. "But the Prentices have been faithful to see that I've been cared for properly."

"All the more reason to use the resources at hand. No one will ever suspect. But you've one important thing to remember—never let anyone see us together. If the military is watching me as William Orr suspects, then we'll simply lead them down the wrong road."

"How will you contact me?"

"You leave me to deal with the details of the matter. I'll organize the means, you supply the hiding place."

Kelsey turned and departed. She allowed his words to tumble over and over in her mind as she mounted the seat next to the driver. Battling against herself, she believed one moment that she could never aid the United Irish and the next moment feared the consequences for herself and her unborn child if she didn't.

The smell of earth filled her senses. A light, misty rain had settled the dust in the road, leaving the air smelling like freshly plowed soil. The thin clouds had drifted some distance away, and blue sky smiled down on the harbor. The warmth and fresh air began to relax her, but only slightly. Suddenly Kelsey stiffened. A slight pang knocked at her abdomen, reminding her of her obligation. Soon her secret would grow public. She had no time to waste. She would begin immediately to search for an empty shanty at Rose Hill. *It will bring the Prentices no harm*, she assured herself. *How can it?*

Kelsey retreated into her fragile shell of composure and fought silently with the guilt that engulfed her. If only she could return to the days when she first met Caleb Prentice. *Aye. He saw me differently in those days*. Now if she chanced to look into the depths of his blue eyes, she beheld only the pity he reserved for her. She batted away the moistness from her weary eyes and settled herself once more on the wagon seat.

The driver chatted gaily while Kelsey rode the remainder of the way in torment.

18

A Silent
Little War

Kelsey rode out across the pastureland, a breeze bending the tall grasses before her. Sitting sidesaddle atop Katy's mare, she would have enjoyed the ride if it hadn't been for the task set before her. After examining the western depths of Rose Hill's land, she spied the roof of a distant building. Bringing the whip to flank, she reined the shining bay mare toward where her sights were set and cantered toward it.

Examining the grounds around the shack, she noted thick foliage and several large trees that all but hid most of the old building. Within a quarter mile, she came upon a small branch of the river, which after a strong rain could possibly float a small boat. But she couldn't bring herself to divulge all the facts to Keegan. He would have to devise his own plan after she informed him of the abandoned shed. When her part of the bargain was fulfilled, she would expect immediate recompense for passage to Ireland. *I cannot wait another month*, she thought worriedly.

After checking the inside of the shed and being satisfied of its sturdiness, she mounted the mare and headed east. She had promised to help Cook with some chores. The sun now crept away from its midday point in the sky and aimed itself toward providing a warm afternoon, which quickly slipped away. Mounting a small hill, she stopped the horse at the crest. The breezes were stronger on the hillside, and she couldn't help but enjoy the wind against her face. Reaching with one hand, she loosened the scarf that held her hair atop her head. She shook free the golden curls and smiled as the breeze tossed her hair up and away from her neck. "Yours is a lovely world, Caleb Prentice," she whispered softly. "Almost as lovely as was mine."

"Perfect day for a ride, isn't it?" A voice broke into her peaceful idyll.

Kelsey turned abruptly. Her eyes beheld a finely tailored riding frock and the white parasol her intruder carried. "Hello, Miss Hill." Surprised but quick to rally, she responded cordially, "It is indeed a perfect day. Rose Hill's a fine place for riding, 'tis at that."

"Once you've accepted my apology, we can take a ride together," Trula blurted all at once. "Please join me, will you?" She closed up the parasol with a firm snap. "I so hate to ride alone." Her eyes wide with apparent sincerity, she allowed a childlike smile to play around the corners of her face.

Confused by her seeming pretense, Kelsey finally responded. "Apology?"

"My curiosity outlasted my good manners at dinner last week. I've given my behavior much thought, and the things I said to you were perfectly inexcusable. You'll forgive me"—she gazed obliquely at her—"won't you?"

Uneasy, Kelsey frowned. "Of course. I've only vague remembrances of the conversation, however. You needn't feel guilty."

"It's all settled then," Trula beamed. "Shall we go?"

Kelsey hesitated. "I can't. I promised to help with the evening meal."

"Let the servants do their own work," Trula said plainly. She lifted her hand to pull an auburn curl from her brow.

Ignoring Trula's faintly arrogant tone, Kelsey couldn't help but notice how the sun glinted in red highlights around the crown of her head. However, she found the girl's beauty less than flawless. In her own estimation, Trula would've been a stunning beauty except for her mouth, which was usually pressed in a sullen pout. Kelsey felt it ruined the looks of her face. "If I may comment, your hair is beautiful," Kelsey finally said, her smile brightening her countenance.

Taken aback but delighted with the compliment, Trula forced a modest blush across her cheeks. "You're too kind." She paused. "So what is your verdict? Shall we ride and leave the servants to earn their keep? I've already informed the Prentices that you would be joining me this afternoon"—she looked askance, her lashes fluttering—"just in case."

Kelsey, apprehensive of the woman's intentions, shook her head. "I can't. I'm sorry. I gave my word."

"Promises are made to be broken," Trula persisted, the look of fondness waning from her face.

"Sorry. But you may accompany me back to the house. Would that satisfy you? We've a good ways to go as it is." Kelsey endeavored to sound optimistic, although her mistrust of Trula caused her to carefully choose her words.

Her face reflecting her dissatisfaction in the matter, Trula turned her steed around. "I'll lead the way, then." Her tone was curt, tinged with irritation.

Biting the inside of her mouth, Kelsey stifled the humor that threatened to surface in her eyes. They rode in silence for a short while, and Kelsey began to ponder if Trula had watched her for long. Even if she had, what would it matter? Exploring Rose Hill was a common pastime of all the Prentices' guests. "You've known the Prentice family for long?" she asked Trula.

"For a year."

"You traveled here from England with both your parents?"

"Only one." Trula's tone emotionless, she spoke matter-of-factly. "After my mother died, my father grew increasingly despondent. Our land in England only served to remind him further of their life together. The enticement to settle as a squatter in New South Wales grew strong, and with all my siblings grown but me, I couldn't perceive being the one to hold him back from his desires."

"You're happy here?"

Allowing a broad smile to light her face, Trula's reply shone from her eyes. "I believe in divine providence, don't you?"

Kelsey licked her lips, her throat quite dry. "No. I do not," she said with a finality.

Trula's brows lifted with interest. "I suppose if your lot has brought you ill fate, then your optimism is low. True?"

"No. Not everyone feels that way. Amelia Prentice is a perfect example. She's seen the worst of misery, yet her faith grows ever stronger."

Pursing her lips curiously, Trula batted her lashes and voiced her thoughts. "I suppose you're right. I hadn't noticed."

"But when others' choices have dictated my future, it's hard to determine whether an outside force has intervened. Every day the sun rises"—her words were colored with cynicism—"bringing a silent little war into my world." Realizing how grim she must sound, she forced a ray of optimism. "For some of us, triumphs come in increments and sometimes in very small packages."

"So I see." Trula kept her eyes straight ahead, her smile evident. "And does the father of your child know of your situation?"

Kelsey hesitated, annoyed by her direct approach. "He does. He's making preparation for us to leave soon for Ireland."

Trula turned her face toward Kelsey as surprise shone from her eyes. "So Mr. Keegan is going with you?" Her eyes narrowed in disbelief.

Observing the change in her demeanor, Kelsey paused uneasily. "Why wouldn't he? He's my betrothed."

"Of course, I agree that he should fulfill his obligation. But not all men are capable of embracing their duties to us. There aren't too many Caleb Prentices in this world."

"Jack Keegan is married to Ireland. He wants to return as desperately as I. He's earning the money now to buy our passage and then to buy land in Kildare when we arrive." She paused, wondering if she strived to convince Trula or herself. "I'm most anxious for this all to transpire. I want my child born on Irish soil. Not the soil of my *jailers*." Kelsey stiffened. She hadn't intended for her words to sound so harsh. She studied Trula's face for her reaction.

"So you see the British as your *jailers*?" A strange satisfaction sparked in Trula's eyes.

Kelsey flinched. "I spoke in haste. Forgive me."

"Why not? You forgave me. Besides, I'm certain that if I were in your position, I would want to leave here, too. New South Wales is not a home for the faint of heart."

Trula's pointed remark threatened to disturb Kelsey's composure. "You've such a way with words, Trula. Perhaps you should be a barrister."

Trula laughed. "My father said the same thing. Can you imagine—a woman barrister? Now wouldn't that be a jolly surprise? They'll allow *that* to happen when they allow women to own property."

Sighing resignedly, Kelsey responded, "I suppose we ladies are all at the mercy of men."

"If you believe that, then you're blind to your own beauty."

Kelsey stared blankly at Trula. She had never tried to use female guile to entrap a man. *Or, is that what I'm doing now?* She thought of the way she had tracked down Keegan. Uncomfortable with Trula's appraisements, she lifted the whip in the air. "We've almost arrived. Let's fly!" Kelsey laughed, hoping her gaiety masked the anxiety that welled inside of her. She raced ahead of Trula, somehow wanting to beat her back to Rose Hill but not understanding why.

"She's leaving soon, you know." Caleb held back the soft ivory drapery from the window. He could see the two women racing toward the house, their horses gleaming from the run. "This Keegan's agreed to marry her. They'll return to Ireland, just as she's always wished."

"You must be happy for her." Katy pressed a needle through her decorative needlecraft. Her eyes widened, but she didn't smile. Pricking her finger, she complained loudly and then tried to wag away the pain. "Blasted needle!" she muttered.

"And why not? If she's happy, then why shouldn't we share in her joy?"

"True." Katy nodded, her eyes fixed on her troublesome handiwork.

"Dwight has told you of my plans to go to England?"

Katy chuckled. "You've told me of your plans. At least a hundred times since you were eight years old."

"Posh."

"Dwight would accompany you, but he sees more profit in remaining here. Besides, he trusts your judgment. You've proven your shrewdness at the bargaining table often enough."

"I'm the only Prentice who hasn't stepped foot on England's shores. I say it's about time."

"I wish you wouldn't travel alone." Her fingers stopped atop the tapestry, her eyes somber. "You've eight months to make your plans. You don't have to go alone."

"You wish to go?"

"No. You don't catch my meaning. You could take someone with you. A wife, perhaps."

He laughed quietly, ignoring the seriousness of her tone. "Between you and our mother, I'll be a lucky man to escape becoming a bachelor."

"And to escape Trula Hill?"

"She has her ways—charming ways, I might add." He raised an eyebrow and winked at his sister, brushing the thought aside. There'd be time for such contemplations later.

"Dear me, I'm quite thirsty!" Trula waltzed into the room, her riding whip in one hand and her parasol in the other. "Where's our little maid when we need her?"

"Assisting Cook, I'm afraid." Katy intervened. "I'll fetch you both a drink."

"Oh no, please." Trula shook her head, feeling awkward with Katy's offer.

"None for me. I should excuse myself anyway," Kelsey offered apologetically. "I've promised my assistance in the kitchen."

Seeing the concern of Katy's gaze, Trula piped up. "Miss McBride's a stubborn one. I told her that guests shouldn't be doing chores delegated to servants."

"We actually all join in from time to time." Katy smiled at Kelsey. "We feel our employees respect the way we Prentices roll up our sleeves. But Trula's correct in her assessment. We can't allow our houseguest to join the ranks of our servants."

"But I've already promised. You see, it's a special Irish recipe we've planned for tonight. Rather than try to explain it, I simply offered to make the dish myself."

"Ooh. I'll bet it's a special dish then, if you're making it."

Katy affirmed her approval with a compliment.

"We'll soon find out." Kelsey smiled. "If you'll all excuse me." She dismissed herself from the room.

Trula waited for Kelsey to disappear down the hallway before commenting, "Such an odd person." She acknowledged Caleb's rueful gaze, countering quickly with, "But delightful. We've had an interesting chat."

Straightening his cravat, Caleb rested his elbow upon the fireplace hearth while clasping his hands in front of him. "I trust your chat proved fruitful."

"I apologized." Trula gazed up like a spoiled little girl. "And she accepted. It's all finished now. Must we ever bring up the subject again?"

"No. That is, as long as there is never a repeat of such an incident." His tone proved he had no intention of relenting. Then reaching out to clasp her gloved hand, he bowed and lightly kissed her fingers. "Thank you, *mademoiselle*. Integrity is paramount to our family, you know."

"And to me," Trula insisted. She shook her head adamantly. "I want no ill feelings from the Irish girl. No matter how much she hates the English."

Caleb lifted his eyes from his bowed posture. "Meaning. . . ?"

She breathed out an apologetic sigh. "Dear. I've done it again. No, I'll not continue with such gossip. Although, if it's absolutely true, would we label such as gossip?"

"I don't need an explanation, Trula." Katy pressed her lips together as she struggled with a knot in her thread.

"Nor I." Caleb studied her face pensively. "Unless—"

"Yes?"

He stepped close, looking down at her intently. "Unless the information would affect our reputation."

"It could, if word spread of her rebellious political views."

"Did she tell you she hated the English?"

"She referred to the English as her *jailers*."

"*Jailers* they've been to her." Katy grew defensive. "As they were to our own parents. We Prentices are all emancipists, no matter from where we originated."

"But, do you *hate* the English?" Trula's persistence became more obvious.

Katy smiled, her eyes sparkling mischievously. "I'm a Christian, aren't I? But if I could hate, I have my list."

"But Kelsey never actually said she hated us, did she, Trula?" Caleb captured her eyes with his.

"No. Not hate. But one can only assume—"

"That we should keep an eye on the matter?"

"For certain." She lowered her tone. "What if she's part of the United Irish?"

He chuckled. "What makes you say that?"

Trula bit her bottom lip.

"You know something?"

After a moment's hesitation, she shook her head. "No."

Caleb stroked her hands, his deep voice persuasive. "Perhaps you'll tell me later. We can't have a rebel spoiling our *prominence* in the colony," he remarked cynically. "Why don't we all adjourn to prepare for dinner?"

Melting in his presence, Trula smiled demurely. "I'll go with Katy, if that's satisfactory."

Katy muttered to herself, "May as well. I'm certainly not skilled at needlepoint." She shook her head and laid the frame aside. Seeing Trula awaited her answer, she welcomed her absentmindedly. "Yes, please join me. Half your wardrobe hangs in my room now."

"Splendid. And then afterward, Caleb, I want to hear all about the trip to England." Eagerness sparked in Trula's gaze.

"Yes, and beyond all that, there's that party tomorrow night at the Franklins' home." Katy's eyes locked on her brother's. "Some of us need escorts."

Caleb, seeing her pointed gaze, countered, "I'll be happy to escort you, sister. That is, if your husband doesn't mind."

Katy straightened her back. "I wasn't speaking of myself."

He glanced away, avoiding her indignant stare as well as Trula's nervous giggle.

They all treaded up the staircase unaware of the one who stood with a tray of refreshments at the hallway's end. Kelsey gazed at the tray she had prepared for them, her eyes pain-filled. She had stood too long outside the door and had heard Trula's venomous assumptions of her. She was glad that Katy had rushed to her defense, but Caleb's interest in the subject had sickened her heart. How could he compare the family's reputation to their friendship? *Reputation.* She pondered his words. If he cared so much for the Prentice reputation, then she would be forced to leave sooner than she had expected.

Returning the tray to the kitchen, she began to formulate her own plan for the United Irish uprising. Jack Keegan had a soldier's heart, but his intuition was dull. She would return to the abandoned shed and fully arrange the plan for the arsenal. Her eyes blazed a blue-green fire. *If there's to be an uprising, then a glorious one it shall be!* Another silent little war had been declared, but now by her own choice. *And by my own choice I will be the victor, at last.* Sadness engulfing her spirit, she disappeared into the next room.

19
THE BARN
DANCE

The Scottish fiddler stood upon an earthen floor with golden straw scattered across it, his fellow musicians tuning their instruments. Beyond the musicians bustled the Franklins' servants, who were busy about stretching tents of bright fabric from the loft, adding festive touches to the barn's interior.

The Franklins' home, modest and practical, could not have held the neighboring families invited from their ever growing guest list, so the party was held in their newly built barn. Outside, a recently dug pit billowed with the tantalizing smoke of a roasting pig. Most of the neighbors arrived early, the women offering up their sumptuous contributions to the Franklin feast. Congregating out on the lawn, the men passed around cigars and joined in the prattle regarding the latest news from England.

Trula's father assisted his daughter from his carriage. "Allow me, m'lady. You look stunning, by the way." He referred to her blue satin gown, which boasted the latest styling from France—a daring neckline.

Her eyes fastened on her father, Trula stepped down while carefully covering her bodice with her fan. "Do you think it too daring, Papa? I don't want the neighbors spreading tales about me."

"Any tales spread here tonight will be out of jealousy," James Hill assured her, his eyes scanning the faces of those present. "I believe the Prentices arrived earlier. Why don't you join the ladies for a chat while I look for Mr. Farrell?"

As casually as she could manage, Trula suggested, "Let me accompany you. Perhaps Caleb will be with them."

"I still don't understand why Mr. Prentice didn't escort you tonight."

"It was his plan to escort me. But his sister, Katy, felt the polite thing for him to do would be to accompany them and their houseguest. You know, the Irish girl?"

"A gesture of sympathy, I'm sure."

"Quite. But I agreed the poor girl should have an escort. At any rate"—her eyes narrowed in a calculating manner—"I plan to steal him away before the night is finished." Her lips spread in a tight smile.

"I'll have no daughter of mine chasing after a man."

"There's no chase to it, Papa. Caleb Prentice will soon be traveling abroad to England, and I fully expect to travel along with him—as his wife." She spied Caleb ahead conversing with Dwight. "Now, please allow me to accompany you." Her eyes wide, she gracefully looped her arm through his.

His thoughts elsewhere, Hill shook his head. "You'll be better off with the women. I'll return shortly." He saw the disappointment of her gaze. "Allow me to handle this young Prentice my way."

Chafed by her father's controlling manner, Trula sullenly complied. She spotted a cluster of men and saw that Caleb was with them, but rather than conversing with those around him, he had turned his attention from the group. Trula lifted her face to look beyond his gaze. Near the barn's entrance several young women had gathered. Wearing another of Rachel's beautiful gowns, Kelsey chatted, oblivious to the eyes that watched her. Flapping her fan indignantly, Trula looked around and found a private place of observance.

After straightening his coat in a dignified manner, Caleb excused himself from the men. "I should see to our guest."

"Mr. Farrell?" Hill joined their circle, lighting his pipe in the process. "May I have a word with you?"

Caleb strolled toward the young women. One of them lifted her face when she saw him approach. "Hello, Mr. Prentice. Won't you join the ladies for some punch?"

"My thoughts exactly." He flashed a noble smile. "Miss McBride, I trust you're becoming acquainted with the families of our neighboring farms. Parrametta has produced some of New South Wales' most beautiful women."

Franklin's daughter gasped. "Why, thank you, Mr. Prentice. And we know of at least one handsome man in our citizenry."

The ladies surrounding Kelsey laughed gaily, but she did not join in their revelry. Instead, she appeared slightly embarrassed at the flirtatious flattery. Noting Kelsey's discomfort, Caleb added, "Yes, but my brother-in-law is no longer available."

Lifting her chin, Kelsey flashed an admiring gaze while the Franklin girl remarked politely, "Mr. Prentice is also modest."

The music suddenly burst forth in a lively dance tune, and the women began to stir excitedly. Some glanced hopefully at Caleb, while others looked confidently for their escorts.

"I would be most gratified if you would allow me the first dance," Caleb said quietly to Kelsey. "Miss McBride?"

"I've promised it to another," Kelsey answered quickly, but her anxious gaze said otherwise.

Clasping his hands behind his back, Caleb glanced all around curiously. "Well . . . it appears your partner has disappeared. Please allow me to take his place until he chooses to arrive." He cupped his hand under her delicate wrist in a dapper fashion.

Pressing together her rose-tinted lips, Kelsey reluctantly agreed. "I suppose, but I'm not familiar with this dance."

"Allow me. It's a French dance called the *quadrille*. We'll need four couples to execute it properly." He pointed to three eager couples. "Shall we all, then?" With courtly sophistication, he led her into the barn and carefully demonstrated the dance.

Kelsey's face poised in firm concentration, she awkwardly

followed his lead, paying special attention to the roles the other women had taken.

"You're quick on your feet," Caleb complimented.

Keeping a modest tone, she replied, "I love music. The sound of it moves me deeply."

"You're so graceful. You're certain you've never danced the *quadrille* before?"

Gazing up into the Australian's handsome face, Kelsey couldn't help but smile a bit at his own agility. "Thank you for asking me to dance."

"Just for a bit, now, until your partner arrives." Caleb twirled her gracefully around, their bodies perfectly synchronized with the other dancing couples.

The voluminous skirts of the young ladies billowed and swirled around the straw-strewn floor as their parents happily gazed on, chatting amiably with one another.

Caleb caught a glimpse of his mother's face, somber yet curiously peaceful. *Is that approval I see in your face, Amelia Prentice?* He convinced himself that it was his promise to Katy that drew him to dance with Kelsey. *Befriend this lonely young woman*, she had graciously suggested. *Just be her friend.* But seeing her now smiling under his approving gaze stirred a strange emotion within him. *She's erratic as a summer storm*, he decided. Yet through her life ran a thread of surety. *I must get to know you better.* He allowed his fingers to intertwine in hers, the tenderness of her touch almost unbearable. The past few years of her life had been a mystery to him, and so the obscurity of her world intrigued him somehow. He decided to chance a question. "Norfolk Island must have been a dreadful place."

Kelsey hesitated, but something about the assurance of his gaze caused her to relax. "Dreadful beyond words. The convicts are treated as dogs—worse, actually."

"They never should have transported you. Therein lies the real crime."

Kelsey stepped back to bow slightly along with the other young women and then stepped toward him again. Her lips parted to reply but no words followed.

"No need to respond." Caleb saw the struggle in her face.

"We shouldn't speak of such horrors on such a lovely night as this, eh?"

"I don't mind. Truly. 'Tis better to speak it out than harbor the memories alone, I suppose."

Seeing that she didn't discourage his inquiry he cautiously continued. "Were there . . . are there many young women at Norfolk?"

"Yes. Although I don't know exactly how many of us were there. Some found their way into the care of a mariner. Others . . . they weren't so fortunate."

"Rachel said they must have starved you."

"Yes. Even though much food was grown there, it gave the authorities more control over us to limit our rations."

"Devils! All of them!"

Kelsey nodded but displayed little emotion.

At first her lack of emotion surprised him. Then Caleb suddenly realized the mental barriers she had been forced to erect for her own protection. What she harbored from the past had now become a barrier between them. How deeply he regretted that he hadn't stolen her off the transport ship that day and spared her the ruination of her childhood. "Are you enjoying yourself tonight? We could leave—"

"Oh no. I don't wish to leave." Unknowingly, she tightened her grip on his hands.

Caleb forced himself to resist drawing her closer. But his desire to spare her any further pain became almost insufferable. *Dance with me . . . all night, Kelsey McBride.* He had to know her better now. It became an obsession.

The longer they danced, the more he discovered of the torturous days she spent on Norfolk Island. She cautiously released bits of her past to him, as though each fact were reluctantly handed to him like a delicate piece of glass. She slowly revealed details of the brutal floggings, the squalor, the starvation, the threat of insidious men. He carefully responded to each account with sincere words of both sympathy and anger, tempered with assurances of compassion and understanding. He could not disappoint her trust.

Caleb now began to understand why Kelsey had grown so defensive. What he could not understand was the strange longing he had to stay near her side. Nor could he explain the bond between them. He was drawn to her as he would be his own sister, Katy, he tried to convince himself. There could be no other explainable attachment. Moreover, her betrothal to another, however corrupt it appeared to him, must be honored. But he continued to question his own feelings, weighing them and comparing them to his feelings for Trula Hill. *The thought is absurd*, he chastened himself, searching his mind for the answer. *But what is it?* He swung her into the circle of his arms.

Staring away from him throughout most of the dance, Kelsey finally brought her eyes up to meet his.

Caleb nodded politely to a group of older women who stood admiring them from the side. Then he brought his gaze back to hers. *Such a shame. The innocence of our childhood friendship was so rudely interrupted. Somehow, Kelsey, I'll make it up to you. I will!*

"Lovely couple, eh?"

Trula whirled around from her perch behind the barn door. She saw that Caleb's friend, Matthew, stood over her. "I hadn't noticed," she said curtly.

"Resorting to spying now, Trula?"

"There's nothing to spy on."

Leaning around the open doorway, Matthew looked at the dancing couples with interest. "So *this* is the Irish emancipist. No one's said how beautiful she is, though. And is that a spark of fascination I detect in young Prentice's eyes?"

"Shut up, Matthew!"

"Temper, young lady"—he stepped toward her, enamored by her angry passion—"certainly becomes you. Perhaps you should join me in the *quadrille*, eh? A little game of 'two can play' is now in order, wouldn't you say?"

Trula looked anxiously into the barn. Caleb appeared to be holding Kelsey tighter than ever, his eyes never leaving hers. "Two can play?" she asked faintly.

"Just follow my lead and act as though I'm the only man on the dance floor."

"That would be petty." She clasped her hands worriedly. "Papa would think me childish."

"Look at you." Matthew smiled, his eyes full of mock pity. "You're miserable. Let us make the evening memorable, shall we? Before the night is finished, you'll have young Prentice bowing at your feet."

Diffidently, she accepted his hand and followed him onto the musty floor.

"I'm famished. How about you?" Caleb clasped Kelsey's slender fingers and stepped gaily around another couple.

"Yes! And out of breath!" Kelsey laughed. "Will it ever end?"

Caleb's eyes clung to hers, contemplating her statement, *Will it ever end?* Without hesitation, he drew her away from the dance and slowed their pace. "Will what end?" he asked quietly.

She looked up inquisitively, her hazel eyes graced by dark sweeping lashes. "Well, the dance of course. When will the dance end?"

Inhaling, Caleb shook his head as though lost in a dream. Something intense flared through his entrancement. "Of course," he chuckled sheepishly, "I knew what you meant." He glanced quickly across the floor. The tempo had changed and the couples had resumed a quiet waltz. "I believe it's finished now."

"Thank you." Kelsey released her hand from his.

Reluctantly, he allowed her to back away. "It looks as though your dance partner has forever lost his way. We may as well find something to eat. The feast is spread just outside these doors."

"Caleb, you don't have to escort me." Kelsey stepped away, placing more distance between them. "I know that Katy asked you to do this as a favor to her. I'm certain Trula would appreciate me relinquishing you of your obligation."

Stunned by her words, he smiled almost apologetically. "I'm most happy to fulfill my *obligation*, as you call it."

"It isn't necessary." Kelsey turned and walked away.

Confounded, Caleb watched her leave the barn, her silk lavender dress trailing behind her.

"Having a jolly time, I trust?" Matthew purposefully waltzed past them. Trula smiled woodenly next to him.

"The best of times, Matthew." Caleb acknowledged them both with a nod. "Be a good lad and take exceptional care of our lovely friend, Miss Hill, will you?" At once, he turned to follow the beautiful Irish vision that had just escaped his grasp.

Trula released Matthew's hold, her mouth agape.

The night sky wrapped the moon in soft sable, with a faint translucent cloud veil kissing the conjunction of sky and moon but not hiding the light. And so those revelers who drifted in and out of the party were apt to gaze up, steal a glimpse of the beauty, and then proceed with their merrymaking. But Kelsey found her preference in the peace of the outdoors and in the glory of the heavenly spectacle.

Setting her refreshment on an outdoor table, she walked to the edge of the packed earth where the grass began. Closing her eyes, she reflected on the memory that had all but become a fantasy in her mind—that wonderful hillside where she once played as a young girl. Inhaling, she sniffed the aroma of moist Australian grass and struggled to imagine the fragrance of shamrocks—*had they a scent?* The shamrock she had hidden so long ago in her pocket had eventually disintegrated or was lost. It was another incident she couldn't remember for certain, nor could she remember the texture of it, which now disturbed her. She wanted it all to be real again and a part of her, to become the ground beneath her and the sky above—all that she called home, all that she called Kildare.

She slipped her feet out of the pale satin slippers that Rachel had given her along with the dress. Stepping forward, she allowed the grass to caress her bare feet. The cool, wet sensation sent a refreshing shudder through her body. She could almost transport herself now to Kildare and imagine it all. But then, as quickly as it had come, the euphoria ebbed away. Childhood had its freedoms, one of which included ignoring reality. But as much as she desired to recall the innocence of those days, she could no longer hide behind a mask of who she once was. The ugly truth of her degradation while imprisoned on Norfolk Island would soon be evident to all. She glanced back at the lighthearted faces that reflected the innocence of youth. *They're all so carefree.* She stroked her stomach. *And I can't enjoy one moment, not one blissful moment of peace. I hate you Jack Keegan. I hate what you've done to me.* She followed her fingertips with her eyes as she stroked the satiny folds that hid her embarrassment. *And I want to hate what grows inside me.* A stifled sob caught in her throat. *But I cannot.*

Her thoughts intermingling with angry guilt, Kelsey sighed and walked slowly to retrieve the slippers. Bending downward, she glanced up at the table where she had set her crystal glass and suddenly pinched her brow in puzzlement. Quickly, she slipped her feet back into the shoes and strode back to the table. *What is this?* She lifted the glass to retrieve a folded piece of paper that had been slipped under it. Her eyes scanning the grounds around her, she glanced back and forth. No one appeared to be watching her. All the guests moved in and out of the barn with ease, conversing gaily as expected.

In the lantern's yellow glow, Kelsey could see Trula's animated face and imagined her to be fatuously engaged in spoken flattery. She couldn't see Caleb, but she assumed he stood just beyond the barn entrance, basking in Trula's shallow admiration. *I don't care.* She shrugged away a feeling of unnatural rivalry. *Not a wee bit.* She quickly unfolded the letter. Her eyes, quick and assessing, narrowed. Fear crept across her face. *My derest darling Kelsey, Aye told you aye would find a way. Aye can see you now from wer aye stand. Come away, but quiet now. No one must see us together, luv. Look and see the biggest wattle tree ahead. Jack.*

Kelsey pondered the letter's words. She wanted to turn and walk away, leaving the note where she found it. But lifting her eyes, she saw the prominent black silhouette of the tree far off in the field ahead. A light flickered, flashed, and then was extinguished. Slowly, she shredded the letter and stuffed the pieces into the empty goblet. Seeing that no one watched her, she disappeared into the shadows.

Caleb stood a short distance from her. His heart ached to follow her, but the scene left him baffled. The ill-dressed man who had stolen up behind her had drawn his curiosity. He watched as the man slipped a bit of paper under a glass and then ran in the opposite direction. At first he assumed the man to be a farmhand. *Could this be Keegan?* he pondered, moving cautiously to the table. Lifting the goblet, he turned it upside down and emptied the contents into his pocket. Seeing that few people fraternized inside the Franklins' home, he walked briskly toward it and disappeared into the house.

"How did you find me?" Kelsey whispered tremulously.

"You're not difficult to find."

"But I thought you didn't want us to be seen together."

Keegan clasped his roughened hands across her wrist and pulled her further into the shadows. "No one sees us, m'dear."

"But the note—"

"I had it delivered. Keegan's no fool." He drew her near, the light of night casting a foreboding shadow across his face. "I must tell you, Kelsey, that until I saw you again, I hadn't realized how much I missed you."

She shook her head. "You're lying, Jack. You've no feelings for anyone but yourself."

"Untrue. I've had you on my mind since I saw you last."

Kelsey couldn't discern the sincerity of his gaze for the darkness. Nor did she care. Her feelings for him were like those she would have for an adder.

"You found a location for us?"

She nodded reluctantly. "Yes."

"Where, then?"

"About five miles west of the Prentice home. It's an old house. Perhaps the Prentices' first house, I'm not for certain. It's overgrown now with foliage." She paused without looking up. "It's well hidden."

"You can meet me there tomorrow?"

Hearing his anxious tone, she remarked, "You're in a hurry?"

"We want to strike quickly, while they don't suspect."

"How do you expect to overthrow the British? It's foolish to assume—"

"Quiet! You leave the details to me, woman. Orr and I are

meeting in two days. I want to give him full confidence in our abilities. Now, you meet me tomorrow—"

The reality of his words flooded her mind. "Wait!"

"What're you saying now?"

"I want you to bring me a boat ticket tomorrow, or I'll not show you the house." She felt his hands grip her arms roughly.

"Don't you be making no demands, lassie!"

"If you want me to take you there, I want the passage to Ireland." She ground her teeth nervously.

"It's too soon."

"You'll no longer need me after I've shown you the building. You only need the storage for the ammunition. Correct?"

"No! You must be certain that no one discovers our location."

Kelsey could feel his hot breath against her face.

"We need you, Kelsey McBride. The United Irish need you."

His piteous tone caused only a slight glimmer of sympathy to well inside her. She recalled the manner in which William Orr could manipulate her mother. She had never understood his power over her, except to call it a strange infatuation. "But *I* don't need the United Irish!" A challenge etched her tone. "I only need a one-way passage to Ireland."

"Well, you'll not get it until after we've made our strike!" He loosened his grip. "If you're not with us, you're against us! I'll have no control over what happens to you then!" The moon glinted off Keegan's coal-black hair as he stormed away, the small lantern in his grasp squeaking.

Kelsey froze, spellbound by his sudden rejection. "Wait!" she whispered. Then seeing that he didn't respond, she ran after him. "Jack! Wait!"

A chore girl handed Caleb a tallow candle, freshly lit. "You can sit in Mr. Franklin's study. He won't mind. Has lots o' books if you've taken a mind to do some readin'," she offered.

Caleb cordially took the candle. "Thank you, miss. I won't be long. There are times when I grow nervous in crowds and parties, you understand?"

"Don't 'ave to explain nothin' to me." She dismissed him

with her hand. "They never asks me to none, so's I wouldn't know."

Her words drifted away, and Caleb strode quickly into the study. Setting the brass candlestick atop the table, he set about at once to try to arrange the torn letter. After several attempts, the letter finally fitted together. The handwriting was rough, and he squinted to interpret the words between the dribbled splotches of ink. *It's from Keegan, all right. He's here!* Caleb pressed his fingers against the wood and leaned over the letter. *My dearest darling*, he mouthed silently. *No one must see us together.* He pondered the statement. *Why?* Remembering Trula's warning yesterday, he began fitting together the mystery. *Why would Keegan want to stay hidden?* He shook his head. *I can't believe it. Kelsey McBride wouldn't involve herself with such a thing—not with the United Irish.* Turning away from the candlelight, he slowly stepped toward a window. He could see the barn well lit and the dark woods behind it. His gaze focused on the silhouette of a large wattle tree. A pale light suddenly flickered. He could see it moving away deeper into the woods. There was a pensive shimmer in the shadows of his eyes. His fear that Keegan would harm her was no longer as real as his latest fear that she was using the Prentice family to aid the rebels. *They're making you do this, Kelsey, aren't they? Keegan's forcing you, isn't he?* Seating himself in an overstuffed chair that smelled of pipe tobacco, he lifted his hand to stroke his chin. *But yet, I can't let you do it, Kelsey.* He made his decision. *I can't allow you to use my family in this way.*

An old clock ticked away more time as he pondered whether the matter could be salvaged. He remembered their dance together. The aroma of her perfume still lingered on his fingertips. For a moment in the barn, he was certain he had detected a spark of attraction in her eyes. Perhaps it had been only his wishful imagination. But yet, her memory hypnotized him as no other woman had the ability to do. And now her image tormented him. *If there is a way*—his emotions battled against his powers of reasoning—*that I could protect you from yourself . . .*

But his reasoning began to strengthen and take precedence, and he shook away his feelings. He must guard himself from her. If she *were* involved, as Trula feared, it was his duty to discover the plan and expose it. If Trula's theory proved correct, he would be forced to send Kelsey away from Rose Hill. *But if she's wrong?* A spark of hope welled inside him.

He stood and gathered the torn paper into his pocket once again and walked quietly from the house to join Miss Trula Hill for the remainder of the evening.

20

THE BOUNTY
OF A STRANGER

"But, you're certain the dress wasn't sent by Rachel Whitley?" Kelsey sat up abruptly in bed, the white cotton sheets folded across her lap. She quizzically eyed the young maid who stood before her lifting a sparkling new dress from a plainly wrapped box.

"No, I can't say I'm certain, miss. I only found the box by the front doorway this morning when I was sweeping beneath the portico." The maid admired the fabric with her eyes. "It's the prettiest one I've ever seen. I will say that for certain."

"And my name is on the card?"

"See for yourself." She handed the white card to Kelsey. Kelsey studied the heavy parchment card, front and back. The handwriting, written in blue ink, was unfamiliar to her. Other than her name gracefully inscribed, the card was blank. "Curious. No message. No way to know who sent it?"

The maid shrugged. "It's all a mystery. I wish I had such an admirer."

"You think it's from an admirer?"

"Who else? Look at that fine stitching. Wouldn't surprise me a bit if it were from Paris or some such place."

Kelsey mused. "A dress from France. Now where would anyone I know find such a beautiful gown?"

"I don't know. Mr. Prentice, now, 'e knows all about France. Went there to study, he did. You might ask 'im."

"That is true. I've heard him speak of it." She shook away the thought. *He wouldn't send this to me without signing it, would he?* "Thank you, Carla. I suppose I'll have to try it on." She smiled lightheartedly.

"I'll help you with it, then."

"All right," Kelsey nodded. "Dear me"—she slipped her legs from beneath the blanket's folds and placed her feet into the slippers on the floor—"my feet do ache."

Carla's brows lifted knowingly. "Ah, must've kept the gentlemen busy dancin' all night."

"Not many. Just a few," Kelsey chuckled. "Met one of Mr. Prentice's friends. Do you know Matthew?"

"Know 'im? Why he and Mr. Prentice, they grew up together. But I thinks Matthew—" She gasped. "If you can keep it to yourself—"

"I swear it!" Kelsey crossed her heart. "Tell me."

"I thinks, to myself, that Matthew 'as 'is sights set on none other than Miss Trula Hill." She blushed and then sighed. "I never kin keep me tongue to meself."

"I won't tell a soul." Kelsey laughed. "As a matter of fact, I saw Matthew vying for her attention all night."

"No! An' right in plain sight o' Mr. Prentice?"

Her eyes lighting almost impishly, Kelsey nodded, amused with the girl's manner. Slipping out of her nightgown, she allowed Carla to drop the brocaded gold gown over her head.

Fastening up the back, the maid commented approvingly, "No corset needed here. You've a fine figure, if you don't mind me saying."

"Thank you," Kelsey answered modestly, thinking of her pregnancy. "But I don't want you to think me vain. I don't usually give much thought to my appearance, although I suppose I should."

"That's what makes you so lovely, I believe," Carla grew reflective. "We've all noticed—all the servants, that is—that you don't walk around with airs like some of the guests do around here from time to time."

"Hah!" she laughed. "I've no reason to. I'm an emancipist."

"So I've heard. An' me as well."

"What have we here?" Katy peered around the partially opened door.

"Look, Mrs. Farrell. A lovely new dress for Miss McBride to wear. Ain't she a sight?"

"It's stunning." Katy slipped into the room. "Where in the world—"

"That's the mystery. I found it only this morning . . . right outside . . . just layin' on the porch wif Miss McBride's name on it."

Studying Katy's face for a reaction, Kelsey queried, "So you've no idea either?"

"No, I swear it." Katy bent and grasped the colorfully bordered hem. She pulled it out and then allowed the folds to relax around Kelsey's feet. "Hangs so gracefully. Look at the workmanship."

"Where am I going to wear it?"

"The next party of course."

Kelsey patted her stomach. "It had better be soon."

"If not, I can take it out in just a few places. A seam or two would do the trick."

"T'would be a shame to alter it, though. If need be, I'd rather save it."

Surrounded by the curiosity of the ladies of the house, the dress was neatly stored in the wardrobe. Over the next few days, Kelsey's surprise over the mystery gift grew to apprehension. She received no less than three more dresses, a bonnet, two velvet purses, and several pairs of shoes. Each article, like the first, was costly, and her embarrassment in the matter grew right along with the rumors that flew about the household.

Bustling into the dinner hall one evening, Kelsey observed Trula eyeing her newest dress with envy. It had come one day prior. Made of aquamarine silk, the elegant color had reminded her of the clean sea waters that swelled near a quiet shore where she once stood on Norfolk Island. Stopping to acknowledge her gracious host and hostess, she glanced self-consciously down at her dress upon seeing their surprised and admiring faces. The gown glistened faintly under the candelabras and billowed beautifully whenever she turned. She couldn't help but be pleased when she walked into the room. Caleb's extraordinary eyes, though visibly held in check, appeared to light with approval. With a tip of his head, he motioned her to the chair beside him. Ignoring Trula, who sat to the other side of him with her pointed stare, she complied with his cordial gesture.

"And yet another?" Caleb quipped, his eyes widening in question.

Seating herself, Kelsey answered, "I don't know what to say."

"What are we talking about?" Trula glanced around the table at the others, but no one bothered to answer. All eyes fastened on Kelsey.

"Well, I swear it isn't from me." Rachel, who had joined them along with her husband, smiled and bit her lip. "I would wish for such a friend myself."

"And I as well," Katy joined in.

"I suppose I'm the only uninformed one, then?" Petulance glared from Trula's eyes.

"It seems our Irish guest has an admirer," Dwight said, finally offering an explanation.

Trula's eyes shifted uneasily toward Caleb. "And who would that be?"

"I've no idea," Kelsey spoke up. "I don't recognize the handwriting on the cards that have accompanied the gifts."

"*Gifts?* There's more than one?"

"She's been handed an entire wardrobe, it seems." Katy laughed quietly. "Do you suppose they're from your Mr. Keegan?"

Kelsey recalled their secret meeting a few days ago at the old Rose Hill shack. Keegan had been tense and demanding. Nothing in his demeanor suggested that he would be in any mood to endow her with excessive and costly presents. "No," she answered, shaking her head. "It wouldn't be within his means," she paused, a disdainful smile curving her face, "or his taste."

"Of course, the sender could be someone you know, and he's hiding the fact from you." Trula drummed the white tablecloth with her fingertips, her eyes narrowed with suspicion.

"How do you mean?" Kelsey listened, intrigue lighting her face.

"Perhaps he's having another sign the cards and paying a messenger to deliver them."

"Ah, there's the barrister arising in you again." Kelsey contemplated the matter. "I hadn't thought of such a thing. If that's true, then he's trusting the secrecy of an accomplice. But of course, we've yet to meet the bearer of these gifts." She hesitated while pondering the events of the past few days. "The maids have all arisen early to try to catch the culprit, but he always manages to allude them." She arched an eyebrow, feigning slyness.

"It's true," Katy reasoned. "One box was found in the hayloft and another under Dwight's wagon seat. We've found them in all sorts of places, actually. But all have borne the same white card." She crossed her arms prettily across her bosom. "The handwriting suggests an educated person. It's quite an elusive fellow we seek."

"How charming," Trula commented, although her expressionless gaze suggested she found nothing humorous about the matter.

"Well, enough about our mystery admirer." Caleb nodded toward the maid who stood waiting to serve them. "On with our meal. Rachel, how is it you keep such a lovely household with all your duties at the prison colony?"

Kelsey attempted to listen with interest as the conversation quickly changed. But she couldn't help wondering if the handsome man who spoke knew more than he divulged. She saw Trula's worried countenance and the way her eyes appeared to question Caleb wordlessly. Perhaps she, too, suspected the heir of Rose Hill to be the secret giver of gifts.

Gently, she brushed her fingers across the silk sash beneath her bodice. *Whoever it is must care a great deal.*

She allowed her thoughts to drift back to the conversation at hand. Tomorrow Keegan's perilous plans would bring a new tension to her life, so she basked in the relaxation of the moment, the quiet enjoyment of chatting with friends, and the private satisfaction in realizing that, for once, someone was looking out for her. She reflected on her talk with Trula, remembering the day they rode horseback together. Trula boasted of divine providence as though she commanded the strings. But perhaps Amelia's prayers for her had worked after all. In the event they did, Kelsey breathed a silent prayer of thanksgiving and hoped that like Amelia, she would someday also believe.

Caleb dimmed the light next to his bed. The dinner party had fatigued him, and he had excused himself early when Heath and Rachel offered Trula an escort home. The household had suddenly grown quiet, and assuming all had retired for the evening, he decided to slip downstairs for a piece of rhubarb pie. Earlier, he hadn't eaten as much as usual. *I'll just have one slice and a cup of hot tea*, he vowed. Padding down the stairs with his lantern held high, he hesitated on hearing a distant murmuring. Making his way downstairs in his stocking feet and wearing only a cotton nightshirt, he realized that Mum had gathered Jared and Donovan into the parlor for a Bible reading. Even as adolescents, his nephews enjoyed the undivided attention of Grandmama.

"Awake thou that sleepest, and arise from the dead, and Christ shall give thee light. . . ."

Leaving the lantern on a hall table, he continued on silently, driven by his stomach. Peering around the corner, he stopped again. He could see the figure of a woman standing quietly in the darkened hallway, eavesdropping on Amelia and the boys. He smiled at the expression on Kelsey's face, her mouth curved in a tender expression. She appeared mesmerized by the scene that had become commonplace to him. It had been years since he had sat next to Mum's rocker for the nightly ritual. He paused to listen as well.

"Walk circumspectly, not as fools, but as wise. Redeeming the time, because the days are evil. . . ."

"Good evening," he whispered, his low voice startling her.

Kelsey flinched and whirled around to face him. "I . . . was only—"

"Eavesdropping?"

A sheepish resignation spreading across her countenance,

she nodded and quietly laughed. "You caught me. I—"

"Don't apologize." Gazing around her, he lifted his chin to observe the loving scene. "They're quite a family, eh?"

"You're fortunate." Kelsey turned to gaze back inside once more. "I once longed for such a family myself."

"Wherefore be ye not unwise, but understanding what the will of the Lord is." The words continued to flow around them.

"You're welcome to share mine."

"Pardon?"

"You said you longed for a family. I said that you're welcome to share in mine."

Kelsey was silenced by his generous offer. How she wished that she could take part in Caleb's family. This was what her heart had longed for when she was but a child in Kildare. But now it was too late. Too much had happened, too many choices had been made for her beyond her control, and now she was with child and headed for Ireland with Keegan. The past could not be changed.

"We'd best head for the kitchen. She's marking her place." Caleb broke into her musings and gestured toward the kitchen. Retrieving the lantern, he soon joined her. The kitchen lit up as he strolled in, and he could see her standing with her arms crossed at her waist, smiling meekly.

Biting her lip, Kelsey eyed him in amusement.

"Something wrong?"

She directed her eyes to the ceiling. "You're wearing your nightshirt."

"Mum has a mad fit if I don't. They're invented for mothers, you know."

Her cheeks reddened slightly, she redirected the conversation. "What is the purpose for our standing here in the kitchen?"

"Rhubarb pie is better after dark. Have some." He quickly opened the pie pantry and drew out the cloth-covered dish.

"None for me. I've been squeamish over desserts of late."

"You're eating for two. Have some anyway."

Settling herself into a chair, she rested her face in her hands. "No, thank you," she answered quietly but firmly.

"The lady knows what she wants. But so do I." He rubbed his hands in anticipation. Stoking the fire beneath the stovetop, he set the water kettle atop it. Noticing her subdued demeanor, he prepared his food in a dish and seated himself next to her. "You're quiet this evening." He remained cheerful but didn't wish to appear meddlesome.

"Just thinking." She paused. Her face filled with reflection. "May I ask you something?"

"Certainly." He savored the first bite.

"How do you feel about your mother's faith?"

"Ah, dangerous ground—discussing religion."

"I don't mean to pry."

"Quite all right." After thoughtful evaluation, he responded. "I remind myself of the need to pray. Perhaps chasten is a better word. Sometimes when the need is great, I can plead to the heavens, if need be." He chuckled, one hand raising dramatically. "But I don't call that faith. Mum tends her faith like a well-kept garden. To her, Christianity is a daily *vigil*, if you will." He wiped his mouth with a cloth and then clasped his sinewy fingers in front of himself. "I feel she's found what we all need, but I haven't embraced it as passionately as she."

"For me," Kelsey hesitated, her eyes guarded, "prayer has been repetitive, to a large degree. But, as you say, I have my moments of desperation, too. Either way, do you suppose God hears?"

"I don't know."

"Your parents have had a difficult life. Yet, they don't blame God."

"It's true that my parents suffered needlessly under the British transportation system. They had every reason to be bitter. But Mum esteems difficulties as a refiner's fire," Caleb answered with mock fervency, although a fondness shone from his eyes as he searched his memory. " 'Count it all joy . . . the trying of your faith worketh patience . . . let patience have her perfect work that ye may be perfect and entire, wanting nothing'—something to that effect."

"She believes it, doesn't she? She believes all of it, the entire Bible?"

"Absolutely." He rubbed his suntanned jaw. "Don't you?"

Sighing in confusion, she shook her head. "Don't ask me."

"Ah, the kettle's ready. Tea?"

"Why not? Allow me, please." Kelsey pushed away from the

table and busied herself with the cups and saucers. "I want to," she finally said. "I want to believe as your mum does."

He nodded but gave no reply. The sound of his nephews thundering up the stairway was followed by Amelia's fading footsteps, and the house grew uncomfortably quiet. He and Kelsey drank their tea in silence, each retreating inside their own thoughts.

PART THREE

AGE TO AGE

21

SCANDALOUS PURSUIT

"Thank you for inviting me, Corporal Chilton." Trula stood in the officer's doorway, her eyes lit with a curious gleam. "I trust your investigation is unearthing the rebels' plans?"

"Come in, please, and close the door." Chilton smiled woodenly. "Privacy, madam, is paramount."

Trula complied and closed the door but maintained a cool demeanor as she strolled toward him. She did not wish to sit, so she remained standing and slid her gloved fingers across the back of an upholstered chair. "News?"

"We've yet to locate Keegan. Our sources discovered that he was employed with a printmaker. But our observations may have been discovered. He's vanished. Have you noticed the McBride girl disappearing for long periods of time?"

"No." A disturbed scowl spread across Trula's face. "But I can't follow her around as often as I wish." The entire affair confounded her. "She seems . . ." Trula paused to formulate her answer. "She seems distant now, as though her thoughts are elsewhere. But I've managed to follow her on her jaunts across

Rose Hill, and I haven't noticed her meeting with anyone I don't know. She's nearly always under escort. Caleb Prentice sees to that detail," she said with deepening frustration.

Chilton drew out a roster from his desk. "I've discovered a bit of news I'm certain will interest you," he said dryly.

"Oh?" Trula walked briskly around the chair and seated herself in front of him.

"It seems your first suspicions were accurate. Kelsey Mc-Bride escaped from Norfolk Island."

Trula straightened upon hearing his words. "I knew it!" Fingering her purse, she eagerly retorted, "Arrest her, then."

"Not so hasty, Miss Hill. She's our only link to finding Keegan and Orr." His eyes narrowed. "And you must help us in this matter as well."

"But if she's escaped—"

"She's but a small fish. Chances are, she's most likely all but fulfilled her sentence. Has she indicated anything at all about her escape?"

"No." Trula gazed at the floor. "Only that she's pregnant. That's why she seeks Keegan."

"All the better. She'll be desperate to find the louse, then."

"I *must* tell the Prentices she's escaped from Norfolk. She's been lying to them." Defiance sparked her gaze.

Chilton stiffened. "You do so, and the military will consider your actions an interference with the investigation! Do we have your cooperation or don't we?"

Now she was the victim of his glare. Dissatisfaction with the military's handling of the matter vexed her beyond words, but she composed herself before answering. "You've my full cooperation," she said evenly. "I've trusted you thus far. But have I your word that as soon as Keegan is found, Miss McBride will be arrested? The colonists would not be pleased at your knowingly allowing an escaped convict to roam free, would they, now?"

Without smiling, the corporal chuckled gruffly. "We aren't guided by colonial opinion, Miss Hill. We answer to the Crown."

"But if you can't locate Keegan, you'll have no answers at all."

"We'll find Keegan."

Trula smiled, but her eyes held a hint of contempt. "I needn't bother you any further, Corporal. I'll keep a closer watch on Miss McBride, and if I see anything suspicious, I'll inform you at once." She stood and nodded politely, but the cold tension between them grew evident. Allowing herself out, she strode briskly away from the military office. Outwardly, she held to a diplomatic mien. Inwardly, she roiled at the thought of Caleb being duped by an escaped convict. *That liar cannot roam free!*

As she mounted her papa's carriage and nodded at the driver, she recalled her own helpless sense of anxiety as she had watched Caleb leading Kelsey McBride around the dance floor. However much she had denied her fears to Matthew that night, she remembered how her stomach knotted when the two of them, Caleb and Kelsey, had looked into each other's eyes. Every time his magnificent blue eyes had met Kelsey's, Trula's heart had pounded in fury. How *she* longed for his tender gaze to be directed at her and to hear his voice say her name as affectionately as he appeared to speak Kelsey's. Any pity she had felt for the convict girl was now swept away by malignant hatred. She vowed in silence, *I'll wait briefly, Corporal Chilton.* Then, bitterly she determined, *I'll give you some time to find your Jack Keegan. But then—Caleb Prentice will know the truth!* "He must!" she whispered.

"I can't do this, Jack!" Kelsey stepped around the rubble inside the old homestead. Keegan had thus far hidden inside it for a week. "I've already deceived the Prentices once. I can't bear to take matters any further. I've decided to tell Caleb the truth." She placed the basket of food next to the blankets on the floor.

Keegan crossed his arms, his glare stern. "We've come this far. You can't back out now. The United Irish—"

"I don't care a dribble about the United Irish, Jack. And they care nothing about me. Nor did they ever care about my own mother."

"Hattie McBride was a patriot. Your mother's name is spoken respectfully—"

"Untrue! She was a pawn for your greed and Orr's political ambitions. She died unnecessarily."

"We were all wrongly arrested and sentenced. Can't you see it all clearly now? The Irish must be freed. Can you now abandon your own people, your own child?"

"How can you say that? I've sacrificed my life, my childhood—"

"And within a few short months, we shall all be back where we belong. In Ireland, Kelsey, in Ireland."

"And I want that, Jack. More than life I want to go home."

"Then let me take us both there." Keegan drew closer. Reaching out slowly and carefully, he clasped both hands beneath her slender arms. "I'm no criminal. I'm a victim of war just like you. Like our child." He slid one hand down and placed it against her stomach. Kelsey watched his eyes open with surprise.

"Yes, I'm growing larger. When will you marry me? I should go to Ireland *now*!"

"I'm the father of this life, and my decision stands. First we help our countrymen, then we leave together. It won't be long. I swear on my own life that we'll be home before we know it."

Kelsey battled her own emotions. His words should have encouraged her. The security of having a husband enticed her. Hattie had never been offered such security. But Keegan's motives distressed her. "And then your obligation will be met?"

His face softened upon seeing her troubled gaze. "You want more?"

She nodded back at him without speaking.

"I love you." He slid his arms around her waist.

Kelsey lifted her face. She couldn't help but recall the hostile side of his nature. "Why can't I believe you?"

"Because you don't return my love."

All of her loneliness and confusion welled together in one devouring yearning. She wanted to love and be loved. Carefully she studied his rugged countenance. He was rough but handsome. He was a skilled craftsman. Together . . . together they could build a life in Ireland, couldn't they?

A probing query came into his eyes. "You could grow to love me, yes?"

Without knowing why, she nodded. Then she felt her eyes

moisten as he placed his lips against hers. His kiss was hard and searching. She found his nearness disturbing but not exciting. And not nearly so disturbing as being close to—*I can't allow myself to think such thoughts. Caleb belongs to another. He belongs to Trula and to Australia.* In mute submission, she returned Keegan's kiss almost platonically. Then she slid her fingers up his sinewy arms and placed some distance between them. "I can show you the path to the river, if you're ready now."

Jack pulled her closer, his eyes lit with desire. His lips recaptured hers, more demanding this time. Kelsey knew that to struggle would only ignite him more. She kissed him again without feeling and then lifted her shoulders up and away from his embrace. She dropped her face to hide her discomfiture.

Keegan's face suddenly went grim. "It's Prentice! You love 'im."

Keeping her gaze downward, she shook her head. "No." Then slowly lifting her face, she replied, "Please give me time, Jack. I . . . I don't know that I feel anything at all. Love, hate. It's all the same to me now." She felt him release his grip and saw the dissatisfaction of his gaze. "You understand what I . . . what we've been through, don't you?"

Keegan nodded, but his dark searching eyes showed the tortured dullness of disbelief. "More time, then," he agreed and opened the door to allow her to pass.

Her shoulders tense, Kelsey strode out. Peering cautiously around the ramshackle building, she checked the horizon for signs of anyone who might observe them. Finding no soul upon the landscape, she mounted her horse and allowed Keegan to slide onto the saddle behind her. "How long until you strike?"

"Soon. We're gathering the ammunition now. Some will be delivered here tonight. To remain undetected, we're moving slower than we wish to move."

"Orr knows that the Prentices must be kept safe?"

"He knows and he agrees. I believe he has a fondness for you."

"Orr has a fondness for no one."

"I believe he must have loved your mother at one time."

"She was blind to him. I know that fact for certain."

"He has the means to set us up with property."

231

Kelsey turned to glance back at him and then returned her eyes to the pathway. "How? He's been in prison."

"Aye, but he's a political prisoner and a wealthy man."

Kelsey hesitated while pondering his words. "Then he should save himself and leave."

The two of them rode the remainder of the way in silence.

Caleb squatted in stunned stillness next to the laborer Frank, who had acted as Kelsey's escort and driver. "Thank you for alerting me. But why are they so secretive? Why doesn't she tell us she wishes to meet with Keegan?"

"That I don't know, sir. I think she fears 'im, most likely." Frank peered around the shrubbery that hid them from view. "I can't see her as a zealot—not Miss McBride, sir—if you don't mind me opinion o' the matter."

"But if Keegan's gone into hiding, he must be sought after by the military authorities."

"I'm sure you're right, sir. But I feared that if I questioned the authorities it would give rise to suspicion."

"Good man. We shouldn't involve the military, not yet, anyway. If I discover Kelsey's involved in a rebellion, then I'll report her myself. But until then, I must assume her innocence."

"She's such a meek young lady. An' lovely, at that."

"Don't be fooled by beauty, Frank. It could be the death of you."

"Or the makin's of a happy future."

"You see an Irish emancipist in my future?"

"Don't be layin' no claims to what I knows. I'm no soothsayer." Frank waved his palms outward.

Caleb laughed and then his eyes narrowed as Kelsey and Keegan disappeared into the thicket.

"Do you wish for me to follow them?"

"Yes, but I'll go with you. We can't allow them to know."

"Of course, sir."

"They're headed toward the river. Let's take the south pass. We'll bypass them by a mile." Caleb bolted over the hill's crest behind them and retrieved his stallion, Frank following closely behind. Kelsey may have discovered many of the common paths that most guests followed, but she had yet to know the secret trails that he had traveled since his childhood.

"Mr. Prentice!" a voice called out.

Caleb whirled around and saw a fieldhand riding fast toward him. "Something's wrong?"

"Bushrangers, sir! Beyond the eastern pastures!"

Caleb blew out a frustrated sigh and gazed toward the cluster of trees where Kelsey and Jack Keegan had disappeared. "These bushrangers—they're armed?"

"Shot two o' the shearers." The laborer's countenance fell. "One escaped alive."

"Blast!"

"Your orders, sir?" Frank asked.

"Go with us. We'll need all hands with firearms to meet in the eastern quarter of Rose Hill."

"At once, sir!" The driver whipped his mare and speedily headed for the eastern quarter.

Caleb realized that his worries about Kelsey would have to be laid aside for now. With one man already dead, it would take all their efforts to stop the bushrangers' thievery. He whipped the stallion without further hesitation and rode away in the opposite direction that Kelsey had gone. *Why, Kelsey? Why won't you trust me?*

22

AFTER THE SUNSET

The distant hills before sunset faded to a pale celadon green. An afternoon shower had cooled the air and filled the pastureland with the pungent aroma of earth and grass, a green fragrance that enlivened the senses and reminded the earth's occupants that all was alive and fresh and awash with colors from the Creator's palette. Small white-and-black mounds of sheep stirred across the green land, throwing in texture and sound. And the birds added their lilting song to the pastoral scene.

Kelsey walked her horse slowly. She desired to drink leisurely of the remaining hours of the day and not have them blur past without distinction or shape or line. The closer she drew to the ammunitions site, the more connected she felt to the land and to Rose Hill. But she couldn't define her thoughts as much as she could feel them—the beauty of earth and sky surrounding her, the sense of harmony between God and man. Although dead, George Prentice lived on through his legacy. Basking in the serenity of the moment, Kelsey whispered, "You would be proud, sir, of your seed." Her escort, Frank, had been so caught up in the roundup of bushrangers that he had scarcely bothered with her all day. A maid had informed Kelsey of the band of escaped convicts caught stealing from the flock, and Kelsey couldn't help but admire Caleb's organization in expediting their capture. The fact that one of the laborers had died saddened him. *He has a tender heart*, she thought. And she knew that he and Dwight and the entire Prentice family would see to the care of the dead man's widow, for they never overlooked a single hurting life. *Including my own*, she acknowledged.

Kelsey hoped that the commotion would aid in masking the evening activities she was about to partake in. With the Prentices and their workers occupied with tracking down the bushrangers, she convinced herself that the ammunitions would be stashed without incident. If all their plans prevailed without a confrontation, the location of the rebels' lair would be of no importance. They would come and they would go, with none the wiser.

Arriving at the old homestead, Kelsey tied her horse to a tree and walked inside with a wrapped parcel under her arm. None of the Irish men would arrive until after sunset when Jack returned with them. She settled herself upon the blankets where Jack had been sleeping. Unwrapping the parcel, she set out several food items: some butter, a loaf of yeast bread, fresh fruit, and several generous helpings of smoked meat. Because of the bushranger crisis, not a single family member had assembled for the evening meal, and to her surprise, not even Trula Hill had graced the household with her usual presence. The cooks and servants, glad for the rest, had retired early, giving her ample freedom to prepare a meal for Jack. Now she settled herself against the roughhewn wall and within minutes her eyes grew heavy. Soon drowsiness overtook her, and she fell asleep.

When the sound of voices startled Kelsey awake, she shook the sleep from her eyes. Not knowing how long she had slept, she gazed toward the window and quickly realized that the day had disappeared. She stretched herself and stood to gaze more clearly through the dingy glass.

"This is the place! Take the crates through that door." An

Irish voice rose above the others.

Kelsey stiffened. Even though she had anticipated their arrival, their sudden presence unnerved her. She pressed her back against the wall and waited apprehensively.

The small house, lit only along the roofline by the moon, lay black against black. An unseen observer sat crouched only a few yards from the scene. A hand moved the brush away, and two eyes stared out anxiously at the men. Driven partly by fear and partly by angry curiosity, the bystander listened to the sound of the Irish emancipists, detecting only a few words— *crates . . . ammo . . . gunpowder.*

Kelsey drew her arms about herself. She flinched when the door slammed open against the decaying wall, kicked open by force.

"We need light!" a voice rasped out.

"No torches!" Keegan's voice sounded above the others. "Remember, this is private land. We can't draw attention to ourselves."

"Why isn't Orr here? Where's Orr?"

"Orr knows our every move. I'm in charge tonight. Just do as I say." Keegan stepped into the middle of the musty room, the moonlight following him through the open door. "Kelsey?" he whispered.

Stroking her bottom lip with a trembling fingertip, Kelsey swallowed hard. Stepping away from the wall, she finally answered, "I'm here, Jack."

"Good girl." He turned his face around to regard her.

"I brought you some food."

"Save it. We stopped to eat earlier." He rubbed his jaw.

Confusion welled inside of her. Keegan had insisted upon her meeting him with a ready meal. "Jack, why am I here?"

"You know the land best. Take your horse and ride to the crest of the hill. If you see anyone—"

"I know every soul who lives at Rose Hill. I won't be party to bring any of them harm."

"What about your countrymen?" His voice held a possessive desperation. "You'd rather have the British military pounce on us without warning?"

"No." Kelsey ran her hands slowly up her arms and shook her head. She loathed the British military as much as he. "If I see anyone, I'll try and lure them away."

"Kelsey, you realize that quite soon there will be bloodshed?"

"No, Jack!"

"But not here. Our plans are to execute the revolt elsewhere, not at Rose Hill. You must believe me when I say it. We mean no harm to the emancipists."

"I'll hold you to your word."

"Understood." Jack's voice hardened ruthlessly. "Now, go and mount your horse. We want no observers."

Resentment trickled through Kelsey as she walked out of doors through the mob of surly men. "I can't linger long. Caleb Prentice will send an escort out soon if I don't return to the house," she called out defensively.

"We'll hurry along, miss." An older Irishman tipped his hat toward her.

After securing her mount, she rode slowly away, her eyes scanning the landscape for movement. Finding all quiet, she rode to the hill's crest and waited. In the distance, she could hear the bay of a shepherd's dog. She often wondered how the shepherds survived the solitude of guarding the flocks both night and day. With the quiet settling around her, she sighed and fell to the task of watching for intruders.

Accustomed to the familiar sounds of the sheep ranch, she momentarily ignored the sound of a horse's nicker. Her mind wandering, she allowed her thoughts to drift back to the night she danced with Caleb in the neighbor's barn. Intent on her return to Ireland, she seldom took time for enjoyable moments and scarcely allowed herself to acknowledge that she deserved a moment of joy. But if she dared to admit it, she would have to confess that she had indeed felt a slight exuberance on that night. So embroiled with Jack Keegan, she hadn't until this moment basked in the memory of having enjoyed a moment of

Caleb's undivided attention. A faint smile played around the corners of her mouth.

Realizing her thoughts had traveled far from the task at hand, she glanced around awkwardly. Then a faint nicker caught her ear. *The men had arrived by boat, not by horseback!* She whirled around. Just beyond her, she could see a form moving rapidly from the dense foliage. Tensing, she glanced back and found Keegan and his men too preoccupied to see the figure stealing away. She flicked the reins. "Go!" she ordered barely above a whisper.

The person leaped onto his mount just beyond her. Kelsey galloped toward the fleeing eyewitness to the Irish rebels' activities. She had no weapon and no plan except to determine the identity of the person. Hearing the sound of a whip, she saw the rider gallop away on a steed as swift as the wind.

Kelsey drew her mare to a halt. A sickening realization swirled through her. The diminutive rider, although dressed in mannish attire, had mounted the horse too gracefully for Kelsey's keen eye. *It's a woman!* she determined regretfully. Unwilling to unleash the United Irish onto the woman's tracks, she sat paralyzed, unable to make a suitable decision. *What had she seen?* She worried, although Jack's decision to work without light had been a wise choice. *Why would a woman be out here and dressed so deceptively?* she wondered. Then a dreaded suspicion struck her mind. Obviously the woman had a motive. *Perhaps I've been too careless.* Kelsey had felt so safe and protected in the solitude of Rose Hill. *She followed me! It's . . .* —her heart pounded in her ears—*the woman is Trula Hill!* Kelsey jerked the horse around and raced back toward the ammunitions site.

Trula galloped toward the Prentice home, her cause clear. She now had proof of Kelsey's involvement with the United Irish. Within the hour, she would gladly expose Kelsey's ruse to Caleb and his family. Imagining his reaction, a smug, satisfied smile stretched across her face. Surely he would be indebted to her for saving Rose Hill the embarrassment of a scandal. *Or will he?* His cool demeanor of late had baffled her. Surely his feelings for the girl weren't of serious intent. Confused thoughts roiled in her mind and a new fear surfaced. *What if Caleb confronts her? She could have the entire operations dismantled and moved to another site before sunup.*

A new plan began to smolder in Trula's mind. First, she would personally lead the military to the site and, she furiously determined, *witness for myself the arrest of Kelsey McBride!* Then Caleb Prentice would have no further distraction in regard to their future together.

After an hour's ride, she observed the lantern lights of the house and saw Frank riding toward her. Her clothes soaked with sweat, she composed herself and steered her horse into his path. "Frank?" she called out casually.

"Miss Hill? What on earth?"

"Kelsey and I have gone for a ride."

"Mr. Prentice 'as been worried about the girl. I don't believe 'e knew you was out an' about today, though."

"Oh, he's so busy with his affairs"—Trula struggled to catch her breath—"he scarcely notices me anymore."

"So Miss McBride is—"

"We raced our horses, and"—she turned to look coyly over her shoulder—"it seems I've won, as usual." She smiled prettily, her sardonic gaze hidden by the night.

"Well, I'm glad to know she's been with you. Perhaps I should go and fetch her."

"No, you needn't," Trula spoke confidently. "She's right behind me." Realizing his discomfort in the matter, she sighed and then offered airily, "I'll go and fetch her myself. Be a dear man, will you, and inform Mr. Prentice that we shall be in shortly. Then perhaps he wouldn't mind escorting me home."

Hesitating, Frank tipped his hat. "As you wish, miss."

Satisfied that he had bought her story, Trula disappeared down the road. She calculated that Kelsey would be forced to return soon. She would wait for a few moments and then report to Caleb that Kelsey was boarding her mare and wanted to take a walk alone. That would explain her delay. Knowing how protective Caleb might be of Kelsey, she would feign a headache and beg him to escort her home at once before Kelsey had a chance to return.

Tapping the horse's flank, she made haste for the stables.

Within moments she had removed the English saddle and secured the horse in a paddock. If Caleb escorted her home in one of the family wagons, she could always retrieve her roan mare later. *Papa will have to understand.* Now to strip off the clothing she had borrowed from a young laborer. If Kelsey arrived soon, she wanted no trace of her previous attire present. The more she confused the convict girl, the better her chances for seeing her arrested.

Expertly, she again donned her dress, a lavender linen outfit accented with an ivory fichu. She could slip into the maid's quarters and straighten her hair and wash her face before meeting Caleb. Smoothing her frock, she congratulated herself in whispered tones. Her face beamed with exultation.

Caleb stood gazing out his window toward the distant hills that hid the old homestead from view. "I thought she had slipped away to meet with Keegan again."

"No, sir. Apparently she's taken a ride with Miss Hill. The two of them are just now returning." Frank answered.

"You've spoken with Miss McBride?"

Hesitating awkwardly, Frank shook his head. "No. Only Miss Hill. She says that Miss McBride's followin' up right behind 'er soon, though. They've been racin' their horses."

"Trula's so competitive. She won, of course."

His words preceded by a chuckle, Frank cocked his hat. "Accordin' to Miss Hill, anyway."

His forehead pinched, Caleb pursed his lips speculatively. "I'm rather relieved that my prior suspicions proved incorrect."

"An' I as well, Mr. Prentice. Miss McBride's a right fine lady."

Nodding his affirmation, Caleb couldn't help but agree. "She is. Both she and Miss Hill are fine young women. I'm happy to hear their friendship is maturing."

Frank stared blankly, his mouth twisted to the side.

"Frank?" Trula stood in the doorway.

"Yes, Miss Hill?"

"I'm thirsty."

Well versed in the proper rank and file of servants, Frank crossed his arms stubbornly. "I can fetch you one o' the maids.

But I vow they've all retired for the evening." He retained his affability, but there was a distinct hardening of his eyes.

Trula glanced aloofly and pretended not to understand his look.

"Don't bother," Caleb laughed diplomatically. "I'll escort our guest into the kitchen myself. Surely we haven't fallen into complete helplessness."

With obvious controlled composure, Trula forced her lips to part in a curved, stiff smile. "Good evening, Frank." There was defiance in her tone as well as a subtle challenge.

Caleb grasped her arm and invited her to follow him with his eyes. "I was about to retire myself. You young women are about to give my mother a fright."

"Where is Amelia?"

"I suggested she go on to bed. If all else failed, I knew I could set the hunting dogs on your trail."

Trula laughed. "Please accept my apologies for my . . . indiscretion. But I *have* promised to be more pleasant to your guest. You cannot fault my efforts, true?"

"As a matter of fact, I'm impressed. You're growing as fond of Kelsey as my sister, Katy, has. She's really quite interesting, if given the chance to be."

From lowered lids, Trula glanced sideways toward him and then straight ahead. Lifting her hand, she pressed it against her forehead. Allowing a faint moan to escape her lips, she stopped and leaned against the wall.

"What's wrong?"

"My head." She lifted her long lashes, a childlike gaze dimpling her face. "I'm embarrassed to say, but I'm afraid I've overdone it today. My head hurts so badly, Caleb."

"I'll fetch Frank at once." Caleb started to turn but felt her firm grip upon his forearm. He turned to face her.

"Why won't you take me home? I want you, not *Frank*." She said the driver's name with contempt.

He chuckled quietly. "Why don't you like our driver?"

"I don't like or dislike the man. But you never see me home anymore. Since the Irish girl arrived, I've become like a forgotten trinket to you."

"I apologize." The sincerity of his gaze melted the hardness from her face. "After today's capture of those outlaws, I'm just

. . . I'm . . . well . . ." He paused, resolve filling his gaze. "You're right, of course. I suppose I owe you an apology."

Lifting her face closer to his, she answered softly, "Accepted."

He felt the eager affection coming from her. "Oh, who needs rest? I'll take you home myself."

"And for that you'll receive"—she stroked her finger across his strong jawline—"my undying gratitude."

Fetching his hat, Caleb did trouble a disgruntled and weary Frank to hitch the wagon. But within a few minutes, they had pulled away from the house. Before they had a chance to reach the main gate, he heard a horse galloping toward them. "Trula, I thought you told me that Kelsey had already boarded her horse in the stable?"

Straightening at once, Trula answered evenly. "Obviously the girl's gone out again. Here she comes through the gate."

Lifting his face to call out, Caleb heard Trula quietly plead for his attention. "Caleb? Please don't mention the race. I'm afraid I may have offended Kelsey. I don't want her to know I've told you anything about tonight."

"Surely she wouldn't concern herself over such trivial matters?"

"She might. I'm getting to know her better. Promise you won't mention our ride together?"

"If you're certain?"

"I am. Thank you." Trula composed her welcome. "Good evening, Kelsey. We'd begun to think you'd gotten lost."

Kelsey slowed her mare to a trot.

"Good evening! You must be famished," Caleb said.

Carefully choosing her words, Kelsey reined her horse to a halt. Glancing suspiciously at Trula, she gazed back at Caleb and shook her head. "No. I had dinner before my ride. You were all so busy with the convict capture and all, I didn't want to bother you."

"Glad to hear you're safe and sound then." Caleb's voice trailed off as he whipped the steed. "I'm driving Miss Hill home. I'll see you at breakfast in the morning, I trust?"

Kelsey nodded warily. "Certainly. I'll see you then."

Trula smiled innocently up at her and smoothed her lavender skirt. "Can't wait to change out of this dress. Quite fashionable, but much too hot for Australia." She waved a polite farewell to Kelsey.

Caleb guided the wagon out of the gate and headed down the road. He failed to see the women lock anxious eyes before disappearing from each other's sight.

23

THE FUGITIVE

Kelsey tossed back and forth in her bed. Assisting Keegan and the others with the supplies had left her too exhausted to think. She had reluctantly informed them of the intruder, and Keegan and his men had searched the grounds and found no visible signs of an observer. But the darkness of night impeded their investigation, and time demanded that they make a decision. Kelsey had returned to the Prentice home to discover whether Trula had indeed followed her to the old homestead.

Her conclusions had confounded and nagged her worriedly. After finding Trula being innocently escorted by Caleb, she chastened herself for believing Trula had spied on the rebels' activities. Studying Caleb's calm demeanor had allayed her fears that he had been alerted. *He didn't know, did he?* She had come to know him better in the past few weeks, she tried to assure herself. His candid mannerisms had led her to believe that he left no matter to consequence. Surely he would've confronted her if Trula had been the one she saw.

Looking around the room, Kelsey observed furniture and

objects slowly becoming more distinct as the dawn prepared to manifest itself. Sliding quickly from the bed, she stood at the window. Soon morning would overtake Rose Hill, and as the day revealed the world, perhaps it would also reveal that she had seen no one at all. *Maybe I imagined it all.* Glimpsing into the mirror, she sighed. *I look a fright.* Having collapsed on her bed the night before, she hadn't bothered to brush out her hair or change her clothing.

She stretched out her exhausted limbs and made her decision. Before dawn, only the housemaids and cooks would be stirring. She would ask if any had yet drawn water and, if so, she could bathe and dress before the others awoke.

She slipped down the staircase and into the kitchen. Within minutes, a maid with a steaming pot of hot water led her to a privately situated washtub near the barn, handed her some linens, and left her to bathe. Tossing aside her soiled clothing, Kelsey felt her muscles begin to relax as she slid into the tub. Knowing that tarrying too long could attract unwanted visitors from around the ranch, she finished washing up, stepped from the tub, and dried herself. Donning a fresh white cotton underdress and an overdress of straw yellow, along with her black slippers, she made haste to gather the linens and soiled frock into one arm.

She rushed around the corner of the barn, busily buttoning the front bodice of her dress. Hearing men's voices approaching, she stopped and modestly examined her dress. She heard two young shearers muttering between themselves. "Look! Me trousers thrown over that mare's stall."

"Wot's that?"

"Me best trousers!"

"So? Why'd you leave 'em here?"

"Not me. I loaned 'em out. Shouldn't 'ave done it, I know."

"Tell the bloke to find 'is own trousers, that's wot!"

The young man chuckled. "Not likely. Not wif those two pretty eyes begging for 'em."

"Are you daft?"

"No, mate. It was no bloke. It were Mr. Prentice's lady friend, Miss Hill 'erself, wot asked fer 'em."

"Go on!"

"It's true. I saw 'er leave wearin' 'em meself."

"It's come to this now?"

"Said she wasn't dressed to ride, so I gave 'em to 'er."

Kelsey waited for the men to leave. A sickening realization flooded her mind. *Trula! It was Trula!* She marched deliberately into the barn and found Trula's mare in the farthest paddock. Frank had greeted her when she arrived and offered to wipe down and put away the horse she rode. So weary, she had accepted his offer and had never thought to enter the horses' stalls. Trula had appeared so calm. But Kelsey couldn't blame her. *It's all my fault. The treachery is all mine. I never should've agreed to Jack's plan.* The fear that Caleb now knew seized her, and she ran from the paddock toward the house. *I'll confess to him now. Surely, he'll not turn me over to the authorities.* Before running in through the rear servants' entrance, she stopped to smooth her hair and tug on her ever tightening waistline. She had to remain calm and collect her thoughts. Once she revealed the rebels' plot, she realized that all hopes for returning to Kildare would be lost. She hesitated. Caleb would have no choice but to report the planned uprising to the military authorities. Jack would be furious. But her own plans had to remain secondary. More than Kildare now, she desired the trust of the Prentice family. *Oh, please don't hate me.* Taking a deep breath, she stepped through the rear entrance.

The maids stood at their stations, faces down, tending to their morning preparations. Kelsey walked past them but noticed an uneasiness in their manner. She lifted her hand to twist the kitchen door latch, but a soft voice stopped her. "I wouldn't go in there, Miss McBride."

Kelsey whirled around to face the young maid who had assisted with her bath. "What's wrong? Something's happened?" A flicker of apprehension coursed through her.

"I don't rightly know all the details, miss. But Mr. Prentice is in the parlor with a roomful of the military."

Nodding her affirmation that she understood, she struggled to speak. In her heart, she had known this would happen. Caleb did know and he had alerted the authorities. Her voice shaken, she forced a polite reply. "I . . . thank you for warning me. I wouldn't want to interrupt their business affairs." Disappointment and panic swirled through her. She was ashamed at having taken advantage of Caleb's trusting nature. She couldn't hate him for his actions, but somehow she couldn't control her mind's accusations. *If only he had come to me—* She stopped. *No. It was I who should've trusted him.* She struggled with her tumultuous emotions. She had to act decisively. Within moments, she would be arrested. *They'll send me back to Norfolk!* She couldn't bear the thought of it. Stifling a sob, she tore from the kitchen out the back and into the wide open spaces of the farmyard. If she rode out to warn Keegan and the others, perhaps he could hide her. After all, it wasn't she who had informed on the rebels, it was Trula Hill. She made haste for the paddock to secure a mount, glancing fearfully behind herself the entire way.

Caleb paced in front of Corporal Chilton, who stood flanked by six armed privates. "So am I to understand that Rose Hill is being used as an ammunitions store for the United Irish?"

"We've yet to explore your land, as I've already informed you, Mr. Prentice."

Dwight and Katy bustled into the parlor, having just been awakened by a timorous maid. "Caleb? What's wrong?" Dwight looked worried.

"Mr. Farrell," Chilton explained gravely, "we feel that your houseguest, Miss Kelsey McBride, may be aiding the United Irish rebels."

Caleb prompted, "They want to examine Papa's old homestead. They say that it's being used as an ammunitions storage." He spoke evenly, although his brow was pinched with anxiety.

"Not Kelsey." Katy's voice adamant, she shook her head. "She wouldn't do that to us."

"Where is Miss McBride?" the corporal persisted.

"I suppose she's still asleep in her bed." Katy tried to sound optimistic. "I'll fetch her." She departed quickly.

Caleb slanted a look at Trula, who had seated herself confidently in a tapestried parlor chair. "You're certain, Trula, that you saw ammunition being hidden inside the old house?" The unwelcome tension stretched ever tighter between them.

"I'll take you there myself." Trula gazed up at him with penetrating eyes.

"No need." Caleb held up his palm, his jaw taut. "I'll conduct Corporal Chilton and his men there. I want to see for myself. But first, I want to speak with Kelsey. Surely she can explain."

Trula stood quickly, her frustration piqued. "Caleb, when will you learn? Kelsey McBride is not one of us. She's a rebel like her despicable friend, Keegan."

His anger at Trula's entanglement in the matter kindled, he glared at her but directed his conversation back to the corporal. "Firstly, why would the Irish be storing ammunitions?"

"That's why we're concerned. If armed, it could spur them into an attack on the British military or worse yet, the colonists."

"They'd be destroyed!" Caleb's tone incredulous, he lifted his face in disbelief.

"But would cause much damage in the course of things." Chilton turned to face Katy, who bustled into the room.

"Dwight? Kelsey's not in her room! The maid said she bathed early and left on horseback."

"Could she possibly know that we've found her out?" Chilton tensed at the thought.

"How could she? I've only been informed this very instant." Caleb walked quickly to gaze out of the window. "I suppose we'd best make haste. Frank?" he called out forcefully.

The footman scrambled into the room. "Mr. Prentice?"

"Make ready three of our best horses."

"I'm going as well," Trula insisted.

"No. You'll stay here with Katy. If Kelsey appears, detain her until we return."

Katy firmly grasped Trula's forearm. Arching an eyebrow, she nodded. "We'll stay."

Pulling away from Katy, Trula followed Caleb from the room. When they had gone up the staircase, she stopped him in the dimly lit hallway. "You're angry with me."

"Why shouldn't I be?"

"I've saved you and your family a great deal of pain, at least by my estimation!"

"Your estimation is distorted by your own selfishness."

"You're blaming me for *her* wrongdoing!"

"You should've come to me first. Not the military!"

"You wouldn't have listened! I wanted to prove it to you. Can't you see?"

"See? I've known all along of Kelsey's involvement and her secret meetings with Keegan."

"You knew?" The color drained from her face.

"Now your interference has ruined any chances for us to help her. Those beasts will ship her off to Norfolk again."

"And well they should!" Defensiveness welled in her face. "She's a criminal." She slid her fingers about his wrists, her eyes pleading. "Please don't be angry with me, Caleb. Can't you see I'm trying to protect you?"

"I don't need your kind of *protection*. But I can see clearly now that Kelsey McBride's in desperate need of protection from you!"

"How can you say that? You're blinded!"

"I'll agree that I've *been* blinded."

She shriveled at his expression.

"But now I know the truth. Your jealousy's driven you too far, Trula." He spoke calmly, with no lighting of his eyes, no tender smile. "When I return, I want you gone from Rose Hill."

"You don't mean it!"

"If you'll excuse me . . ." He attempted to pull away from her desperate grasp, but Trula refused to release his arms. Firmly, he lifted his arms in front of her, no longer moved by her tears. Without another word, he studied her piteously.

Overcome by sobs, Trula released him and turned away to disappear alone into Katy's bedroom.

Caleb spent the next quarter hour preparing some fresh water for the ride and quickly consuming the breakfast prepared by an oddly silent staff. The food seemed tasteless to him, so he numbly departed the dining area saying nothing to Dwight and Katy, his disappointment in the entire affair evident.

Dwight followed him out to where Frank had reined their mounts. "Caleb?"

"I'm sorry if this has embarrassed you all."

"We're not embarrassed. We aren't certain it's true, are we?"

Caleb confessed, "I've been following Kelsey out to the old house." He kept his voice low, not wishing for one of the military guards to hear. "She's been meeting Keegan for several weeks."

"Why didn't you tell me?"

"I saw no ammunitions, I swear. I've waited for a chance to confront Kelsey before she got herself into trouble. But I see now I've waited too long."

"So you believe Trula's story."

"As much as I hate to admit it."

"You don't have to ride with us. Why don't you remain here?"

"No. If she must be confronted, then I'll do it myself." Seeing the military guard circling to leave, he lifted his heel into the stirrup and mounted at once. Dwight followed immediately behind. Securing his musket inside his leather pouch, he rode to the head of the search party and waved his arm for all to come after him. The early dawn warming their backs, they departed for Papa's old homestead.

24

BEFORE THE SIEGE

The soldiers gathered quietly at the crest of the hill that overlooked the old house. Peering intently down at the abandoned building, they soon realized that a closer look on foot would be necessary. Caleb glanced back at their horses reined several yards away under Frank's careful watch. Then he nodded at the corporal that he would be the first to go ahead. Intent to keep Kelsey from harm, he had insisted upon leading the search party into the house.

"Please stay until I signal for you," he requested of the corporal. Keeping himself low to the ground, he crept around the dense shrubbery that surrounded the house. His fond memories of the place now clouded by its present ill use, he pressed his lips together and determined to forge ahead. Within minutes he lay a few feet from the back doorway. He could see the door that once hung loosely had now been propped up against the frame to block the exit.

With stealth, he secured his musket at his side and made his way to the tall grass beneath a partly broken window. Seeing a military hat rise just above the hill's crest, he turned quickly and propped himself upon his knees. Hearing no voices, he stared inside the house and, much to his furtive relief, found it completely empty.

The Irish rebel boats floated silently away from the Rose Hill billabong. When Kelsey had arrived with her distressful news, the men who had stayed and made their beds inside the old house had scrambled to remove all evidence of their arrival. Even the horse ridden by Kelsey galloped not far behind the flotilla, mounted by one of the rebels. In their eyes, Kelsey had salvaged the rebellion. But in her own eyes, she loathed her part now more than ever before. Now she would be forced to follow them into an attack against the British. Her only solace lay in knowing the attack would not be fomented from Rose Hill.

"Jack," she whispered.

"Hmm?" Keegan's eyelids fluttered. Exhausted from the morning's frantic retreat, he had leaned against the stern and rested his eyes. "What is it?" he answered gruffly.

"Why can't we leave right now for Ireland?"

"What? A mutiny?" He laughed but didn't smile.

"We've helped them, haven't we? Now we should concern ourselves with the well-being of our unborn child."

"Patience." His mouth curved in a smile. "There's a boat leaving in a few days for Ireland."

Kelsey felt her throat tighten, although the news didn't gladden her as she had supposed it would.

"We'll have to work fast to muster our forces, but Orr feels he'll be calling the strike at any time now. It's believed we'll convey our men to Castle Hill settlement. It's not guarded as well. We can overtake the military easily and seize their weapons to add to our own supplies."

"Boat ahead, Mr. Keegan." An oarsman peered anxiously.

Keegan sat up immediately and then settled himself down again. "It's one of our own." He waved a torn shirt to flag the man.

Kelsey glanced at the approaching boat and then turned her

eyes again on Keegan. "You'll hide me, then? I'm no use in battle."

"I'll see if Orr will make arrangements. I can't be bothered now. Leave me to my tasks! I've much to decide." He shoved her away roughly.

Catching herself on the rim, she glared at him, visibly shaken. "I've risked everything for you, Jack Keegan." She held her own. *If only you knew*, she thought regretfully.

"Mr. Keegan?" The approaching boatman called out.

"You've news, I trust."

"I do at that, sir. William Orr's sent you a message." Keegan's boatmen pulled aside the other boat. One reached out and grasped the envelope in the messenger's hand. Anxiously, Keegan ripped away the seal and snapped open Orr's quickly scrawled letter. *Strike tonight. Castle Hill. On to Parrametta to muster forces. March on Sydney. Password is St. Peter. William Orr.*

His dark eyes glistening with pleasure, Keegan read the letter thrice and then shredded it into minuscule pieces. "Now hear this!" He stood rigidly in the boat, his back erect. "We strike tonight!"

The Irishmen cheered. "First we'll march on Castle Hill and take the military by surprise. Seize all the weapons you can marshal. We'll then proceed to Parrametta where we'll garner all the Irish convicts into our troops and arm them."

"Parrametta? But what of the settlers?" Kelsey desperately attempted to interject.

"Kill anyone that stands in your way!"

"No, Jack! Don't!" Kelsey called out, trying to make herself heard above the noise of the men's gleeful cheers.

"Once we've freed all the Irish convicts and gathered the emancipists, we'll march on to Sydney!"

Her face colorless, she leaned against the boat's rim. Added to her fear was a horrifying feeling of guilt. She regretted that she had fled to save her own life. For now it meant risking the lives of the Parrametta colonists. *Somehow, I must warn them. I must escape from Keegan and find Caleb.*

The boats meandered down through the settlement of Parrametta and onward toward Castle Hill. It occurred to Kelsey that today was Sunday. She would normally have dressed and accompanied the Prentices to Reverend Whitley's church for a morning service. She wondered if in lieu of dressing for church, they instead searched Rose Hill for her whereabouts. The thought sickened her.

Her disappearance could never be explained away. Facing Caleb now, she would be forced to divulge all the truth if she hoped to aid in smothering the rebellion's flames. Caleb's trust in her would cease, but at least no blood would be upon her shoulders.

"As we muster the Irish emancipists, our password is *St. Peter*." Keegan aptly informed his men, who passed it on to the rebels on the other boats.

"We're nearing a bridge, Jack." Kelsey sat forward. "Allow me off and I'll catch a ride to Sydney Harbor."

"For what purpose?" Keegan asked warily.

"I'll need to secure our passage. Once you've marched on Sydney, then we'll need to make our escape to Ireland. We can hide out until the ship departs." She chose her words carefully in hopes that she would appear completely sincere.

"You wish to travel alone to Sydney Harbor?"

"As I said, I'll secure a ride with a settler. I know many of them, and—"

"Shut up!" Grabbing her collar, he yanked her close. "You'll be taken where I say. You must think me a fool!"

"You're hurting me!" Her eyes moistened but she refused to cry.

"You think I don't know that you'll return to Prentice and warn him?"

"Please, Jack!"

"If I didn't know better, I'd say you care for him more than you do me." He pushed her away. "Am I right?"

"All right!" Kelsey felt her blood pulsing. "I admit it! I *do* care for Caleb Prentice. He's befriended me and asked nothing of me in return. And his family are all nothing but honest people—people of faith and of kind deeds. All traits that completely escape *your kind*, Jack Keegan."

"Now the truth is known, lassie," he said between clenched teeth. "Now you're telling the truth to ol' Jack." He shot forward and growled, "MacPherson! We'll meet the horseman at the bridge. See that Miss McBride is taken into . . . *safekeeping*, shall we say?"

"No! I won't go!"

"You've no choice."

Kelsey saw the mare she had ridden earlier gallop toward the bridge with the rebel rider astride it. Now her earlier means of escape would become her present mode of entrapment.

Keegan directed his men to steer the boat to shore beneath the bridge. Kelsey gripped her fingers tightly against the boat seat, her knuckles white. *God—Amelia's God—please help me. I'm in trouble—again!*

Caleb, glancing carefully around, stepped cautiously into the old homestead. He stuck his head back out through the doorway and motioned for the others to proceed toward the site. Before the others joined him, he stepped around the room he once called home. The morning sunlight streaked in through the window's broken glass, veiled with the dust of his family's history. The rotting twigs that had fallen from the wattle-and-daub roof lay crushed around the floor. Larger pieces of wood had been kicked aside to make way for whatever had been stored here. But without any signs of ammunition or supplies in the room, Colonel Chilton would be none the wiser. The more time he could buy for Kelsey, the greater his chance for one last attempt to try to reason with her. But if the military's suspicions about an uprising proved accurate, then he could not delay. He heard the men's voices, the sound of their boots tromping onto the porch. Turning around, his own boot kicked a hard, round object that skittered across the floor. *Musket fire!* He walked quickly to retrieve the telltale sign. With one fluid motion, he bent and scooped up the musket ball into his hand and stuffed it inside his trousers pocket.

"Kerns, you take two men and search the foliage!" Chilton barked. "Holtz and the rest of you, come inside with me!"

Caleb crossed his arms at his waist. "I'm sorry to say, Corporal, that you've made a needless journey."

"No supplies?" Chilton's eyes scanned the empty room. "Mr. Farrell?"

Dwight followed the officer into the room, his face reflecting the same relief as Caleb's. "Yes, Corporal."

"You know this property." He bent to grasp a freshly broken twig with his gloved hand. Holding it up to Dwight, he asked somberly, "Has anyone, a laborer perhaps, had any business in here? Or does the room appear to have been tampered with?" Examining the twig, Dwight sighed, his lips pursed speculatively. "It's hard to say, I—"

Caleb stood with his hands clasped casually behind him. Arching one brow, he widened his eyes and gestured by slowly shaking his head.

"No." Dwight caught his meaning. "We have laborers milling about the entire property. But I see no gunpowder traces or a single splinter from crates being moved."

"I've made the same assumption, Dwight," Caleb agreed at once. "I'm afraid our dear Miss Hill is a bit *excitable* at times. If I'd known of her involving you, why—"

"Don't say?" Chilton rubbed his chin with his finger and thumb. "But she's made several visits to my office the past few weeks." He eyed them both suspiciously. "She seemed quite precise and specific in her explanations, not excitable at all."

The realization of Trula's detailed involvement ignited Caleb's temper, but he held his words. Pausing, he inhaled deeply and countered with, "You've not seen the manipulative side of this young lady, then. She's quite biased regarding emancipists. It would please her greatly if every emancipist in the colony were loaded up and shipped off to Norfolk."

Chilton shot his eyes sideways. "So, you believe that Miss McBride is an emancipist?"

Caleb studied the officer's skeptical face. "I happen to know that she's an emancipist, sir. I've known the girl since we were children."

"Then you don't know all there is to know of her," Chilton said complacently. "Kelsey McBride escaped from Norfolk Island. She stowed away on a transport and then stole a johnboat to escape the harbor authorities at Sydney. She's a fugitive wanted for escaping prison and now for aiding in an insurgency against the British government!"

Caleb and Dwight exchanged a worried gaze. "If that's true,"

Caleb asked cautiously, "then why haven't you already arrested her?"

He commented as if the answer were obvious. "We've waited to catch a bigger fish."

"You feel Kelsey's involved with the United Irish?"

"I *know* she is."

"Corporal Chilton!" A private bolted through the doorway, breathless.

"Private?"

"We found tracks—men's tracks. They lead to the river."

"They're traveling by boat." Chilton turned to politely acknowledge Dwight and Caleb. "If you'll excuse us, gentlemen."

Caleb nodded but struggled to formulate a reply. The military men clambered out of the room, leaving Dwight and him alone.

Dwight waited until Chilton and his men had ridden quickly away from the site. "Caleb, you realize—"

"I know. She deceived me. Admittedly, she's made no secret of her desire to return to Kildare, but I didn't want to believe she would aid the rebels. Not Kelsey."

"I suppose she'll be arrested soon." Dwight stared at the floor.

The two of them stood in solitary silence, their thoughts roiling.

"If you could only speak to her . . ." Dwight hesitated, his eyes gazing up, tentative.

Caleb sighed. Ruminating without reply, he stroked his chin, deep in thought.

"Perhaps she would allow us to help her out of this situation."

"She's a criminal." Caleb's comment surprised even himself, sounding forced and without emotion. A pained resignation spread across his countenance. His shoulders relaxed and he lifted his face to return Dwight's pointed stare. "What do you expect me to do?"

"Go to her, Caleb. At least give her a chance to present her intent. She cares about you, I believe."

"Why do you say that?"

"Can't you see it when she looks at you? Don't tell me you feel nothing for her?"

"We've always been friends."

"Friends always make the best life's mates, the best lovers."

"She doesn't love me. She loves Keegan."

"I don't believe it and neither do you."

"I'll not make a fool of myself, Dwight."

"You'll feel a bigger fool if you don't intervene. Kelsey's in danger. And what of her child?"

"Keegan's child. He'll see she's taken care of, no doubt." Caleb blanched at his own words. He meant none of what he said. Keegan had never proven worthy of Kelsey. The harder he tried to ignore the truth the more it persisted. "I agree I should at least investigate the matter to be certain she's safe."

"I'll go with you." Dwight smiled.

"We should inform Katy."

"I'll send Frank." Dwight glanced out the window and saw Frank tending to their horses. "But he's not to inform Trula Hill of anything."

"Agreed." Caleb paused, a shadow of pain darkening his face. "How blind I've been," he whispered mostly to himself. "And selfish."

"How so?"

"Kelsey's had many questions regarding our faith. I've shown her so little personal conviction."

Dwight nodded.

"I've many matters to correct." Caleb straightened his hat and pulled his gloves from his coat pocket. "Let's go!"

He ran quickly from the old homestead, his heart pounding half in anticipation, half in dread.

25

THE UPRISING

Stepping onto the bridge, Kelsey stared down at Keegan and the others. The sunset beyond the river reflected blood red in the waters that flowed around the johnboats. "Please don't do this, Jack." Her eyes narrowed as a strange pity swept through her. She almost felt sorry for him. "You could stop it all now."

"Take her out of here, out of sight." Keegan waved her away with his hand. "Hide her away until we've marched on Sydney."

"At least allow me to warn the Prentices—"

"Shut up!" Keegan shouted. "Set a guard on her. She can't be trusted."

"You'll be killed, Jack, you and all these men—"

"I told you to shut up!"

Kelsey felt herself roughly shoved from behind. She stumbled sideways and reached out to grab the bridge railing for support. Straightening immediately, she saw the rebel who acted on Keegan's commands. She turned away to walk toward the rider standing next to the stolen horse. Without another note of protest, she allowed him to hoist her up onto the back of the saddle. Waiting for him to mount in front of her, she turned her face away from Keegan.

Taking his place again in the boat's aft, Keegan glanced up at her. Seeing her turn away in insolent defiance, his face hardened. "Griggs." His voice a whisper, he lifted his face conspiratorially.

"Aye, Mr. Keegan," Griggs responded.

"When we march on Parrametta—"

"Sir?"

"You'll see the Prentice property is duly pillaged?"

"The land we just departed, sir?"

"One and the same. And, Griggs—"

"Aye, sir?"

"Leave no survivors at Rose Hill."

"As you wish, sir."

"We'll cut through the northern pass." Caleb gestured in the direction and nodded anxiously at Dwight.

"Let's hurry! If Chilton and his men find them first, Kelsey's without hope." Dwight whipped his horse and tore past Caleb.

Caleb followed fast behind. Driving hard into a narrow thicket, he felt the foliage whir past him, blurring and swirling much the same as his confused thoughts. His conversation with Dwight nagged at him. Dwight had never interfered in his past relationships, a fact that nurtured great respect between them. Although Dwight and Katy knew of his affection for Trula Hill, neither had tried to force the relationship. Even after Trula's father had approached Dwight at the party, demanding to know of Caleb's intentions regarding Trula, Dwight had merely mentioned the matter to him. But he hadn't insisted upon an answer. Struggling with his doubts about Trula, Caleb gratefully hadn't fallen into a decision that might have entrapped him.

But now he struggled with the new question that Dwight had posed. *Have I feelings for Kelsey?* True, he had caught himself reveling in her beauty on more than one occasion. And he couldn't help but stop outside her closed door each evening.

Only hesitating for a moment, he enjoyed the perfume that lingered outside her room. But yet, at times, he found it torturous, as though she had purposely left behind the fragrant trail to taunt him. She had never given him the slightest indication that she felt anything other than friendship for him. Opportunities had been available. They had eaten nearly every meal together for the past few months. They had enjoyed evenings on the verandah with his family. He recalled their lively conversations and his secret disappointment in how, too quickly, they ended each evening. He at least had to admit to how dearly he loved her company.

What about the dance? He had recalled the evening on numerous occasions. It was all so visual in his mind. She had moved fluidly in graceful concert within his embrace. She had spoken openly that evening, blushing beautifully when his gaze traveled over her face and searched her eyes. In that brief moment, he *had* detected a spark in her eyes. *I'm sure of it!* The tempo of the music had accelerated enough that he seized the need to tighten his grip on her hand and waist. Kelsey hadn't pulled away. Instead, she relaxed and smiled warmly up at him. That's when his heart had melted. That's when the platonic friendship of their childhood had leapt into a higher realm— *dear Lord!*

"Look ahead!" Dwight called over his shoulder and held up his hand.

Caleb, caught up in his thoughts, nearly plowed into Dwight, but he yanked back on the reins when he suddenly saw the steed halting ahead of him.

"We're nearly to the river. Look! There's been a rider through here."

"More than one?" Caleb pulled his horse up aside Dwight's.

"No. The military party's not been through here yet. But the tracks are fresh. It could be Kelsey's horse."

Caleb's heart raced. He brought the whip around, stinging the stallion's flank. The horse whinnied its protest, reared its gleaming black head, and then lunged down the pathway toward the river. Caleb didn't even bother to look back and ascertain that Dwight charged close behind. Now driven by his emotions, he had but one thought—*I must find you, Kelsey, and tell you . . ."*

Kelsey leaned against the rider. She could feel the horse's flanks heave beneath her. Griggs wouldn't answer her when she asked their destination. But she could tell as he wound the mare in and about the trees that lined the river that their journey was no different than that of Jack Keegan's. *We're headed for Castle Hill!* She pressed her cheek against the man's leather coat and closed her eyes, her mind tossing with dread. She wanted nothing to do with the uprising. She wanted nothing to do with Keegan. She only wanted to return to Rose Hill and warn the Prentices and the neighboring settlers of the Irish invasion that would soon be upon them. She moaned and a single tear fell from her eye, but it was dashed into the wind.

The rider drove the horse nearer and nearer to the Castle Hill settlement. Kelsey knew that many Irish had been incarcerated in the Castle Hill prison colony. But many squatters had settled around the colony with their families as well. She couldn't bear the thought of bloodshed. *So many innocent—* Helplessness washed through her. She had been useless both to herself and to those who had cared about her. Caleb surely hated her by now. She felt the driver stiffen. He reined the mare down to the river once again. Without hesitation, he pulled his musket from the holster and said gruffly, "Need to water the horse. You get down first."

Sighing, Kelsey complied. Holding tightly to the rear of the saddle, she slid from the horse's flanks and landed awkwardly on the grassy shore. She stepped back when he aimed the weapon toward her. "Don't try nothing, now, or you'll get some of this!" he threatened.

She shook her head, her eyes wide with worry. "I wouldn't risk the life of my child." She placed her arms around her stomach.

"Keegan didn't say you was with child."

"It's his child I carry."

"Don't say." The rebel showed no emotion. "Stand here." He pointed toward the shore's edge with the musket's tip. "You get yourself a drink, now, lass. We've not much farther to go."

Kelsey turned to face the rushing water. Seeing the tumbling foam, she wished she could fall into it and be swept away.

But her captor would surely kill her for trying it. She knelt and allowed the water to swirl into her hands. Quickly quenching her thirst, she stood and faced the rebel again. "At least tell me where you're taking me."

"You'll be kept at an emancipist's shanty until we've overtaken the British in Sydney."

"You'll surely die."

"Keegan's right. You talk too much."

"The British military are trained. You're raising up a pathetic group of men who are weakened from imprisonment. Most are half-starved."

"It's not our might, it's our will that drives us. You're Irish. You should know. . . ."

Kelsey stared at the bank while he ranted about the Irishman's will. Her eye detected a small grass snake gliding through the tall grass. Appearing harmless, it gave rise to an idea, however foolish it might seem later. She gasped, her eyes wide, feigning fear.

"What? What do you see?"

"Look there! A hideous snake! It'll spook the horse!" She took several steps away.

"Don't you move!" He trained the gun on her, but as if on command, the mare nickered nervously and bobbed its head.

"I'm not lying. See?" She pointed to where the snake moved, bending the tall grasses around it.

The rebel whirled around and aimed his musket toward the grassy fronds. "Yah!" he shouted while snapping the trigger. The musket fired and the water exploded around the horse's head. He ran to yank the reins before the horse could rear up in fright. Calming the mare, he quickly glanced toward the bank and saw the small snake slither into the water. He grunted. "Harmless! You females are too easily spooked." The air, quiet and still except for the sound of the rushing water, suddenly seemed too quiet. He snapped around, anxiously scanning the thicket of trees just beyond him. "She's gone!" He cursed furiously. "She's gone!"

Not believing the man had fallen for her ploy, Kelsey ran

blindly into the wooded glen, the branches tearing at her face and clothes. Her foot slipped into a rut and she tumbled over a berm and down an embankment. She could hear the angry rebel ranting in the distance. On horseback, he would be upon her quickly. Not knowing which way to run, she bolted ahead, panic rioting within her. Suddenly realizing that the density of the thicket no longer hid her, she ran into an open field of tall grasses. Finding a thick cluster, she dove beneath it and waited fearfully. She breathed in short, shallow gasps. Without warning, she heard the rider approach, the horse galloping madly. She choked back a terrified cry and hid her face in the grass. This time he would surely kill her, if from nothing else but sheer anger. The ground pounded beneath her, but she dared not look up. Fully expecting to hear the sound of musket exploding, she tensed as if a hand had closed around her throat.

"Where is she?" Caleb lay on his stomach, peering out from a bramble of underbrush.

"I see men. But no Kelsey." Dwight gazed down upon the flotilla that glided past, oblivious to their presence.

"But if she's not with them . . ." Caleb paused. A new fear seized him. "What have they done with her?"

"Perhaps we've been wrong all along. She may be gone. What if she's gone to Ireland?"

The question was a stab in his heart. "I can't believe she'd leave without telling us. Not Kelsey."

"Certainly there's no sign of her here."

"She's in danger, Dwight. We've got to find her!"

"Calm yourself." Dwight curled his gloved hand around Caleb's wrist but kept a steady gaze on the flotilla. "Where next? You say the word and we'll go, dear brother. But as for direction, I am at a loss."

Caleb drew up his fists and lay his forehead against them. He felt a terrible tenseness seize his body. His eyes tightly closed, he breathed a quick, silent prayer. *I'm the most selfish human on earth. God, I'm sorry. Please . . . please help me find Kelsey. Keep her from harm, please!* He felt Dwight's hand grip his shoulder. He turned to face him. "We must pray, Dwight."

Dwight nodded. "Let's do it now."

Again closing his eyes, Caleb silently affirmed what he had needed to affirm for some time. *I can't do it myself, dear Lord. My mother's faith alone cannot sustain me. I need you, Christ Jesus, to live in me as you live in her. Help me now . . . be my Guide.*

"Help us, dear God. We're lost without you." Dwight lifted his face. "Amen."

Caleb uncurled his hands, but his eyes remained closed. He had to be certain he had connected with his Creator.

"Ready now?" Dwight asked quietly.

Caleb nodded and slowly opened his eyes. Although he was still uncertain of the direction they should take, a peacefulness had overtaken him.

Waiting until the boats had passed, Caleb and Dwight scrambled to mount their steeds. They chose to take a path a mile from the river to prevent the United Irish from detecting them. Caleb's uneasiness returned. The day would soon fade, and traveling by night in the wilderness with the Irish rebels afoot would be treacherous. He slowed his mount. "Dwight, I don't know where I'm going."

"I know," Dwight answered quietly. "But at least we're going there together."

They continued to travel on. The air cooled and the late afternoon sun disappeared behind some clouds. "We need to water our horses."

"The river's too great a risk." Dwight shook his head. His stallion nickered and reacted uneasily. "Quiet," he whispered and held a finger to his lips.

Sensing Dwight's disquiet, Caleb glanced around and then slid from his saddle. Tying his horse to a tree, he crept to the edge of a grove and waited, his pistol in his grasp. A moan broke the silence. He grasped his weapon with both hands and stiffened both arms straight out in front of him. "Who's there?" He crouched behind the tree and then moved quickly forward. Detecting movement in the tall grass, he charged ahead. "Don't move!" he ordered to the figure that lay crumpled beneath the grass.

"Don't shoot," a weakened voice cried out.

"Dwight!" Caleb shouted. "Over here! I've found her!" He

stepped carefully around the tall mound and put away his gun. "Kelsey!"

Opening her eyes, Kelsey came out of the haze her mind had been in. "Caleb?"

"Thank the Lord!" Caleb slid his hands beneath her head. "You're hurt?"

"No," she smiled faintly. "Just so tired." She struggled to sit up. "You've got to listen—"

"I'm taking you home."

"No," she insisted determinedly. "We have to stop the United Irish. They plan to attack Castle Hill."

"Castle Hill?" Caleb glanced worriedly at Dwight, who stood over them. "We aren't far from there now."

"They plan to ransack the colonists' homes and take their weapons. If they aren't stopped by the British, they'll invade Parrametta next. Then Sydney."

"We'll have to move fast!" Dwight shouldered his musket. "We can notify the authorities and then ride back to Parrametta before they can execute their plan."

"Kelsey, you can't ride into Castle Hill." Caleb knitted his brow in worry. "You should be abed."

"You've no choice but to take me with you. I wish at least one chance to rectify the wrongs committed here today."

"Why *are* you here?"

"I made a mistake and followed the wrong man. He planned to hold me captive until Sydney's invasion, but I managed to escape. Keegan and Orr—"

"Yes, we know," Caleb said quietly. "But aren't you concerned for Keegan? For his welfare?" He waited, studying her reaction.

Kelsey licked her lips and paused, her eyelids heavy with fatigue. "I don't want to see anyone killed. I just want to go home."

"So Keegan's taking you to Ireland?"

"I'm not going with him. I've decided to go alone. I'll earn the money myself."

"I see." Caleb felt relieved in part. "Nothing could convince you to stay here?"

"Why . . . why would I?"

"You've friends here." He helped her to her feet.

"I know." She smiled. Her air of calm and self-confidence encouraged him.

Dwight hurried them along. "We've no time to waste!"

Caleb offered his mount to Kelsey. "You don't mind riding with me?"

"Not at all." She placed her toe into the stirrup, lifted herself with the help of Caleb's steady hand, and settled herself behind the saddle.

Caleb hesitated once more. He hadn't said any of the things he'd planned to say. Girding himself with resolve, he slid into the saddle ahead of her. "Hold on!" he called out and tapped the horse's flanks. He felt Kelsey quickly throw her arms about his waist. He settled back, enjoying the feel of her arms around him. "Dwight, have we plenty of ammunition?" he called out.

"Not a lot," Dwight yelled back, increasing the steed's gait.

"We should head straight for the military authorities, then. No time to waste." He aimed the stallion for the main road that led to Castle Hill. "If any time left at all."

26

THE BATTLE OF CASTLE HILL

The Castle Hill prison compound, lit by only a few torches, presented a dreary image to Kelsey. She had grown up inside a British prison colony, so the thought of entering one again gave rise to anxious fears. She stood next to Caleb and Dwight, her arms wrapped about her waist and eyes cast to the black ground.

"You don't have to go inside, Kelsey," Caleb gently offered.

"I must, Caleb. There's something I haven't told you."

Caleb glanced knowingly at Dwight and then back at her. "Go on."

"I had all but fulfilled my prison sentence at Norfolk. I believe I was only weeks away from my release. But something . . . it was dreadful." She drew up her shoulders.

Caleb stepped toward her, his blue eyes somber and sympathetic. "You don't have to tell me, you know."

"I want to. I've lived a lie before you and your family. I don't deserve any of you."

Caleb sighed inwardly.

"When Keegan and Orr departed after my mother died, I found myself completely alone. Not that I felt a friendship with either of them, but the Irish looked after one another while on Norfolk." She pursed her lips uncomfortably. "A British officer, seeing my fiancé had departed, wanted to"—her lip quivered—"to force me to come and live in his tent. I had to escape, you understand. I had no one to protect me."

Caleb lifted his finger to catch the tear that trickled across her cheek. "You do now."

"We'll speak on your behalf to the authorities. You're now aiding the colonists. The British will recognize that fact." Dwight secured his horse to a hitching post.

Kelsey stepped ahead of them both. Courage and determination rose up like rocks within her. She led the way past the guards, through the compound, and up to the officers' quarters. During the next half hour, she told everything she knew to a British lieutenant. She watched with relief as the lieutenant quickly scrawled a temporary letter granting her pardon.

Handing her the letter, the officer barked orders to his assistants. "Prepare for an attack! Muster arms!"

But before the assistant could step through the doorway, the sound of musket fire echoed across the dark compound.

"They've come!" Kelsey ran fearfully to stare out the window.

Caleb lunged for her, his eyes wide with fear for her life. "Get down, Kelsey!"

Kelsey crumpled to the floor, feeling Caleb's body atop hers. But a sudden explosion of glass brought a scream to her throat. "Caleb!"

"Quiet! Don't anyone move!" The lieutenant doused his lantern. "You all stay here. I must inform the commander of the details!" Cautiously peering out his rear door, he slipped away.

Caleb shook the debris from his back. "Kelsey! Are you all right? Dwight?" he anxiously whispered.

"My hand's cut, but I'm fine," Kelsey answered, her voice strong.

"I'm over here!" Dwight sat squatted beside the front doorway. "We've got to get her out of here."

"No, we should stay. We can't go out now," Kelsey insisted.

"Dwight's right. We'll have to find a back way out of here.

Think of your child, Kelsey." Caleb brushed shards of glass from her hair. "They couldn't have surrounded the compound yet—not enough men."

Kelsey, staying low to the floor, moved away from the broken glass. "We don't know for certain. Orr's been rallying his men for many months now."

The musket fire increased and the open window allowed in a brilliant glow. "They're setting houses afire!" Caleb lifted his face above the windowsill. "The entire colony's ablaze!"

"It's madness! I've got to get back to Katy and the boys!" Dwight headed for the rear door. "Are you staying or coming with me?"

"Kelsey?" Caleb awaited her response.

"Let's go!" Kelsey followed Dwight, and they ran for the rear of the compound. Kelsey dodged alerted soldiers, who ran past snapping up their trousers and tallying their ammunition. The sky behind her lit up a brilliant gold and vermilion against a backdrop of black. She saw the lieutenant marshaling a group of soldiers into line. An Irishman shouted in the distance, "He sang out, Now My Boys, Liberty or Death!" Kelsey recognized the Irish treason song. She could hear the shouting of the rebels and the soldiers. "Look, Caleb!" She saw hostile convicts pouring out of one of the stone buildings. "They've escaped!"

"This way!" Caleb pulled her toward him and led her behind a building. His back against the wall, he stood silently, his arm protectively across Kelsey's shoulders.

"We've lost sight of Dwight!" Kelsey felt her heart hammering against her chest.

"He'll make it to Parrametta. Nothing can stop Dwight Farrell."

Glancing up at Caleb in the dark, Kelsey could only see a golden outline framing his noble profile. "I'm so sorry for everything I've caused."

"You've helped save Parrametta and Sydney."

"But I've destroyed our friendship."

"That's for me to decide."

"Can you forgive me?"

"I'm sure we can make some sort of arrangement." Caleb smiled confidently.

Kelsey paused, unsure of his intentions. She turned to face

him fully. She could sense something different about him, but she couldn't determine what it was. A breeze stirred his gold and auburn hair about his face. His eyes, deep sapphire, penetrated hers as if he wished to convey a silent message. He was so disturbing to her in every way. "Caleb, I—"

"Don't speak." He held his finger to her lips.

A slender delicate thread began to form between them. Without thought, she lifted one hand and allowed her fingers to wrap around his. His nearness kindled a fire she had long denied herself.

Caleb slipped his other hand around the back of her head. He gently stroked her hair and then drew closer to her face.

"You don't know what you're doing—"

"I know perfectly well." Caleb pressed his lips against her cheek, allowing his touch to linger across her face.

Kelsey's eyes closed, and she felt herself allowing him to kiss her face again. Turning her own face slightly, her lips found his. She reveled in the moment, praying it was not a dream and that she would awaken again on Norfolk. His lips pressed against hers and they embraced as though no battle raged around them. At this moment her world was filled with nothing but him.

Slowly Caleb pulled back and smiled into her eyes. "I love you, Kelsey McBride."

She could form no words but closed her eyes and felt his lips softly brush across hers again.

He continued speaking softly, as though raising his voice would shatter the moment. "I've always loved you. But I had to nearly lose you before realizing how much you mean to me."

"Caleb, how could you love me?" She felt her hands trembling as she rested them against his chest. "I've deceived you."

"I've deceived myself, Kelsey. How could you tell me anything at all? I've been so wrapped up in my own ambitions. Forgive me for being so blind."

Kelsey felt as though her heart would explode. "But I carry another man's child."

"Against your will. But the Lord will see to the child if we trust Him, Kelsey."

"You sound like Amelia."

"My mother is a wise woman."

"She is at that." Kelsey allowed a weak smile to play around the corners of her mouth while her eyes moistened. "She taught me to pray."

"God is with us, Kelsey. No matter how great the battle, He is our defense."

His words stirred her as no other's could have done. "I love you, Caleb. You've no idea how much I've longed to tell you. But I thought it could never be—"

Caleb laughed, his eyes alight with joy. "Then I am your undying servant. Your every need, Kelsey, I will somehow meet." He stepped back and held her at arm's length. "If you wish to return to Kildare, I will take you there myself. Just say the word."

Kelsey stepped quickly forward and embraced him. "Thank you!" She could no longer hold back the tears.

A sudden explosion rocked the building next to them, wrenching them apart.

"Let's run!" Caleb grasped her wrist and pulled her away.

Kelsey, fast on his heels, ran with him past a guard post and toward the front gate.

"My horse!" Caleb shouted.

A rebel ran away from them, holding the reins of Caleb's horse, the stallion whinnying wildly behind him.

Caleb pulled out his musket and fired over the rebel's head. "Halt!"

The convict jerked around and lifted a fowling piece above his head.

"Look out!" Kelsey tried to pull him away.

The rebel fired but Caleb fell behind another building with Kelsey firmly at his side. Quickly reloading his ammunition, he came around the corner and steadied his aim. The tip of his musket kicked up when he fired. The rebel shrieked and hurled the reins from his grasp.

Caleb signaled at once. "Now, Kelsey! Run! Follow me!" Quick to retrieve the horse, Caleb led them into a thicket to hide while he helped her remount, then leaped atop the stallion himself. Kelsey held tightly to Caleb as they headed toward Parametta. Rounding a dark road, she suddenly spotted torches lighting the deep woods beyond them. "Caleb, more croppies!" she shouted to him.

Caleb drove the horse into the opposite woods. Kelsey could hear the drunken singing of the voices joined in a capella.

It was early in the spring,
The birds did whistle and sweetly sing,
Changing their notes from tree to tree,
And the song they sang was Old Ireland free.
It was early, early in the night,
The yeoman cavalry gave me fright,
The yeoman cavalry was my downfall,
And taken was I by Lord Cornwall.

Kelsey remembered the rebel anthem from the uprising of ninety-eight. *I was just a girl then*, she thought. Her mother would sing the song tearfully, as though Ireland were her life's blood. Now the song drove through the bush like a banshee. More fires erupted. A distant colonist ranted through the night, "The croppies are coming!" *At least the colonists are being warned.* She felt relieved at the thought.

"We're nearing the Parrametta River," Caleb called over his shoulder.

Kelsey peered around him. Ahead, she could hear more voices. Caleb reined the horse to an abrupt halt. Assisting her down, he tied up the steed. Cautiously, they crept toward the riverbank.

Kelsey saw three figures moving quietly. "Someone's getting into a boat."

"Let's find out who," Caleb answered.

A mist floated above the water, partly hiding the man and two women. Two military guards ran from either side.

"No rebels in sight yet, Reverend Marsden!" a guard called out to the minister.

"Good man," Marsden answered nervously. He helped his wife with her belongings and then turned to assist the other woman. "We must hurry, Mrs. Macarthur!"

"Kelsey!" Caleb whispered. "It's Elizabeth Macarthur—Lieutenant John Macarthur's wife—and Reverend and Mrs. Samuel Marsden."

"They're fleeing the Irish." Kelsey shook her head in disbelief. "And well they should. Marsden's flogged enough Irish convict men to fear for his life."

"Macarthur's notoriety has earned him no respect either. I

can imagine Elizabeth Macarthur's apprehensions." Caleb grasped her hand again. "Let's go. If I stay much longer, I'll be tempted to expose them to the United Irish."

"Agreed."

They departed Parrametta River as quickly as they came. Avoiding the main road, they traveled farther into the brush, hoping to put as much distance between them and the sound of the rebel drums as possible. The entire settlement now glowed ethereally from the burning sheds and shanties.

"Halt!" a British voice shouted. "Identify yourself!"

"Caleb Prentice, a British subject!" Caleb answered without a moment's hesitation.

"Prentice?"

"Corporal Chilton!" Caleb recognized his voice.

Chilton beheld Kelsey and turned to call to his men at once. "Seize the girl! She's one of them!"

Kelsey stepped back, momentarily rebuffed.

"No!" Caleb pushed his way between them. "You're wrong, Chilton. She assisted the British only an hour ago with the rebels' entire plan. She's the salvation of Parrametta and Sydney."

"You're lying, Prentice."

"I'm not. Ask the commander at Castle Hill."

"Castle Hill's in flames."

Caleb countered, "But the troops are defending her, true?"

"I've heard they were alerted by one of the Irish, sir," a private piped up but then saluted respectfully to his officer.

"Where are you going now, Prentice?" Chilton demanded to know.

"Parrametta, to Rose Hill."

Resolve marked his countenance. "It's best you hurry then. Governor King's ordered a detachment of the New South Wales Corps out of the barracks. They're headed for Sydney and Parrametta at this very moment. There are no less than two hundred and sixty croppies garnered for this blighted effort!" Chilton turned to confront Kelsey himself. "You've had no involvement with the United Irish?"

Looking straight into his questioning eyes, Kelsey refused to live out another lie. "Sir, I can only say that my past involvement was a grave error on my part. I've divulged the rebels' entire strategy to the British authorities. According to the Castle

Hill authorities, I'm to be granted a full pardon." She pulled the letter from her sash.

Examining the official paper, Chilton conceded. "We'll allow you to pass, Prentice. I trust I'll not hear later that you've misled the military."

"I swear it, sir, on my family's own honor. You shall find us all defending Rosè Hill if you've further need of us."

"Godspeed, then." Chilton waved them on.

Kelsey felt a renewed sense of restoration. With one stroke of an official's pen, she had been granted a freedom she hadn't known in years. "I'm free, Caleb," she whispered while leaning against him atop the stallion.

"You are free, Kelsey. But now we're running out of time. If Keegan and his men are planning an assault on Parrametta, there's no limit to the destruction they'll wreak. Rose Hill may be their next target."

The hour-long ride to Rose Hill was long and precarious in the darkened settlement, and Kelsey felt the weariness of the strenuous day overtaking her. But she dared not complain, for now she feared for Katy, Amelia, and the boys. She hoped that Dwight had by now mustered the settlers along with their weapons as a defense against the coming assault.

"I'm taking us back to the main road. We're almost to Rose Hill now. The path along the river hastened our journey." Caleb sounded stronger and more encouraged.

But Kelsey felt the horse slowing. Caleb's arms pulled back on the reins. "Why are we stopping?"

When Caleb gave no reply, she cut her eyes around him. Lined across the road stood several darkened figures with weapons aimed at them both. She tightened her grip around Caleb's waist. "It's the rebels!" she said tremulously.

Caleb spoke calmly while winding the reins around the saddle horn. "I know. Say nothing."

Kelsey dropped her face, hoping she wouldn't be recognized.

"Miss McBride," a petulant voice rang out.

Her breath taken away by the familiar sound, Kelsey uneasily lifted her face and stared out at the croppies that now blocked their path.

"Jack Keegan," she heard herself say. "What do you want?"

27

IRELAND FOREVER

"Let the girl come to me." Keegan raked his fingers through his hair with one hand while waving a pistol with the other.

"She doesn't want to come to you, Keegan." Caleb brought his arm protectively behind himself to shield Kelsey. "I'm taking her to Kildare where she belongs."

"She's coming with me. It's my child she carries."

"She doesn't love you, Keegan."

"I'll be needing to hear it from her, Prentice! Now get out of the way before I get too careless with my weapon." He curled his fingers around the pistol and readied the flintlock.

"No, Jack! I'll go with you." Kelsey would allow no bloodshed on her behalf. "It's as he's saying, Caleb. He's the father of my child. I'll go with him." Before sliding from behind the saddle, Kelsey lifted one hand and gently stroked his back. She wanted to whisper her intent, but she dared not take the risk.

Caleb quickly glanced back at her covertly. "You've no need to do this!" he said between bared teeth.

"She's every need to do this, Prentice. She's one of us. She's

Irish and she'll return with me to Ireland. Not with the son of a British beggar."

Caleb continued to hold his words.

"I'm here, Jack. Now what?" Kelsey stared intently, hands clasped in front of her and her jaw set determinedly.

"We ransack Rose Hill. Then on to Sydney as planned. Mulligan, seize his weapon and any other possessions of value."

"The British are waiting for you, Keegan." Caleb glared down at the surly Irishman who rifled through his belongings and yanked his musket from its leather sheath.

"A paltry amount of military against our numbers? They'll never defeat us. Now, stand down on the ground, Prentice. We've need of your horse."

"Aye and a fine piece of horseflesh, it is," the rebel commented as he ran his hands over the stallion's neck.

"You can't leave him here, Jack." Kelsey looked first at Caleb and then at Keegan.

"Of course not." Keegan lifted his weapon toward Caleb. "We can't leave behind a witness for the British, aye. Turn around, Prentice. I don't want to see your face."

Several of the rebels chuckled and then gazed at another from their ranks who emerged on horseback from the shadowy woods.

Kelsey stepped toward Keegan. "I won't allow it!"

"Out of the way." Keegan shoved her.

"No!" Kelsey persisted. "You'll not shoot him!"

Whirling around to face her, Keegan snapped, "Why do you care?"

"Because I love him, Jack! Can't you see?"

"You're a traitor! You'll not live to see him die." He turned his weapon on Kelsey.

"Don't think of it!" Caleb stepped toward them both. "I'm warning you, Keegan—"

Two of the rebels seized Caleb, pushing him away from their leader.

Deliberately, Kelsey stepped back. Seeing Keegan's hostile countenance, she beheld him as she knew him to be—a malevolent man with a hunger for vengeance. "You're evil, Jack!"

Fingering the pistol, Keegan leveled his arms and prepared to fire.

Kelsey hid her face. "My baby!" she shrieked. A barrage of gunfire sounded all around her. She turned instinctively away but felt no pain from the shot. Slowly, she opened her eyes. Before her stood the Irish leader so long esteemed by her own mother. "William Orr?"

Orr stood glaring down at the body of Jack Keegan from atop his stolen mount. "He was . . . going to kill you." His voice shook, along with his trigger hand.

"You?" Kelsey's forehead furrowed in bewilderment. "You shot Keegan? Your own man?" She felt Caleb's arm slip around her waist. Biting her lip, she embraced him. Relief flooded her mind, and tears welled from her eyes. "You're safe. Thank God!"

A murmuring of discontent rippled through the rebel ranks.

"Silence!" Orr commanded. "Keegan took matters too far! It's his own fault this happened!"

"I don't understand." Kelsey felt her fingers interlace with Caleb's. She glanced back up at Orr. "You chose to take his life over mine. Why did you save my life?" She looked once more upon Keegan's lifeless form and then turned her face to Orr.

Orr nodded somberly. "Because of a promise I made to your mother."

"My mother? I don't understand."

"When Hattie died, I was at her side. You arrived later, if you recall. Hattie informed me of something that she had kept from the both of us."

"What was that?" Kelsey asked, her face clearly marked by confusion.

"Hattie and I, when we were young, had grown close."

"No. Mother never loved any man. She told me so herself."

"She thought she loved me at one time."

"It isn't true—" Kelsey gazed defensively at Orr and then tried to convince herself it couldn't be true. "She loved Ireland. That was her only love."

"Not her only love, lassie. She loved you dearly, far beyond measure. But driven by a bitter spirit, she knew nothing about displaying her love to a gifted daughter, although she told me herself of her love for you."

"I know she loved me in her own way," Kelsey agreed, but her words were guarded. "Mother simply refused to show her affections. She thought it proved her weak."

"You knew her well, in part. But none knew her weaknesses better than I."

"How can you make such claims? It's foolishness you're saying—"

"And she told me in her own words the truth about you, Kelsey."

"Stop it! You torment me!"

"Hear him out, Kelsey." Caleb stroked her arm comfortingly, his tone steadfast.

"Yes, do hear me out, lass. For I, William Orr, am your father, although I've done little in the way of expressing it."

"It's a lie! And you've done *nothing* in the way of expressing it!" Tears drenched her cheeks.

"You've received my gifts?"

"The dresses?" she asked.

Caleb nodded as the realization struck.

Kelsey shook her head in disbelief. She asked Caleb, "They weren't from you or Rachel?"

"We told you they weren't. We were honest about the matter."

"You . . . William Orr . . . you're my father?"

Orr nodded, his eyes reflecting an inward pain. "We must take our leave, my daughter. The British will soon be upon us."

"If what you say is true, then abandon the rebels. I'll help you with your clemency," Caleb offered. "All of you men, surrender now, and I'll speak on your behalf."

"We've our liberty at stake, Mr. Prentice." Orr reloaded his pistol. "To arms!" he called out. The small party of rebels clustered about his horse. "But mark my words, not a rebel soldier is to step foot upon Rose Hill. On to Sydney—"

Kelsey ran to him. "You'll die. Don't go. Not now that I've just found you."

Orr turned his face from her, unable to bear her pleading eyes. He looked away momentarily, then turned back to Kelsey. "I nearly forgot. I've something else for you." He reached into a pouch strapped to his saddle, and pulling out a small velvet bag, he opened it. "Inside is a little memento your mother asked me to keep for you."

Kelsey peered into the bag. Allowing him to dump its frail

contents into her hands, she wept openly at the sight. "The shamrock! I thought it had decayed."

"Your mother found it inside an old book you once kept. She took it for safekeeping."

Kelsey grasped the bag with one hand and slid the dried shamrock back inside its folds. Lifting the bag to her lips, she closed her eyes and kissed it. Now her tears flowed from pure sentiment. "Forever, Mum, I'll love Ireland forever," she whispered. The tears running freely down her cheeks, Kelsey waved a sad farewell to the father she'd always dreamed of knowing.

"Sorry to have been such a dismal disappointment, my dear."

Kelsey pressed her lips together and attempted to quell her riotous emotions. She could think of no appropriate reply.

"Mr. Prentice, you'll see she's taken care of, won't you?" Orr asked Caleb.

Caleb nodded. "Kelsey, let us take our leave. Dwight and Katy will be worried."

Kelsey rode with Caleb back to Rose Hill, scarcely noticing the shanty fires that dotted the landscape. A purple haze lightened the horizon behind them. Soon the dawn would be upon them, and the events of the last few hours would fade into history. But she would never forget the father she had known but for a brief moment in time.

Katy and Dwight greeted them with great relief when they turned onto the property. "We've worried so! What detained you?" Katy asked, frowning in concern.

"Katy, help me assist Kelsey to bed. She's seen too much strain for one in her condition." Caleb threw his leg over the saddle horn. "Dwight, some water, please?"

Amelia waved at them from the front porch and then bustled into the house to order food prepared for everyone.

Following the Irish rebels' speedy defeat by the military, Kelsey slept for what seemed to be days. Katy kept a steady stream of maids at her side, and Rachel Whitley stopped by to examine her almost every day. She began to feel stronger, and the Battle of Castle Hill seemed like a distant dream.

The news arrived that the Irish dissidents had been captured and sentenced to execution. Some had been executed without trial. Kelsey grieved when she read the notice from the authorities that William Orr and his United Irish rebels had all been hanged. She handed the letter back to Caleb. "I still find it difficult to believe that Orr was my father." She sighed, then gave a resigned shrug. "I never tried to become better acquainted with him. Had I only realized—"

"No. I won't allow you to torment yourself so," Caleb somberly interjected.

Kelsey stopped to reflect upon the memory of her mother and William Orr standing on the bow of the English transport ship. She had always thought of Hattie McBride as an iron woman, without feelings. But now she realized her mother had only hid her love for William Orr behind the cloak of her political activities. If only the two of them had been free to declare their love for each other and to marry. Perhaps the bond of marriage and family would have been enough to settle them down to a normal existence. Perhaps life would have been different for Kelsey. . . . But Kelsey knew she could not dwell on the past.

"How sad, Caleb, that I know my mother better now than I did back then." It would take a long time to erase the pain of what was and what could have been in Kelsey's life. But she now realized that a seed of forgiveness had taken root in her heart and had begun to grow within her.

During those dark days, Caleb refused to leave her side, offering what comfort and aid he could with his presence.

Kelsey finally had to insist that Caleb busy himself with his farm duties, for he languished at the foot of her bed, reacting to her slightest complaint. When he wasn't reprimanding the servants for their minor mishaps, he was delivering flowers and sweets to her bedside.

"You're spoiling me, Mr. Prentice." She smiled up at him.

"Flowers, dainties—I wouldn't refer to those things as spoiling you."

"What then?"

He handed her an envelope. "Perhaps one could say that *this* is spoiling you."

"What is it?" She slid her finger under the wax seal. Swiftly examining the contents, she shook out two tickets onto the blanket. "Ship's passage?"

"To Kildare."

"Caleb, I don't truly expect you to deliver me to Kildare. What of your duties here?"

"I've a selfish motive as well. First, I'll deliver you to Kildare. Then it's off to England, the homeland of my parents."

Kelsey managed a faint smile. "I'm happy for you." She dropped her lashes quickly to hide the hurt.

"Something's wrong?"

"No." She immediately shook her head. "We both shall have our heart's desire. I'll have my Ireland and you'll have your England." Her gaze was clouded with tears.

"We've both always known what we wanted, true?" His eyes lit mischievously.

She nodded numbly.

"But then, of course, I could really be a selfish lout if I so desired."

"How so?" she whispered but kept her eyes downcast.

"I could insist upon your hand in marriage. Then I could make your life utterly miserable by taking you first to Kildare and then on to England—"

"What is it you're saying?"

"And then of course, with my being the heir to Rose Hill, we would be forced to return and take up our dreary duties as owners of a sheep ranch."

"You're demented!"

"Or you could take the small fortune left to you by your father and live out your days as a wealthy spinster in Ireland."

"Now you're truly deranged. Stop it, I say! You're teasing me."

"I'm not teasing you. Your father, William Orr, left a testament naming you his beneficiary. You're quite wealthy now." Caleb lifted his chin proudly.

Rachel Whitley entered the room. "It's no small wonder that he would ask you to marry him, Kelsey. He's after your money, you know."

Reverend Whitley followed his wife into the room. His dark eyes flashed, full of humor. "Has she answered you yet, old man?"

"Not yet." Caleb heaved a heavy sigh. "She needs more time to ponder, I believe."

"No!" Kelsey sat up.

"It's 'no,' then, I'm afraid." Heath Whitley patted Caleb, his eyes sympathetic.

"That's not what I meant!" Kelsey, swift to respond, turned to face Caleb. She fought the urge to laugh. How she loved his gentle camaraderie, his subtle wit. "I mean to say that I need no more time to ponder."

"No?" Caleb's brows lifted with interest. Her reaction appeared to amuse him.

Kelsey shook her head. Her trembling lips could no longer hide her smile. "I can give you my answer now." She clasped her hands over his. "My answer is—yes, of course I'll marry you, you mad man."

"How am I mad?"

She offered a quiet reply. "Mad to want me—and my child."

Caleb bowed to place a kiss atop the blanket that covered her stomach. "I want you and *our* child."

Rachel broke into an infectious laugh. "Congratulations, Mr. Prentice. You've been snared!"

Caleb stood and straightened himself. "Are you ready, Reverend Whitley?" He caught Heath's eye and winked conspiratorially.

"Completely." The minister nodded. "I'll fetch your family. I'm certain they would wish to witness this auspicious occasion." He started for the door.

"What?" Kelsey stared at both of the men quizzically. "Marry you now? From a sickbed?"

"You said yes, I believe," Caleb affirmed.

"But I can't marry you here—now. I want a church wedding. Rachel . . . *help me!*"

"I should have you both flogged." Rachel pinched Caleb's arm affectionately. "Leave us women to plan the ceremony."

"But our ship leaves in five days." Caleb wagged the passage papers in front of her.

"Then we've little time to make Kelsey's arrangements.

Out. . . !" Rachel ordered. "Out!"

Caleb laughed and bent to kiss his bride-to-be.

Kelsey drew his face to hers in a joyous embrace, and Caleb sealed his promise with a kiss.

In her heart, Kelsey realized that her earlier longings had been founded on the daydreams of a child. But now, by trusting in God, she could encounter a future she had never dreamed possible. For God was giving her the loving family that her heart had always yearned for. Parrametta would be a challenging environment in which she and Caleb would rear a family, but she no longer feared tomorrow. While she recuperated, Amelia had read her a Scripture passage from Joshua that she brought to mind every morning when she awakened: *Have I not commanded thee? Be strong and of a good courage; be not afraid, neither be thou dismayed; for the Lord thy God is with thee whithersoever thou goest.* " She would cling to the Scripture just as she would cling to her newfound faith in God, which Amelia had led her to embrace. She had much to be thankful for.

Katy and Dwight walked into the room. "What's the answer?" Katy asked, eyeing her younger brother.

"She said yes," Rachel answered ahead of Caleb.

"Does everyone know?" Kelsey arched a cynical brow.

"What did she say?" Amelia peered around the doorway.

They all threw back their heads and laughed, filling the room with the rich sound of happiness.

"We've much to plan for, Mum." Katy drew Amelia out of the hallway. What with a wedding and so many babies—"

Heath, Dwight, and Caleb gazed at one another in numb astonishment.

"What *babies*?" Dwight scowled.

Katy linked arms with Rachel. "Why, naturally I speak of all the babies. Kelsey's, Rachel's, and mine, of course." She patted her stomach.

"Oh, my dear!" Amelia scolded. "We don't dare speak of such things in the presence of men!"

Caleb observed Dwight as he swallowed hard, the color draining from his face. Then seeing the stunned stupor of Rev-

erend Whitley, he laughed aloud. "The good Lord's full of sur-
prises, eh, blokes?"

The house fell silent except for the quiet laughing of the
women.